W9-ABE-790

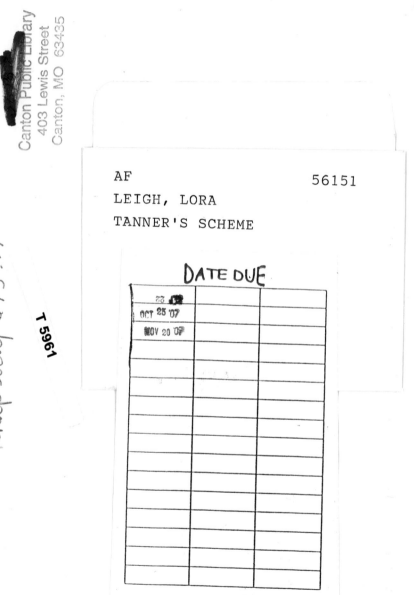

Canton Public Library
403 Lewis Street
Canton, MO 63435

T 5961

Rhapsody $13.95

SEPTEMBER 2007

AF   56151

LEIGH, LORA

TANNER'S SCHEME

DATE DUE

22		
OCT 25 '07		
NOV 20 07		

Tanner's Scheme

Lora Leigh

BERKLEY SENSATION, NEW YORK

THE BERKLEY PUBLISHING GROUP
Published by the Penguin Group
Penguin Group (USA) Inc.
375 Hudson Street, New York, New York 10014, USA
Penguin Group (Canada), 90 Eglinton Avenue East, Suite 700, Toronto, Ontario M4P 2Y3, Canada
(a division of Pearson Penguin Canada Inc.)
Penguin Books Ltd., 80 Strand, London WC2R 0RL, England
Penguin Group Ireland, 25 St. Stephen's Green, Dublin 2, Ireland (a division of Penguin Books Ltd.)
Penguin Group (Australia), 250 Camberwell Road, Camberwell, Victoria 3124, Australia
(a division of Pearson Australia Group Pty. Ltd.)
Penguin Books India Pvt. Ltd., 11 Community Centre, Panchsheel Park, New Delhi—110 017, India
Penguin Group (NZ), 67 Apollo Drive, Rosedale, North Shore 0745, Auckland, New Zealand
(a division of Pearson New Zealand Ltd.)
Penguin Books (South Africa) (Pty.) Ltd., 24 Sturdee Avenue, Rosebank, Johannesburg 2196,
South Africa

Penguin Books Ltd., Registered Offices: 80 Strand, London WC2R 0RL, England

This is a work of fiction. Names, characters, places, and incidents either are the product of the author's imagination or are used fictitiously, and any resemblance to actual persons, living or dead, business establishments, events, or locales is entirely coincidental. The publisher does not have any control over and does not assume any responsibility for author or third-party websites or their content.

TANNER'S SCHEME

A Berkley Sensation Book / published by arrangement with the author

PRINTING HISTORY
Berkley Sensation mass-market edition / August 2007

Copyright © 2007 by Lora Leigh.
Cover design by Rita Frangie.
Interior text design by Stacy Irwin.

All rights reserved.
No part of this book may be reproduced, scanned, or distributed in any printed or electronic form without permission. Please do not participate in or encourage piracy of copyrighted materials in violation of the author's rights. Purchase only authorized editions.
For information, address: The Berkley Publishing Group,
a division of Penguin Group (USA) Inc.,
375 Hudson Street, New York, New York 10014.

ISBN: 978-0-7394-8735-8

BERKLEY® SENSATION
Berkley Sensation Books are published by The Berkley Publishing Group,
a division of Penguin Group (USA) Inc.,
375 Hudson Street, New York, New York 10014.
BERKLEY SENSATION and the "B" design are trademarks belonging to Penguin Group (USA) Inc.

PRINTED IN THE UNITED STATES OF AMERICA

For Scheme.
Thanks for being a friend.

Berkley Sensation titles by Lora Leigh

TANNER'S SCHEME
HARMONY'S WAY
MEGAN'S MARK

⋆ P R O L O G U E ⋆

General Cyrus Tallant sat in his office with only his desk lamp for light, his gaze trained tearfully on the picture he held in his hands.

His daughter. His little Schemer.

His lips turned up in a sad smile as he thought of the name. It had been his idea, of course, to name her Scheme. He'd been unable to help himself. The moment he held her tiny body in his arms, he had known she would be a little manipulator.

And he had been proud. Proud of the chocolate brown eyes, the thick sable hair, the way she stared up at him as though wondering, even then, how she could maneuver this male to her benefit.

A watery chuckle whispered through the room. She had been quick and calculating, just as he was, just as her mother was. Unfortunately, perhaps she was too much like her mother.

Sweet Dorothy. She had conspired against him. She had helped those nasty Breeds escape. The ones who tormented him now. Callan Lyons and the small pride he led. She had aided their escape and the destruction of the New Mexico labs when Scheme was barely ten.

He should have known then that his child had been corrupted by Dorothy's sudden attack of scruples. Dorothy had spent much time with Scheme. She had bonded with her as only a mother can. He admitted he should have suspected his daughter had inherited that lack of the mental strength that it took to do what must be done. To force the Breeds to heel to their masters.

And now Dorothy's legacy had carried over to his precious child.

He wiped at the tear that fell slowly from his eyes.

She meant to destroy him. And if she managed to actually contact Jonas Wyatt, then she *would* destroy him. He couldn't allow that to happen. He couldn't allow her to escape to the creatures she had obviously been secretly helping for years.

Luck had aided him this time. He had managed to draw Wyatt out of Washington; all he had to do now was take care of his daughter.

Kill her.

He gazed around his office. He should have taken care of it before she left for the party where she intended to betray him, but he just hadn't found the strength.

He couldn't kill her in the home she had grown up in. Where he had played with her as a toddler, laughed with her before the years she spent at the Academy.

He couldn't spill her blood in the home where she had been born. It wasn't right.

He lifted his head and gazed across his desk at the man still awaiting his orders.

Chazzon St. Marks was an excellent assassin. Stealthy, never leaving evidence, and always following orders. One couldn't ask for a better killer.

And it was because of this man that his daughter so hated him. Perhaps he had been wrong, he mused silently, to order Chaz to become her lover all those years ago. To steal his daughter's heart and learn her secrets.

Not that Chaz had learned much. Just her suspicion that Cyrus had murdered her mother, her regret that she had grown up without that bitch's influence. Her dreams of a life away from him.

And then she had conceived.

Chaz was a good killer; he wasn't heir material though. And Cyrus couldn't allow a grandchild to be born of him. Especially a grandson.

As her father, he had made the decision to have the child aborted.

She had never understood, Cyrus realized now, that he was looking out for her. That he was trying to guide her, to lead her.

"Do you regret the child?" he asked Chaz.

Cold, cold blue eyes stared back at him as hard lips tilted mockingly. "I drugged her for you. If I had wanted the brat, I would have taken her and run."

Yes, he would have. Chaz gave his loyalty freely. He wasn't above taking anything if it suited his whims. It was one of the things Cyrus respected about him.

"Do we have proof?" Grief weighed on him.

He had punished her many times over the years in his efforts to train her, to strengthen her and teach her the value of giving him her loyalty. He had been hard on her, he admitted. Once, he had even killed her, to teach her the meaning of death. The punishment should she betray him. He hadn't had proof then, only suspicion, and the weight of remorse had grown inside him each time Scheme stared back at him with accusation in her eyes.

He couldn't kill her permanently without proof. Those accusing brown eyes would haunt him for eternity if he did such a thing. He needed to know for certain.

"Her ID was logged into the message relay system. She took great pains to erase her tracks, but I found proof of it." Chaz handed him the ID log.

It was there in black and white. Her attempts to erase her presence from the relay system and to destroy the message that they knew had been sent to the Bureau of Breed Affairs earlier that day. A message requesting asylum from Jonas Wyatt. It had been sheer luck that his spy had been in the offices in

Washington when that message came through. Cyrus restrained his sigh, his regret. "She obviously didn't have the time to do the job right," he murmured. He knew well that she could have done it, given time.

"And I would suspect she knows that. She thought she had destroyed enough of the internal memory to give her the time she needed instead to get to Jonas Wyatt. She's our spy, Cyrus. It's time to admit it. The question is, what information did she take with her? Do you think she knows about the kidnapping of the Breed child?"

Admit it. He had suspected it several times. He had tortured his own child to force the admission out of her, only to fail each time. For years he had hated himself, felt flayed by the guilt of it, only to learn she had been more deceptive than even he had believed possible.

The beatings he had ordered. The times he had buried her alive. The one time he had allowed her to die before quickly reviving her. Because he suspected her. Because he was desperate to turn back the tide of her possible betrayal and to avoid the need for her death.

Cyrus lifted his gaze to the oil painting on the far wall. His Scheme, resplendent in fiery silk, curled in his office chair. Long sable hair cascaded over her shoulder, dark lashes shielded the expression in her eyes. He pretended often that she hid her love for him there. Her understanding.

"It doesn't matter what she knows. Our agent is in close enough now that taking the child will be no problem. She won't know the exact date, only an approximation. Telling them won't affect the outcome."

But she knew other things. Things she might not have proof of, but that could destroy him anyway.

"She's a liability now, Cyrus. You've made the right decision," Chaz assured him.

"She's attending a party for Reynolds, that bastard Bengal. I want her dead before sunrise." The words choked him. "Mercifully, Chaz, if you please."

Chaz tilted his head in agreement. "I wouldn't hurt her, Cyrus," he promised softly. "I'll take care of her."

And Chaz would. He felt affection for Scheme, Cyrus knew that. But unlike Scheme, Chaz understood the future and what they were working toward.

"Do you think allowing her to keep the child would have prevented this?"

That question often haunted him.

"I doubt it, Cyrus. She was working her way toward this since the day her mother died. She's always known you killed her, despite your story. You would have just had to kill a grandchild later."

Yes. Cyrus nodded at the assassin's words. As he had killed his wife, now he was forced to take the life of his child. He couldn't have borne doing the same to a grandchild he had helped raise.

"Very well." He nodded, setting the picture back in its place. "I trust you to take care of it then."

Cyrus rose to his feet, only to pause before turning.

"I couldn't have murdered my child, Cyrus," he said. "I would have killed you over a kid, had it been born. You made the right decision. That child would have made us both weak."

Yes, it would have. Weaker than Scheme had managed to make them. He nodded again. "Mercifully, Chaz. Gently."

Regret flickered in the younger man's gaze before he turned and headed to the door. Chaz, like himself, would regret the loss, but he would carry through.

"Good-bye, Princess," he whispered, his finger reaching out to caress her face in the picture as another tear slipped down his cheek. "I'm sorry."

✦ C H A P T E R   I ✦

She was the epitome of grace, mystery and beauty. Tanner
Reynolds watched as Scheme Tallant skirted around the edges
of the room, chatting here and there, that cool smile tempting
him, challenging him.

He should have ordered her death the moment he learned
she had accepted the invitation to the party. But something
stopped him. Something always stopped him. Not for the first
time where she was concerned, his lust was guiding his actions.

She was General Cyrus Tallant's daughter. The seed of
evil itself. Cyrus Tallant had headed the training program for
the Breeds until their rescues ten years before. Manipulative,
destructive, he had managed to cover his ass and make certain there was no true proof of the position he had held, but
Tanner and the Breeds he had followed out of the labs in New
Mexico years ago had known the dark malevolence that infected him.

And it infected his daughter. She worked with him, worked
for him. She had signed the orders for Breed deaths and she
had destroyed vital information to cover the tracks of the
Genetics Council.

They had managed to have dozens of Council members indicted, but the head of the beast was still intact. The twelve-member inner Council head had yet to be penetrated. Until they were destroyed, there would be no peace for the Breeds.

If they could take Cyrus Tallant out, then the head Council would be seriously compromised. Scheme Tallant was her father's weakness. Unfortunately, no one had been able to get her to talk.

Tanner was certain he could.

A smile curled his lips, one he was certain was filled with lust and anticipation. Tonight. He was going to take her tonight. Jonas Wyatt, the director of Breed affairs, was out of town; he couldn't veto the mission. And when it was over, Tanner swore he would have the information he needed. Or Scheme Tallant would be dead.

He was sick of Jonas standing between him and the woman. As director of Breed affairs, Jonas had ordered Tanner to wait. To see what happened. To give Tallant a chance to mess up.

Tallant wasn't going to mess up. He wasn't going to make a mistake. And neither was his daughter. And Tanner was tired of waiting.

Tonight, he was going to take her. Her father would guess who had her, but he would never have proof. And Tanner knew how to hide her. He could hide her where no man or Breed would ever find her.

It was time to make Scheme Tallant pay for her part in the orders that had sent countless Breeds to their deaths. It was time to take the gloves off and get the information they needed. Not just against her father, but the identity of the spy in Sanctuary and locations of the purist and supremist factions moving closer by the day to penetrating the defenses the Breed compound had managed to put in place.

It was time to fight back.

◆　　◆　　◆

The golden boy of the Breed society was in attendance and being fawned over and loved by all. Tanner Reynolds. Playboy,

PR genius and possibly her executioner if he managed to actually get his hands on her in a dark alley.

She had come to the party to find safety. To find the Breed she had been working with for the past eight years. And he wasn't here. He wasn't, but many others were.

Scheme moved slowly about the room, tracking the Breeds present, placing names with the files she had studied over the years. Cabal St. Laurents, Tanner's genetic twin, wasn't present, though that wasn't unusual. He rarely attended the parties.

None of the married Breed couples were present, though Scheme knew they had been invited. There were several enforcers dressed in their black Breed uniforms, the insignia of each particular Breed's DNA stamped on the uniform's shoulder. There were many lions, a few panthers, she was certain she had glimpsed a cougar earlier, but no Bengals.

The only Bengal in the room was Tanner, and he wasn't an enforcer. At least, not that the Bureau of Breed Affairs admitted. But Scheme knew better. She knew the vicious retribution he could mete out when the situation warranted it. Hadn't she once died after destroying the evidence of his vengeance? That thought had a mocking smile dragging at her lips. Being a double agent for the Breeds could be hazardous to one's health. Especially when the only Breed aware of her status as a double agent seemed to be MIA at the moment.

Carefully, she made her way around the ballroom. There were at least two dozen Breeds present. But the one she was searching for hadn't attended. Jonas Wyatt was noticeably absent from this event. Which was rare. Too rare.

Sipping at her champagne, Scheme skirted the edges of the room, heading for the patio doors and the gardens beyond. Escaping the stifling atmosphere of the party filled with suspicious gazes was imperative. Almost as imperative as finding Wyatt. Damn, he was supposed to have been here.

Lifting the skirt of her blazing scarlet evening gown, Scheme stepped from the marble patio, following the stone path that led into the dimly lit gardens. It wasn't the safest place for her to be, not with the number of Breeds milling around, but she needed the silence, needed to weigh her options now that her main objective had made himself scarce.

Coming here was a risky move. Not just because there were any number of Breeds willing to put a hole in her head, but because too many eyes were watching for what she had intended to attempt. Betraying Cyrus Tallant wasn't a good idea, especially as openly as she had planned.

With the induction of Breed Law several years past, Scheme's life had been placed, more or less, on hold. Working as her father's assistant, she had been the liaison with his Council contact, and once that contact had been arrested and tried for his crimes, Scheme had come under fire as well. And under suspicion. She had been her father's shield and she hadn't even known it.

Moving through the gardens, she drew farther away from the party and deeper into the shadowed peace the lush landscaping afforded her. Here, there weren't as many eyes following her, the gazes sometimes condemning, always suspicious.

"It could be dangerous roaming around in the dark, Miss Tallant. You're not exactly well liked these days."

The voice drew her to an abrupt stop. Deep and smooth as aged whiskey. Tanner Reynolds slid from the darkness and faced her from within a small grotto echoing with the soothing sound of a nearby fountain.

The atmosphere was pure romance. Dimly lit, water trickling in the background, shadows lengthening around them. For a moment, just a moment, Scheme let herself regret. Regret that the atmosphere and the sudden heightened tension in her body wasn't for a lover, but rather a man who considered himself her enemy.

And he was dressed in a tux. Sweet heaven, men like Tanner Reynolds should never be allowed in a tux. It should be criminal. It was like putting a bow on a tiger. It only served to emphasize the primal danger of the beast wearing it.

"I was invited," she assured him, wondering at the husky sound of her own voice.

"Of course you were," he said softly. "I made certain of it."

Now that was enough to make a girl's nerves clatter in sudden shock. It also had her nipples peaking in interest. That wasn't a good thing, for the simple fact that she was well aware that Breeds could sense and smell female arousal.

"You made certain of it?" She tilted her head to the side, allowing her hair to fall over her shoulder and shield the side of her face. "And why would you do that?"

To kill her maybe, a cynical, suddenly less-than-pleased voice reminded her. Forget the sudden warmth between her thighs and the sensitive budding of her nipples. This Breed was liable to kill her rather than fuck her.

And she couldn't blame him. He was aware of nothing but the impression she had sought to give for the past ten years. That she was indeed Cyrus Tallant's daughter, not just by blood but by mercilessness. That she was a part of factions determined to destroy them, an enemy of the very species she had risked her life countless times to save. And she couldn't reveal the truth. Not now. Not until Jonas learned who the spy was within the Breed community. Not until she found Jonas and insured that the information she had made it to the right hands.

"Let's say, I thought it was time we should meet," he informed her. "We've been dancing around each other for years, making certain to stay out of one another's space. I've grown impatient with the game."

"We're playing a game then?" She arched her brows curiously. "The rules must have been lost in the mail."

"I think you're very well aware of the rules." He moved from the shadows, stepping onto the path beside her, seeming to suck the oxygen out of the air as he did so.

"You'd think I would be," she murmured. "But I'd have to understand the game first. What do you want, Mr. Reynolds?"

"You aren't calling me Breed," he reminded her chidingly, the sound of his voice stroking along the sensitive nerve endings. She actually had chill bumps racing up her spine. "Wasn't it your father's opinion that by giving us names we

were given the mistaken impression we were of worth? That
we could be human."

Warning tension filled the air. His warning. She chose to
ignore it. She had been avoiding this for far too long; she was
growing tired of the battle. Tired of avoiding him and making
excuses. Tired of the fear, the blood and the death.

"I work for my father, Mr. Reynolds, I don't live his opin-
ions," she stated.

His chuckle was low and dangerous. It was so dark here,
this far into the gardens, that as she stared up at him she could
see nothing but the golden glitter of his eyes. And they too
were mesmerizing.

Another chill raced up her spine as his hand lifted, his fingers brushing back her hair. Long, thick, the silken strands
brushed across the bare flesh of her shoulders and heightened
her awareness of him.

The low cut of her strapless gown was no protection
against his fingers as they trailed over her bare shoulder, or
when they outlined her collarbone. Warm flesh, slightly
rough, touching her, easing her. She could feel it easing her
even as it heated her.

Her heart was racing, banging between her breasts with
fear. Or excitement. Fear, she told herself; she wouldn't allow
herself to be excited by something so small as the whisper of
his calloused fingertip over her flesh.

"Your father should protect you better," he said softly.
"Blood was shed last month in the attack against Sanctuary.
We know the two of you were involved. All we have to do is
prove it."

"And you have no proof," she reminded him just as softly.
"Accosting me in the dark isn't going to provide that."

He paused, his nostrils flaring as he watched her, his gaze
quizzical. He was dangerous, much more dangerous than the
other Breeds, and she knew it.

There was no hiding her arousal from him; she knew he
sensed it. She could see it in the ready tension of his body and
the glitter of lust in his eyes. Tanner was the Breeds' answer to

a Hollywood playboy. The bad boy. The one that reveled in his sensuality and his sexual hungers.

"Tell me, Scheme." He bent closer, blocking out the light, his eyes mesmerizing as she stared up at him. "Aren't you the least bit frightened? I could peel your flesh from your bones and hide your body in such a way that no man or Breed would ever find you. And I could show you pain unlike anything you've ever known."

"It's not pain you want to show me," she whispered back. "And it's not murder you're considering at the moment. Is it, Tanner?"

"Don't tempt me." His dark voice deepened, carrying an unmistakable sexual edge now. "You could never handle what I could give you."

She forced her lips into a little pout. "But, Tanner, tempting you would be so much fun," she drawled. "Surely you know it's my favorite sport? Tempting otherwise good men to be bad boys."

"I'm already a bad boy," he growled, suddenly looming nearer. "Of the worse sort. You don't want a piece of me; you wouldn't be able to handle it."

"Oh, a dare." She teased him, actually enjoying the repartee. "If I weren't on such a tight schedule, I'd be sure to take you up on that."

"And actually let an animal fuck you?" he asked. "Why, Miss Tallant, your father would have a stroke."

If only that were true.

"All men are animals, no matter their birthright," she assured him, fighting to hold back the bitterness. "Don't worry, I'd never let that affect my decision."

He leaned closer, his lips suddenly at her ear, caressing the fragile shell as he whispered, "Pretty girl, you've never had me. I could show you what being with an animal is really like. I could make you beg for more."

She had no doubt in her mind. If the state of her body were any indication, begging for him would not take long.

"You'd have to actually get me in a bed first." She moved her lips until they touched his ear as well, allowing her tongue to peek out, to flick over the tough earlobe. "And I make it a rule to never fuck men who hate me. That counts you out, Mr. Reynolds."

He held himself perfectly still, his hands at her hips, barely touching them, his body tense, ready, as though scenting danger.

"I never claimed to hate you, Scheme," he finally whispered, nuzzling her hair aside, his lips suddenly at her neck, his incisors raking a burning path across the vein at her neck. "But one of these days, you will fuck me. Unless I kill you first."

He nipped her neck, causing her to jerk back in surprise, her hand flying up to the smarting skin as she frowned back at him with a spurt of anger.

"That was uncalled for." She hardened her voice as she straightened her shoulders and glared back at him. "Don't you know the rules, Tanner? You don't bite on a first date, let alone a chance meeting in the dark. The mark of a civilized male is his control."

"Who said I was civilized?" He was laughing at her now. The flash of a smile, his wicked incisors gleaming in the dark. "That was just a warning, pretty girl. Once I get my dick inside you, you'll be begging me to bite you."

Yeah, that was what she was afraid of now. Dangerous. Very dangerous. She was playing with a fire hotter and with a greater potential for destroying her than the one she had been playing with for the past ten years.

"In your dreams." She scoffed him with much more confidence than she felt. "And if you will excuse me, as entertaining as this little adventure is, I really must be leaving. It's getting late."

She moved to pass him, only to come to an abrupt stop against the chest suddenly blocking her way.

"You're running away," he accused, one broad hand reaching up, his finger running down her cheek. "Do you think I conspired to get you here just so you could get away so easily?"

"I think I've had enough of your charming company." Her body was begging for more, but hell, it didn't have the good sense to pick decent lovers, so why should she begin paying attention to it now?

"I'm going to have you, Scheme. Fighting it isn't going to do anything but prolong the battle."

"And I'm just shaking in my shoes." She rolled her eyes before moving to the side and, this time, succeeding in skirting around him. "Haven't you heard, Tanner? The chase is half the fun." Actually, she had found it was the only fun, but it wasn't considered an intelligent move to insult the male ego. Let alone a Breed male. "And you will have to excuse me now. I've had enough of the party and the witty sexual innuendo. It's time I leave."

"Miss Tallant," he murmured as she walked back toward the party. "It has definitely been a pleasure."

✦   ✦   ✦

Tanner watched her walk from the garden, the light from the house spilling around her, causing the scarlet dress to blaze on her slender frame and darken the lush fall of sable hair.

He ran his tongue over his teeth. No swollen glands there. For a moment, just a moment, he had tasted something so unfamiliar in his mouth that his heart had tripped in suspicion. Could Scheme Tallant be his mate? The woman he had been plotting to kidnap for years, watching with an almost fanatical fervor, held a fascination for him that no other woman ever had.

The signs of mating heat were firmly established within the Breed community now. The swollen glands, the unusually vicious sexual heat that gripped the mind and body. His hunger for her was ripping through him, stronger than anything he had ever known. But none of the physical signs of the heat were making themselves apparent.

"She's leaving the party," he reported, knowing the team on the other end of the earpiece would receive the transmission.

"So we heard," Cabal growled in response.

Tanner's lips quirked. Despite his sexual abandon in private, Cabal was rarely comfortable with public flirting.

"Follow her," he ordered, heading back toward the party. "I want to know when she arrives at the house and whether or not she's alone."

"Are you certain this is the best course of action, Tanner?"
Cabal asked. "Following a snake into its den is never smart."

"That's lion," Tanner informed him with a smile. "Just make
certain the house is clear."

"We swept it for bugs before heading here," Cabal responded. "Evidently Daddy dearest doesn't trust his little
princess. Every room in the place is wired."

Tanner grimaced. "Have a jammer ready for me. I don't
want this recorded."

"Ready and waiting." Cabal sighed. "Covering your ass on
this one isn't going to be easy. You're damned lucky Jackal
has a perverted sense of humor when it comes to these games
of yours."

Jackal snorted in the background. He was one of the few
human enforcers within Sanctuary.

"He was just bored this week." Tanner smothered his laugh
as he neared the patio. "I'm out. See you at the castle."

The castle. The princess's town house in the middle of D.C.
had been searched from end to end over the past few days.
They found the bugs and little else. Strangely, the princess
had no intimate family photos other than a simple four-by-six
of her dead mother that sat by her bed.

Her home was sterile. Cold.

"Merc is bringing the limo around for you." Cabal spoke in
Tanner's ear as he reentered the ballroom and made his way
through the crush of political and not so political guests.

Making his excuses to the hostess, Tanner moved through
the lavish foyer of the house, for once ignoring the heated
feminine looks thrown his way.

It was rare for him to leave a party alone. But he didn't intend to be alone for long. Tonight, Scheme was going to get up
close and personal with a Breed in a way that didn't involve
blood or death.

First, he would fuck this fascination he had for her out of
his system, then get the information he needed, then just as
coldly as she had signed the death warrants on Breeds in the
past, he would turn her over to Breed Law.

He finally had the proof he needed against her. Pictures, signed orders, and her ex-lover's confession. All he needed now was one last confession by a council soldier or member to take her out. Scheme Tallant was about to become nothing more than a memory to the Breeds.

She didn't go home. Scheme couldn't bear the thought of the electronic listening devices scattered in her home, or the knowledge that her father had finally begun to suspect that his daughter was his greatest enemy.

That was the only answer. He had her home swept for listening devices weekly, and had been claiming none were present. But the small handheld device Jonas had given her proved differently.

She checked into her favorite hotel instead. As she followed the bellboy to the executive suite, a wave of weariness washed over her. She shouldn't have attended the party. Staying as far from Tanner Reynolds as possible would have been her safest bet. Unfortunately that particular Breed was her weakness. Not that she had ever been as close to him as she had been tonight. She had watched him from afar, studying his press releases and watching every interview and news program he was a part of. But until tonight, she had never pitted her own wit against him.

Bad Scheme. A smile tugged at her lips. At least she knew

her libido still worked; after the years it had remained silent, uninterested, she had wondered.

"Here you go, Miss Tallant." The bellboy inserted the key card and pushed the door open as he carried her small suitcase and laptop in.

He moved through the room, turning on the lights and setting her laptop on the desk before heading to the bedroom with her suitcase.

Seconds later he reappeared, a smile creasing his lips.

"We're very pleased to have you with us tonight. Is there anything room service can get you before I leave?"

"Not at the moment, thank you." She accepted the key card from him with a brief smile of thanks and a hefty tip. "I'll be fine for now."

Left alone in the well-lit suite, Scheme looked around the sitting room with a sense of unreality. Why the hell was she here? And where the hell was Jonas?

Pushing her fingers through her hair, she moved to the door, engaged the security locks and then moved to the bedroom.

Scheme opened her small luggage bag and pulled a pair of velvet lounging pajamas from inside. She tossed them to the bed, then reached back, pulled the zipper of the dress free and stepped from it.

She needed a shower; then she had to contact Jonas. If she didn't contact him soon, then everything she had worked for in the past years was going to go to hell.

If it hadn't already.

She couldn't discount Tanner's sudden appearance on the scene. After years of playing a subtle cat-and-mouse game, he had finally met her face-to-face, revealing a very tempting reason for suddenly confronting her.

Desire.

She grimaced at the thought as she adjusted the shower and stepped beneath the stinging spray.

Desire on her part, perhaps. He had always held a certain fascination for her. One she had never truly managed to deny herself. And he would know that. As manipulative, calculating and deceitful as he was, he would never have approached her for desire alone. He was up to something more. He knew something.

That made Tanner doubly dangerous. It meant he had inside information, information that possibly only the Breed spy for the Tallant organization could have gotten.

She closed her eyes as the water pelted over her face. It was too coincidental, and she didn't believe in coincidence. The very night she had attempted to meet with Jonas and he wasn't where he had agreed to be? He wouldn't have missed that meeting if it were safe. Which meant he could have suspected the spy working within Sanctuary would be there.

Could it be Tanner?

That sucked too. It sucked because it would have been much simpler and much more enjoyable for her if he were just who he was supposed to be. Sanctuary's playboy. The loyal public relations genius that had nations clamoring to help the Breeds.

She would contact Jonas tonight and arrange another meeting. There was no staying within her father's organization, not once he managed to discover who had disabled the message relay machine the night before. Her life was hanging by a thread and she knew it.

"Stupid. Stupid," she muttered as she hurriedly finished showering.

She had taken one look at the message that had come in, and she had panicked.

Plans in place. First child will be taken within fourteen days. Prepare exit.

Scheme had immediately contacted Jonas for pickup, then tried to erase her presence on the machine, but she knew she hadn't done so effectively. She hadn't had time. After her father had picked up the message from his spy, unaware she had seen it first, Scheme had known she had to run and do so quickly. Once Jonas had this information, Callan's son David would have a shield around him that no one could penetrate. And then her father would know what she had done. Because the cameras in the office would have placed her as the only other person in the office that day.

If her father managed to take the first known naturally born Breed, then the Breeds would retaliate with savage force. Which she knew her father would be gleefully looking forward to. It was his chance to rebuild his reputation with the Genetics Council. In one move he could acquire a first-generation naturally conceived Breed and, at the same time, cause the Breeds to attack in a way that would definitely turn world opinion against them. She had bought herself some time by sabotaging the message relay system. There would be no way of telling when the data processor had been corrupted—at least not for a while—or who had corrupted it. The cameras in the office would show nothing but her working diligently at the computer for several hours. Until they managed to get into the relay systems log-in files, she was safe.

Breathing out in frustration, she rinsed before wrapping her hair tightly in a towel and drying off her body. Half an hour later, her hair was more or less dry, her body was lotioned, smooth and softly scented.

Checking the wristwatch she had laid on the bathroom counter, she calculated the chances of contacting Jonas before midnight. The man kept some very odd hours. He hadn't answered his cell phone all evening, and he hadn't returned the coded messages she had left despite the message she had sent earlier to his personal relay system within his office. Something was very wrong here, and the potential for her death was rising.

Scheme tightened the towel around her body and moved purposely toward the sitting room. Then, she came to an abrupt stop. Directly in front of Tanner, who lounged on the overstuffed couch facing her.

Jacketless, the top buttons of his dress shirt undone, his golden eyes darkening in lust, the Bengal moved with deceptive laziness, pulling himself to his feet as his gaze moved slowly over her scantily covered body.

"Well, you are persistent," she murmured, her fingers moving to tighten on the tuck of the towel at her breasts.

His gaze licked over the swell of her breasts above the towel as her nipples tightened, rasping against the material.

It was instant, her response to him. Her nipples tightened violently, her clit instantly came to life and a damp warmth glazed the folds of her sex.

"You didn't return to your home," he said softly, his voice rumbling erotically. "Why a hotel instead?"

She arched her brow. "Perhaps I'm expecting company."

"So why not in your own home?" he asked her again. "Most women prefer to have sex in their own beds. A form of intimacy, I believe." His lips quirked with endearing male charm.

"Perhaps the intimacy isn't what I'm after." She shrugged, turning back to the bedroom to dress in the lounging pajamas rather than conducting this conversation in a towel.

And she really didn't relish the thought of dying naked. If he were there to kill her, she'd just as soon be dressed, thank you very much.

As she moved to close the louvered door between the rooms, a broad hand pushed it open and Tanner's hard male body leaned against the door frame.

"I have a feeling letting you out of my sight might be a very bad idea right now." His gaze flicked over her again. "You don't have to dress on my account. You'll just be removing the clothing later."

"Oh, certain of yourself, aren't you?" She arched her brows mockingly but moved to the bed anyway.

Some imp of scandalous amusement filled her. Dropping the towel, she ignored him as she picked up the violet silk and lace thong and pulled it over it her legs.

She dressed casually, convincing herself that being naked in front of him didn't affect her, though she knew better.

The soft, light, velvet sleeveless lounging top came next. Pulling it over her head, she let her gaze connect with his and nearly lost her breath.

His eyes were glittering with hungry lust now, stroking over her high breasts before the material dropped over them. Picking up the loose bottoms, she inserted one leg, then the next, before pulling them on, feeling his gaze on her flesh almost as clearly as she would have a physical touch.

"You know I can smell your arousal." He did a growly thing with his voice that had shivers racing up her spine. "Why bother to dress?"

"Are you hungry?" She ignored the question. "I was about to call down for room service."

"Oh, I'm hungry," he murmured. "But I don't think food is going to still my particular appetite."

Her womb flexed, spasmed. For a moment, regret sliced through her so heavily that it nearly stole her breath. Another place, another time, she could have enjoyed the byplay, the sensual threat. She was a woman who enjoyed the chase, the thrust and parry before the foreplay moved to the bedroom.

She had enjoyed it until Chaz had taught her how very deceptive it could be. Until she had learned the pure evil that inhabited her father's heart when he destroyed her unborn child, and how easily Chaz had aided him.

Sexual byplay was now a threat. No matter how enjoyable. No matter how tempting.

"Food is the only offer being made. At the moment," she informed him, allowing a small smile to tip her lips as she gazed up at him through the screen of her lashes. "Are you particular or do you trust me to order?"

She moved for the doorway, intending to move between him and the frame.

"Why the game?" His hand caught her upper arm. "You want to be in that bed with me as much as I want to be there."

The touch was soft, light; the only restraint it evoked was that of her own response to him. She slammed to a stop, staring at the strong fingers curving around her flesh.

"What I want, and what I allow myself, Mr. Reynolds, are rarely the same thing," she warned him tightly. "Restraint builds character. Perhaps you should try it."

"Too bad it doesn't build honor and decency," he retorted as he released her arm, following her into the sitting room.

"I've actually heard it does." Her lips twitched in amusement. "The good sisters at Our Lady's Academy assured me it would strengthen those qualities in me."

While they were laying the strap to her back.

"Ah yes, Our Lady's Academy," he mused. "You were expelled, yes?"

"I was." And it was a very fond memory. "The good sisters there decided I was a lost cause that even they couldn't save." Her father hadn't been nearly as understanding as she had hoped he would be. The healing bruises from the nuns' beatings had been added to exponentially. It had taken her weeks to recover.

"Are you a lost cause, Scheme?"

She turned to him, wondering at the sudden somber vein in his voice as she tried to match it to the almost angry glint in his eye.

"Completely," she answered quickly, honestly. "Really, Tanner, you seem disappointed. Did you expect anything less?"

Punching the button for room service, she ordered a selection of meats, cheese and bread, and her favorite wine. If Tanner was here to kill her after he fucked her, then she was going to enjoy her last meal.

After hanging up, she moved to the balcony doors. Sliding the curtains open, Scheme opened the doors and stepped onto the shadowed expanse of the balcony overlooking D.C. They were twenty floors up, and the view was breathtaking. And she hoped the shadows outside would help to still the nervousness rising inside her.

"I don't get to stay here often," she said as she felt him move behind her, crowding her against the railing. "But I love the view. From here, you can feel the pulse of the city below."

"Why here and not at your home?" he asked her again, the warmth of his breath caressing the shell of her ear.

"You're tenacious." Her fingers tightened on the rail as she felt his hands move to her hips. "It's peaceful here. Almost anonymous." There were no hidden eyes watching, no malevolent ears dissecting each word, each move she made. Until his arrival, she had been safe here.

She turned, unable to bear the threat of his large body behind her without the benefit of seeing his face. Would he show a shift of expression? A subtle warning tense of his body if he made his move to kill her here?

When she stared up at him, his head tilted to the side and his eyes gleamed oddly in the dim light.

"You think I'm going to kill you?" Sensually full lips curved into an amused grin. "I wouldn't kill you, Scheme. Fuck the hell out of you, yes. Turn you over to Breed Law, definitely. But I won't kill you."

"You can't turn me over to Breed Law, Tanner." She sighed as she regarded him calmly. "I haven't done anything."

She was a double agent for the Bureau of Breed Affairs. Jonas might be a son of a bitch, but he wouldn't see her pay for the very crimes she had committed to gain evidence against her father and the Council.

If only she could trust Tanner. If only she were certain he wasn't her father's agent, that he would believe her need for asylum and the information she had. She was half tempted to spill her secrets to him and take her chances, but she couldn't take chances with another child's life. Not until she knew for certain.

"Your signature is on kill orders, pretty girl," he whispered, leaning forward to lay his lips against her ear. Wicked incisors scraped over the tender shell. "Pictures of your meetings with several suspected Council members. All we need is the confession of a Council soldier or member to crucify you. Do you think that's possible?"

Her lips quirked wryly. "I think, Tanner, that you could acquire just about anything you wanted, if you wanted it bad enough."

He frowned, his brow furrowing with a hint of frustration as his fingers tightened on her hips.

"You're so confident of escaping Breed Law," he said softly. "You should know better. Your father has headed the training branch of the Council for decades, and for the past ten years, we know you've been involved. Proving a definite isn't all that hard to do."

Breed Law. The statutes that were made into law years before gave the Breeds not just the right to govern themselves, but the right to seek vengeance. Not that vengeance was easily sought. It first had to be approved by the Breed

Cabinet, comprised of twelve Breed elected members, it would then go to the Oversight Committee in D.C., which was comprised of eight humans and four Breeds.

So far, there had been only a few executions of high-level Council members, and many incarcerations. But the pressure against the Breed Cabinet as well as the Oversight Committee to execute those found guilty of the attempted slaughters of the Breeds was becoming overwhelming.

"So prove it." She shrugged.

It would never happen. No one would dare betray her father in such a way, except her of course, and even if someone did, she had the agreement she had signed with Jonas years before.

It was too bad Jonas trusted no one at Sanctuary. Having a fallback position was always important. In this case, there was no safety net other than the place she had found to hide the agreement they signed. And until she knew for certain who her father's spy was, then she could give her information to one person only.

"You could come clean." He lowered his head further, his teeth rasping over her shoulder, followed by his tongue.

Scheme forced herself to breathe normally, and nearly failed. That should not be erotic. She shouldn't be creaming helplessly in response to something so simple.

"I just showered," she whispered at his ear. "I promise you, I'm very clean."

He nipped her shoulder. The sensual little pain brought a gasp from her lips and sent weakness shuddering through her body.

"I smell you," he growled then. "You're wet. So wet the scent of your arousal is like a drug."

Scheme tried to force herself to focus—she really did try. Her lashes fluttered against her cheeks, though, as his lips were suddenly on hers.

Sweet heaven. She hated kissing. She really did. But this kiss. Her hands tangled in his hair immediately, holding him to her as his lips slanted over hers and his tongue took immediate possession of her mouth. This kiss, hot, blistering with sexual intent and lustful demand, literally swept through her senses.

His arms wrapped around her as he dragged her from the rail only to turn and press her into the wall of the balcony. He surrounded her. He was around her, inside her, heating her, warming her. Sending shards of brilliant heat to explode around her clitoris as her hips arched against him.

Damn, he needed to bottle this kiss. He could make a fortune.

One big hand moved to tangle in her hair, pulling at it, causing her scalp to sting erotically as he pulled her head back, breaking the kiss before his lips singed her neck.

Scheme's eyes drifted open, not that she could see much; her vision was hazy, dazed.

Lifting to the tips of her toes, she sought to push the aching flesh between her thighs against the stiff length of his erection beneath his slacks.

Oh, that was good. A whispering moan fell from her lips as she finally managed to rub the aching center of her body against him.

Then his hips thrust back to her, one hand gripping her ass to lift her.

"Put your legs around my waist," he panted at her ear, doing that growly thing again. It made her want to lick his lips, to feel the vibration of it against her own.

Her legs moved around his waist, and then she saw stars.

Oh my. This was dangerous. She whimpered—and she never whimpered—when his cock pressed fully against her thighs and his hips rotated against her.

"I've been dying to shove my dick inside you." Explicit. He did not mince words in the slightest.

"Oh geez, you're such a romantic," she gasped, in no way turned off by the dangerously erotic statement.

"Did you want romance?" He nipped the line of her jaw. "Pretty lies to soften this?"

This being his teeth raking over her desperate nipple above the velvet before he drew the hard point, material and all, into his mouth.

The tight, muffled scream that left her lips shocked her. Oh shit. She was going to orgasm. Right here, pressed against the wall, from nothing but his teeth working the tight bud of her nipple.

And she wasn't even embarrassed.

Then he purred.

◆ CHAPTER 3 ◆

She orgasmed.

Tanner felt it ripple through her, felt her breath catch and smelled the excitement and shock that poured from every pore of her body.

Son of a bitch. She was hotter than dynamite. The smell of her need clouded his senses; the sweetness of the syrup he knew gathered between her thighs nearly made him drunk from the smell alone.

"Naughty, naughty Schemer." He pressed his dick tighter against her pussy, feeling the heat and wild wetness gathering there.

"Don't let it go to your head," she panted. "Been a while."

And she was lying. Unlike other liars, the scent of her little deceit wasn't nauseating. It was soft, with a hint of mockery and a soft undercurrent of surprise. He liked the smell of her lies. That didn't mean he was going to let her get away with it.

"Liar," he accused her softly.

"We won't go there." Her head fell back against the rough wall behind her as her eyes glittered behind her lashes.

"Where do you want to go then?" he asked her instead, rolling his hips against her heated pussy.

"Where you're about ten feet away from me."

She flexed, her knees tightening on his hips as though to hold him in place.

"Ten feet?" he mused. "It's going to be damned hard to turn that little ripple of release into a burning orgasm that far away, pretty girl. You sure that's what you want?"

He could smell her need for more. It was burning inside her, taunting both of them with a hunger he could barely resist.

"It would be a very good idea." She licked her lips. He wanted to lick them.

Before he could cover them again, she was pushing at his shoulders, her legs dropping from his hips. He was a fool to let her go. Giving her time to rebuild her defenses against him wasn't a good idea. But the challenge it presented called to him, had him smiling in anticipation as he released her.

"Impressive." She smoothed her hands over the soft velvet top before adjusting the hem and turning to stalk back into the room. "You can leave now."

He chuckled at that. "I don't think so."

Her hair whirled around her like a silken cape, thick, falling nearly to her hips as her eyes sparkled back at him in anger and desire.

"Play time is over, Bengal."

Rather than arguing with her, he closed the balcony door and pulled the curtains together.

"Play time has only begun."

Turning back to her, Tanner hid his smile as he sensed the sudden insecurity running through her. Scheme was said to be without vulnerabilities, without weaknesses. He had always known better. What he knew about her and what he sensed from her wasn't meshing. Until it did, there wasn't a chance in hell he was letting her go.

For years he had plotted to kidnap Tallant's little darling. First, because he wanted Tallant to suffer. Now, he didn't give a fuck what the general felt; he wanted the woman. The secrets. And now he wanted the hot kisses and shuddering releases. And until now, Jonas had always managed to foil his plans for one reason or another. Tonight, he would die before he released her.

And that thought brought a shadow of discomfort. Nothing should be this imperative. He shouldn't need any woman this desperately.

He checked his tongue again. Nope, no swollen glands. It might not be mating time, but it was definitely play time. And Tanner did like to play.

Her lips parted, her lashes drifting over her eyes as he stalked toward her, moving slowly around her.

"Tanner."

He could hear the warning in her voice, but he also heard the excitement. And that was good. Real good. Because the next time that sweet pussy clenched in climax, he intended to have his dick buried so deep inside it that he felt every luscious ripple.

"I smell you." He nipped her ear, his hands tightening on her waist as he pushed her against the wall.

"I said no," she panted.

"No, you didn't." He chuckled against her neck. "You're not a coward, Schemer. Or are you?"

His fingers spread open just below her breasts before sliding down slowly, burrowing beneath the soft elastic at her hips.

Her fingers curled against the wall as she rolled her forehead against it with a moan.

"I think I hate you."

"That's not hatred, that's hunger. Admit it, you're as hot for me right now as I'm hard for you." He pressed his erection against her ass.

Damn, he loved that curvy, rounded ass. A bubble butt. It lifted against him, grinding against his cock as his fingers slid into soft, drenched curls.

"Stay put." He held her to the wall as she tried to turn. "I just want to touch you."

If she turned to him, he was going to fuck her where she stood.

"This is insane." Her cheek pressed to the wall now, her lashes lowering over her flushed cheeks.

"Just let me feel," he crooned, pressing a kiss to her cheek, holding her steady as his fingers grazed her swollen clit.

It was still sensitive. The light orgasm moments before had affected only that tight little bud. He could feel the needy clenching of her pussy even now as his fingers rimmed the small opening.

"Do you want me?" he whispered at the corner of her lips. "Tell me, Scheme, do you want my fingers inside you?"

"I want . . ." She bit her lower lip, a grimace crossing her expression as her breath caught.

"What do you want?"

She shook her head.

"Tell me, pretty girl." He needed the words. Needed them with a ferocity he couldn't have imagined before.

"I want you. To fuck me."

He caught her as she tried to turn, held her steady, and thrust two fingers into a silky heat so tight, so fucking incredible, he nearly came in his pants.

✦ ✦ ✦

Scheme went on her tiptoes, her head slamming back against his shoulder as her eyes burst open, colors and heat shimmering in front of her gaze as he filled her.

And he stroked.

She tried not to scream, not to beg. Her thighs clamped on his hand, holding him in place, his fingers inside her, his palm cupping her, rasping her clit.

"There, pretty girl." That growly thing again.

She shuddered, pleasure swamping her as a whimper left her throat.

"Come for me now," he purred. "All over my hand, Scheme. Come for me."

Wicked, carnal, his fingers reached deeper inside her, finding a nerve ending she didn't know she possessed, stroked, thrust and sent her senses careening.

She came with a cry. She never cried from something so tame as this. She cried in arousal when being spanked. She cried at the carnality of anal sex, but rarely, rarely in orgasm.

This one shook her. There was nothing forbidden in the act. Nothing to tempt the most depraved senses. But it rocked through her until she was gasping, whimpering, her nails biting into the arm crossed beneath her breasts, holding her against him.

And she wanted more.

"Enough." She was surprised when he allowed her to push away from him, his fingers sliding slowly from the clenching depths of her pussy, stroking over her clit before he let her jerk his hand from her pants and stumble away.

"You need to leave. Now." Her voice quavered. She could feel her nostrils flaring, the tight jerk of her lips as she fought to push back needs she had never known before.

Sex was a sport. A hobby. A manipulation. External pleasure was all she desired. A good hard orgasm was all she needed. She didn't need *this*, this clawing desperation she could feel building inside her.

Then she shook, shuddered as he brought his still-damp fingers to his mouth and licked. His expression tightening, gold eyes gleaming with a brilliant, fierce hunger.

"You taste like sunshine," he rasped, clearly enjoying the taste of her, relishing it. God, had any man ever done such a thing?

"It's the soap," she snarled. She had to fist her hands at her sides to keep from reaching for him. She couldn't do this. She couldn't handle it. Not now.

His lips curled in satisfaction. "It's sweet, hot pussy. I want my lips there next, Scheme. I want to go down on you so bad my teeth ache."

Her knees went weak.

"Stop that," she hissed, hating the hunger on his face, the open, wicked gleam in his eyes. This wasn't a game anymore. For the first time in her life something inside was responding, a part of herself she kept hidden, even from herself. "I want you to leave, Tanner."

"It's not going to happen, pretty girl."

"Then I'll call Security." Yeah, right, she was going to let the tabloids have this one.

"No, you won't." He was openly, clearly laughing at her.

"Daddy might not be pleased that you're cavorting with Breeds, sweetheart."

No shit. If her head weren't already on the chopping block here, it would be then.

She had opened her lips to at least try to bluff her way out of this one, when a sharp knock sounded on the door. Her eyes widened as alarm skittered through her. Dammit.

✦　　✦　　✦

Tanner winked. Grabbing his jacket from the couch, he pointed to the bathroom. There, he slipped inside, leaving the door carefully cracked as he pulled the silencer-equipped handgun from the inside pocket of the jacket.

He didn't have a good feeling about this. He could feel something odd, smell it—cold, yet tinged with regret.

"Chaz." There was a note of fear in her voice, almost undetectable except for the scent of it suddenly whipping in the air.

Scheme didn't linger by the entry door. Tanner caught her scent moving closer, entering the bedroom. She was suddenly off balance, uncertain.

"What the hell do you want?" She questioned her visitor.

Anger and hurt mixed with the fear now.

The bedroom door closed softly.

"Chaz, this isn't a good idea right now."

Why did he have a feeling she wasn't talking about sex?

"You took one chance too many, Scheme." Chazzon St. Marks, an ex-lover and her father's assassin for hire. Tanner knew his voice, his scent. He stiffened at the note of death in the other man's voice. Hell no. This had nothing to do with sex. "Wasn't the beating last month enough? Did you have to keep pushing our luck?"

"What are you talking about?" Cool, composed. Her voice was a direct contrast to the fear bleeding from her now.

"You're busted," Chaz said gently. Too gently. "Did you really think you would get away with this?"

Terror. She wasn't just frightened now. She was terrified. Tanner could smell it, almost taste it.

"Excuse me?" Her tone was scathing. Oh yeah, she definitely lived up to her name.

"He didn't even order you to be brought in for questioning," Chaz sighed. "He doesn't think you can be broken, Scheme. I had hoped he was wrong. I hoped that last beating you received from him would convince you to change this course you seem to be on."

Ice built in Tanner's veins.

"Nothing to say?" Chaz asked her then.

Tanner could feel the other man preparing to kill. He couldn't smell a weapon, and that meant only thing. He intended to break her neck. That was St. Marks' specialty.

"I don't even know what you're talking about," she bit out, obviously retreating from him. "And I wish you would leave."

"You've hated him for eight years," Chaz sighed then. "He was watching out for you, Scheme."

"Shut up!" Agony resonated in her voice. "Just shut up."

"You had no business getting pregnant. I didn't want the brat, and your position didn't afford you the luxury of unwed motherhood. Would you have really wanted him to have such a hold over both of us?"

"I won't discuss this with you!" Ice dripped from her voice. "How are you going to kill me, Chaz? I don't see a gun, or a knife."

"I'm going to break your neck." His voice was heavy with regret now. "It won't hurt, Scheme. There's no pain, no blood. You'll be as beautiful in death as you are in life."

Like hell! And Tanner would be damned if he would wait around to see if the bastard was going to change his mind.

He jerked the door open, seeing the pale shock in Scheme's eyes as St. Marks turned. There was no time for a defense. The bullet struck right between the bastard's eyes, dropping him to the floor as Tanner palmed the syringe he slid from his pants pocket.

"Sorry about this, pretty girl." He grabbed Scheme, twisted her around, laid the pressure syringe against her neck and pressed the inject.

She collapsed into his arms.

"Shit." Laying her on the bed, Tanner crossed quickly to the fallen assassin, running his hands over his body with quick, sure movements.

St. Marks carried nothing on him. No weapon, no identification. Grimacing, Tanner pulled the earpiece and sleeve mic from his pants pockets. Inserting the receiver, he lifted the mic to his lips.

"Cleanup, boys. Pronto."

Cabal's and Jackal's curses filled his ear, the sound of movement assuring him they were on their way. He dropped the electronics into his pants pocket before jerking his jacket on, pocketing his weapon and lifting Scheme into one arm.

His arm curved around her back, holding her to him, her head on his chest. If they were seen, the assumption would be much different than the truth. Not that he intended to be seen.

Moving quickly from the suite, he headed for the stairs, pushing through the door as the elevator sounded on the other end of the hall. He knew it wouldn't take Jackal and Cabal long.

Tanner didn't wait around for them. Why it seemed imperative to slip past the other two men, he couldn't be certain. But from the moment he blew Tallant's man away, the animal inside him had taken over.

The shock of it might hit him later, but as he lifted Scheme in his arms and moved down the stairs, he didn't let it bother him now. Savage, protective, the animal instincts were imperative. Her life was in danger and nothing mattered past getting her to safety. Complete safety.

SANDY HOOK, KENTUCKY

There was no one to notice the black SUV that drove quietly along the mountain roads that night. The flare of headlights bounced off houses that now sat on once-thriving farmland, pierced curtained windows, then curved and gleamed along immaculate lawns before moving on. Mobile homes, red-bricked stately residences and modest farmhouses shared the same narrow roads as Tanner Reynolds drove steadily, heading for the turnoff that would lead him home.

The GPS for the vehicle wasn't just disengaged, it was dismantled and floating in a river somewhere. There were no eyes to see him, no ears to hear him as he headed for the last true sanctuary he knew.

He knew where he was going, but only he knew his impatience to be there. Only he was aware of the primal determination to find the hidden caves he and his family had discovered years before and to hide.

He checked his rearview mirror. There were no lights behind him or in the distance. The stretch of road was dark and rarely traveled this late at night.

The soldiers sent from the Council to find the small Breed pride Callan raised during the years they had lived in this county had never discovered the caves he was heading for. They weren't even part of the network of caverns that lay below the house their pride leader had lived in before the world discovered them.

It had been a mistake, Tanner thought now. Revealing themselves to the world hadn't been the assurance of safety that they had believed it would be. The remaining members of the Genetics Council would never let them live in peace. And those Council members would always fuel and aid the pure blood and supreme race societies that had risen in the wake of the Breeds' revelation to the world.

Tallant and his supposedly spoiled, well-loved daughter were rumored to be head of those organizations.

Tanner inhaled roughly, drawing in the scent of her, letting it permeate his senses. And God, she smelled good. She didn't smell like the gutter slime he'd once believed her to be; she smelled like fucking summer. Like roses on a desert wind. Like goddamned nirvana, and he was waxing poetic about what could still be a murderous bitch. Forget the fact that animal instincts he had relied on all his life roared in denial.

Who the hell was Scheme Tallant? She sure as hell wasn't the spoiled little bitch he had believed her to be. Not after what he'd heard in that fucking hotel room.

Her father had sent an assassin after her.

And instead of just killing the assassin and turning her over to Sanctuary, he was running with her.

He had lost his mind. That was all there was to it. The animal was clashing with the man in a battle Tanner knew he was going to lose. Something, some inborn sense he couldn't escape, wouldn't let him release her.

Tightening his hands on the steering wheel, Tanner felt his lips curl back from his teeth in a primal snarl. He had to physically restrain a growl. His hold on the animalistic side of his nature was tenuous at best at this point. The more he immersed himself in her scent, the less he fought it.

And the thought of that terrified him. This weakness worried him. He couldn't countenance it. For years, more years than he wanted to consider, he had made certain he had no weakness. No lovers that meant more than the good times they shared. No friends except those he considered family. No associates that could be used against him.

But this woman weakened him. She made the animal inside him stronger.

Growling at the stupidity of saving her bubble ass, he flipped off the lights on the SUV and made the turn on the graveled road that led into the cliffs below.

He needed to get her to shelter. She had awakened only once during the drive from D.C. to eastern Kentucky, enough to assure him that she wasn't in any real danger from the tranquilizer he had pumped into her.

Getting her into the hidden caverns was imperative. He had everything he needed to protect her there. And there he would get the answers he needed. She would know who the spy was in Sanctuary; no doubt this was how General Tallant was aware of every move made at the Breed base. That meant Scheme must know the spy as well.

Damn, her daddy had named her right. If reports could be believed, and Tanner was beginning to doubt those reports, then Scheme was personally responsible for several of the attacks made against Sanctuary.

She plotted. She planned. She schemed. She was the Schemer. Except he was starting to suspect that rather than scheming *for* her father, she may well have been scheming *against* him.

✦ C H A P T E R   4 ✦

She wasn't dead. It was the first thing Scheme could think with any certainty. She was breathing. For now anyway.

There was no confusion, despite the grogginess. She knew exactly what had happened right until the moment Tanner's arm had gone around her neck and darkness had washed over her.

Funny, she had been certain he was going to kill her. She had seen death in his hard, suddenly brutal gold eyes, and felt it pulsing in the air around her as he moved from the bathroom.

Her hand moved to her neck, feeling the slight soreness where something had pinched her. She had a feeling she was royally fucked in a way she didn't want to be. But what didn't kill you made you stronger, right?

Bullshit.

Well, at least she wasn't buried. She could feel the sense of space around her, a blanket lying over her, clear, clean air moving into her lungs rather than the feeling of dwindling oxygen. That would have sucked.

"You can open your eyes. I know you're awake."

Her eyes flew open, and it took every ounce of control she

possessed to stare back at Tanner with even a modicum of control.

Yep, she was screwed. Not in a good way. Not even in a decent way. She was royally FUBAR, as her father's second in command like to say. Fucked Up Beyond All Repair.

The man standing at the end of her bed wasn't the suave, charming, sophisticated public relations liaison to the Breeds. Oh no. This was the animal the Council had created. Savage, intense, dangerous.

And she was now at his mercy.

Lucky her.

Her gaze shifted from the dark fury in his eyes. She couldn't bear to hold it, to see the accusation in his gaze, the judgment. Not that she could ever expect anything else. She'd worked hard over the years to gain the Breeds' total hatred, and she had succeeded. It made her job easier. Her life less complicated. It was just harder to see the truth in his eyes now, rather than the playful desire.

Her gaze touched on stone walls, stone floors. The bed she lay in was made of heavy wood with thick posters. Above, heavy material spanned the connected posters before draping to the floor. It was old-fashioned, almost medieval in design. Wildly romantic. There wasn't a chance in hell the man staring at her from the end of it had had anything to do with its design.

There was a large overstuffed couch and several chairs at the other end of what appeared to be a large cave. An old-fashioned cast-iron stove sat not far from the sitting area, along with a circular table and four chairs. Cabinets were overhead and along the stone walls. Several metal pipes ran along the ceiling before disappearing into the stone walls, conduits of some sort. There was a television, stereo system, a small shelf of books, CDs and DVDs. All the comforts of home. Surrounded by stone.

"Where am I?" She had a feeling she really didn't want to know the answer.

"Safe. For the moment." Powerful arms crossed over his chest as he stared back at her, his eyes cold.

"For the moment?"

A heavy black brow quirked mockingly.

Scheme resisted the urge to swallow against the fear that tightened her throat. She could do this, she assured herself. He might be a rogue Breed for the moment, but eventually he would have to check in, right?

"May I have some water?" She licked her dry lips, fighting the fear and nausea as she had so many other times in the past. She faked it.

"For a price."

"It would appear I'm most likely rather penniless at the moment." She sighed. "Father has a habit of canceling credit cards and bank accounts on those he has assassinated."

He had really done it. Cyrus had really grown tired of the game and decided to have her killed. It was like throwing out the trash, he had once told her. You had to get rid of the filth in your own organization sometimes. It seemed she had become part of the filth. Tanner's head tilted to the side, his eyes, unique even among the Breeds, glittered with ice as a satirical smile shaped his sensually full lips. Thick, ropy muscles flexed in his arms as his head straightened and he continued to stare down his nose at her.

"What's the price for a drink of water?" That look went hand in hand with the art of negotiation.

Amusement lit his gaze then. Just his eyes. A glimmer of it, nothing more before his gaze dropped to the blankets covering her.

"Whatever possessed you to sleep with an assassin?" he finally asked.

"A question is the price?" Negotiation was never that easy.

His lips quirked. "I told you, sweetheart, I have every intention of getting my piece of that tight little body. I was just wondering why your taste in men is so damned lousy."

Years of control stilled the flinch that a whiplash of pain brought.

"I'm not that thirsty yet," she said calmly.

"I'm not that horny yet, but I could get there fast," he assured her, his smile turning cold once again. "Maybe you'll be thirsty by the time I'm ready."

Her gaze dropped to his hips then jerked back to his face. Okay, he looked pretty damned ready right now. It was almost amusing. Tanner Reynolds was reported to be one of the most docile Breeds ever created. Created approximately thirty-five years before, escaped with pride leader Callan Lyons at the age of fifteen and raised in Sandy Hook, Kentucky, until Lyons revealed their existence ten years before.

The New Mexico lab he had escaped from had been considered one of the most severe. The members of the Genetics Council, as well as the scientists and soldiers who oversaw the Breeds, had known no mercy. Mercy was said to breed weakness, and the Council refused to allow any of its creations to be weak.

All but one. Her mother. Twenty years ago, the only person willing to help the Breeds had been on temporary assignment in New Mexico to run a series of tests on a Breed known as Sherra. The only Breed to have conceived at that point, only to miscarry.

Scheme knew that much for a certainty. Her father had on several occasions pointed out how her mother had paid for her decision to aid the Breeds. She reportedly died of a massive stroke days later. But Scheme knew her father had had her killed. Just as he was willing to have his daughter killed now.

Tanner wasn't the pleasure-seeking, laugh-a-minute American boy he was made out to be. It was there in his eyes, in the hard curve of his lips. He could fool others, but Scheme had spent her life traversing the dangerous waters of the Council. She knew exactly what she had managed to somehow get herself into here.

She was imprisoned with one of the most merciless, conniving Breeds ever created. As well as one of the most curious. And that was dangerous for her. Extremely dangerous.

"No compromise?" she asked, aware that her voice was weakening.

God, she was tired. And thirsty, the need for water almost torturous. And she needed a restroom. That one was becoming overriding.

"Breeds weren't trained to compromise," he reminded her.

"I believe that was one of your father's predecessor's first orders when he began the training of the Breeds."

Yes. Good ole Grandfather Cyrus Tallant Sr. The bastard.

"Is the price lower for a trip to the restroom?" She sighed wearily. There should be a rule that negotiations could only be conducted when both parties were at their best. Or their weakest. The playing field really should be even.

Whatever the hell he had done to her had her head fuzzy as hell.

"Restroom breaks are free." He shrugged. "So is the water. Take a bath while you're in there. It might improve your disposition."

Yeah, sure. Why didn't she just do a few laps while she was at it? She wondered if she would even have the strength to carry her ass to wherever the hell the bathroom was located. Whatever he had used to knock her out with had made her weak as a kitten.

"Where is it?" She forced herself to move. Forced. Focused every ounce of strength she possessed into moving her legs, shifting her body. A person might never realize how much they used their backs, until those muscles cramped with the pain.

She hadn't been so stiff the night before because she had worked out the soreness through the day. Now, after the enforced sleep, however long she had slept, she had stiffened to the point of agony.

No tears. She blinked back the moisture the pain of movement brought as she slid to the edge of the bed, careful to keep the blankets over vital parts of her naked body.

"Behind the curtain." He jerked his head to the rich maroon velvet curtain hanging on the wall several feet from the bottom of the bed.

"Figures," she muttered to herself. "Of course it couldn't be anywhere close."

"This far underground, pretty girl, you have to put the facilities in the best plumbable area." There was a shrug in his voice, but the only thing that really caught her was the underground part.

As she sat on the edge of the bed she turned to stare at him in resignation. "Underground?"

He flashed his teeth. Especially those wickedly sharp incisors. "Deep underground, sugar. You got phobias?"

"If I did, I'd be screwed at this point, wouldn't I?" Forcing amused derision into her voice wasn't easy.

"Well, you might be screwed anyway," he murmured. "Do you have any preferences there?"

Scheme almost laughed at the thought of that one. Oh, she had many preferences, and she was certain he could handle most of them.

"Sorry, I've decided Breeds are off the list this year. Try next year," she suggested lightly.

"Let's see if we can't change your mind for this year first." His smile was predatory. Almost frightening.

Scheme stared back at him in surprise.

"All this for a roll in the sheets? You killed my assassin, carted me to only God knows where, underground, so you could get fucked? Isn't that a little extreme?"

Even for Tanner it was extreme. Even the Breed community itself recognized that their Bengal brother was a little outside of what Breeds considered normal behavior. But this was more than Scheme had expected.

"Getting fucked will be an added benefit," he said. "Go get your bath; we can discuss terms later."

Fine. They could discuss it later. Just chickie. Suited her. She didn't know if she had enough mental capabilities to discuss the weather right now, let alone the terms to anything.

She gripped the sheet, intending to pull it with her as she rose.

"No sheet." Hard. Growling. The tone had her gaze jerking back to his and then to the hand gripping the sheet through the quilt that covered it.

Now, why hadn't she just expected that one? Son of a bitch, she was supposed to be protected from Breed kidnappings or attempted hits by Jonas. What? Did the director of Breed affairs forget to send out that memo? Tanner was supposed to be contained and his movements reported to her if he came anywhere close to her, because of his rumored declaration to see the Tallants wiped off the face of the Earth. And she was after all a Tallant. What the hell had happened to Jonas protecting her? First she had seen he had ditched that stupid party, and now this?

"Fine. No sheet." She rose to her feet, letting the sheet and quilt slide over her body.

She had learned a long time ago not to let her own nudity distress her. *No weakness* was her father's motto as well. And that meant none. He had raised her with the same iron fist that he had trained his marines with when he was in the Corps.

Holding her head high, she gave him a mocking little smile and moved without haste to the bathroom.

Suck it in, Breed, she thought with a spurt of amusement as his eyes heated and his hard body tensed. It was like teasing a hungry animal, and something inside her decided it was fitting punishment. For both of them.

◆   ◆   ◆

Tanner leaned against the thick post of the bed, crossed his arms over his chest and watched her. Bad mistake. It was all he could do to keep the mocking amusement on his face rather than go to his knees and drool like a cur dog as she walked past.

Bengal Tigers did not drool.

But damn if she wasn't a sight worth drooling for. Sleek, well-toned flesh, long silky hair and a grace that had him clenching his teeth to hold back a sliver of respect.

Small, high breasts, a rounded little tummy and curl-covered pussy. Most women waxed or shaved their pussies, keeping the flesh there soft and silky smooth. And Breeds had no true body hair themselves. Which meant he was fascinated by it. Loved it. He couldn't wait to find out what those soft curls hid from his gaze, flesh only his fingers had known so far.

Long sable hair fell to her waist, tangled but silky and thick, caressing her back and hips with a flirting sexiness he found definitely appealing.

She was beautiful. Simply beautiful. And weaker than a kitten. He was going to have to have a little talk with Jackal about the strength of the dosage in that sedative. Fuck, he was a mess and he hated being a mess. Calm and controlled, that was his motto. Unless he was between a pair of beautiful thighs belonging to a hot woman. That was worth letting go of a little control. But not this much. Never this much.

Tanner sighed wearily as he heard the water running in the bathroom, before pacing to the cabinets Callan had set along the side of the cavern wall, while keeping a careful ear on Scheme in the bathroom.

She was muttering to herself. He couldn't catch what she was saying, but if he had any parentage, it was definitely being called into question.

Shaking his head, he drew the microwave, hot plate and coffeepot from below the counter and set them in place before plugging them into the outlets set into the stone wall.

Getting electricity down here had been a pain in the ass. He bet Callan had spent three years running their asses into the ground to wire this place. It was their last safe hole— caverns so deeply imbedded beneath the ground and layered with so many different minerals and ores that even the ground-penetrating satellites above the earth couldn't find them. There were small pockets of rough diamonds, rubies, gold and silver, iron ore and other mineral deposits that he had finally lost track of.

The caverns were unexplored, unknown, so well hidden that even the locals were unaware of them. And Callan had gone to great lengths to keep it that way. Hell, he had been working on the caverns long before he had been recaptured by the Council and taken to New Mexico.

Tanner prepared the coffeemaker quickly before pushing his fingers through his hair and grimacing at the sound of a muted feminine groan from the bathroom. Then a smile kicked at his lips as she cursed herself.

Tanner listened to the water running in the big claw-foot bathtub as he set out food for a meal. He had left her alone long enough. He needed to check on her. If a Breed had nerves, then his were rioting with concern. He could have sworn she didn't have the energy to drag her ass into that big tub, let alone get herself out later.

He stalked to the curtain-covered entrance and jerked the velvet curtains aside, his gaze going instantly to the tub. And he swore the breath froze in his chest but flames began to lick at his balls.

Water still flowed into the deep, old-fashioned tub, hot, steamy water that had barely reached the tips of those damned luscious tits. His cock jerked, throbbed. He swore he felt cum boiling up the shaft as he stared at the hard rosy nipples bobbing in the water.

The animal growled, and unfortunately, the sound slipped past his lips.

Scheme's lashes drifted open as the water slowly eased over those perky, berry-ripe nipples. His mouth watered. What he wouldn't give right now to taste those sweet tits.

"Negotiations for privacy?" she murmured, her voice lazy, drowsy.

"Sure." Damn, he could still form words. He was doing good. "Tell me why your father sent your ex-lover to kill you."

Tallant was a dead man for that alone. There would be no way in hell that he could stop himself from killing the other man now.

Her eyes closed as she turned her head from him.

"Watch all you like." Her lips quirked. "Exhibitionism excites me, didn't you know that?"

Oh yeah, he knew that. He knew all the nasty erotic adventures she had experienced over the years. Knew about them and relished the thought that when he got her beneath him, he would have a woman who understood pure pleasure with a dash of the extreme.

She wasn't promiscuous really. After Chaz St. Marks, she had chosen her lovers outside her father's organization. Men who understood the brief affairs she was looking for, men who tried to give what she needed without asking for more themselves. He wondered if she had found exactly what it was she was looking for in those affairs. He knew that for himself, he never had. No matter how extreme, how depraved, nothing had ever stilled the hunger for her that rode him.

"You haven't answered my question." Anything to hear her voice. It stroked over his senses in a way that made him check his tongue against his teeth again.

Her lashes peeked open once more, giving him a glimpse of chocolate brown eyes so deep, so dark, he swore there was a chance of drowning.

"Which one?"

"Why did your father send St. Marks to kill you?"

"The assassin." Her smile was bittersweet. Son of a bitch, she felt something for the bastard willing to kill her. "You enjoyed killing him, didn't you?"

"What do you think?" The only sign of emotion was the slight flinch of her lashes.

"I think you enjoyed it very much. In answer to your question, he believes I betrayed him."

"And did you?"

Her expression was weary, sad. "Perhaps I've just been sloppy. I've made a lot of mistakes in the past few years. I've become a liability."

It wasn't exactly a lie, but Tanner could detect a shadow of deceit. It wasn't sitting well with him.

"So you heard everything?" she asked then.

"Pretty much."

She didn't say anything more. Instead, she lifted one gracefully turned ankle out of the water and used it to shut off the water.

Her expression wasn't cold, but neither was it one of emotion. It was reflective. Almost thoughtful.

"And then you kidnapped me," she said. "Why?"

"Some would say I saved your ass," he pointed out.

"I'm free to leave then?"

Tanner grinned at that. "I wouldn't go that far."

"And why did I expect that answer?"

She was avoiding the discussion coming. He could see her need to hide from it, to distance herself from what she knew he'd heard.

"You should have guessed it," he agreed, moving away from the entrance and stalking slowly toward her. "Sit up and let me wash your hair. It's so damned long, it dragged the ground a time or two."

"I can wash my own hair."

He doubted she could wash her own face at the moment. She was stiff from the bruises and from sleeping so long. Abused muscles stiffened up after time, and he had been forced to keep her under longer than he would have liked.

"Don't make me force you to sit up. It's going to end in something you don't want."

Moving stiffly, she sat up in the tub as he collected the girly shampoo and conditioner his pride sisters Sherra and Dawn had stocked the bathroom with.

"Lean forward," he ordered as he lifted the detachable showerhead from its holder above the tub. "Let's see if we can't get you cleaned up here."

He pushed her hair forward, suddenly as reluctant to ask the questions as he knew she would be to answer them. Sometime in the past Cyrus Tallant had killed her child. Tanner had heard the pain in her voice, the bitterness as she refused to discuss it with the father who had aided Tallant in the vile act. But that didn't mean she had any loyalty to his enemies. Until he knew for certain, he would have to play his game very carefully.

The scent of honor he had detected from her, mixing with deceit, anger and bitterness, could have been there for many reasons. She could believe in what she was doing. It was possible. She could hate her father and yet believe in his battle against the Breeds.

At this point, nothing was certain except the need to learn the truth.

CHAPTER 5

Why was she letting him do this?

She was never this weak. It wasn't acceptable.

Scheme stiffened her body, attempting to lift her head, to deny the erotic thrill of calloused fingertips working over her scalp.

"Shh. Relax." Those diabolical hands gripped her neck, and strong fingers began to work the tense muscles as she forced back a moan.

She had never had a man bathe her. Ever. And now she knew why. The intimacy of the act was a weakness itself.

Swallowing tightly, she kept her head down, forcing her breathing to become regular while he wrung the water from her hair and twisted it expertly into a towel.

"Lean back." His voice was insidiously soft, his hands firm as he gripped her shoulders and forced her to recline against the back of the porcelain tub.

"There you go. Just rest," he murmured. The sound was a purr of male satisfaction, one she wanted to fight.

She was in dangerous territory here and she knew it. Her father could have more than one spy in Sanctuary, and she knew that at least the one she knew of was in a very high position. She couldn't discount Tanner.

At this point, anyone within Sanctuary was suspect. Especially Tanner. He was trained in non-weapon warfare. Before he was fifteen years of age he had excelled in guerilla infiltration and subversive techniques. The Council scientists had determined he had the mental capabilities and lack of emotion to excel at it. He could just as easily be one of the spies her father had managed to secure within Sanctuary as any other Breed could be.

Trusting him was too dangerous.

Just because Tanner had rescued her from Chaz didn't mean he could be trusted. Her father knew about the message she had destroyed; he knew she wouldn't break if he hurt her, or if he buried her. Tanner could have been her father's insurance. He could have been in place to gain her trust, even if it meant killing Chaz.

General Cyrus Tallant was nothing if not diabolical, and he left very few things to chance. He would have wanted that information above all things, if possible.

"What do you want from me?"

"There are a lot of things I want from you." He eased around the tub, a bath sponge in one hand, a bottle of bath gel in the other.

Scheme watched as he squeezed the gel onto the sponge then set the bottle on the floor.

"Like?"

His eyes were alive. The colors within them brightened and dimmed, shifted and shadowed.

"Should I make a list?" He dipped the sponge into the water before lifting her arm and beginning to bathe her.

"Yes, make a list," she said. "I'll read it later. And I can bathe myself."

Strength. All she needed was a little more strength. Moving jerkily, she had gone to push herself upright, when firm hands, not rough, but firm, insistent hands, pressed her back.

"You're as weak as a kitten," he purred. "You don't have to fight me, Scheme."

"No, I just have to lie back and allow you to molest me."
She didn't fight him. She had learned long ago there were better ways to meet force rather than head on.

"Molest you?" The sponge paused on her arm. "How am I
molesting you?"

"I prefer not to be touched by you, Tanner."

"I didn't ask your preference." His jaw tightened.

Scheme shrugged lazily. "Then the technical term for such
force is molestation, Mr. Reynolds."

He dropped her arm into the water. For the smallest second, she assumed she had won. Now, what did they say about
that word? *Assume.* Something about an ass, she thought in
amusement.

A second later he had reached across the tub and gripped
her other arm.

"Fine. I'm molesting you." His hard shoulders shrugged
in return. "Breeds weren't trained to be politically correct
or sexually polite either. We were trained to take what we
want."

And it was obvious that among other things he might want,
he wanted her.

"Do you ever take no for an answer?" she asked as he let
her arm drop into the water once again before dipping his
hand below and lifting her knee.

"Rarely," he answered. "Now prop your foot on the edge
of the tub."

"You're pissing me off." But she did as he asked, her gaze
focusing on the sponge traveling over her leg.

How much more humiliating could this get?

"Why did your father beat you? And don't deny it, I heard
every word St. Marks said."

Damn Chaz and his loose lips. He should have just broken
her neck and kept his damned mouth shut. She didn't need
all these questions.

"Because I'm into pain?" She glanced at him from the corner of her eye as she let a smile tug at her lips. She did mocking amusement rather well when needed.

"Do you practice that look in the mirror for effect?" he

asked as he lowered her leg back to the water before lifting the opposite knee.

"Do you get off on torturing women? What the hell do you want? You've been watching me for years. I know you have, you know you have. Why? Why rescue me? Why kidnap me? And why the hell do you think I need you to bathe me?"

She jerked her leg back from him and jackknifed upright as she glared back at him. His hand snapped out and wrapped around her neck as the growly thing turned dangerous.

There was no pressure. Only the threat of it.

"Do it," she lashed out at him, amazing herself with her own daring. "Go ahead. Snap my neck. You know you want to. Get it over with."

She had lived with the fear of punishment and death for twenty years. She had sacrificed more than he would ever know and in doing so had come to realize that death wasn't the terrifying specter she had once imagined.

Cause for regret, yes. Terrifying, no.

She had realized it long before she knew that the man she had once loved was going to kill her.

"Your father ordered your death," he snapped. "He sent your former lover to do the deed. *The father of the child you never had.* And he was going to kill you, Scheme. He wasn't having second thoughts. Why did General Tallant suddenly decide to kill his only child?"

"Why do you want to kill me?" She kept her voice cold. Hard. "Really, Tanner, do you think I give him any less trouble than I've given the Breeds?"

"Your father beat you!" Rage flamed in his eyes. She swore the swirling amber nearly blazed.

"And you care why?" Her fingers locked around his wrist as she reminded herself that his fingers weren't tightening on her throat. That she really could breathe.

"I'm going to kill that son of a bitch," he suddenly whispered, his face coming closer, his lips pulled back from his teeth to reveal the wicked incisors, top and bottom, at each side. "Do you hear me, Scheme? I'm going to gut him with my bare hands."

"Are you—"

She gasped, the words cut off as his lips suddenly covered hers and an explosion of pleasure began to storm her body.

It was just a kiss. That was all. Lips meeting. His tongue pressing forward, invading, licking . . . Oh God, he was licking at her mouth, purring into the kiss, and flames were searing her.

This wasn't just a kiss. This wasn't just pleasure. It was a claiming. And she was helpless beneath it.

The hell it was. This was a kiss that stole into the soul and stoked flames she had never known existed within her. It was a fiery invasion that had her reaching for more, had her hands moving to his hair, tangling in the silky mass to hold him to her. She heard her own moans slipping past her lips to his and reveled in them. For the moment.

It was the closest thing to ecstasy she had ever known in her life.

"Damn you!" Just as quickly as he had taken the kiss, he broke it off.

Scheme stared back at him in shock as he jerked back from her, surging to his feet with a force that stunned her.

"Get out and dry off," he snarled, his expression filled with disgust. "And don't take all day. If I have to come back in here, I'll bend you over the damned tub and drown your ass while I show you what it's like to be fucked by a Breed. Let's see what you think about pain then."

She could only stare back at him. For once, her normal glib responses were absent, her brain in chaos. For some reason this kiss was more destructive than the orgasm he had given her in that hotel room.

He turned and stomped from the bathroom, jerking the curtain so hard he nearly ripped it from the heavy rod holding it.

"Oh hell," she whispered as she stared at the closed curtain, fighting to swallow. To taste something other than the fierce, heated taste of Tanner's lust. And damn if his lust didn't taste good.

⋆ CHAPTER 6 ⋆

There had to be a way out of here. Somehow he had managed to drag her into these caverns, and that meant there had to be an entrance. He was a Breed, not a ghost. Well, not the dead kind of ghost, anyway. In the last forty-eight hours he had snuck out of the cavern without her seeing him and disappeared for several hours. And she had yet to even find the damned exit.

There had to be twenty tunnels running around in a maze that led directly back to the main cavern. There were no extra tunnels, at least none that she could find.

She had to get out. She had already been here too long and she knew it. She had to find Jonas, give him the information she had and secure her own safety. Then she could deal with Tanner on her terms rather than his.

This was incredibly bad.

Moving through the narrow tunnel she had been investigating, she reentered the storage cave and made her way back into the cavern and the man waiting on her. He sure as hell hadn't been there when she began investigating tunnels, so he had to have slipped in while she was searching. Which just pissed her off.

"I'm getting tired of playing this game," she snapped as she came face-to-face with Tanner's mocking smile.

Tightening her hold on the large bath towel she used to cover her body, she glared at him, not in the least surprised that her anger wasn't affecting him in the slightest.

"You won't find the exit, Schemer; you can stop looking." He turned his back on her, moving across the room to the bed, where he dropped a large black bag on the mattress.

When he turned back to her, his gaze was considerably hotter, though his lashes drifted over his eyes with drowsy sexuality. He had been giving her those looks for two days now. Sexy, body-licking looks. She could almost feel his tongue stroking over her flesh.

"You can't keep me here forever, Tanner." He wasn't listening now any more than he had listened to her before.

"I brought you some clothes." He indicated the black bag. "I assumed you were growing tired of running around here naked."

She glanced at the bag. There were enough clothes there for several weeks if he had any clue at all when it came to packing. She assumed he did. She hoped he did.

"Tanner." She crossed her arms over her breasts, holding the towel in place. "There are things at stake here. You have to let me go."

"What's at stake, Scheme? Another strike against Sanctuary? Another plan to kill Breeds? Tell you what, tell me what your precious daddy has planned and I'll think about letting you go. Better yet, tell me what he was willing to kill you for." His expression was friendly; his eyes were roiling with danger.

"Father hasn't shared his plans with me in years and I have no idea what Chaz was talking about."

Tanner's snort of disbelief assured her of his opinion concerning that one. It wasn't good. And of course he knew she was *lying*. Bastard's sense of smell was off the damned charts.

Then, he really surprised her.

"Your father has two teams after you, both headed by loyal coyote Breeds. The order is dead or alive," he informed her softly. "I'm going to ask you one more time. What do you know that your father is willing to kill you over?"

She felt the blood drain from her face. Damn, Cyrus was serious about this one. Not that she had expected anything less.

It wasn't as though she hadn't lived with the threat of her own death hanging over her head for years now. She knew how dangerous Cyrus was, just as she had known that she couldn't get away with betraying him forever. She couldn't trust Tanner with that though. She couldn't trust anyone except Jonas. He and the pride leader, Callan Lyons, were the only two Breeds that were without a doubt not a Tallant spy in Sanctuary. The information she held now was too important, too explosive, to trust to anyone but those two men.

"Who knows why Father does the things he does," she finally said and sighed. "I've outgrown my usefulness to him, one would assume."

"So he sent an assassin guaranteed to kill you mercifully, just because you had outgrown your usefulness? Because you made some mistakes?"

"Go figure. But to be fair, I've been messing up a lot lately. Why not let me go so I can ask him about it? Then I'll get back to you."

"No." He crossed his arms over his chest as he smiled arrogantly. "I think I'll keep you for a little while longer."

"And Sanctuary has ordered this?"

"I think you know better than that. You don't exactly have friends at Sanctuary, sweetheart."

No kidding there.

"So I'm here for what reason?"

"Because I want you here."

"Because you want me here?" she asked in surprise, a mocking laugh leaving her lips as she stared back at him. "For what? Excuse me for being just a bit surprised, Tanner, but you're not exactly on the allies' side of my personal contacts."

"Does it matter why I want you here?" He frowned then. "You're safe for the time being. Content yourself with that."

"And my safety matters to you why?" None of it made

sense. "Why the hell would you care if a dozen coyote Breeds were after me? You're not making sense." This was not part of the profile she had done on him over the years.

Tanner gave a good impression of the classic playboy, the lazy Breed raised outside of the labs, taught mercy, family and values. Bullshit. He was taught how to hide the killer he had become before Callan Lyons ever stepped foot in that New Mexico lab.

"I don't want you dead before I have the chance to fuck you myself."

"And once you've fucked me?" She forced the words past gritted teeth. Going to bed with this man would be the ultimate mistake.

"Would once be enough?" He moved forward slowly.

And she didn't like that. She could feel the air thinning, his very presence taking up the oxygen, almost leaving her light-headed.

"You're very confident." Too confident, and she was weak. She could sense her body's weakness to him and she hated it.

"Is it merely confidence?"

Scheme steeled herself for his touch, for his fingers as they touched her collarbone, moving slowly over the slight ridge and sending a rapid fire of response racing through her body.

"I won't have sex with you."

"Yes, you will. It's just a matter of time." His eyes gleamed with the knowledge.

"And you have all this time to waste? Don't you have a job at Sanctuary, Mr. Reynolds? News releases to send out, press conferences to prepare for?"

"I'm on vacation. Sanctuary allows those, you know." His hand cupped her neck, his fingers curling around her nape. "We're not in the labs anymore, Scheme. No matter the attempts your father has made to have us returned there."

"He doesn't want your return, Tanner. He wants your death."

His fingers tightened slightly at her statement as his unusual amber eyes stared directly into hers.

"How will it feel?" he asked her. "To get all sweaty and wet beneath one of the animals you've helped track? To feel my cock burying inside you. Taking you. Marking you. And I will mark you, Scheme. I'm going to come inside you so deep and so hard, you'll never remember what it was like to lie with another man."

It would feel like nothing she had ever known before. She knew it. Sensed it.

"I'm liable to puke," she said and sighed, rolling her eyes at him as his narrowed on her. "That could get messy, Tanner."

"Oh, we're going to get messy all right," he assured her, his smile tight. "Real messy, Scheme. But in ways you might not imagine."

"No, Tanner." Her hands slammed against his chest as he leaned forward. "Don't do this."

She could hear the desperation in her own voice, the fear.

"Why?"

His lips were close. Too close. The brush of them was like a whisper against her own, a heady temptation she had to fight to resist.

"Because you don't really want me. You want to strike against me. Hurt me. That's what the Council taught you."

"Don't." His hand cupped over her mouth before she could say anything more. "The Council didn't teach me to jack off watching you sleep in your bed. It didn't teach me to shadow you, or to become bewitched by you. And it didn't teach me to care if you lived or died. Until I find out the reasons for those anomalies, Scheme, you are stuck with me."

He was snarling. Furious. She could see the flames of anger sparking alongside the lust in his eyes. And none of it made sense. Nothing should be there but killing rage. No emotion, no regret, and sure as hell no attempt to protect her.

"You watched me sleep?" She walked this edge of danger carefully.

"I watched you sleep, fuck, masturbate and stare out that damned skylight for almost ten years. Since the month you turned twenty, sugar," he growled. "From the moment I figured out how to direct our fucking satellites where I wanted them, I've watched you."

Watched her fuck. He had watched her each time she had

brought a man to her bed, each time she had used her vibrator. She should be throwing up in disgust rather than creaming in excitement.

"Why are you doing this? Did Sanctuary somehow miss a psychopath in their ranks?" She jerked away from him, trying to hide her reaction as her fingers knotted in the towel. "Are you forgetting who I am, Tanner? Scheme Tallant. Remember me? General Cyrus Tallant's daughter? His right hand. Breed killer." She was pushing it and she knew it. Tempting her own death, and it wouldn't be a painless death if Tanner were the one meting it out.

His nostrils flared, his eyes gleaming with predatory awareness as he advanced on her.

This was why she'd fought to avoid him throughout the years. Why she had made certain there wasn't so much as a chance meeting until that stupid ball. It was in his eyes now, primal, primitive, the same hunger she had felt growing within herself throughout the years. The more she tracked him on the television, received reports about him, the more he had fascinated her.

"Are you forgetting how hot and wet you were in my hand?" he countered. "The feel of my fingers fucking you, stroking that tight little pussy until you came for me?"

He stopped stalking her, but only because her back met the stone wall and there was no place left for her to go.

"That was a mistake." Oh yeah, big mistake. That was why every cell in her body was reaching out for him. *Good going, Scheme, just keep up the good fight there,* her inner voice of reason chided her.

"The mistake is in lying to me, pretty girl," he growled, his eyes flashing with a dangerous mix of lust, danger and anger. "Now, we'll assume the good general has decided his daughter is no better than his coyotes and you've just become a liability. So why stay?"

Ahh, the reasons. Just let her count them. Of course, it could take days.

"And go where?" she asked. "By the time I was strong enough to run, your people were free and many of them would have eagerly killed me if they had caught me. They would have hunted me. Just as my father would have hunted me."

"You had enough information against him to turn evidence during the hearings in the Senate and secure your safety."

Scheme gave him a droll stare. "I was twenty years old, and I was still fighting the conditioning Father had used to raise me. When you train a child rather than raise it, Tanner, you condition it to certain things. I was conditioned. By the time I had the strength to break away, it was too late. And I knew it. He would have never let me live. And he'll be even more determined now to see me dead."

To a point, it was the truth. Once she had found the strength to break her conditioning though, the hatred had been all she lived for. It was then that she had secretly met with Jonas Wyatt and made her bargain. In exchange for her complete safety when the time came, she would help him bring her father down. He had enough information now. And she had more that she had held back for insurance when that time came. She could have waited. She could have tried to gain the last vital pieces of information that she needed to access the inner sanctum of the Genetics Council, but her time had run out.

If she didn't get away from him soon and get to Jonas, then it would be too late for the pride leader's son. And if that happened, then the Breeds world would quickly go to hell in a handbasket. Because nothing would restrain their rage then.

Her time had run out. And Tanner was deceptive enough, merciless enough, that he could be trying to gain her trust for one reason only. To gain the information her father's agent had sent, the location of the first Leo and his child. That information couldn't get into the wrong hands. Until she knew, beyond a shadow of a doubt, that Tanner wasn't her father's spy, then she couldn't trust. She couldn't afford to ever trust her heart or her hunger again. Chaz had taught her better than that.

✦   ✦   ✦

Her eyes were cold. The dark chocolate gaze was unemotional, uncaring. She could have been talking about the weather. But what he saw and what he could smell were two different things. His eyes saw a cold, hard shell. But he rarely depended on his eyes alone.

He could smell her pain, just as he could smell her fear and the anger she was tamping so deep inside her that it festered like an open wound.

She was fighting desperately to shut it all down. He could sense that. She had to obliterate all emotion to survive the darkness her father had placed inside her. And he couldn't allow that. Smelling her fear made the animal inside him pace and thirst for blood. It did nothing to keep the man he was in control.

He knew all about conditioning and training. He had lived beneath Tallant's guidelines for the first fifteen years of his life. As an animal. A weapon that had to be molded for effectiveness.

"Once you had the strength to break away, why was it too late?"

Her gaze flickered with shadows of deceit. He hated that deceit.

"I was already created," she whispered then with a mocking smile, her gaze meeting his with icy knowledge. "It was too late. And it's too late for this, Tanner. Go ahead and kill me. You'd be doing the world a favor. Wouldn't you?"

"I won't hurt you." He forced the fury back and focused on his desire rather than his rage. On the hunger rather than the bleak memories he glimpsed in her eyes. "As a matter of fact, pretty girl . . ." He let his lips brush hers with the barest touch.

He was rewarded with an almost imperceptible intake of breath on her part. Her expression didn't change, and neither did the look in her eyes, but her scent did. Once again, he could smell the heat of her need. It was there, sweet, soft, edging around the harsher scent of her forced detachment.

"As a matter of fact what?" Her curiosity was almost as legendary as her cold, unemotional facade.

"As a matter of fact, I intend to make you feel very, very good. I'm going to make you so damned hot you'll burn both of us alive."

"As I said, you're a little overconfident, Breed." The derision in her voice belied the scent of her passion. But it was the scent he went with. The scent that calmed the beast raging inside.

"Let's see if that's true."

Nothing mattered but kissing her, holding her, sheltering her from the past that he wasn't sure he could protect her from. And from the moment his lips took hers fully, he was lost in her. Not that he had expected anything less. Pleasure began to wrap around him, to emanate from her and lick his body with burning flames.

God, her kiss was good. She wasn't hesitant; she reached for him, ate at his lips as eagerly as he ate hers. Slender arms twined around his neck; sharp nails scraped against his scalp and had a growl rumbling from his chest.

He had to touch her. Not just kiss her. Nothing mattered except this. Her body flush against his as he lifted her, her knees lifting, thighs parting, the towel falling away and her swollen breasts pressing into his T-shirt.

God yes, this was what he wanted. One arm wrapped around her back, the other moving to the firm mound of one tit. He had to taste her. Have her. Just one taste of those pretty, berry-ripe nipples.

He tore his lips from hers, scraped his teeth down the graceful column of her neck, then moved to the delectable fruit awaiting them.

And it was good. The growl that tore from his throat joined her cry as his lips covered the flushed, eager tip. His tongue lashed at it as he sucked it in deep, his teeth scraping tender flesh with lush eroticism as she shuddered against him.

"You taste like candy." He would have winced at the gravelly sound of his voice if he'd had enough mind to do so.

"We can't do this."

He didn't want to hear her denial, he wanted her to cry out his name, wanted her to beg him to fuck her.

That's what he wanted to hear from her lips.

He nipped at the hard peak.

"Tanner."

"Sweet nipples, perfect tits." He groaned. "I could suck your tits for hours and never get enough."

He went back to her, filling his senses with the feel of her, the taste of her, the heady scent of her wet pussy in the air.

"This is crazy." Her voice was weak, but the scent of her lust—now, that was strong. Strong enough to intoxicate. Strong enough to mesmerize.

"Naw, darlin', not crazy. Hot. Wicked. Never crazy." He pressed closer between her thighs, feeling the heat of her pussy through his jeans, searing his dick.

"You're forgetting who I am again," she whimpered, but her head came forward, her lips pressing to his neck as every muscle in his body clenched in response.

"I know who you are, pretty girl." His teeth scraped her other nipple as her responding cry sent a shock of satisfaction raging through him.

This was why she was still alive, why he couldn't hurt her, could never harm her. For this pleasure, the taste of her, the heat of her. Nothing else. When he was finished, when he had sated himself with the need clawing at his insides, then he would pack her ass up and haul her to Sanctuary. Callan could do whatever the hell he wanted to with her then. If there was honor in her, Callan would find it.

"I can't do this," she whispered again as he continued to nip at one berry-ripe nipple while he bore her to the bed. "You don't understand."

"I understand my dick is so hard I'm going to come in my pants if I don't get inside you," he growled as he laid her back on the bed. "I understand you taste as sweet as sugar and you're hotter than fire. What the hell else do I need to know?"

He leaned back, staring down at her pale face, her wide chocolate eyes. Sable hair spread out around her head like a silken fan, and excitement had flushed her breasts the color of a pale sunset.

She wasn't exactly beautiful, except to him perhaps. Her irregular features—the little stubborn chin, pert nose and high cheekbones—and the faint Asian set of them combined to make her infinitely unique.

"I don't want this, then." Her head shook as her face mirrored some inner desperation.

"Don't you, Scheme?" Before she could tighten her thighs to evade him, his hand slid between them, cupping the fiery mound of her pussy as his teeth snapped together at the heat filling his hand.

"You're so fucking wet I could drown in you," he said accusingly, using his fingers to part the swollen curves and find the honey beyond.

She jerked, shuddering as his finger slid along the narrow cleft to find her swollen clit.

"You're close," he growled. "I can smell your heat. Feel your pleasure growing. You're so close to coming you're having to fight it."

"No." She shook her head, fighting him, fighting the pleasure.

"No?" When she was this close? "Sweetheart, you're so primed I could get you off with a few licks of my tongue. Wouldn't you like that? To feel your hard little clit in my mouth, sucking you, tonguing you?"

"I don't fuck animals," she snapped, desperate anger filling her voice as the words whiplashed in his mind, causing him to still above her, his fingers poised to rub against the distended little knot of nerve endings awaiting his touch.

Before he could stop himself, an enraged snarl left his lips, causing her to pale further before he managed to jerk back from her, whipping the blanket over her naked body as he fought for control.

"You'll fuck me," he growled furiously. "Before you leave here, you'll be on your knees begging me to fuck you."

"Not even if you had the finest carpet covering the floors," she shot back furiously. "If I wanted to fuck one of your kind, I could have had my pick of you at any time. Coyotes aren't the only Breeds still beneath my father's command, Tanner. Remember that."

He bared his teeth, the predator raging inside him, roaring for release, for surrender. Her surrender.

"Get dressed," he snapped. "Now. And the next time you call me an animal, Scheme, I'm going to show you exactly what your goddamned father helped train for all those years."

He stalked from the room, taking the nearest tunnel, and headed topside again. If he didn't get away from her, if he didn't get the smell of her out of his head, then he was going to end up forcing that surrender. And that was something he had sworn he would never do.

◆ C H A P T E R 7 ◆

Oh God, what had she done? She had a death wish; it was that simple. Because she had seen murder in Tanner's eyes the second she'd thrown that final remark at him.

Desperation. Fear. Scheme Tallant was rumored to never know fear. She was ballsy. Deceptive. Scheming. She did not know fear.

Not true fear anyway. She had grown used to the threat she lived under beneath her father's command. That threat, to a point, had been controllable, though, until she began taking more and more chances.

Running her hands over her face, she fought for a way out of this one. Even now, her skin felt fevered, burning for him. One touch and he made her hotter than she had ever been in her life. He made her weak. He made her remember what it was like to be young, to need to feel warmth. The brief affairs she'd had in the past were pale comparisons to what she needed now.

She was thirty years old, but sometimes she felt twice that age. Right now, she felt a hundred. As long as Tanner had been watching her, she had been watching him. He was on her short list of suspects where the Breed spy was concerned. He was privy to the Breed Cabinet's innermost secrets. He knew security, communications and long-range plans. Things her father's Breed spy seemed to know as well. He was exactly where he would need to be to destroy the Breeds. And to destroy her. He was a weakness.

Pushing herself to the edge of the bed, she let her feet dangle, watching the soft shadow they cast from inches above the floor.

She had needed to be touched like this once before, years ago, and she had let Chaz into her life. Chazzon St. Marks. He had played the game so well. She had needed someone so desperately that she had let him convince her that he loved her. That he needed her. What he had needed was to follow her father's orders, track her movements and learn if she could be trusted.

She had covered her tracks well enough to keep herself from actually getting killed. But she hadn't escaped the beatings for being ineffective in her job.

The job of tracking and seeing to the killing of Breeds who'd been entrusted with high-level information and assignments during their training within the labs had fallen to her. And she had gathered much of that information.

Some of the Breeds had escaped. And some—their deaths would always weigh heavily on her soul.

Crossing her arms over her breasts, she gritted her teeth and fought the arousal still burning through her. It had never been this strong with another man. It had never sensitized every cell in her body and made her ache for his touch.

Even her need for Chaz had never been this strong.

Chaz. She fought back the pain again. He had taken the job to kill her, coldly, methodically. She had loved him once, before she had learned that her father was paying him to fuck her. Before she had learned he was an assassin. Before she had found out he had been part of her father's plan to abort her child. Her father was well capable of sacrificing Chaz to learn the secrets she was holding, though.

She had to get out of here. By the second it was becoming

more imperative that she get as far away from the deceptively lazy Bengal Breed as possible.

Especially now.

Clothes. She got wearily to her feet before turning and dragging the heavy black bag Tanner had brought in toward her. Gripping the zipper, she pulled it open, then flipped the top back before staring into it in shock.

They were her clothes.

Her comfortable clothes, the outfits she wore to relax in, to be herself in. Soft velvet lounging pants with matching sleeveless tops and overshirts. There were silk shorts, silk pants, comfortable shirts, socks and jeans. And on top of the carefully folded clothes was her favorite vibrator. What the hell? He had packed everything but damned shoes.

She pulled a black silk, French-cut thong from the top of the pile. No bra. And she knew she had bras.

How the hell had he managed this? How close to home was she? Or had he done this after he drugged her?

She dressed quickly in the panties and black velvet lounging pants and sleeveless top. And on her feet she pulled on matching velveteen socks. Who needed carpets?

And what was she supposed to do now? Pace the floors more? Check out tunnels she had already checked a thousand times, top to bottom, and still not found the entrance?

The television didn't work. She had tried it earlier. The stereo didn't work, but the appliances did.

She was stuck. Until she could figure out how he was getting in and out, she was stuck there.

"There's a washer in one of the connecting caves if you need to wash anything," Tanner growled as he reentered the main cavern. "And you can hang your clothes—"

"In the smaller cave off this one." She turned to face him as he exited the bathroom cave. "Are you trying to drive me insane? How the hell do I get out of here?"

"You don't." He stalked across the room to the suitcase, lifted it from the bed and carried it to the smaller cave on the other side of the bed. "Remember that if you decide to kill me in my sleep, little Schemer. I die here, so do you."

She clenched her fists at her side.

"All this just to get fucked?" she asked derisively. "Fine, Tanner. Fuck me and get it over with."

He grunted, obviously still angry. "All this to get the answers I want," he retorted. "When you give me that, then I'll let you go and make certain you're safe."

Oh, she had a lot of information her father would kill for. Information he would do anything to attain if he learned she held it, and that she was still alive.

Not the least of which was the message she had destroyed.

Her smile was mocking.

"My father knows everything I know," she said softly. "I'm not hiding anything, Tanner. I hold enough information that I'm a risk. It's that simple."

She was a risk. She would have only one chance to walk away from her father when the time came, and even that could be jeopardized if she didn't find some way to reach her contact.

"It's that simple?" His expression was calculating, disbelieving. "Why don't I believe you, pretty girl?"

"Who cares?"

"Why did Tallant send St. Marks to kill you? He was once your lover. The father of your child?"

"Because he trusted Chaz to get the job done," she whispered, swallowing tightly. "You heard what he said, Tanner. He agreed with Father's decision."

"Why did you stay after that?" Tanner snarled furiously. "Why, Scheme? Why give your loyalty to that bastard after he killed the baby you so obviously wanted?"

What could she say? She couldn't force the words she'd thrown at her father when he questioned her on it. General Tallant was maliciously efficient.

Why do you still love me, Scheme? he had asked. *I took your child, yet I have your loyalty?*

You did what you thought was best, Father, she would respond sadly. She would do it so well that the Coyotes trained to smell a lie never detected the deceit.

But she couldn't say it now. She couldn't betray that child

she had wanted so desperately by excusing even one more time the monster that had taken it away from her.

"Get ready for bed. It's nearly midnight," Tanner snarled when she refused to answer him.

"I'm not sleepy." Her skin was itching and she was tired of his attitude. She was tired of being a captive. Tired of the emotions that refused to stay locked away. "Really, Tanner, have you considered the black mark this is going to become against the Breeds? Kidnapping General Tallant's daughter? Father will let me live for years more once this becomes known. It could bring the entire Breed community down."

"Who says you're going to come out of here alive?" He didn't even pause. He stripped off his shirt as he asked the question, before tossing it to the end of the bed and staring back at her. "I didn't say anything about it."

"Oh well, that puts me in my place," she snapped back. "So what, you get the obligatory fuck before you break my neck?"

"I wasn't trained to break necks," he pointed out as his hands went to the buckle of his belt. "I was trained to rip your heart from your chest with my bare hands. Remember? Thought you had my file, pretty girl."

Yes. He was. He was trained to kill painfully, as well as silently.

"You would have killed me by now if that was what you meant to do." She spoke with more confidence than she felt.

"I haven't fucked you yet. Spread your legs, keep your damned mouth shut and let me get off, then I'll kill you."

Her lips twitched. He was angry, and because of it, he was striking out at her. What had he said before? He had spent nights jacking off watching her sleep.

Then she frowned.

"You actually watched me. Have sex?"

"Of course." He arched a brow at the question.

"Why?" Outrage colored her voice and she knew it. "There's no way you could have monitored me. You're lying."

She refused to look down. He had already removed his boots and now he was pushing his jeans over his hips. She would not look.

"When you use that cute little blue vibrator, you always run it gently, so gently, around your clit first. It takes three times to get it in your tight little pussy. But when you do, your lashes flutter before you force yourself to hold them open. Afraid someone's going to come in on you, darlin'? I packed the vibrator, by the way."

He wasn't lying. He had been watching her.

"Why?" She could feel herself trembling. Shaking. If he had been watching her, in her bedroom, then she could be in more trouble than she had ever imagined.

"Because I loved watching you trying to find what I knew didn't exist anywhere but with me." He tossed his jeans to the bottom of the bed, and before she could stop herself, she looked. And looked.

Oh. My. God.

Surely that couldn't be real. It wasn't that he was overly large, though he was large. Heavily veined. Darkly bronzed. And so fucking tempting her mouth was watering.

Her eyes jerked back up.

"You're crazy," she whispered, suddenly knowing beyond a shadow of a doubt at this moment that his insanity was entirely possible. Just as she knew he had no intention of hurting her. Yet.

She knew General Tallant didn't have the control over his spy that he would have liked. That there were weeks, sometimes months before a report came through, and when it did, it was often sarcastic and bordeline insulting. That would suit Tanner's profile. He did what he wanted, not what others expected.

For the moment, maybe, she was safe.

"Get undressed and get in the bed, Scheme. If you're a good girl, I'll even turn the television on for you while you're going to sleep."

The television? Her eyes narrowed as he smiled back at her benignly.

"That is so not fair," she grated out. "Put some pants on at least."

"Take your clothes off and get into bed or I'll go to sleep

while you're standing there and there will be no television for a week."

Her teeth clenched. "Do not talk to me as though I were a child."

He slid into bed before pulling the sheet over his nude body. His eyes gleamed back at her, rich, golden, daring her. He was daring her to get into that bed with him.

"I can do without the television." She shrugged, moving for the seating arrangement and the overstuffed couch. It looked more than comfortable. "Good night, Tanner."

One minute she was walking to the couch, the next she was practically flying through the air and bouncing on the bed. Just that fast. He had moved just that fast across more than ten feet of space, counting the king-sized bed, and tossed her to it as though she weighed nothing.

Scheme fought to push her hair out of her eyes as she glared back at him.

"You're being childish." She kicked at him as he jerked the bottom of her pants, pulling them off. "I just put those on, you damned pervert."

Before she could fight him off, he gripped her arms and had her up and the top wrestled off her body faster than she had managed to put it on.

"Damn you, you son of a bitch." Breasts heavy, anger thundering through her system, her fingers curling, she tore her arms from him and went for his eyes.

"Tsk, tsk. Ladies don't fight like that." He batted her clawed fingers back, laughing at her. The bastard was laughing at her.

"Fucking pussy," she snarled, her fist curling as she jumped for him.

She didn't know who was more surprised, her or the Breed who had been laughing, when her fist connected with the side of his face.

They stared at each other in shock.

"Now . . ." He pushed her back to the bed, following her down, his hands pinning her arms above her head, his hard body covering hers. "You can kiss it and make it better."

Kiss it and make it better? Scheme froze, wide-eyed, her nipples rasping over his broad chest as she fought to breathe.

Breeds were thought to have no body hair. Few people knew the truth: that the hairs on their bodies were so tiny, the color so perfectly matched to their flesh, that it was like a thin pelt. And at the moment, she could feel every tiny hair her nipples were raking as her breasts heaved beneath him.

The sensation was exquisite. Fiery. So heated she could feel herself melting against him, losing strength, losing control.

"God, you're warm," he murmured, lowering his head until his lips were close to her ear, his abused face next to her lips. "Now kiss me better, pretty girl, so we can go to sleep."

Helplessly, hopelessly she turned her head, her lips touching the small spot of blood she had drawn at the side of his mouth.

His body tightened violently; his breathing became harder, heavier, as his jaw clenched. A violent groan tore from his lips as she licked at the cut at the corner of his lips, the salty taste of his flesh mingling with the coppery flavor of his blood.

And it should not have been erotic. It shouldn't have gotten her so wet she could feel her juices gathering all along her pussy, thick and hot and making her crazy with the need to be touched.

"Enough." He was gone as fast as, if not faster than he had grabbed her.

Hard-on bobbing out from his body, his expression set and furious once again.

Scheme sat up as he threw himself back into the bed and jerked the blankets over his body. She wondered if he had any idea how close he'd come to making her beg that time.

"Has anyone ever mentioned that you're not exactly stable?" she finally asked.

"Yeah, every time they caught me and Cabal double-teaming one of our lovelies," he snarled. "Now fucking go to sleep before you find out exactly what one-half of the last two surviving Bengal Breeds can do."

Her breath caught. Her eyes widened, and she turned slowly

as he picked up a remote, pressed it, and the sound of a television droned behind her.

"Double-teamed?"

"Double-fucked," he clarified.

She blinked. He smiled. And it wasn't a comforting sight.

"Night, night, pretty girl."

✦   ✦   ✦

She couldn't sleep. The television had flipped off more than an hour before, the lights were dim, but sleep had never been further away.

She ached. Every time she closed her eyes, she swore she felt Tanner's fingers sliding between her thighs, the heavy weight of them inside her, stroking her, burning through her common sense. And her eyes would jerk open to stare miserably into the cavern once again.

Despite the width of the bed—it was a king-sized bed, after all—she could still feel Tanner's heat. It blazed against her back, wrapped around her and made the quilt he'd tossed over her stifling.

She was dying. She needed to be fucked worse than she had ever needed to be fucked in her life.

God, she was so pathetic. She had already had one close call with one of her father's assassins and now she was looking to form an emotional bond with another? And she knew it would end up being emotional. She wasn't stupid. Tanner touched not just her body but something inside her. Some part of her that she hadn't known existed.

And she wanted it touched again. How stupid was that? Chaz had been her father's killer; could Tanner be his spy?

"You know . . ." She flinched at the silky rumble of his voice. "There's always the vibrator."

Scheme flipped around, clutching the quilt to her breasts as she stared back at him.

"And do what?"

His hand lifted, the long fingers wrapped around the thick length of the blue vibrating toy.

"I loved watching you use this," he murmured with a wicked smile. "Want to try it now?"

Her lips parted.

"I could help you."

The suggestiveness in his voice had heat pulsing through her.

"How?" Oh Lord, was that really her voice? That breathless phone-sex murmur that had his eyes nearly glowing with lust.

He grinned, a shiverlicious kind of grin that made a woman want to just eat his lips up. Not to mention other parts of his body.

The quilt moved slowly away from her, revealing her an inch at a time as she watched the blue dildo come closer.

"Do you know what really turned me on?" he asked her.

"What?" It wasn't a question, it was a whimper of hunger and she knew it.

"Watching your tongue curl over it after you came, tasting yourself."

She was shaking. Her hands, her lips—her entire body was shaking. God, she had never been so excited in her life as she was watching him press that dildo closer until it touched her mouth.

Her tongue peeked out, licking over the fake head as his gaze locked with hers.

"I can smell how hot you are." He moved closer, his other hand flattening on her stomach before sliding slowly upward and tucking between her breasts.

"All those years I watched you in your bed, alone and with your lovers, you want to know what I saw?"

She shook her head. She didn't want to know.

"You were never satisfied. You wanted to be. You tried to be."

"Not true." She was not abnormal. She had always climaxed.

"Very true." He pressed the dildo to her lips, his eyes narrowing as they parted, accepting the toy. "I saw your eyes. That's what I watched, Scheme, when you were with those men, your eyes. And I saw a woman desperate to find that final certain something. That orgasm that went all the way to the gut."

Her eyes widened.

The dildo slipped free of her lips, only to draw a wicked, damp path down her chin, between her breasts, then along her stomach.

"On your back," he whispered. "Let me give you a taste."

Common sense screamed no. Yet she was turning, moving to her back, fighting to breathe as carnal, wicked lust filled the room with its heavy scent.

"There we go, pretty girl," he purred, stroking the dildo on her thighs. "Now open up just a little bit for me."

Her thighs parted.

"Little bit more, darlin'."

They were both breathing hard now, their gasping breaths filling the air around them.

She spread her legs further.

"Mmm. Those pretty curls are beaded with the sweetest juice." His eyes locked between her thighs; his hand trailed the dildo over the saturated area.

It skimmed her clit as she lifted closer, watching his expression. It was tight, savage, bordering on animal lust as the head of the dildo tucked between the swollen folds of her pussy.

"Bend your knees. I want to watch it go in."

She bent her knees, lifting closer as Tanner slid between them. She hadn't expected that, but she really didn't care as long as the horrible, aching hunger in her womb went away.

His nostrils flared as he drew the scent of her in.

Tucking the dildo against the desperate entrance to her sex, he pressed slowly inside.

"Oh God. Tanner." She shook her head, her eyes wide, locked on the sight of the erotic toy pressing inside her.

She was so wet it didn't take the usual three tries to get it in.

"Damn, you're tight." He pulled it back, ignoring her little cry before pressing forward again. "I'm thicker." He grinned up at her with carnal intent. "Longer." The dildo pressed deeper inside her. "Are you sure this is what you want?"

Hell no. Not if she had a choice.

She shook her head frantically.

Pausing, he stared back at her. "What do you want, pretty girl?"

"I want you to stop playing." Okay, this was the point of no return. "Fuck me or get the hell away from me."

The dildo slid free before being tossed away, in which direction she didn't really care.

"All you had to do—"

She didn't let him finish the sentence. He was on his knees, the lickable length of his cock spearing out before him, flushed, sun-kissed gold, heavily veined and mouthwateringly engorged.

She had reached the end of her patience. She wanted a taste.

"Scheme." There was that growly thing again. He had to know it just made her wetter. But that was okay; she intended to make him harder. If possible. She doubted it was possible, but she was sure as hell going to try.

She went to her knees, spreading her legs and bracing against the mattress as she leaned forward and enveloped the head of his cock in her mouth.

His taste exploded on her tongue. Rich, male, earthy. Like a storm. Like a mountain lake on a summer night. He tasted like pure male ecstasy.

"Fuck. Damn." His hands clenched in her hair. "Hot little mouth. Sweet, hot little mouth."

She tightened her lips on him, sucking greedily. One hand gripped his cock just below her lips, not that her fingers could surround him, but she could stroke, while her opposite palm cradled the hard sac below.

"Beautiful. So damned pretty," he groaned, his hips rotating, moving, thrusting against her lips in tight, hard strokes.

She expected to weaken him. Get a guy's cock in your mouth and that was what usually happened to him. But not Tanner. A second later she felt a stinging, highly erotic slap on the cheek of her ass. A second later, the opposite cheek.

Her mouth was filled with the bulging head of his cock, her excited little squeal coming out as a strangled scream as he struck again.

She might like that a little too much, her common sense warned her.

She wanted more, the hormonal inner slut screamed out. Oh yeah, way more.

His hand landed again, right there on the rounded part of her cheek where the flesh was so sensitive, where the sensations could streak through her nerve endings, attacking not just her clit, but the tender, nerve-laden entrance to her rear.

She lifted to him, feeling deliciously wicked, sexy.

"You like that, don't you, my little Schemer?"

Like? Like? That was supposed to describe this?

She screamed around his cock as his hand landed again. Then she rewarded him. She sucked him to the back of her throat, swallowed, massaged her tongue on the underside of his shaft and moaned at the erotic pleasure of it.

"Damn you." His voice was strangled.

Tightening further, the muscles of his abdomen and thighs were corded now, standing out in taut relief, rippling powerfully beneath his golden flesh.

His hand smoothed down her rear then tucked lower and two broad fingers pressed inside her.

Oh yeah, oh yeah, she chanted silently. *Deeper. Just deeper. Just all the way to the interesting little spot . . .*

Her eyes widened, her lips and tongue drawing on his cock desperately as Tanner's fingers found that spot and he *rubbed.*

The other hand tangled in her hair, pulled as she resisted, and sent flames whipping over her.

More. Just more. She was dying now.

She worked her mouth over the head of his cock greedily as his fingers retreated from her aching pussy, smoothed back, returned to the dripping opening, teased, pulled back. It took a second to understand. Just a second before one of those strong, long fingers pressed into the ultrasensitive entrance of her ass.

She tore her mouth away from his erection. She had to breathe. She had to.

"I want that pretty ass," he whispered. "I want to cover you and sink inside it. I'll remember the hollow look of dissatisfaction when I saw you taking it from another man, for all of two seconds—until I hear you scream for more. I'm going to show you what you should have received the first time."

His finger retreated. Panting, desperate for air, Scheme pressed her head into his thigh, whimpering, insensible as his finger pressed deeper inside her.

"Mmm, you like that." It wasn't a question.

Hell yes, she liked it. It was wicked. Forbidden.

This was sex the way she had always fantasized about. Lacking self-recrimination, no doubts, no fears beyond the one that he would stop.

He bent over her. The sound of the bedside drawer opening barely pierced her consciousness or intruded on the sensations ripping up her back. His finger wasn't still. It didn't thrust or raid, it rubbed, the calloused pad rasping over tissue so delicate that she shuddered with the pleasure.

Nothing mattered—spies, blood, death—fuck it. Nothing mattered now except this. Here. Now. Just this.

• CHAPTER 8 •

The way beneath his little Schemer's defenses was her pleasure. He sensed it, knew it. The years he had spent watching
her, he had felt it to the soles of his feet. She needed mindless
pleasure, the kind that gets in your gut and turns you inside out
because it's too damned good to be borne. The kind that
makes you weak in the knees, makes your mind shut down and
your nerve endings sing. And he was going to give it to her.

She had known pleasure. She had known release. But she
hadn't known the gut-wrenching, soul-searing fulfillment that
came from having her needs sated, fulfilled. He intended to
sate every hunger she had ever known. He intended to show
her hungers she had never known she could possess.

It wasn't about the act, or acts, she had participated in. She
had pushed her own boundaries, had explored her sensuality,
only to find that the tease was more exciting, the promise
much more tempting than the actual act.

Until now.

Now he would show her exactly what she had been missing. A man who understood her hungers, her needs and her
pleasures. A man willing to lose himself in them with her.

It wasn't about control. It wasn't about submission. It was about feeling, from the inside out, feeling the radiance of complete satisfaction.

Sliding the tube of lubricating jelly from the bedside drawer, he straightened on his knees once more and slid his finger from the ultra tight clasp her rear had on it.

"No. Don't stop." Her hips lifted to him.

Damn that was a tempting ass. So softly rounded. So damned pretty when it blushed.

His hand descended, laying a sharp little caress to her rear as she shuddered in response. She liked that. Liked the biting pleasure/pain, the sharper sensations as her arousal grew.

She lifted to him again. Her shoulders coming off the bed, struggling to support her weight as she fought to regain a measure of control.

"Stay there." He pressed her back to the mattress. She didn't need control right now. She needed release. She needed him.

His hand smoothed over her ass again.

God, she had the prettiest butt. Rounded and creamy, though blushing now from the erotic little spanking he had given her.

He flipped the top open on the lubricating jelly and spread a line along his fingers, grimacing at the hunger eating at him. God, he needed to fuck her. He had to fuck her or he was going to die from the hunger.

Laying the tube aside, he used one hand to part the rounded cheeks of her rear before preparing the tiny entrance for a deeper caress. He smeared the gel over the opening, pressed the tip of one finger against it, smiled tightly, then added the second finger.

And she took him. She opened up like a dream, taking the penetration, begging for it.

Her back bowed. Her cry echoed around him. The scent of her pussy had his mouth watering and his dick jerking in demand.

A hard, gravelly growl left his throat as his fingers slid inside her, feeling the tender muscles tighten around them as her hips jerked back, driving him deeper.

He twisted his wrist, rotating his fingers in the little hole.

The scent of her arousal was invading his brain now. He could smell nothing else. Taste nothing else.

Gripping his cock, Tanner moved closer.

"Tell me to fuck you," he snarled. "Ask for it."

"Damn you!"

"Ask for it."

He couldn't take her without it. He wouldn't take her without it.

"Tanner, please."

He pushed his fingers deeper, scissored them, felt her shudder.

"Ask me for it, Scheme."

"I hate you!" she snarled.

"You want me." He pressed his other hand between her thighs, feeling the saturated curls before he ran his fingers around her straining clit. "Now ask me for it."

"Fuck me!" She drove her hips back.

His fingers buried inside her as the head of his cock slid against moist, swollen curves.

Pulling his hand back from her wet curls, he fought to breathe as he positioned his straining flesh. Pressing into her pussy was like entering a super-heated, super-tight furnace of liquid silk.

Sweat ran down his face, his chest, as he eased into her. Hell, she was so tight. Too tight.

"How long?" he snapped. "How long since you've had another?"

"You watched me," she stuttered. "You know."

He paused. It had been more than a year, perhaps two since a man had been to her bed.

"Outside your bed," he growled.

Her head shook desperately, her hips straining against him. "Only my bed. Not theirs."

He snarled again, pulled his tortured cock back before working inside her again.

"Does it hurt?"

"God yes!" she cried. "More. Just do it. More."

His head tipped back on his shoulders as his hips pressed

forward. Pulled back. Gave her more. Her sharp cries were breaking his control. He needed to bury inside her. He needed the full length of his tortured dick surrounded by all that tight, wet heat.

"Please, Tanner."

Her strangled scream, the scent of her need, her pussy flexing around his cock and her tight little rear tightening on his fingers were too much.

His control broke.

Scheme screamed. She couldn't help herself, not that the sound held any true power. You had to breathe to scream effectively. She couldn't breathe. She was too hot. She was burning, fevered with lust and so full, stretched so tight the pleasure/pain of it was just short of too much.

Her shoulders fell to the mattress, her fingers clenching in the quilt as she cried. Tears actually squeezed from beneath her lashes. There was too much pleasure. Too much of the sensations she had never experienced before but always reached for.

"Fuck, you're tight." He was snarling behind her, growling. "So fucking tight."

His fingers moved in her rear, rotating, rubbing. His erection pulled back, spreading the excess moisture along the sensitized channel before spearing inside her again.

It was too much. The first orgasm was a hard, drowning wave. It rushed through her, over her, shuddered up her spine and sizzled in her brain. It caught her so off guard that she was gasping, clawing at the bed, her own mewls of ever-increasing ecstasy stealing what breath she had left.

"Damn you!" he cursed.

He stilled inside her, his cock throbbing, the needs inside her far from sated.

She needed it again. Oh God please, just one more time.

"Please . . ." She was barely aware she was begging, pleading. "More. More."

The hand gripping her hips snaked around the front of her thighs, his fingers finding her clit. His fingers moved more demandingly in her rear, and his hips thrust. Hard. Powerful. Deep plunging strokes as his fingers milked her clit.

And that growly thing.

The heat in her rear.

The overstretched flesh of her pussy.

More deep plunging strokes. Hard, forceful, stripping away her inhibitions, tearing past her restraint.

The second orgasm destroyed her. It exploded in every cell of her body, every molecule. She felt the muscles of her vagina tightening on him, heard his curses behind her, and felt the deep, hard pulses of her juices meeting the forceful spurts of his release. She was lost within a maelstrom she could have never imagined existed. A whirlwind of so many sensations, so much pleasure, that her brain just couldn't process it all.

But when it did, the fever was calmed, sated, exhaustion washing over her and sending her collapsing to the bed.

She was barely aware of him falling to the mattress beside her. For some reason, she was very aware of his arms coming around her though, pulling her tight to his chest as he jerked the quilt over her rapidly cooling body.

For the first time in her life, after sex, she was sated. Even more, she was content.

◆   ◆   ◆

BUREAU OF BREED AFFAIRS
WASHINGTON, D.C.

GENERAL'S DAUGHTER MISSING

Jonas stared at the newspaper laid out on his desk, one finger rubbing thoughtfully over his pursed lips.

"Any leads?" he asked the Breed agent standing across from him, staring back at him, his expression grim.

"Nothing." Lawe sighed. "Her house is bugged though, and not by us. The electronics are identical to those Tallant and his purist and supremist groups use. He's been watching her."

"Interesting."

He knew all this, but he held his tongue. He had known what was getting ready to happen when he found the message on his PDA from Scheme Tallant. She had been at the ball. She had been with Tanner. Now she was gone. He was adding up two and two and coming up with the proper answer, he was certain. He had to ensure that this played out exactly. It was a risk, using Scheme and Tanner to catch the spy at Sanctuary. But fate had handed him the chance and he was going to take it.

"The night she disappeared she had a room reserved at an upscale D.C. hotel. She had ordered a late platter of meats, cheeses and breads. When room service arrived, she was gone. Luggage, laptop, purse, the whole nine yards."

Jonas relaxed further in his chair. If Tallant had her, he wouldn't have bothered taking her luggage. They would have found her body and nothing more. She was still alive, he was almost certain of it. But if Tanner had her, that was another story.

"Scents?"

Lawe narrowed his eyes. "The room had been inundated with her perfume."

Jonas restrained a smile. Heavy perfume could affect Breed senses, hide the scent of another Breed or even a person. "I'd suspect damn near a full bottle of something even I couldn't pronounce. Cabal said French, around two grand an ounce. The place had been sanitized, but Merc managed to identify the scent of blood in the carpet. Not hers, male blood though."

"A Breed has taken her," Jonas mused as he stared beyond Lawe, eyes narrowed, his brain working with possibilities. "Tanner was at the party that night?"

Lawe nodded. "He left a little before ten and returned to his hotel, from where he headed out to Sandy Hook on vacation. He's currently incommunicado and refusing to take messages. Callan refuses to send them."

Jonas's lips twitched. "Tanner's been planning this vacation for over two years." That and much more.

"We need him here, Jonas. This is a public relations nightmare."

"They can't lay this at the Breeds' feet," Jess Warden, the Bureau's lawyer, spoke up from where she sat on the couch across the room.

Jonas turned his eyes to her. Tall, cool as a mountain lake in winter, as blond and composed as an icy peak.

"I wasn't worried about that in the least."

"I'm aware of your concerns." Her brow drew into a frown. "Anyone with a modicum of public speaking ability can handle this. Popular opinion will hold in the Breeds' favor."

"Tanner is our public relations genius," Jonas reminded her. "It doesn't matter if anyone else can do it. Tanner can do it better."

She shook her head at the futility of arguing with him. She had been doing that a lot lately. It wasn't a good sign.

His attention turned back to Lawe.

"What did Callan say?"

Lawe grimaced. "He said he will contact Tanner if need be. Until then, as he reminded me, Tanner does have an assistant now."

This time, Jonas grimaced. "Geez. His assistant stutters."

"She's on standby to fly in to Washington if you change your mind."

Jonas sighed. The timid little panther female Tanner had chosen as his assistant and trainee wasn't exactly a prime choice in his opinion.

"Hell, I couldn't do any worse than she does," Jonas sighed.

Jess piped up in a droll challenge. "I dare you."

He glanced at her from the corner of his eye. She was focused on the papers though, as if his ire or disapproval didn't matter in the least.

"We'll continue as we are," he finally said. "Continue to investigate the disappearance. Has Cabal checked the room?"

"He was first on the scene. He and Jackal were still in D.C. after Tanner left."

Jonas covered his smile. Ah yes, and so the threads were indeed coming together. Tanner would have left Cabal and Jackal behind to foul any attempt Jonas made at tying Scheme Tallant to Tanner.

"Where are Cabal and Jackal now?" Jonas asked.

"They're in the barracks below. Waiting on orders." There was a faint vein of mockery in Lawe's voice.

"Let them wait." He pursed his lips. "I'm certain they need the rest. Tell them they're on call."

It would be best to keep both men close at hand for the time being.

He loved it when a plan came together. Jonas was certain Cyrus Tallant thought he had managed to keep Jonas out of town with that piddling attempt at an attack that a group of purists had made against him that evening. They hadn't come close.

Evidently Tallant had learned that Scheme was betraying him. Jonas had found the message on the relay system when he returned to the office. Her request for pickup and asylum and the information that she would meet him at the ball that was held that evening in D.C.

There wasn't a doubt in his mind that Tanner had Scheme Tallant. Which meant she was exactly where Jonas wanted her to be. With Tanner. Safe for the time being while he pulled the rest of the threads of this little web. Shift a pawn here, pull in one there, whisper the proper words and then wait for the fallout.

"Put Alpha team on covert alert at Sanctuary," he ordered Lawe. "I want anything out of the ordinary reported to me. Any Breed behaving out of character, asking any questions concerning Ms. Tallant, anything that seems suspicious. And monitor each outgoing transmission, no matter the means made. Cell phone, sat phone, landline and broadband. If so much as a drum taps in rhythm, then I want to know about it."

Suspicion glinted in Lawe's gaze. Alpha team was the special, highly organized team of investigative agents working within Sanctuary to uncover Tallant's spy.

Lawe nodded slowly. "Got it, Boss."

Jonas's lips twitched. "Take care of it, Lawe. I expect you to coordinate from here. Check with Mia and she'll set you up an office."

Mia, his superefficient, stranger-than-hell secretary. If he hadn't seen her file himself, he would have never believed she was a Breed.

"Don't put me behind a desk, Boss," Lawe snarled, his incisors flashing. "That's just going to piss me off."

Jonas arched his brow and stared back at the agent. He just stared. No expression. No comment.

"Goddammit," Lawe cursed.

Jess spoke up then, her tone chastising. "There's a lady present. Act like a snarling animal when Jonas lets me leave. Until then, remember a few manners."

Lawe frowned before jerking his gaze back to Jonas. "Where did we learn manners?"

Jonas sighed.

"You don't curse in front of women, Agent Justice," Jess snapped. "Doesn't matter who she is, where she comes from, how she talks or your opinion of her. Pretend she's a child. Would you speak like that in front of a child?"

Lawe frowned, his gaze suddenly flickering in indecision. Jonas held back his smile. He knew damned good and well that the only child Lawe allowed himself to interact with was David Lyons. And David's vocabulary at nine years old was impressive.

"My God," Jess muttered, turning to make a note on a legal pad. "We're going to have to work on this."

"Boss, I'm going to find that office now." Lawe cleared his throat. "I'll uh, let you deal with this."

Jonas watched as Lawe turned and hurried from the office, casting Jess one last suspicious gaze.

"This isn't going to work, Jonas."

"Not now, Jess." He wiped his hands over his face as he blew out roughly. "First things first."

"And when one of your Breeds makes the mistake of speaking to the wrong person at the wrong time in that manner? Visiting dignitaries? Allies? What then?"

"Not now, Jess."

One mess at a time. Yeah, that was going to happen. He was presently juggling close to a dozen messes. This one just happened to be his pet project.

She rose to her feet, sophisticated perfection dressed in a short, navy silk skirt and jacket with a creamy-colored silk blouse beneath. She was buttoned up, composed and disapproving.

"You're going to have to get your men into social training."
She paced over to his desk, her regal expression a challenge.

"Jess, not right now," he growled.

Her lips lifted into a condescending smile. "Yes, your plots
and schemes are so much more important at the moment." She
braced her hands on his desk and leaned forward. "Tell me,
Jonas, what are you going to do when everything and everyone you've manipulated backfires on you?"

His brow quirked. That was an interesting scenario.

"Enjoy the battle?" he queried with faint amusement.

A frown snapped between her brows. "This isn't a laughing matter."

"Jess, I'll tell you what, you do your job, the legal mumbo
jumbo you enjoy so well, and let me do mine. I won't tell you
how to argue a case and you don't tell me how to conduct my
missions. Agreed?"

Her eyes narrowed. "I can't wait until you fall."

"Join the club," he snorted. "I'm going to start charging for
that particular membership. Now, why don't you get back to
covering our ass on that latest strike against the purist camp
and I'll get back to my job."

"Manipulating people?" She straightened, staring down
her aristocratic little nose with haughty disapproval.

"I do it so well." He grinned. "Can I get back to it now?"

"You do that, Jonas." Her shark's smile would have made a
lesser man wince. "And I'll consider your defense in case you
get caught. Of course, you could always plead insanity."

He growled warningly. Not that the rumbling of danger affected Jess in the least. She smiled back at him complacently,
turned and sauntered back to the sofa.

Damn woman. Thank God she hadn't turned out to be his
mate; they would have killed each other.

CHAPTER 9

She couldn't allow him to ever touch her again. She wasn't going to allow him to touch her again.

What the hell had happened? Since when did Scheme Tallant allow her hormones to drown out her common sense?

The next evening, her head propped on her hand, Scheme watched what had to be the sixth hour of some insane rerun.

Of course it wasn't any more insane than the urges she was fighting within herself. The need to join Tanner on the couch, to stretch out along his hard body and run her tongue over every inch of his golden flesh.

Instead, she was forcing herself to watching some incurably deranged sitcom.

Gilligan's Island? It had been ancient even when she was a child. Not that she had ever watched it. Her father hadn't considered television a productive form of entertainment for his child. But sometimes, at the girls' academy she had attended, the other students had watched it.

Scheme had managed to drown it out then while she studied. There was nothing to study now. Except Tanner.

He was stretched out on the couch, his feet crossed at the

ankles, his arm thrown behind his neck as he watched the show with a quirk on his lips. He was impossibly relaxed despite the obvious hard-on filling out his jeans. Despite the tension building inside her.

"CNN is much more informative," she finally said, dazed from yet another of Gilligan's bumbling accidents as well as her own arousal.

"CNN is depressing," he grunted with a spark of amusement as he kept his gaze on the television. "I'm pretty up on world affairs. And this is my vacation. I don't watch CNN on vacation."

"Do you do anything besides watch television while you're on vacation?" she asked, frustrated. "As long as I've been here, I have yet to see you do anything worthwhile."

"I fuck while I'm on vacation too," he answered, not taking his eyes from the television. "Want to provide that little entertainment for me? We had fun with it last night."

She glowered back at him.

"Didn't think so." He still hadn't taken his eyes off the screen. "You know, darlin', you need to decide one way or the other what you want here."

She sighed in complete boredom. Even the books on the shelf were light reading rather than anything thought-worthy. There were even romances. Not that she didn't enjoy romances, as long as they were explicit in nature and hot enough to singe. The ones on the shelf weren't.

"You're killing me," she said and sighed. "If you're out to torture me, you've succeeded."

He flicked his gaze over to her with a hint of sexual heat.

"How did I manage that?" The action on the screen drew his gaze back.

"You've watched at least six hours of this, Tanner. Gilligan is getting on my nerves here," she sneered. "He's a twit. He couldn't walk down a city street without being shot for stupidity."

"He's not on a city street." He grinned, a chuckle leaving his lips as a man in an obvious gorilla suit terrorized the castaways. The show wasn't exactly heavy on special effects.

"It's a good thing. A twelve-year-old has more common sense."

"It's a show, Scheme," he chastised her gently. "It's for your enjoyment. It's not attempting to mirror reality."

"Good thing." She rolled her eyes. "A little reality break would be nice though. A half hour of CNN might save my sanity."

"Your sanity isn't high on my list of priorities," he assured her, chuckling at Gilligan's predicament once again.

She pulled herself to her feet, wrapping her arms across her chest as she began to pace the room. Not that it bothered him. In the past hours she had learned there was very little that pulled his attention from that asinine rerun.

"Where are we at least?" she asked. "You could tell me that much."

"In the middle of a mountain," he answered drolly.

She hated men. She really did.

"Where is the mountain?" she grated out.

"In a mountain chain."

"Which frickin' mountain chain, Tanner? For God's sake, you could at least tell me where I'm at."

She turned and glared at him. He hadn't taken his attention from the show. He was, for the most part, ignoring her.

"What would it hurt?" she asked.

"What would it hurt to tell me why you received that beating you took before that your ex-lover was talking about?" he retorted, his voice casual, almost unconcerned.

Wasn't the beating last month enough? Did you have to keep pushing your luck?

Chaz's words vibrated through her mind. Hell, what would it hurt to give him that much? To play his game to a point.

Scheme stared at him for long tense moments. "Will you let me have a half hour of CNN?"

His head turned, his thick lashes shielding the expression in his eyes.

"If it's the truth."

She inhaled roughly. "I didn't turn in a report that came

through of a Breed mission in New Mexico. Because of it, Father wasn't able to make certain there was an experienced team in place to gain information he needed."

Information on the first Leo, a Breed Cyrus had spent decades searching for.

That got Tanner's attention. His eyes narrowed further.

"Do you know what the information was?"

"That wasn't part of the question," she reminded him tensely. "I answered you honestly."

"But not fully." He shrugged. "I don't want half-truths." His attention went back to the television show.

"The information was on the first Leo," she answered. "He's been searching for him for decades and still has no clue where to look. The information he lost out on, to an unknown source, was supposed to be that location. Now will you please change the fucking channel?" she yelled back at him.

The channel flipped. CNN blazed back at her with glorious color. Monday, September 5, 2023, and it was ten a.m. A time, a date. A quick calculation told her she had been there four days. She moved back into her chair, her attention focused on the television and the world events she'd been missing out on.

She was a CNN junkie; she couldn't help it. She could watch the world news and sometimes predict what her father would put into place.

"Father will send a team into Colombia," she murmured as the reporter announced a story concerning terrorist activity in Bogotá. "He likes the South American factions the best. They're easier to control than those in the Middle East."

Tanner sat up slowly.

"What makes you think that?"

"The name of the group the reporter gave," she replied. "The leader of that group has been in contact with Cyrus several times. Each time they make the news, Cyrus sends a team down with cash and training support. The leader kisses his ass and makes him feel like a father figure. He likes that."

"Who would he send?"

Scheme's lips twitched. "He would have sent Chaz. Now

that he's dead, I would guess he'll send Dog. Dog is his top Coyote Breed. Very cold-blooded, with an excellent record of success in his missions."

"Dog has failed every mission against the Breeds," Tanner growled.

"Did he?" Scheme asked archly. "Or did he gather information the Council needed concerning Sanctuary's defenses and their teams' security protocols? You would do well to begin creating shifts in how you defend the base as well as how your teams call in for support or to report in. It won't be long before the Council programmers crack your security codes if you keep using the same ones. The spy he has within Sanctuary has already managed to help crack several key points to the code."

He leaned back in the couch and watched her as she continued to track the news.

"And you're telling me this why?" he asked.

"Because I want another half hour." She watched the next report intently. "Take that senator, for example." She nodded to the screen. "Father has been courting him for years; he's certain to have enough information against him soon to begin blackmailing him in any vote concerning the Breeds that comes up in the Senate. That particular senator has a daughter who isn't always as careful as she could be. Father will have what he needs within the year, I expect."

"That information has already come through the Bureau," Tanner informed her.

She shot him what she hoped was a surprised look.

"Someone is on the ball then."

"So it would appear," he muttered thoughtfully.

Scheme ignored him. As the news stories flashed across the screen, she settled back and watched intently. She knew of several missions her father was putting together to go into the Middle East and help heat up yet another conflict there. The more politicians were concerned with the terrorists reaching out from the desert states, the less focus they put on racial issues flaring up at home. Specifically, the Breed issues.

As world news shifted from overseas to the States, the

story of the general's missing daughter flashed across the screen.

Scheme tensed as her father's expression, lined with supposed grief, filled the screen.

"Whatever Scheme has done, she doesn't deserve to die," he was saying in response to the reporter's claim that she might have been kidnapped in retaliation for the attack against the Breed base, Sanctuary, several months before. "If she's used my contacts and my resources to inflict more pain on the Breeds, then it should be dealt with through the proper channels. Justice will not be served by hurting her or, God forbid, killing her."

Her lip curled as the screen blackened.

Her gaze swung to Tanner and the remote he was lowering to the couch beside him.

"Turn it back on," she snapped. "I want to hear it."

"Your half hour is over. Actually, it turned into close to forty minutes. You owe me for the extra time."

"Like hell. Turn it back on."

The lying bastard. She knew her father was a monster; she had known it for years, for most of her life, but she had never realized what a consummate actor he truly was.

Tanner stared back at her, unconcerned. "No."

Her fists clenched at her sides. "Why?" she snapped. "Afraid I might actually believe his lies? That I might cause you more trouble to return to his loving arms?" she sneered.

"No," he said softly. "I'm more worried that if I have to smell the scent of your pain much longer, I'll end up losing control and go after his throat myself. Which would do nothing to help you."

She sneered hatefully. "Of course it would bother you that he beat me," she snarled. "Now, why didn't I think of that? A Breed would, of course, be concerned for a Tallant's welfare."

Not.

She knew better than that.

"You didn't rescue me from Chaz, Tanner—you kidnapped me for your own ends and you're keeping me here for the same reason. Is it all about fucking me?" she bit out sarcastically. "Oh, yeah, I can just see that one. You're just dying to fuck the daughter of the man who tortured your entire fucking family." Cold, hard mockery finished the sentence. She knew better. "Just tell me what you want, Tanner. What is the cost of my freedom?"

"Your safety."

She glared back at him, her expression twisted with disbelief. Only her father's spy would care how she intended to cover her own ass.

"My safety," she repeated chillingly. "Tell you what. Release me, give me a secured cell phone, and within hours, I'll be safe. I promise you that. All you have to do is let me go."

"Tell me who you would call first." He rose from the couch with a smooth flex of muscle. "The same bastard who stole that information in New Mexico last month?"

"I could only get so lucky," she snapped. "No, Tanner, my contact isn't your unknown thief. And who it is is none of your business. Now let me go."

She stood in place as he stalked closer to her, his body rippling with tension, his eyes swirling with it. Like this, he reminded her more of the animal than the man. He had the same controlled, graceful movements of the Bengal. Almost lazy, calculating, every bone and muscle flexing with an innate animal grace.

She couldn't control the shiver when he touched her though. When his hands settled on the thin silk covering her hips and his chest brushed against her suddenly distended nipples.

"I can't let you go," he said softly, his head lowering until her vision was filled with the sexual intensity in his gaze.

"Why?" Her hands settled on his chest, not to push him away, not to pull him closer. Just to touch him, to feel the warmth of him. "You've had me. It's time to end this game now."

One hand moved from her waist to cup the side of her face, his thumb brushing over her lips as they parted helplessly. Anger was melting beneath pleasure despite her attempts to hold on to it. She needed to stay angry with him. She needed a defense against his touch other than the suspicion that he could be her father's spy.

"I don't know." His brow gathered into a frown. "Maybe

because I don't trust you. Because too many people are out to kill you. And maybe because I need more of this."

His head lowered and his lips were on hers again. Parting them, his tongue slid inside as she whimpered against it.

Tearing herself away from him was almost impossible. Almost more than she was capable of. As she backed away from him, she was aware of her weakening thighs, the soft, heated dampness between them and the tingle of pleasure that lingered on her lips.

"You can't keep me forever."

"Don't bet on that," he sighed roughly. "At this point, Scheme, don't bet on anything. Not until I figure out the puzzle you've become. Fucking me won't change that; it will just make the time pass more pleasantly."

"I'm not a puzzle for you to figure out."

His short laugh was mocking. "Sorry, love, that's exactly what you are. From the reason your father wants you dead to the reason you don't like old reruns. I could make a list of questions to start with if you like." His eyes were suddenly gleaming playfully, inviting her to join in.

"I'll find my way out," she warned him desperately.

"Not going to happen, darlin'." He sighed, moving back to the couch. "But I tell you what, come here and cuddle with me and I'll let you watch the INS. I like it better."

The International News Service. It was better than nothing.

"Cuddle with you?" she asked in disbelief.

"Yep. Cuddle with me." He sat down, stretching one long leg out on the couch as he propped the other foot on the floor. "Come on, Sugar, we'll watch the news together or I can watch Gilligan. There's several hours left."

She shuddered as he patted the area between his legs. "I dare you."

Her eyes narrowed as he lifted the remote. "News or Gilligan. Make your choice, Sugar."

If only she didn't want to sit there, cushioned by his broad chest, his arms around her. Feeling a warmth she had only dreamed of, feeling a need she had never allowed herself to recognize before Tanner.

She was weak. So weak.

"You aren't allowed to molest me," she snapped.

"You aren't allowed to make the rules," he grunted. "Now come here, pretty girl, before I change my mind. You know, I've been looking forward to that *Gilligan's Island* marathon for months. You're lucky I'm making the offer."

She should feel guilty for knocking him out of the show, she was sure.

"They're reruns, for God's sake." She settled carefully on the couch, between his thighs, turning toward the television and leaning back distrustfully.

"They're in order," he argued lightly, pulling her fully against his chest. "But cuddling you could compensate me. You know, Scheme, I don't cuddle women much," he told her as he flicked the television on.

"Cabal does the cuddling for you?" She snorted.

He chuckled against her chest. "Naw, Cabal's not a cuddler either. But I think I like holding you." One arm draped around her stomach. "I think I like holding you a lot."

✦   ✦   ✦

How had he known that world events and news would fascinate her? Tanner wondered as he settled back into the corner of the couch and watched the news.

Scheme was a pleasant weight against his chest, her head on his shoulder, her hair spreading out across his chest.

How many times had he entered Callan and Merinus's private suite to find them on the couch just like this, watching soap operas. Their pride leader was fascinated with his mate's soap operas.

For a man who had never cared much for television before he mated, Callan had become a regular couch potato during the quiet evenings at Sanctuary. That, or he really didn't give a damn what he watched as long as he could hold his mate with close intimacy as they watched the shows.

But Scheme wasn't his mate. He had been checking closely for the signs of it, close enough that his tongue was nearly raw from rubbing the sides of it over his teeth to check the glands there. There was nothing.

He wanted her.

He ached for her with a strength that made him half-crazy, but there was no mating hormone, no unusual sensitivity in his flesh.

Was it possible for a Breed to fall in love without mating? Even the scientists researching the phenomenon had no answer to that one. So far, every mated couple seemed deeply in love. The mating always came first though. The chemical, biological matching of two souls that would have been compatible, that would have loved anyway. But the heat had ensured it.

There was no mating heat with Scheme.

He should feel relieved, carefree; instead, the regret nearly choked him.

As they watched, news of the Breeds was reported. Jonas was standing in front of the offices of the Bureau of Breed Affairs, denying involvement in Scheme's disappearance and stating the instances that the Breeds had always turned suspected Council members or collaborators over to the federal authorities once they had proof against them.

He answered the reporters in that hard, growling voice of his, a scowl on his face as Tanner chuckled.

"Jonas hates the media," he said against Scheme's hair, drawing in the scent of her.

"He's not bad at handling them though," she commented, her voice much calmer than the scent of her arousal.

"He bitches for hours after he has to hold a news conference." He nuzzled his face into her hair, the thick sable silk stroking pleasantly against him. "Then he normally calls me and bitches at me for not handling it."

"I didn't hear the phone ringing," she pointed out. "That news clip was made yesterday."

"You were asleep." He smiled against her hair, allowing the fingers that rested on her belly to rub against the silk of her shirt in little circles. "He threatened me, Scheme. Something about stuffing the trout I was catching up my ass."

"You aren't catching any trout." Her voice was a bit breathless, husky.

Confronting Scheme with the hungers that rose between them wouldn't work; he had found that out last night. A man had to wait until the hunger was more than she could bear. Not that she was entirely comfortable with it, he thought with a smile. His Scheme was as wary as a little cat.

She was also a damned control freak.

"This is more fun than catching trout." He licked at the shell of her ear. "Takes more patience. Callan says I should work on that patience issue I have."

A soft, feminine snort had a silent laugh tugging at his chest.

She was settling against him, relaxing a bit more, and as she did, the scent of sweet female heat became thicker. Damn, he'd loved that smell before he'd met her, but her particular scent he had become addicted to. It was sweet and tinted with spice, like syrup on a crisp winter morning. It had his mouth watering and his dick throbbing.

"I could see you with a patience issue," she said softly. "That lazy Bengal Breed act of yours doesn't fool everyone."

"Most people it does," he argued with a grin. "You're just a perceptive little thing, pretty girl. You see me for what I am."

"I studied you," she admitted. "For years. Studied your lab files against the persona you project. You lie to a lot of people, Tanner. I can almost tell when you're lying on television."

"Hmm, dangerous thing to admit to," he grumbled, feeling warmth he shouldn't have felt, because she had managed to learn anything about him. "I can see you sitting in front of the television telling your daddy what the Breed plans are as you watch me lie."

She was silent.

"Did you?" he whispered.

"No," she said with a hint of sadness. "It was what he had me trained for, observation. He was very upset that I couldn't tell him what he needed to know."

"So he beat you?"

"Not always." She was lying, and she was a very adept liar,

so he could barely detect the scent of it. She didn't want him to know she was lying. For some reason, this woman who should have been his enemy didn't want him to know he had been the reason for any pain she had felt.

He nipped her ear.

"What was that for?" Her head tilted back, a frown creasing her brow as she glared back at him.

"That was for lying to me, pretty girl," he growled, lowering his lips to hers because he couldn't resist them. Because he needed the taste of her, needed it to clear the scent of her lie from his head. "Never lie to me."

He didn't take her easily, he didn't ease her into a kiss, and he sure as hell didn't ask for permission. Asking for permission from this woman was an instant debate.

She struggled without force as he shifted to the side, moving her into the crook of his arm to allow for a deeper penetration of her mouth.

One hand pressed into his chest, the other into his side. Her sharp little teeth nipped at his tongue; his nipped at her lips.

She pulled back; he buried his hand in her hair, cupped her scalp and forced her mouth back to his and let her teeth nip at it.

Damn, it was good. The sharp little sting, a flick of her tongue, and he was ready to come in his jeans. His other hand gripped her jaw, holding her still, his fingers controlling her ability to bite as his lips covered hers, his tongue impaling her mouth with a hunger that should have worried him.

Flickering, inquisitive, her little tongue met his, battling, a heated erotic battle that ended with one of her hands buried in his hair and her breasts pressing into his chest as she turned to him, her legs straddling his hips, rising over him, taking control.

Fuck. He gripped her hips, pulling her down to him, grinding her pussy against his jeans-covered cock. Slender fingers tangled in his hair as she began to ride him, the silk of her pants sliding against his jeans, her heat seeping through and raking over his dick.

Hell. He was going to fuck her. If he didn't fuck her, he was going to die. Last night wasn't enough; it had only whet his appetite for more.

He had unclenched his hands from her hips, lifting for her breasts, when suddenly, just that fast, she was gone. Stumbling, whirling around, her hair creating a silken fan as she faced him, pushing it back impatiently.

"Watch Gilligan," she rasped. "I told you not to do that."

"Hell." He laid his head against the couch and stared up at the stone ceiling, almost to the point of begging her. Damn, if he'd thought begging her to ride his cock would work, he'd have been on his knees in front of her.

"Yes, hell," she snapped in agreement. "Find something else to amuse you while you hold me here, Tanner, because I'll be damned if I'll stand in for your stupid reruns."

He lifted his head as she stalked to the cavern doorway.

"Where are you going?" he called out on a sigh.

"I'm finding my out of here," she retorted. "Right now. I've had enough of you and enough of stone walls. And when I do, I'll find those stupid trout and shove them up your ass for Jonas."

With that, she stalked down the darkened tunnel, soft lights glowing to light her way as Tanner's lips twitched. If she could find the hidden access, then she was welcome to it.

He picked up the remote and changed channels, chuckling as he caught Gilligan working the bike-powered washing machine.

He might be so horny he was about to explode, but he had time, he assured himself. Time to figure out why she pulled at him, time to figure out how to save her.

Scheme hadn't found the exit out of the caves, and the dark mood it put her in did little to ease the frustration rising inside her. In desperation, she crawled into the bed, pulled the blankets over her head and prayed for sleep.

Sleep that finally came despite the knowledge that Tanner was naked beside her. Naked and hard and waiting to still the warmth growing inside her. It was a restless sleep though, one plagued by bad dreams and a certainty that Tanner would be the death of her. They followed her, shadowing the landscape of her sleep, until finally, she forced herself awake, and faced the real nightmare.

It was dark.

But her eyes were wide open.

Her eyes were open and her heart was racing as panic began to set in.

It was pitch-black dark.

"Tanner?" She sat up in bed, her fingers clenching in the blankets as she listened.

There was no light, no sound.

"Tanner, where are you?" She was not going to panic.

Forcing the fingers of one hand from the blankets, she felt across the bed, ignoring the tremors beginning to build in her body.

She had been here before, she reminded herself. In the dark, lost, uncertain where she was or what awaited her.

"Tanner, don't play these games with me," she snapped, her voice loud in the dark as she found only emptiness on his side of the mattress. "Where are the lights?"

She hadn't found light switches in the past two days. If they were here, they were very cleverly hidden, just as the exit was.

"This is going too far, Tanner," she cried out, staring around frantically, seeing nothing but the darkness, hearing nothing but the sound of her own heart beating, her own gasping breaths.

She was not going to lose it, she promised herself. She hadn't lost it yet, and she wasn't going to start now.

But it was so dark. Her breathing hitched in her throat. With the lights out, it was like . . . She shook her head as she inhaled roughly.

She was not buried alive. She was in a bed, a very comfortable bed. The cavern was at least ten or twelve feet high, she remembered. She had plenty of room. Plenty of air.

And she was buried alive.

"Tanner. Tanner, where are you?" She screamed out his name as she struggled to get herself out of the bed.

Suddenly, the mattress wasn't a mattress, it was a coffin, enveloping, smothering. Her feet tangled in the blankets, tripping her, tossing her to the cold, hard floor as her fingers clawed at the stone.

She could feel the rock biting into her knees as she tried to find her feet, only to collapse again as her legs refused to hold her up.

It was fear, that was all, she told herself frantically. Her mind had been screwed with too many times, the dark used against her in too many ways. She had survived it then without giving away her secrets; she could do it now. She was stronger than this, she told herself. She could survive this.

But she knew her father's weaknesses. She had no idea

how far Tanner would go, or if he would even return. He could have left her there to die in the dark. To smother in her own fears.

"Tanner, don't do this to me," she screamed, shuddering, feeling the chill of the air wrap around her. It was cold. So cold.

It was too dark. She had to find light. There had to be light here somewhere. Appliances. Where was she in the room? Where were the appliances?

Inhaling roughly, she tried to push back the fear. It took what seemed forever, each second filled with the sound of her heart thudding and her gasping breaths.

She could do this. This was a cavern; it wasn't a coffin. All she had to do was get her bearings.

Still kneeling on the rough floor, she reached out around her, feeling the stone slowly. Methodically. She had to take this a step at a time. She had to be patient.

She was whimpering. She heard her own panicked gasps as her hands found the footboard of the bed. Okay. She was at the bottom of the bed.

She knew this cavern. She had spent days pacing it off, getting to know her territory. All she had to do was make her way across the room to the counter. There was a light inside the dishwasher.

She looked around desperately, realizing that the digital light that had been on the dishwasher before was no longer there.

There was no power.

No power.

"Oh God, Tanner, please don't do this to me." She couldn't scream now. Her voice was weak, and she hated the pleading sound of her voice.

She was not going to do this! Scheme clenched her fists as she bent over, pressing her clenched fingers into her stomach as she fought to hold back the bile boiling there.

She wasn't going to be sick either.

She should have known she couldn't trust him. She had been close though, so close to considering it. He had seemed so concerned, so furious for her sake that Chaz had tried to kill her.

And as she had suspected, it was all an act. Just an act. A trick to get the information her father wanted. He needed to know what was on that fax. He had worked decades for that information.

"I don't know anything." She keened before slapping her hands over her mouth to hold back the sobbing pleas. She had stopped begging years ago. She had learned to accept that her father was a rabid psychopath; no amount of pleas would change whatever he had planned for her. And no amount of pleas would change whatever Tanner had planned.

But she did know something. She knew too much. She knew David Lyons, Callan Lyons's son, would be kidnapped. She knew that the first Leo still lived and where he could be found. She knew the rumors of the Breeds mating rather than just loving were true. She knew enough to ensure that her father faced Breed law rather than just federal law.

She couldn't breathe. Her hands moved from her lips to her throat as she gasped for breath.

It was so dark. She rocked forward slowly, fighting to hold on to her composure as she felt the coffin surrounding her, smelled the scent of her own fear and urine around her.

It wasn't real. Her hands swiped out around her desperately. There was no coffin. Just a cavern. And there was an exit somewhere.

And Tanner would be back. He would wait, wait until she was completely hysterical before he came back. He would try to soothe her. To make it better. Then while she was weak, broken, he would ask her questions. He would probe.

She didn't try to stop the tears from falling. She was fucking terrified; hysteria wasn't that far away—there was no way to fight that. She knew her weakness, and so did her father.

The dark. Complete darkness, restraint, though at least this time her hands and feet weren't tied. She was mobile. Hysterical, but mobile.

"You bastard!" she screamed. "You son of a bitch. You think burying me alive is going to get you something I don't have to give?"

She laughed. The sound was sharp, desperate and disinte-grated into sobs.

She really, really hated the dark.

◆   ◆   ◆

Tanner dropped from the opening in the tunnel's ceiling be-fore reaching up and pulling the stone cover carefully back into place.

The lights blinked on, activated by the motion sensors hid-den in the stone, providing a faint glow to light the way through the tunnels.

The motion-activated lights allowed for greater freedom of movement as well as an early warning system if the tunnels were ever breached.

Small pinpoints of warning activation would now be light-ing through every tunnel, cavern and cave that Callan had wired. The tiny red sensors would emit a pulse of sound, sim-ilar to a hum of electricity.

He flipped open the panel at the side of the wall; the fake stone hid a small digital keypad that he punched his password into automatically. The hum would evaporate and the cavern's motion-activated lights would flip on as he made his way to the main cavern.

Scheme was obviously still sleeping. He had left the sen-sors active there when he left. If she had awakened and gotten out of the bed, the lights would flip on. Once she got into the bed, they would dim and within an hour extinguish, just as the lights and television had the night before.

He had just spent longer than he would have liked fielding several very heavy suggestions from Callan Lyons that he re-turn to oversee any potentially harmful media that arose from the disappearance of one Scheme Victoria Tallant.

That middle name never failed to make his lips quirk, whether in disgust or amusement he was never certain.

As he turned to the next tunnel, Tanner paused, a growl rumbling in his throat at the sound of an almost animalistic keening echoing from the cavern.

There was no way anyone could have invaded the caverns without him knowing. Jerking the electronic remote to the sensors from the holder at his side, Tanner deactivated the automatic lights before crouching and moving quickly toward the main chambers.

He could smell terror, thick and cloying. Scheme's terror.

The small, guttural sounds of uncontrolled hysteria sliced through his soul and brought the Bengal lurking just beneath the surface to violent life. Tanner could feel his lips peeling back in a silent snarl as he tested the air, but found no scent other than Scheme and her terror.

His night vision picked up the area, if not perfectly, then with enough clarity to be certain no enemies were lurking or waiting for him.

A frown pulled at his brow as he slid silently into the cavern.

"I don't know anything," she sobbed. "Please. Please turn the lights on. Please, Tanner . . ." Her weeping was strained, exhausted. Hysterical.

"Scheme?" Tanner moved quickly across the room, finding her huddled in the middle of the cavern floor, naked, her hair and arms wrapped around her body as she curled on the cold stone defensively.

Kneeling next to her, he reached for her, his fingers curling around her arms when she erupted.

Clawed fingers raked his cheek as her cry shattered his senses. There was no sanity in that cry. There was only pain, fear and the need to escape.

"Scheme." He gripped her wrists, jerking her to him, trying to hold on to her as she fought like a wildcat. One small fist found the side of his head, her knee came impossibly close to his sensitive balls.

Fractured sobs echoed around him as he restrained her. He wrapped his arms around her from the back, locking her to his chest as one powerful arm held her and the other reached for the button of the remote at his side.

Soft, gentle light filled the room as she suddenly stilled. And then he got his first look at her face.

Deathly pale, her brown eyes nearly black, her face streaked with tears. The sight of it was heartbreaking. Enraging. This was not a normal reaction to being caught in the dark.

"I don't know anything," she cried again as he allowed her to jerk away from him, rising quickly to his feet as she stumbled back to the bed. "Leaving me in the dark won't change that."

"You think I left you in the dark to punish you?" he asked her slowly, grief filling his soul at the implications of her hysteria.

"Didn't you?" Her voice was shaking, hoarse, as she jerked the quilt from the bed and wrapped it around her shuddering body. "The lights wouldn't come on. There was no power to the appliances." She was gasping, fighting for breath as she tightened her hold on the quilt and moved to the bottom of the bed. "Do you really think it's going to work?" she screamed, her expression twisting painfully.

"Think what is going to work?" He wanted her in his arms. He couldn't bear to see the remnants of terror that filled her expression.

"Do you think turning the lights off here is worse than being tied hand and foot in a fucking coffin? You son of a bitch, you don't have a clue."

Rage, uncontained, filled with pain, fear, with the resounding echo of horror, filled her voice and filled Tanner's soul.

"Someone buried you alive?" It was all he could do to keep his voice calm, to keep the outrage and fury out of his voice.

Her laugh was bitter, cynical. "Oh, really, Tanner. You've investigated me. Watched me. For how long? Were you watching me the last time I disappeared for a few days?"

He had been. He nodded slowly.

"Would you like to know where I was?" Her voice was low, guttural.

"You were at your father's estate," he said. "You stayed a week."

"I was buried alive in a coffin, in my father's basement, because my profile of his favorite Coyote was weak. The Coyote was spying on Father for the Breeds and got away with it. I paid for it. Or did you already know that, Tanner? Tell me, did you know the punishment I would receive when Cyrus found out your Coyote was working for you?"

His hand clenched at his side. That had been his decision, placing the Coyote in Tallant's camp, using him to gain information not just on Tallant, but on Scheme. But this wasn't in that Coyote's report.

"For three days, Tanner," she snarled. "I was locked in a coffin, my hands and feet tied while a goddamned electronic voice counted down the hours of oxygen I had left."

The animal inside him roared in rage. A rage so black, so violent, he had to restrain the need to leave, to go hunting for the bastard who would dare to do something so evil to her.

"He took me out two minutes after my oxygen expired," she said. "You left me air. You can't die if you can breathe."

You can die of sorrow, Tanner thought grimly as he felt grief well inside his soul. And he was ready to expire from it.

"The lights are on motion sensors with a remote backup." He stared around the room, seeing the tangled blankets trailing over the side of the bed, their disarray indicating that she had fallen, or stumbled, from the bed. "Once you move from the bed and actually stand up, they come on. You have to stand up."

She stumbled again; obviously shuddering so hard she could barely stand.

Fuck this. She was shaking like a leaf, adrenaline and terror still racing through her. He could smell her refusal for comfort, her distrust of him, and that was just too fucking bad.

He had to hold her. If he didn't hold her he was going to break apart himself.

"Don't you touch me." She fought him. He had known she would.

Lifting her into his arms, Tanner ignored her struggles as he wrestled her to the couch, sat down, then pulled her into his lap.

"It's okay, Scheme," he whispered against her hair. "It won't happen again."

"I don't need you to comfort me, cat," she spat furiously. "I don't need you to touch me at all."

Tanner tightened his arms around her, burying his face in her hair as he forced back the snarl that tugged at his lips.

God help him, he wanted to kill. He wanted to gut her father and watch him bleed for what he had done to her. The hunger to kill was almost overwhelming, but stronger was the need to hold on to her, to calm the scent of terror still emanating from her.

If he didn't, then the beast was going to break free, and if it ever broke his control, then it might never be reined in again.

"Maybe I'm the one that needs comforting," he growled into her hair. "I'm sorry, Scheme . . ."

"I don't need your platitudes." Her fists clenched tighter, the muscles of her wrists tensing further as he held on to them.

The fact that she wasn't fighting him hurt. Deep inside, in places he hadn't known existed within himself. She was just sitting in his embrace, unresponsive, fighting to distance herself.

"I don't have platitudes." He buried his face deeper in her hair, inhaling the scent of peaches and of fear. He had to get rid of that scent of fear. "I don't have excuses." His lips brushed her ear. "It will never happen again."

"I survived. I always survive." She jerked her head to the side, and he had no choice but to follow. His lips grazed her neck, and for less than a second, he smelled her response.

"You always survive," he whispered against her ear. "It was your father's favorite mode of punishment, burying Breeds alive. He released you. He never released a Breed."

A low, keening moan left her lips as her head lowered and a tear dropped to his arm.

"You survived, Scheme," he whispered. "For this."

✦   ✦   ✦

Long, rough fingers touched her cheek, turning her face to him as Scheme felt the regret, remorse, the destructive emotions that always came with the knowledge that she had survived. She had survived when so many had died.

"I have always survived. Even death." She stared into his

eyes, gold and green, shifting with lust, rage and undefined emotions.

She fought back the sobs that wanted to escape, that wanted to break from the self-imposed exile she had placed them in so many years before. "Sometimes, it's the only way to succeed. Sometimes, failure *is* an option, Tanner."

"You don't fail." His lips touched hers, and she swore she wouldn't respond, that she didn't care. She didn't need the pleasure; she didn't want it. Not now, not ever. It weakened and destroyed from the inside out. "You survive. I won't let you die, Scheme."

What was he doing to her? He was a liar. A deceiver. He was created and trained to deceive and to kill. He was created to destroy her. Because only destruction could come of the pleasure whipping through her from just the touch of his lips. Slightly rough, like dark velvet, brushing over hers as his tongue peeked out to dampen the seam.

"I want to taste you." His eyes stared into hers, darkening, filling with heat. "Just like this."

His tongue lined the seam of her lips again as they parted, flickering, caressing with damp heat.

"All over your body," he sighed as she felt herself melting. She couldn't melt.

"Don't," she pleaded roughly, feeling another tear as it tracked down her cheek and his hold shifted, lowering her further back in his arms as he leaned over her.

"I have to, Scheme." One hand moved below the quilt, flattening on her bare stomach. "Don't you see, pretty girl? I can't fight it. Can you?"

"I'm not weak." The shudder that raced through her body belied her declaration and she knew it.

"Never weak," he agreed, his voice roughening, rasping. "So strong. Show me how strong you are, Scheme. I can't defeat you, can I? No matter what I do."

No matter what he did.

Her lips parted as his brushed against them again.

"Be strong for me," he growled. "Because I don't know if I'm strong enough to survive knowing what he did to you."

Her cry lacked fear; it lacked strength. It was filled instead with hunger. With need. Her lips parted fully, her arms reaching for him, curling around his neck as pleasure began to swamp her.

"Yes. Fuck yes. Take me, Scheme," he growled again between nips to her lips. "So strong."

And she was devouring him. Had any kiss ever been so good? Enraptured. She could taste his arousal, smoky and dark, causing her senses to reel as she reached for more.

Her tongue twined with his, drew it in and savored the wild taste that filled her senses. It was so sharp, so deliciously intense that when he filled his hand with the heated weight of a swollen breast, it felt natural—his fingers on her flesh, surrounding her nipple, pressing in on it and sending fiery shards of sensation to tear through her pussy.

She needed to be touched. Sweet God, from the inside out, she needed his touch. The hunger for it, the overriding desperation was ripping through her body, making her not just need, but crave.

"I'm going to make you scream for me," he growled as his lips pulled from hers, his teeth scraping over her jaw before moving to her neck. "Beg me. I want you to beg me to hold you, to take you. Beg for my cock pushing inside you."

Her head fell back on his arm as his explicit demands sent spasms of destructive need to attack her vagina.

"I don't beg," she moaned.

"You beg." He moved suddenly, twisting until she was beneath him, her legs spread, his hard body stretched between them. "I watched you," he snarled. "Hours where that bastard assassin touched you, made you beg. Made you come. You're going to beg harder now. You're going to come harder."

She should have been embarrassed. Humiliated. He had watched her have sex. He had watched her search for something she had come to believe didn't exist. Something she had found with Tanner. Satisfaction.

But she wasn't embarrassed, or humiliated. It was exciting. Enthralling.

"Touch me. Don't let me think, Tanner." Her nails raked

down his shoulders and her fingers came to the buttons of his shirt.

She gripped, ripped, her breath catching in excitement as the buttons popped from the shirt, scattering around them, revealing his hard, bronzed chest.

"I've dreamed of doing the things they never did." His lips peeled back from his teeth, revealing the sharp, wicked incisors at the side of his mouth. "I made lists."

Hands still gripping his shirt, she stared back at him in shock.

"Years." His head lowered. "I watched you for so many years, aching, dying inside because I couldn't have you."

Her lips parted, but not for his kiss.

"Why did you watch?"

"Because I needed to know you," he whispered. "To see you. I needed to assure myself, each time, that even though they touched your body, those bastards didn't own you."

She saw it in his eyes. He might be lying about many things; he could very well be the spy her father fought to control. But in this, he was telling the truth.

She shook her head slowly. "No man owns me."

"I do."

Scheme stared up at Tanner in bemusement and shock as he shrugged the remains of the shirt from his shoulders. Muscles rippled over his chest and biceps, the restraint he had placed on himself clearly visible in the tense set of his expression and the brilliance of his eyes.

Did he own her? If he didn't now, then he would soon.

"You watched everything?" She was naked beneath him, the quilt lying beneath her and falling away from her body as his eyes raked over her.

"Everything." His voice was an exciting, roughened hiss. "Your lovers were good. But I'm better."

Her heart raced as his hands dropped to the belt cinching the jeans beneath his waist.

"Prove it."

"I'm the best you've ever had." He smiled tightly. "I saw that the other night, Scheme. I knew it."

"Prove it." She needed him to. She needed to still the screaming demand pulsing through her now. Terror, pleasure and danger combined as the rushing adrenaline began to build inside her. "Prove it, Tanner. Now."

Scheme watched in anticipation as his head lowered, his lips parting. She ached for that kiss. Needed it.

But it wasn't a kiss that came. His teeth raked over her neck, the incisors sharp and wicked, scraping over her pulse before moving to her shoulder.

Then he bit her. Not deep. Not enough to break the skin, but the flashpoint of pleasure/pain that had her arching to him, a moan sizzling past her lips.

"Do you think I can't?" He growled as he moved from her then picked her up quickly in his arms.

The next second she was bouncing on the bed, hard fingers gripping her ankles to jerk her forward, pulling her sex directly to his waiting mouth.

She hadn't expected it. That was the only excuse she had. She had expected soft, gentle. Plenty of foreplay and lots of teasing. That's how men reacted when they felt they needed to compete with a woman's past lovers. They teased. They drew out the foreplay and the pleasure until she lost all desire to finish the act.

But this wasn't teasing.

She screamed his name, and she'd sworn she wouldn't. But the pleasure exploded through her body as his tongue slid through her saturated flesh, before his lips capped over her clit and his tongue grew hungry.

The orgasm that tore through her was exquisite. Terrifying. There was no warning, no reason for the detonation of ecstasy that ripped through nerve endings and convulsed her womb in spasms of release, but there was also no containing it. And no stopping him.

As the rippling pulses of ecstasy convulsed through her vagina, he was there. His tongue licked, lapped, pushed her higher, sending her blazing into an intensity of pleasure she couldn't have expected.

"Tanner . . ." She screamed his name as her hands buried in his hair, her upper body lifting, jerking in response to the sudden, fiery release that attacked her again.

Her thighs clenched around his head as her hips rocked,

her lungs struggling for air as she stared sightlessly toward the ceiling.

He gave her no respite. He touched her, from the inside out. His hands, his lips, his tongue. Heated sensations, trigger points of electric ecstasy vibrated through nerve endings that had gone without touch for much too long.

He touched her body; then he reached inside and touched her soul, whispering his need for her, his hunger for her, driving her to the limits of her own sensuality before she flew higher, reached for more. Perspiration dampened her body, making her slick, wet, inside and out, as the sounds of his pleasure ricocheted around her. This was touch. Pure touch. How had she lived without it before this? How had she lived without Tanner's kiss, without his husky voice whispering his pleasure to her, without his hands drawing her closer, soothing her, arousing her, warming the cold places inside her?

Never. She had never known this. She was lucky to orgasm once during sex, let alone twice, with another building, burning, exploding through her as she arched, driving her pussy tighter against his mouth as her legs trembled in response to the grip she had on him.

Bucking beneath him, she did as he had sworn she would. She begged. She pleaded, and she swore the dampness on her face was perspiration rather than tears as she felt the darkness inside her soul reaching for the heated warmth that began to build inside her chest.

Before she could anticipate or even consider his next move, he jackknifed away from her, his hands gripping her wrists as he pulled her up off the bed.

And he was naked. Gloriously aroused, his cock standing out from his body, flushed and engorged.

"You taste like fucking sunshine," he snarled as his hand gripped her waist only to toss her back on the bed. The next second he was on one knee in front of her, the other foot planted across her body as he pulled her back into a sitting position. "Now, darlin', let's see how hungry you are for more."

She was hungry. Hungry for all of him. Desperate. Aching.

His one hand gripped her hair as the other gripped the straining length of his erection.

"Come on, Schemer. Undo me, pretty girl. Make *me* beg now."

His eyes were gleaming gold as her lips opened, her tongue swiping over the engorged crest. She could feel rising within her the dangerous, destructive sexuality she had always fought.

Some things could be too good. Too addictive. Like breathing. Like Tanner.

"Hell yes," he groaned as he slowly fed the damp head into her mouth. "Take me, darlin'. Show me how hungry you are."

And she *was* hungry. Hungry enough that now nothing mattered except his pleasure and her own. Because each growling moan that came from his throat only fed her lust.

"Oh yeah." He was watching as her mouth surrounded the straining length of his cock. His eyes centered, not on hers, but on her lips. "There you go, pretty girl. Suck my dick. Show me how good you are."

And he knew how good she was. Scheme felt her face flame at the wicked knowledge that he had watched her do this at other times. With other men. And as he had promised, nothing that had come before him could compare to this pleasure.

"There's no pulling out, Scheme," he warned her then. "You'll take it all. Every fucking drop of cum I can spill into that hot little mouth."

She whimpered, as much from the domineering eroticism as from the act itself. But if he thought surrender would come from her, he was wrong. She would accept only what she wanted. And she would be damned if she would give it to him easily.

Her eyes narrowed as she pushed at his wrist, forcing him to release the hold he had on the treat she craved.

Her hand couldn't surround him, but she knew how to compensate. Her favorite vibrator had often played her lover, and he knew it. He knew how she longed to taste, to touch, and she gave him what he had watched and more.

Her other hand cupped his tight balls, her fingers playing them, rolling them as her palm gripped the sac firmly.

He snarled again, a hard growl leaving his throat as the muscles of his thighs flexed and the head of his cock throbbed.

"I watched you with that damned vibrator you played with sometimes," he told her then. "Sucking it, filling your mouth with it."

She moaned in response.

"I felt it. I felt your mouth on my cock as you sucked it. Felt your teeth . . ." The little roar that left his lips had her juices spilling from her vagina. "Fuck, yeah." Her teeth raked over the bulging head before her mouth sucked him back in and her tongue began to play with flickering caresses.

His hands tightened in her hair, his fingers flexing against her scalp, pulling at the strands, sending racing arcs of pleasure/pain to streak to erogenous zones she hadn't known she possessed.

"I loved watching you pleasure yourself." Both hands were in her hair now as his hips began to move, his cock fucking her in short, hard strokes. "Seeing what you wanted and couldn't give yourself."

She was ensnared by his eyes, the golden amber flecked with green, glittering behind the thick, gold-flecked lashes.

"I would dream about fucking your mouth." His voice deepened, roughened.

Her tongue raked beneath the head, pressed, stroked, and she was rewarded by a pulse of pre-cum, heated, earthy, the taste of it firing an almost explosive response inside her.

"Dream of feeling your tongue. Fucking over it." He pulled harder at her hair. Her eyes nearly closed at the pleasure. "Watching you." His strokes increased. "Feeling you. Suck it deeper. Deeper, baby." He slid nearly to her throat, where no man had been allowed before, until now.

Her tongue flattened, raking the sensitive flesh beneath his cock, and she felt another pulse of liquid fall from the engorged flesh.

"I'm going to come."

Her fingers tightened at the bottom, her middle finger finding the heavy vein that led up the shaft, stilling his release.

His head fell back, his body tightening further, his hands gripping her hair harder as she began to suck him deeper, filling her mouth with the thick, hard flesh throbbing erotically over her tongue.

The sound of their breathing filled the room, rough, harsh gasps. His growls, her moans as she worked her mouth over the thick crest and impossibly hard shaft.

"There you go baby, work my dick," he snarled. "Show me how bad you are, sweetheart. Give it to me."

The hand working his scrotum moved to the thrusting shaft as he threatened to go deeper than she could bear. The fingers of her other hand continued to play the vein at the back, holding off his release, forcing the sensitivity in his cock higher.

She had dreamed of doing this. Of controlling her lover's release, finding a lover willing to let her play as well, to let her taste, touch and work them both into a frenzy of need.

And Tanner liked to play. One hand dropped from her hair, ran down her shoulder, then cupped a swollen breast.

His fingers gripped her nipple, tweaked it, plumped it, alternating caresses of fiery splendor with delicate strokes as his cock fucked her mouth.

"Hot little mouth." He grimaced. "Fuck, you love this, don't you, pretty girl? My dick filling your mouth, controlling it?"

Oh, she did. She was flying on it, each snarling growl, each purring hiss as she pleasured him. Driving not just him insane but herself as well.

And she was losing control. The need to taste him, to feel his release, was overwhelming her need to play, to tempt and control.

Her fingers moved on the shaft, stroking him as she gloried in the hard-driving rhythm of his cock in her mouth. The pressure at the base of his erection lessened, and within seconds a roar filled the cavern as he drove into her mouth, his hands locking her head in place as his semen began to spurt into her.

Hard, deep pulses of release forced her to swallow, to moan, because the taste wasn't unpleasant. It was silky, smooth, dark and masculine. Like a heated storm, filling her senses with the rich taste of him, her soul with the knowledge that she would never forget it.

"Damn you!" He moved again, flipping her to her stomach, his hands pulling her hips high as he covered her.

And just that quick she felt his cock pushing into her.

"Fuck. Too tight." His hands clenched on her hips as he pulled back, pushed forward, working his way inside her as her back arched and a high, keening cry left her lips.

She had never made such a sound in her life. But she did now. Her hips rocked against him, her juices flowing, easing his entrance, preparing his way as burning spears of almost painful sensation whipped through her.

"It's too much," she suddenly screamed, the feel of his cock parting her, stroking hidden nerve endings, burrowing inside her.

She couldn't bear it. She couldn't survive it.

"The hell it is." His voice was so rough, so deep that she could hear the animal inside him fighting to be free. "It's not enough. Not yet."

Her fists clenched in the blankets beneath her as her head fell to the bed, her upper body collapsing. Another scream tore from her throat as he surged fully inside her, impaling her, invading her.

"Please. Tanner, please . . ." She was shaking apart, shuddering so hard from the pleasure that she didn't know if she would survive.

"That's okay, baby," he panted behind her, moving, drawing back, surging in return.

Her eyes closed against the sweat dripping down her face, the burning in her body.

"It's okay," he repeated. "Remember? I took notes. I know what you need."

Be prepared. The Breed motto, she thought irrationally as he began to move inside her. Long, hard thrusts. Each stroke sending biting impulses of sensation through her, working through her vagina, her womb, her muscles tightening, preparing.

"Not yet."

She screamed, her voice so hoarse now that the sound barely registered as the strokes inside her lessened, built, lessened again.

This wasn't teasing. This was torture. This was a pleasure so destructive it stole her breath.

"Please . . . ," she begged. "Don't do this. Please don't tease me."

"Tease you, baby?" His hand smoothed over a buttock. "I wouldn't tease you, darlin'. Only please you. Please you so much."

He drove in hard and deep, pulled back slowly, then thrust in with a striking surge of pleasure so hard, so swift she nearly blacked out.

"Harder again," she gasped. "Please. Please, harder again."

Hard. An impalement that had her reaching back for him, her fingers gripping his thigh, her nails digging into his flesh at the same instant that his hand landed on her rear in an erotic little slap that threw her higher.

Stars danced in front of her closed eyes; her muscles were so tight she wondered if she would ever relax again. She just needed a little, just a few hard thrusts, that was all. Just a few.

"So sweet and hot," he panted over her, coming fully over her as his legs spread her thighs further and his thrusts continued to power inside her. "Keep tightening on me like that, pretty girl. Milk me with that sweet pussy. Give to me. Give me everything you've never given before."

Was there anything left to give?

As his thrusts increased, became rhythmic, hard and driving, she found there was more to give.

Her orgasm caught her by surprise again, exploding, detonating and washing her body with such pleasure she could only shudder beneath him and take what he had to give.

And he had a lot to give. Harder. Deeper. Faster.

Until she felt everything inside her unraveling, tearing apart and reaching for him as his roar echoed around her again and sent her flying.

She felt him drive deep one last time, then the hard explosion of his heated release, the hard, pulsing dampness filling her, soaking into muscles clenched around his cock, spasming with a shuddering force she couldn't even breathe through.

She collapsed fully beneath him, drained, exhausted, aftershocks of pleasure rippling through her vagina and causing her to gasp with halting little cries she could barely believe she was making.

She couldn't move. She was lost, drifting. So drugged on the pleasure she had endured that she could only whimper as she felt him pull slowly from her and come down on the bed beside her.

"Sleep, baby," he whispered at her ear then. "I'll keep the lights on. Just sleep."

Her eyes fluttered closed, her last thought following her into sleep: Tanner Reynolds would be the death of her.

• CHAPTER 12 •

Sometimes, a man had to admit when he'd been a fool. He had to look inside and realize that he had let his hatred, his suspicions, rule his logic rather than letting his logic rule his emotions. He had to look beyond the surface, and dig past the emotions for or against the situation, and feel for the truth.

His gut had told something wasn't right with Scheme Tallant all along. Nearly ten years he had been watching her, and he had known something was off. Something was wrong. But hatred and suspicion had clouded logic; the need to hate had clouded reason.

The proof the Breeds had gathered on her over the past ten years showed a spoiled general's daughter as merciless and bloodthirsty as the monster who had sired her. Proof such as orders carrying her signature to execute Breeds still beneath her father's command, for no other reason than whatever perceived weakness they possessed. Proof such as the surveillance videos the Breeds had managed to acquire of meetings between Scheme, her father and high-ranking soldiers within her father's organization. Her cold, deliberate plans to strike against Sanctuary.

But the gut had warned him, even during the investigation, that something was off. That something wasn't right with the evidence they had against her. As though he were seeing only part of the picture, and the rest was in shadow. He should have paid attention to his gut.

There were too many inconsistencies in the evidence they had gathered on her. A Breed marked for execution only to escape at the last moment because of a mistake she had supposedly made. Scheme's profiling reports before the escape that the Breed was trustworthy and wasn't an escape risk. Attacks Sanctuary had been warned were coming, or a transmission suddenly appearing that hadn't been there before. Little things. Things that made it appear as though fate were on the side of the Breeds. Tiny little fuckups that, taken by themselves, were meaningless. No organization or person was perfect. But when put together—

And then there were the short disappearances she had made each time those little mistakes had been made.

She had been punished during those disappearances. Punished in ways that made Tanner's skin crawl and his suspicions rise.

He knew Jonas had managed to find a spy within the Tallant ranks eight years before. One he had never revealed to the Breed Cabinet. That spy had been one of the successes that had allowed him to step in as director of the Bureau of Breed Affairs.

Jonas was a sneaky son of a bitch. He had managed to place spies in areas that the Breed analysts had considered impossible. He knew weaknesses and strengths and how to exploit them. And he had had an ace in the hole.

Somehow, Jonas had recruited General Tallant's own daughter. He had to have. It was the only thing that made sense. Why else would her father beat her, bury her, in a search for information? And Tanner knew that was the reason why.

Cyrus Tallant was as evil as they came. He was a monster who believed in his cause. He wasn't there for the power or the money, but because he believed in what he was doing.

To the general, the Breeds had no soul because man, rather than God, created them. They were tools, no more or less than a dog or a rifle. The only difference being in how they were trained.

Their humanity was stripped from them as babes. After they were weaned, they were placed in pens and taught to fend for themselves. Once there, they were watched every second, studied until each surviving toddler was finally placed in what was considered an appropriate training program.

Psychologists, psychiatrists and doctors created individual programs for each Breed, designed to create the weapon the Council envisioned.

They believed in their own rhetoric. That Breeds weren't truly human, and therefore had no rights. They had no souls, and therefore the Council could not be held accountable for their deaths.

They believed in what they were doing just as desperately as the Breeds believed in their right to freedom and life. And General Tallant believed more strongly than most in his right to rid the world of the Breeds now that they were no longer controlled.

He wouldn't hesitate to use his daughter in that battle. And if his daughter showed the same weakness his wife had, then she was as disposable in the war he was fighting as his spouse had been.

Not that there was any proof that the general had ordered her death. Dorothy Tallant had been a scientist within the Breed lab Tallant had first been assigned to oversee.

A petite Asian-American with an IQ off the charts and a talent for genetic engineering, she had supposedly died of a massive stroke twenty years before.

He breathed wearily as he continued to go through the information he had pulled up on his laptop. The surveillance on the Tallants had begun even before the revelation to the world that the Breeds existed.

Only in the past year or so had the Breeds managed to actually formulate a case against Tallant. After all, it wasn't illegal to hire Breeds as security personnel. Just as it wasn't a law that Breeds had to register with the Bureau of Breed Affairs, though most did to assure their own safety.

Tallant's Breeds didn't. The dozen Coyotes he employed

had never registered, which meant no fingerprints, no way of identifying them. And they were damned good killers. The best the Council had ever created from the Coyote DNA.

He pushed back from the laptop as he disconnected the link into the Breed satellites and sighed wearily.

Something was eating at him; he could feel it. Something that just didn't set well with what he knew about Scheme Tallant so far.

Forget the lust and the raging hunger. He knew himself; he didn't lust after whores and killers. And he could smell them; the animal inside him could sense them.

Scheme was neither a whore nor a killer. And that definitely didn't fit with the profile the Breed analysts had put together on her.

So where did that leave him? The minute he walked into Sanctuary with her, she would be placed under Breed Law, convicted and possibly executed.

Her only chance had been a mating. If he had mated her.

He stared at her, his lips flattening in anger as his teeth clenched with it.

And there lay his problem. There was no mating heat.

He had almost been certain she was his mate. The emotions were there. The lust, the need, the overwhelming, primal protectiveness. He was falling in love with her. The animal inside him was claiming her. But there was no mating. Occasionally, at odd moments, an unusual taste would tempt his senses. The taste of wild lust and heat, similar to the tastes mated couples described. But it was never there for long. And the glands that held the mating hormone beneath his tongue didn't swell and release the hormone created from the biological and chemical reaction to a mate. It could be that his DNA was just almost compatible for the mating. Which meant she might be another Breed's mate. A Breed whose DNA matched his own.

He ran his tongue over his teeth. The glands hadn't inflamed, and even more, the barb hidden deep within each Feline Breed cock hadn't shown itself. The hormone within the saliva and that barb marked the mate even more surely than the bite to the shoulder that reportedly always occurred, unknowingly, by the Breed. They rarely remembered the need to bite their mate and only became aware of it after the taste of blood filled their mouths.

Shit. Shit. Had he been taking Cabal's mate?

He moved almost violently from the chair and paced the rough stone floor of the cavern. He couldn't think about that. He couldn't allow it to take hold in his mind or the animal inside would certainly break free.

He had to concentrate on her safety.

He couldn't take her to Sanctuary, and she couldn't return to her home. There had to be an answer. He had searched every database he could find and hacked into more files at the Bureau of Breed Affairs than he wanted to count. There wasn't even a hint that Scheme Tallant was the spy Jonas had recruited within the Tallant organization.

And without proof, Tanner was screwed, because he was running out of time. He barely had a week left on his vacation, and if he didn't return, Callan would send someone out to find out why.

No excuses would be acceptable. Callan knew his family, and Tanner was part of his family. He would know something was wrong, and there was no way the pride leader would understand this one. Not considering who she was and her connection to the general.

Damn, he had been so certain the mating heat would begin. It didn't make sense. He had never been so obsessed with a woman in his life. He had teetered between hate and lust for ten years, only to have the lust, the hunger for her, completely overwhelm him and the hatred dissolve in the face of the horror he was suspecting she had experienced at her father's hands.

She was so small. Delicate. Yet with a strength he hadn't expected. Her bones were so small he wondered how her father had kept from shattering them when he beat her.

Hell, he didn't know how to work this now. He had envisioned arriving at Sanctuary with his mate, and now he had no defense to offer her. Breed Law or her father's assassins. He couldn't allow her to face either. Unless she was Jonas's mole. Or Cabal's mate.

He wiped his hand over his face.

Cabal's mate.

It couldn't be true, but he couldn't ignore the signs that it was possible. Mating heat was a biological, hormonal mating, as well as emotional.

Emotionally, he was so firmly tied to her now that he wondered if he could ever breathe without her scent in his head. But what if the mating heat was more physical than emotional? What if she wasn't his mate at all? What if she belonged to the only man whose genetics matched his? Perhaps matched enough that he reacted to her as a mate, without the mating hormone. A mating hormone Cabal would release once he came face-to-face with her.

Could he survive it? Could he live with it?

"You're thinking too hard." Her voice had him turning swiftly toward her, his brows drawing into a frown at the weakness in her voice.

The touch of her gaze upon him had him hardening instantly beneath his jeans, his body eagerly anticipating her touch. But as he watched her move and detected the scent of physical pain, he knew that wouldn't be an option, not until she managed to loosen those still bruised muscles.

"There are some bath salts in the bathroom." He moved for the bed, helping her to ease out of it despite the suspicion in her gaze.

She wasn't used to being cared for, but hell, he wasn't used to caring for anyone. In her case, he couldn't seem to help himself.

"I'll be okay."

Why the hell was she always pulling away from him? He was constantly trying to get closer to her while she was constantly moving away from him.

"I'm sure you will be, but I prefer to make certain of it." He stared into her dark eyes, seeing the response in her gaze as his hands slid slowly down her arms. "I didn't mean to be so hard on you when I took you."

"I don't break easily, Tanner," she assured him, moving away from him again and heading for the bathroom. "I'll take you up on those bath salts though."

He followed her into the bathroom, his lips quirking as she moved naked through the cavern. She wasn't self-conscious about her nakedness; he liked that about her. She didn't pretend coyness or shyness. She gave as good as she got and didn't make excuses.

Moving into the small cave that held the bathroom, he reached beneath the sink and pulled free the bottle of scented salts.

"My pride sisters Dawn and Sherra like to keep their smelly stuff around." He uncapped it for her and set it on the sink cabinet. "Take your time. I'll fix breakfast now that you're up."

"So it's morning?" she asked casually.

His lips quirked. "About ten."

She stiffened as she adjusted the water running into the tub.

She finally sighed as steam poured from the hot water. "When do you intend to let me go?"

Straightening, she turned to face him, her long hair falling over her shoulder, framing her unique features.

"This isn't a game, Scheme. The minute you walk out of here you're dead, and you know it. Your father won't let you escape, and even if he did, Breed Law sure as hell wouldn't. Without his protection, you'll be taken by the Breeds. Once in Sanctuary, you'll be placed under Breed Law."

"Then why waste your time like this?" She stared back at him somberly. "You confuse me, Tanner. What do you want? A few hard fucks before you turn me over to your pride leader?" Her lips turned down sadly. "Why don't you go ahead and do it? Stop torturing both of us."

"Do you think I want to see you dead, Scheme?" he snapped back, enraged that she would accept death so easily. "I didn't waste my damned time bringing you here just to see you executed under Breed Law or by your father's hand."

"So why did you waste your time?" She moved to the sink and picked up the salts before turning back to the tub and pouring a healthy amount into the water there.

She acted as though dying meant nothing, as though her life had no worth, and it was pissing him off.

"You could turn evidence against your father," he stated. "Sanctuary would protect you, Scheme, for that information."

She paused, biting her lip, her expression concentrated as she stared back at him. "I wish it were that easy."

"Scheme, time is running out," he urged. "I can't stay here forever, and neither can you."

"Then let me go." She turned back to the cabinet, pulling towels, a washcloth and a bottle of bath gel from it before laying them on the small stool by the tub. "The answer is pretty easy, Tanner. I didn't ask you to bring me here."

"You're asking me to let you die," he snarled, furious. "You could live."

"For how long?" Her expression enraged him. Cool. Composed. They might have been talking about the weather rather than her life. "If you truly want to see me safe, then prove it. Give me a secured cell phone and let me go. I'll be safe."

Her words made him crazy.

"Are you Jonas's spy in your father's organization?"

He watched her tense, pale. "You have another spy in Father's organization?" she asked hesitantly, almost fearfully.

His teeth locked together. He could smell neither deceit nor guilt, but he did smell fear.

"Trust me, Scheme," he whispered.

"Trust me first, Tanner," she rebutted. "Just take me out of here and drop me off far enough away from the Coyotes searching for me, and give me a cell. I'll contact you within hours."

If she were still alive. And there wasn't much change of that.

"I can protect you, goddammit," he snarled. "Give me that much at least."

Her gaze flickered with indecision, with hope and fear and a flash of agonizing pain.

"I can't."

"I won't let them fucking kill you." He was surprised to hear his voice rise. His voice never rose. He was the calm Breed, the playful one.

She stared back at him, a cynical twist to her mouth that told him more than words how little she trusted him.

"I can't give you what you want, Tanner." Desperation filled her voice. "I don't have what you need."

"Why do I have to keep telling you that I can fucking smell your lies?" he growled.

"Have I ever mentioned how little I care?" she cried out, the lie obvious not just in her scent, but in her voice and in her eyes. "You seem to be under the misconception here, Breed, that I'm willingly playing this little game with you. I'm not. I didn't ask you to bring me here, and I didn't ask you to interrogate me. All I asked for was a bath."

The tiger he fought to keep hidden awoke with a dangerous shift within him. He could feel the warning snarl in his chest, the opening of extra senses, the added determination that nothing ever hurt her again.

"You're still protecting him." He clenched his teeth against the knowledge. "That bastard has beat you, buried you alive how many fucking times, and killed your child. He hired his own man to be your lover and used him to find reasons to punish you, and you still protect him?"

She turned back to the tub, her hand running beneath the water again before she gripped the lip of the high, claw-foot tub and moved to lift her leg over the side.

She didn't make a sound, but he saw the discomfort the effort was costing her.

"Goddammit, Scheme, can't you even fucking ask me for help?" He gripped her waist and lifted her in as he fought back emotions he had never known in his life. For the first time, he knew fear. Without her help, he couldn't save her.

"If I needed your help, I would ask for it." She lowered herself into the hot water with a small, sighing gasp, the heated liquid washing to her hips as she pulled her hair out of the way and let it flow over the edge of the tub.

"Scheme." He hunched next to the tub and stared back at her imperatively. "Give me something. Anything I can use to help you. Don't go down like this. For both our sakes."

Her lips quirked. "I'm nothing to you, Tanner," she said softly. "You aren't even part of the equation."

Scheme watched as Tanner's face hardened, his eyes gleaming with an almost unearthly light as he straightened, staring down at her with a predatory intent that she knew should have frightened her.

"I won't let you die like this." His voice was guttural, animalistic. "No matter how willing you are to die for that bastard who sired you."

He turned and stalked from the room, snapping the curtain closed behind him as she closed her eyes against his rage.

He was good, she thought, in regret, fighting back her tears. God, she was not going to cry over this. She had never cried for anything short of unbearable pain, until Tanner. She didn't cry because her emotions were ripping her apart inside. And they were ripping her apart.

For the first time since Chaz, she wanted to believe in a man. She wanted to believe so bad it was eating her alive inside, breaking her heart, destroying a part of her mind that she hadn't known existed. She could have sworn she had outgrown fairy tales. But she wanted the fantasy Tanner was offering so desperately that it cut like a knife inside her.

She had lost her child because she had trusted a man. Believed in him with all her heart. Loved him until she had overlooked the tiny inconsistencies that warned her of his betrayal. And now she was on the very edge of doing it again. Placing her trust and the lives of others in the hands of a man who could betray her.

Her soul screamed out in denial. But she remembered that the moment she realized that Chaz had aided her father in destroying her child, her soul had screamed out the same denial. Could she survive such betrayal again?

If he was sincere, then once he learned the truth of what she had been doing, he would understand. That was love, she told herself. He would forgive her, wouldn't he? He would understand why she hid the fact that she was working for Jonas, that she couldn't trust him until the information she had made it to the only man who knew what she had been doing for the past eight years.

Her lips quirked at the thought of that silver-eyed Lion Breed. Very, very few people knew his secrets. She was one of them. And because she knew them, she had trusted him. He would have bled out in the most painful ways before betraying his own people. Or betraying someone attempting to help them. He was her only chance. All she had to do was get to Jonas. She couldn't trust Tanner, no matter the demand inside her that pushed her to do just that. No matter the pain that holding her silence cost her.

A part of her was certain that Tanner wasn't her father's spy. But there was that dark voice within her soul, the one that had awakened the day she realized her lover had helped destroy his own baby. The voice that whispered of Cyrus's manipulative, calculating evil.

Breeds were deceptive; it was part of their training. And Tanner's training, even at a young age, had been extensive. And Cyrus had been part of his training. To date, he still controlled more than half of the Breeds he had helped train himself. He had helped train Tanner before the escapes from those New Mexico labs. He could still have enough hold over Tanner to control him.

So why did she need to trust him? Why was it such a battle to force herself to remember what he was, and what he could be?

Because she loved him. Because he had touched her inside when she was certain she could never be touched there again.

Because a part of her believed so strongly in him that it was willing to give him anything, everything he asked for, and to trust him. Everything inside her wanted that but that shadow of realism that kept reminding her of her child. Kept reminding her that the one person who should have been willing to die for it was its father. The man who had helped destroy it.

She could afford to wait, she told herself. She could afford to trust that if Tanner loved her now, then he would love her later. First, she had to get to Jonas. And time was running out. She had only a few weeks left before everything would be in place to kidnap Callan Lyons's son. Such a small amount of time to save a child.

⋆ CHAPTER 13 ⋆

He was a good cook.

Scheme laid her fork on her plate and breathed in deeply before picking up her coffee cup and finishing the last of the rich brew he had placed in front of her with the ham, eggs, homemade biscuits and surprisingly good grits.

She had never eaten grits in her life, had turned her nose up at them and laughed if anyone suggested she would eat such a thing. If she managed to survive this little venture, then she would have to learn to make them.

"More coffee?" He lifted the pot suggestively.

"Please." He filled her cup, and she ignored his gaze as she lifted it and sipped, hiding her pleasure in the taste. His lips curved knowingly though. His damned sense of smell. He could probably smell her pleasure as easily as he could smell her lies.

She inhaled slowly, trying to ignore other things as well as his amusement. Her arousal, her knowledge that he could smell it. The longer she sat there across from him the stronger it was growing. Her nipples were pressing into the dark violet velvet of her top, her breasts so swollen they were sensitive.

Between her thighs, her clit was engorged, throbbing, and her panties were damp.

She ached for him. Needed him. Never, not even in those first tempestuous months with Chaz, had she been so aroused.

If she survived, doing without Tanner's touch would be hell. She needed to feel his hands stroking over her body, his lips against her flesh.

She flicked him a look, watching as he leaned back in his chair and drank his coffee silently. He hadn't said much since she came out of the shower; his lazy tiger personality was fully in effect though. The gleam of amusement in his eyes, the quirk of a smile on his sensual lips. His long, black-and-gold striped hair fell to his shoulders, framing the fallen angel features perfectly.

He really was too good-looking for any woman's peace of mind.

Her emotions, her attraction to him and this unexplained hunger were getting the best of her. She had to escape. Now. Before he broke her. Before his promises and his insistence that she trust him broke through her woman's heart.

Today, she had to escape.

"So where's your brother?" She lifted the cup and sipped again, staring at him over the rim as she attempted to distract his attention from her.

"My brother?" His brow arched perfectly. Damn, she wished she could do that.

"Cabal," she intoned mockingly. "You two are normally shadows of one another."

"And what makes you think we're brothers?" he asked curiously, setting the cup back on the table.

Scheme breathed in deeply. "You forget, the Council had your full file, Tanner, not just the remnants that survived the lab's explosion. I know you and Cabal are identical twins. You don't have to lie to me."

He crossed his arms on the table and leaned forward slowly. "And how extensive are your files?" he asked.

She shrugged easily. "Somehow, the files in the Council's database were destroyed. Most of what Father has is from memory only, which isn't extensive. But I remember reading the file when I first took over the job as his assistant."

His eyes narrowed. "The files were destroyed?"

"You didn't know?" She arched her brows in question. "I assumed the Breeds had found a way to get a spy into the main headquarters of the Council databases. Most of the files on the Breeds were destroyed several years ago when a virus was implanted into the network. The Council is still trying to recover from that one. I applaud whoever managed it."

She had managed it, along with Jonas's help. The headquarters in Sweden were considered impenetrable, their computer and backup networks impossible to infiltrate. But they had done it.

His eyes narrowed. "We had no idea how extensive the damage was."

"It was catastrophic." She sighed. "Somehow, someone implanted a virus that corrupted every file with the Breed extension. An explosion at the secondary facility that housed the disc backups took care of those as well. We assumed it was a Breed assault."

Jonas was even more closemouthed than she had given him credit for. Once he had managed transferring the Council file databases, he had implanted a virus so insidious that it had taken the Council computer geeks months to catch it. By then, every Breed file they possessed, as well as backups, had been corrupted. The explosion at the secondary facility had been a stroke of genius as well.

"So there's nothing left?" he asked softly.

She shrugged again. "There were hard copies of some files, though those contained very little information. Mostly training stats, genetic source, and so forth. Many of the photos are lost forever though. They're still attempting to put their files back together."

Tanner's lips pursed. "We knew about the explosion, and the virus, but we had no idea how extensive the damage was."

"Of course you knew." She smiled. "I remembered your file though; I read it several times after you were appointed the head of Public Relations at Sanctuary. You and Cabal were created as twins, then separated after the first year for training purposes. If I read correctly, he wasn't as cooperative as you were with the training."

Her chest clenched at the thought of how uncooperative he had been. Cabal had been horribly abused at the German lab in which he had been confined.

"He was nearly dead when we found him," he stated. "Which makes me wonder why you're asking about him. Your father was the head of the committee that decided life or death, Scheme. His signature was on Cabal's cancellation papers."

"Mine wasn't," she pointed out.

She hadn't known of the cancellation orders that had gone out that month. If she had, she would have made certain that one was shredded. The mode of death had been particularly horrific.

"I found him in that pit," he suddenly snarled. "Half-dead, surrounded by the Breeds that had been thrown in there with him, their bodies already decomposing. He had almost bled out from the strikes those knives had made at him."

The only thing that had saved Cabal was the fact that the soldiers had overfilled the pit with Breeds. The smooth stone walls were fitted with deadly sharp daggers that struck in a random pattern. The fact that he had evaded a deadly thrust was a testament to his training. He had managed to calculate the timing and direction of each thrust as other Breeds died around him.

Her father had helped design that pit. It was first implemented as a training pit; the random thrusts of the dagger-sharp blades were used to train and test the Breeds on their ability to sense where and when danger would strike. One or two Breeds at a time in the pit and the blades did little damage. But once it was determined that as a training tool, the pit was ineffective, then it had been used instead as a means of mass murder. It was quite effective in that.

"He survived," she reminded him, steeling herself against the knowledge of the horrific crimes committed against the Breeds.

"And now you're asking about him." He leaned back in his

chair, crossing his arms over his chest and staring back at her with a glint of anger.

"I was merely curious. The two of you are rarely seen apart now."

"You don't want to know about Cabal, Scheme," he half-snarled. "His hatred for your father is deeper than most Breeds'. He would break your neck before I could stop him."

"What difference, him or another?" She rose from the table, lifted her plate and cup and carried them to the sink. "Forget I asked."

"Are you ready tell me why your father wanted you dead?"

She had known that question would return.

"I assume he believes I'm betraying him. It's normally the only reason he goes to such extremes."

She slipped the knife she had managed to slide her fingers over into the hand she had placed behind her back as they talked.

"He didn't entrust me with as much information as the Breeds assume he did. I was a very small cog in the whole organization. But I know enough to make him uncomfortable with a few things that have happened lately."

"Such as?"

She shrugged, forcing a mocking smile to her lips. "Various plans he had made with the pure blood societies, a few reports he gets on missions going out from Sanctuary. Nothing too incriminating, but as I said, uncomfortable."

And he could tell she was lying. She could see it in his eyes.

"This isn't helping you." His golden eyes were narrowed on her and filled with suspicion as he rose to his feet.

Scheme tucked the knife into the band of her pants before pushing her hands into the pockets. He barely glanced at the movement as he rose from his chair and collected his own dishes before moving to the sink.

Dammit, she needed him to sit back down.

"I believe I told you I didn't need your help." But she did. She needed his help, his heat, his honest passion for her. And it was destroying her.

She retrieved the coffee she'd set on the counter and moved back to the table. Seconds later he did the same.

She had to escape and contact Jonas as soon as possible. She had to get away from Tanner before he stole her soul. She was desperate, suddenly more terrified of herself and her own emotions than she was of the risk she was preparing to take.

She needed that electronic remote she knew Tanner carried. It had to be the way out of there. She had checked every corner, every crack and crevice. There had to be a hidden doorway that remote worked.

He continued to stare back at her, the brilliancy of the green-flecked gold eyes almost mesmerizing. The Bengal was perhaps the most dangerous of the Breeds created, which was one of the reasons so few were designed. They were naturally, deceptively lazy, appearing to heel easily. The tiger genetics had taken decades to manipulate, and the scientists had learned early that the animal, as well as the Breed, wasn't always dependable. The moment you thought you had tamed one, he struck. That made them a threat.

"Do you know why I was appointed head of the Public Relations Department of Sanctuary?" he asked then.

She rolled her eyes. "You were appointed as head of Public Relations because you have the looks of a fallen angel and the social graces to match. You're considered the epitome of what the Breeds truly are: playful, caring and as threatening as a lap cat purring for attention."

His lips curled into an amused smile as he propped his arms on the table and leaned forward once again.

"That's the reason we leaked to the public," he said softly. "I took the job because of those things, as well as the fact that my sense of smell is so highly developed that I can walk into the room and give the crowd what they need to hear. What they need to reassure themselves. I can smell more than a lie, Scheme. I can smell the slightest deception. I know you're still lying to me."

She stared back at him silently, cursing her own weakness. She wasn't lying, exactly. She just wasn't being totally honest.

"Do you think I'm really going to give you enough to let you hang me?" And that was total honesty.

He stared back at her intently, so intently that Scheme wondered if he could see into her soul.

"I wouldn't hang you. Trust me, Scheme. Let me help you," he told her, and her heart believed. Her mind screamed out in warning. She had heard those words before, from Chaz. He had sworn he would protect her. Sworn he loved her. Sworn she was his life, his love and all things in between, and God help her but he had nearly destroyed everything she was instead.

She had to get out of there and get hold of Jonas. It was imperative, because her need to trust Tanner was overruling her need for caution. She rose to her feet, doing nothing to hide her nervousness, hoping, praying that the scent of her arousal and her nerves would overwhelm the scent of the knife at her back.

"You're very confident of yourself." Her voice shook as she moved around the table.

"Confident of my ability to help you, if you'll let me." He stared back at her, his expression suddenly serious, almost sad. "But you would have to believe in me first, wouldn't you?"

"I don't need your help." Her fingers trailed up his arm as he leaned back in the chair, his eyes drifting closed as she came around him, her fingers caressing up the shirt-covered shoulders to his neck as the beat of her heart threatened to strangle her and tears suddenly dampened her eyes.

She lowered her head to his neck, placing a heated kiss to his pulse as she slid the knife from her waistband. Her hand shook as a tear fell from her eye.

She had to do it. Her tongue tasted his neck as she shuddered, gripping the hilt desperately as her hand lowered to her side.

He would be okay. Breeds healed amazingly fast. She wasn't going to kill him. She knew where to strike. Her father had taught her how to maim and how to kill. She could do it. Easy.

She fought to breathe, bringing the knife up further as he sat relaxed in front of her, his arms on the table. The perfect position. The knife would slide in just under his ribs, missing the spleen.

He would be disabled until she could bind his hands and then the wound. He would live.

Do it, she screamed out at herself. *Now.*

Her hand trembled.

Her breath hitched as a sob filled her throat.

This was her only choice. She had to escape, and he had already proved he wasn't going to just let her go.

"Do it, Scheme," he whispered gently. "Hurry, pretty girl, before you lose your nerve."

He knew. She would have frozen if a shudder hadn't shaken her body and the sob hadn't escaped her throat.

"It's easy." His voice was amazingly tender. "The knife you chose is perfect. If you keep hesitating, I'm going to get impatient."

"You son of a bitch," she screamed, jerking back before she threw the knife, the tears finally falling as she stumbled back from him, watching as his head lowered and shook slowly.

He rose from the table lazily, turning to her, his expression somber, filled with sadness.

"It's not so easy to kill when your hand holds the weapon, is it?" he asked, his tone so understanding that holding back the tears was impossible. "If you want to convince me that you're a killer, that you've cold-bloodedly worked with your father all these years, then you're going to have to do better than that."

Another sob broke free as he moved toward her, staring at her with eyes so gentle, so filled with emotion that she felt something inside her soul rip open—a wound so intense, so destructive that it weakened her knees and left her on the floor, crying.

"You have to let me go," she cried. "Let me out of here, Tanner, please." If he didn't, she was going to lose her strength; she wouldn't be able to hold back the need to trust him much longer.

Let him think it was claustrophobia; she could handle that.

The truth could get her killed, could get her returned that much faster to her father, and the death that awaited her there wouldn't be easy.

"Come here." He knelt in front of her, lifting her, holding her close to him as he moved her to the couch. "Right here." He sat her down, then opened the laptop he was working on. "Look at this, Scheme."

The screen flared to life, six small windows glowing on it.

"This is the area around my cabin, several miles from here." He pointed out four of the screens. "What do you see?"

The screens were thermoactive, showing bodies moving, weapons held ready.

"Those are Council soldiers, looking for me," he told her. "They've been watching the cabin for days, hoping to find you. Reports are coming in from Sanctuary that several transmissions have left our communications base, concerning you and the assignments that have gone out from Sanctuary. Your father wants you bad enough to make his spy work overtime to find out if the Breed community is searching for you, or if they have you."

"So why are they here?"

"Because every Breed in Sanctuary knew I was gunning for you. His spy would have known. His spy would have informed him that I'm missing from the compound. Very few people know I'm on vacation right now. If you walk out of here, he'll find you. He'll kill you. Trust me. I can save you."

She stared at the computer, fighting the need, fighting the words on her lips that would reveal everything.

"He hired your ex-lover to kill you, Scheme. He murdered your child before it ever had a chance at life. Do you really want to die too?" he said gently.

She shook her head desperately. She was trying to protect herself. Oh God, she wanted to trust him. She needed to trust him, and she knew she couldn't.

One hand flattened on her abdomen as she reminded herself why. She was empty, her life was empty. Her child had been cut out of her body and a tubal performed while she was unaware. She would never conceive again without the general's permission. She would always remember the consequences if she did.

Jonas had warned her to trust no one but him. That even he couldn't vouch for any one Breed until he was certain of the identity of the spy working within their ranks. He had made her promise. Made her swear it. If he couldn't vouch for Tanner himself, how could she be certain?

Because she loved him, her heart whispered.

And she had loved before, the dark part of her soul reminded her. Remember where that led?

"Don't . . ." She shook her head desperately. "I don't have what you want, Tanner. I don't have your answers."

"Scheme, help me save you. For both our sakes."

She lifted her gaze to his, his features blurry through the tears that still fell from her eyes. Why couldn't she strike? She had killed, regardless of what he thought. A Coyote that had caught her helping another Breed escape. A soldier who had slipped into her room intending to rape her. A knife was her preferred weapon; she knew how to use it. Dammit, she knew how to kill, how to maim; why couldn't she strike against this one man?

"There's no saving me," she finally whispered, accepting that fate. "For both our sakes, Tanner, stop trying."

CHAPTER 14

Sighing wearily, Tanner pulled Scheme into his arms before lifting her gently into his lap. She lay in his arms like a babe, fighting to control her sobs, her breath hitching as tears dampened his shirt.

He had taken a risk, he knew. The chances of her sliding that knife into his side had been high. Too fucking high. He could have been bleeding out on the stone floor rather than wrapping his arms around her and holding her against his chest.

So why wasn't he bleeding? He'd been almost certain she would attempt the blow. What bothered him was the fact that at that point, he had almost decided to let her have it.

She had to trust him. There wasn't enough time left to gain her trust or to hope for the best. He had so little time left. Even less if Callan or Jonas became suspicious and guessed where the general's missing daughter really was. He didn't worry about anyone else, but Jonas was naturally paranoid, and Callan, well hell, Callan just knew him. He didn't doubt that his pride leader had already guessed what he was up to. What Callan decided to do about it would be anyone's guess.

"You've never had a problem doing what you had to before," he murmured against her ear. "Why couldn't you do it, Scheme?"

"I don't want to die in these stupid caves." She jerked at the hold he had on her.

"Stop fighting me." He held her closer, one hand cupping her head and pressing it to his shoulder. "And stop lying to me."

"I don't need you to hold me," she cried out. "I'm not a baby. I don't need your comfort. I need you to let me go."

His jaw clenched with the effort to hold back his frustration.

"Did you see those soldiers on the monitor, Scheme? Who the hell do you think they're looking for?"

"You!" she screamed. "It's your stupid cabin, isn't it?"

He laughed at that. "Come on, baby, even the Council is smarter than that. They know what killing me will do to their cause. Don't you listen to the news? The world loves me. The outcry against the Council and the pure genetics groups would be horrendous. They wouldn't dare. They're here because they suspect I have you. Not because they want me dead."

It was amusing to even consider it. How many times had he sneered at the Council soldiers who trailed him whenever he left Sanctuary? As much as they hated him, they couldn't kill him, and what's more, they couldn't allow him to die, not yet. Not as long as public sentiment toward him was so high.

She struggled against him again, her breath hitching, her deliberate restraint over her tears breaking his heart.

The scent of her, a mix of guilt, fear, pain and longing, twisted inside him. He couldn't have expected this when he kidnapped her. How she would set him on fire and break his heart at the same time.

She made him feel things he had never felt before, and that scared the living hell out of him when he paused long enough to consider it.

He nipped her ear gently. "Do you really want me to let you go? You're scared, Scheme. I can take that fear away."

A surprised, almost cynical laugh left her lips. "Are you crazy?"

"My pride leader says I am." He bent her back in his arms, much as he had done the day before. "Want to test his theory?"

Her chocolate eyes were nearly black, staring back at him in confusion, passion and anger as her hands gripped his fore-arms, her lips parting just enough to cause his cock to jerk in response.

"You're a hazard to your own health," she bit out. "How did you know I wouldn't use that knife?"

"I didn't," he admitted with a small smile. "I think I even expected you to go through with it."

Her gaze flickered heatedly. "Why would you let me, Tan-ner? Why would you do something like that?"

He reached out, his thumb brushing over her cheek, catch-ing a tear before staring at it thoughtfully for long seconds. How could he explain that to her when he couldn't explain it to himself?

"Because I had to know if I'm more to you than just your captor." He lifted his gaze back to hers. "Because you are much more to me, Scheme, than you ever should be."

She swallowed tightly, her gaze becoming shuttered now.

"That's crazy."

"Yeah, it is," he admitted with a smile. "But no crazier than this is."

His head lowered to her. He had to taste her lips, dampened with her tears. The sweet salty taste of her went to his head like a narcotic. The touch of her lips against his, like warm satin, her tongue a stroke of fire, sent raging impulses of plea-sure to tighten his cock further and draw his balls tighter.

Her kiss heated him faster, hotter than a volcano at erup-tion point. It was like being in the middle of an inferno.

"I went crazy every time I saw another man touch you," he growled against her lips, his hand threading into her hair to hold her in place as her eyes jerked open in surprise.

"Someone had to watch the surveillance." He nipped at her lips with his teeth. "In case one of you talked business in the fucking bed." He caught her lower lip, pulling at it, scraping over it with his teeth as her eyes narrowed back at him. "I went crazy," he repeated. "Every goddamned time I would be feral for days."

Her lips trembled. "Then why did you?"

He couldn't keep himself from touching her face, from smoothing his fingers over her delicate jaw.

"Because I couldn't bear for anyone else to do it." He would have had to kill anyone else who dared to see her like that. Naked. Vulnerable. Reaching for something she never found. He had seen it in her eyes, that dissatisfaction, that need. Just as he felt it in his soul with every other woman he had been with.

"Why doesn't it bother you?" He would have been enraged to learn his privacy had been invaded in such a way. She should have been clawing his eyes out instead of lying back in his arms and staring up at him.

Not that her rage would have made a difference. With his luck, it would have only made him hotter.

Resignation tilted her lips. "Because you didn't let anyone else see it." Her whisper sliced through him. "And because it was you."

And for the first time he paused. "Why does that matter, Scheme?"

She shook her head slowly as her hand lifted to curl around the side of his neck. "I don't know why it matters," she said, her tone so stoic, so somber, it clenched his heart. "But it matters."

Then her head lifted, her teeth catching at his lower lip as she tugged at it erotically.

"You said you made lists?" she asked then.

He smiled slowly. "I made many lists, pretty girl, and all on exactly how many ways I intended to please you."

"So please me, Breed," she whispered heatedly. "Show me everything I've been missing."

It sounded like a dare, a brazen challenge. But he heard the desperation in her voice, saw it in her eyes. She needed this as much as he did, needed to lose herself in the pleasure and the heat that built with each touch between them.

Lifting her in his arms, Tanner carried her to the bed, keeping his eyes locked with hers, his senses focused on her.

She was confused, desperate. He could feel the raging pain inside her, the need to understand the fires that built so quickly between them.

Why wasn't she his mate?

As he laid her on the bed, Tanner stared down at her, memorizing her features, the soft pale skin of her face, the dark chocolate of her eyes. Her sable hair fanned out around her; the violet velvet of her outfit whispered over her slender body.

She would have made the perfect mate. Strong-willed, passionate, built for endurance and survival. She should have been his mate.

She would be his mate. Fuck science and the damned scientists at Sanctuary. This was his woman, no matter what nature or blood tests decided. He would lay down his life to protect her.

"Take off the clothes. Slowly," he told her, his voice hoarse from the strength of his lust, his need.

Her hands moved to the elastic band of the lounging pants before her hips lifted to push the material over her sensuous curves.

Her silken tummy slid into view, slightly rounded, soft. Kissable. Then rounded, well-toned thighs, the bare, glistening curves of her pussy. And those curl-shrouded folds were more than kissable. They were devourable.

"You have the prettiest damned pussy I've ever laid eyes on," he said and sighed as she finally kicked the soft pants free. "I could spend hours eating you."

He glanced at her eyes just in time to see the flare of response.

"He never did that for you, did he, baby?" His fingers went to the buttons of his shirt as hers gripped the hem of her shirt. "St. Marks didn't appreciate that pretty pussy. He gave it no more than a lick and a promise, didn't he?"

His shirt dropped to the floor as his hands went to his belt.

"You were watching," she whispered. "What do you think?"

"I don't think, baby, I *know* he didn't know how to appreciate what he had," he growled.

He had watched those surveillance videos. St. Marks hadn't

known what to do with a woman who felt that sex was more than an itch to be scratched.

The shirt cleared her swollen breasts, then came over her head. Her eyes gleamed dark and hot, her face flushed with excitement now. Nearly as flushed as the swollen folds of that slick, wet pussy.

He kicked off his jeans before reaching down and pulling off the socks he wore. But his eyes never left her body. He wondered if he could watch her enough, ever stare long enough that he wouldn't be surprised every time he saw something he had missed the time before.

Like the silken shimmer on the underside of her breasts. The mature curves, not overblown, not really slender. Sweet, soft differences that proclaimed her an adult woman in every way.

"Are you going to do anything, or do you intend to think it to death?"

She was impatient in sex. It was one of the things he had learned about her through those surveillance videos. But then again, St. Marks hadn't exactly gone out of his way to hold her interest.

"I don't need to think about it." He reached out, touched her thigh, then trailed his fingers to the silken wetness between her legs.

There, his thumb circled the swollen little bud of her clit peeking from the apex of the folds. She trembled beneath his touch and his cock jerked in response.

"I can't wait to bury my lips there again. I'd rather eat you than breathe."

Her legs shifted, falling further open as he removed his fingers and came to the bed. Last night had been hard and rough. This, he wanted this to last. He wanted to make her come so many times that by the time he finished she could do nothing but shudder in the grip of an orgasm that seemed to never end.

"First on my list was feeling you come around my tongue," he growled as he settled his knees between her thighs and leaned over her. "And that was good, Scheme. That was really good."

He stared into her eyes as he bent to her mouth, sipping at her lips as her fingers moved hesitantly to his shoulders. She always touched him hesitantly. As though she wasn't certain if she should even touch.

And oh, she should definitely touch.

"Come here, sugar." He rolled to his back, pulling her with him, grinning up at her as she stared back at him in shock. "I'm all yours," he growled, helping her to her knees before pushing his head between them. "And you're all mine."

"Tanner, this doesn't work." She didn't bend forward as he'd expected.

His hands slid up the outside of her thighs as he turned his head and pressed a kiss just above her knee.

"Have we tried it before?" He raked her lower thigh with his teeth, smiling as a tremor rippled beneath the flesh.

"I don't like this position." Her voice was smoky, breathless.

"Have we tried it before?" he asked her again, nipping at her thigh with enough force to make her moan.

Oh yeah, she liked that. He raked along the side of the opposite knee. Her hands flattened on his abdomen.

"I've done this before," she gasped. "I didn't like it."

"Hmm." Yeah, he remembered that one. That one hadn't pissed him off too bad, because he remembered watching her eyes. St. Marks had been less than ineffective. "Maybe you'll like it better with a pro."

Tanner lifted his head, distended his tongue and swiped it through the drenched slit directly above him. While there, he made certain to flicker his tongue over the sensitive flesh before rounding her clit with a delicate, purring lap.

She jerked, a gasp coming from above him as he raked his fingernails along the outsides of her thighs.

"I can't do this," she moaned as he gripped her thighs and flicked the tip of his tongue over the curves of her pussy again.

"Why can't you do this, baby?" He kept the purr in his voice. Damn, she liked that sound, or the touch of his tongue, because the dampness increased exponentially.

He tried the purr again. This time without words. Just a

long, drawn-out purr as he laid his lips against the swollen folds.

"Oh my God, Tanner." She weakened, bent, her head falling to his thigh as her long hair cascaded over his cock and balls. And oh, he liked the feel of that, almost as much as he liked the feel of her hard breath against his flesh.

"Sure you don't like this, pretty baby?" He purred again, just over her clit, and was rewarded by the prettiest sight in the world. A small, hot little drop of cream that he caught with his tongue.

But Scheme. Ah, his sweet little Schemer, she wasn't without her own brand of torture.

Her sharp little nails dug into his outer thighs as her head lifted, her hair sliding over her shoulder and his thighs like living silk as she flicked it back and her hot breath washed over the sensitive head of his cock.

And damn, that was good. His hips jerked up in reaction as he let a growling moan slip past his lips. But that didn't stop his tongue. He flicked teasingly over the curves, lapping at her, licking at the sweet drops of syrup beading on her flesh.

"Mmm. Sweet." He caught one of the curves between his lips, drawing the cream from it before moving back, flickering his tongue around her clit with purring strokes and checking for more of the sweetness.

Ohh, yeah, there it was. Dew drops. Sweet, syrupy, feminine dew.

He smiled and licked. Purred. Whispered a growl over her flesh and then got a chance to devour ambrosia as the dew drops increased.

Luscious.

Rawr.

She exploded.

Scheme jackknifed upright, a muted scream tearing from her throat as fiery ribbons of orgasm began to tighten through every muscle of her body.

"Damn you." She shuddered, her thighs clenching around his face, holding him in place. Oh God, she had to hold him in place as her hips rocked, dragging her enraptured wet flesh over his lips and tongue as she forced the pleasure to echo and re-echo through her clit, vagina and womb.

Oh, it was so good. Nothing had ever been this good. And never had this position even come close to good. Let alone this good.

He chuckled as his hands pressed her thighs open and his head lowered.

"Can you keep up, Schemer?" His voice held a dare. "Am I better than you are?"

Better than she was? He was better than a fantasy. He was better than her vibrator. Hell, yes, he was better than her.

But that didn't mean she couldn't keep up. It didn't mean that she didn't know a few tricks of her own.

She shivered as she heard him purr again. That damned purr was going to steal her mind at this rate. She couldn't stand it.

Bending forward, she trembled, shuddering as he flickered his tongue over her saturated flesh again. She had never been so wet in her life, or so desperate for the sensations racking up inside her.

This position had always been less than comfortable. Until now. Now, instead of tension filling her from the expectation of the male beneath her, pleasure and determination filled her. Determination to give as well as she was getting. Or at least to try.

The thick length of his erection rose to his navel, pulsing and throbbing, the mushroomed head damp with pre-cum as Scheme gripped the shaft and lowered her head.

There wasn't a chance of keeping up with him, but unlike her previous experience with this position, she really didn't give a damn. The flames flickering over her body overrode her sense of fair play. If he wanted to get as good as he was giving, then he was going to have to agree not to touch her while she was touching him, because his touch was destructive.

She could taste him though. She could completely immerse herself in the pleasure he was giving her, the sensuality building inside her. The hunger riding her with a desperation she didn't know how to fight.

Her lips surrounded the head of his cock, drawing him in, tasting the wildness of him in the damp essence that covered the hard, satiny flesh. She felt his lust, his hunger, in the hard pulse of blood through the fiery flesh and the hard growl that vibrated against the lips of her pussy.

She jerked at the sensations that came from that sound, panting as she fought to breathe, her hips lowering further, her body demanding more, always more.

His tongue flickered, licked, painted her flesh with fire and left her gasping as she tried, she really tried to bring him the same pleasure, to tease his cock, to suckle it into her mouth and tempt his control the same as he was tempting hers.

But he was touching her, eating her with hungry lips and tongue as she shuddered above him, then exploded with a force that had her back arching and a scream tearing from her throat.

It was never-ending. It ricocheted from nerve ending to nerve ending, cell to cell, and left her writhing as she suddenly found herself beneath him rather than above him.

"I can't keep up," she cried out, her hands gripping his shoulders as she stared back at him, disappointed in herself, in the lack of pleasure she had given him.

A smile pulled at the tight, controlled line of his lips.

"Baby, if you can keep up, then I'm not doing my job." A wicked flash of white teeth came a second before he shifted between her thighs and pressed home.

Her vision dimmed as the breath paused in her lungs. Oh God, it was so good. The way he filled her, pressing in slowly, stretching the sensitive tissue in her vagina to reveal hidden nerve endings and erogenous zones. Tender places she had never known she possessed.

He stroked over them. Working in and out, back and forth, rocking his hips against hers until he filled her completely and left her trembling beneath him.

"God you're beautiful," he whispered then, his voice hoarse, filled with hunger. "So beautiful you steal a man's breath, Scheme."

She was so close. Too close. She could feel her orgasm just out of reach and her own desperation to jump into it.

"There now," he groaned as his elbows held his weight above her, his hands clasping her head as her hands gripped his hips. "I like this, Schemer. I like this a lot."

"You're killing me," she whimpered. "Don't tease me."

"A little bit of tease is good, darlin'." His head lowered, his lips sipping at a hard nipple as his hips shifted, the head of his cock rubbing inside her and setting off small tremors of impending release.

"Not like this." The pleasure was killing her.

Scheme jerked beneath him as the fiery wedge of heat glanced over flesh so sensitive that the tremors of pleasure shook her to her core.

"Just like this, little love." He continued to rotate his hips slowly. "Just relax for me. You don't have to do anything, sweetheart. No thought required. Just feel good."

She stared back at him, gasping for breath. Something was always required. Her head shook in denial as she fought for enough control to do something, anything to return the favor.

"Being buried inside you is like being plugged into pure pleasure," he growled as his head lifted, his eyes such a deep, burnished gold that they stopped her breath. "Pure hot sensation that steals the mind."

Lust, pleasure and so much more reflected in the heated depths, terrifying her with the need to respond, to give him everything inside her, to give him all of herself.

"Let me show you pleasure, Scheme." He kissed her lips gently. "Just close your eyes. Close your eyes and let me show you how good it can be."

Her lashes fluttered shut before jerking open once again. She was trusting him. Trusting him was dangerous.

A chuckle left his lips as his fingers threaded through her hair.

"I dare you."

"What?" She could barely follow, barely think.

"I dare you to close your eyes. Just lay back and feel me

taking you. No responsibility, Scheme. No need to think. Just feel for me. Feel good for me, darlin'."

His lips covered hers then, his tongue licking at her lips, sliding inside, taking the last of her resistance as her nails bit into his flesh and his hips began to move.

"Feel good" didn't describe the sensations tearing through her now. With each stroke of his cock inside her, he was filling her with demented ecstasy, soul-destroying pleasure. A pleasure that would haunt her, torment her even after death.

"There, sweet darlin'." He jerked his lips from hers as she began to moan, to cry out with the sensation ripping through her. "You're so sweet and tight. So hot. I could stay inside you forever."

Her hips lifted beneath his, finding a rhythm to match him, to increase the pleasure building with such catastrophic demand that she couldn't lie still.

Yet she couldn't keep up. His rhythm would change, level, quicken, then slow. Perspiration ran in rivulets along her body, causing Tanner's body to slide against her, to stroke with silky precision along her sensitive skin as his cock thrust hard and deep inside her vagina.

She was dying. It was too much. Too much pleasure. Too many sensations. She had to back off, she needed at least a modicum of control. Just a little.

"Oh no you don't." A primal growl left his lips. "Don't you stiffen on me, Scheme. Give it back to me."

His strokes changed. His lips nipped at hers. His hands clenched in her hair and he began to fuck her hard, deep. Powerful strokes that sent his cock shuttling in and out. Stroking, burning. Each thrust threw her higher, tossing her into a maelstrom of sensation that finally, blessedly, culminated in an implosion of such strength, such depth that there was no control, no restraint. She was helpless, tossed about within an inferno of twisting, searing sensation.

As she collapsed beneath him, she felt a last, desperate thrust before Tanner tightened and drove so deep inside her she was certain he'd pierced her soul. And then she felt his release spurting wet and hot inside her, his cock throbbing, pulsing as he let go.

And she knew she would never be free of him. Alive or dead, the need for this pleasure would follow her. The need for this man would haunt her for an eternity.

Scheme tried to remember how to breathe without gasping as Tanner rolled to her side and pulled her against his body. He was breathing hard as well, his chest rising and falling in fast bellows as he buried his head in her hair and nipped at her shoulder playfully.

"Next time you pull a knife on me, I'm going to spank you," he panted.

"Remind me to use it next time." A smile twitched at her lips as he nipped at her again.

"Remind me to keep the knives hidden," he grunted.

Scheme shook her head with a soft laugh as her hand moved to her lower stomach, covering the slight warmth she could feel deep beneath her skin. In her womb. She caressed the area, bitterness seeping into her soul at the memory of all she had lost the last time she had dared to let herself believe in a man. Reminding herself of all that could be lost if she let herself believe in this man.

◆ CHAPTER 15 ◆

Tanner was gone, right on time. Sleeping with a man helped you to learn the strangest things. How responsive he was to you, even in sleep. But also, how responsive a woman became to a man, even subconsciously.

She didn't have to fully awaken to know when he left the bed, and she noticed, within a few days, that she knew when he left the room.

When he left the bed the next morning, she felt him move. She was more asleep than awake, as the lights flared behind her closed eyes, then just as abruptly darkened.

He wasn't up to fix breakfast.

Swimming up from the deep sleep she had been immersed in after the bouts of sex he put her through wasn't easy. Especially with the knowledge that he would sense her waking.

So she dozed, doing as she had done during the years she lived on her father's estate. Coyotes patrolled there, and her father's punishments were brutal for slipping around the house after lights-out.

She timed the Coyote patrols and learned how to fool them. The brain could do miraculous things when it had to. She had learned how to place herself in that state between sleep and awareness, in a place where her brain was aware of every move, every sound, every scent that drifted around her.

Humans were very much capable of certain animal aware-nesses. She could hear Tanner walking; she had no idea the tunnel he had taken, but several long minutes after he'd dressed and left the room, she heard the scrape of stone. Faint. The sound was so faint it took precious moments for her brain to identify it, and even longer for her to force herself to awaken.

She slid from the bed, blinking at the lights that flared around her as she bent to retrieve her clothing from the floor.

The velvet pants were on the other side of the bed table, the top at the bottom of the bed. One sock was under the bed; the other had her gritting her teeth in frustration before she found it tucked at the bottom of the mattress.

Tanner really was going to have to start taking more care with her clothing.

Jerking the socks on over her feet, she moved for the tunnels. A smile tilted her lips as she found what she was looking for.

Tanner was definitely a Breed, but he had forgotten one major rule. Always watch for anomalies. Tanner had missed one. The very faint dusting of loose dirt on the stone tunnels.

She now had the faintest impressions of footprints, so faint she would have missed them if the day before she hadn't found the small flashlight hidden in the supply room.

She had spent days working on the tunnels, breaking loose the packed dirt, scattering it here and there, one tunnel at a time, and checking for footprints.

Second day and bingo. Her luck was looking up.

This was escape day, she told herself. Today, she was getting the hell out of there and finding the nearest phone. Jonas would be waiting on her call now; he would know something had fucked up bad.

She pushed back her sorrow at the thought of leaving Tanner. Especially like this. But she had to find Jonas and give him the information she had; then she would deal with Tanner. First things first. She couldn't trust this easily. She refused to let herself trust this easily.

Once she got out of the caves, she could get her bearings and avoid the Coyotes. They were around the cabin, and she had studied the area where that cabin was located extensively over the years. The caves would have to be located away from the general area of the cabin, because it took Tanner much too long to return after his excursions out of the caverns.

And if they weren't . . . She breathed in deeply. She would solve that one once she got her bearings and figured out the location she was in.

Biting her lip, she followed the trail, faint though it was. She nearly lost it more than once, and each time found her heart in her throat as fear rushed through her.

She had to get out of there and find Jonas because she was caving bad where Tanner was concerned. She could feel it. She was within days of giving him anything he wanted; however he wanted. And risking everything.

She was falling in love with him.

Accepting that was one of the hardest things she had done. Because it wasn't like loving Chaz had been. With Chaz, there had always been something missing, something not quite complete within herself.

There was nothing missing with Tanner, and that terrified her. Because she knew if he had used sex to question her, then she would have caved. She would have folded and told him everything he wanted to know.

All he would have had to do was withhold one orgasm. Made her wait, and then asked her anything. The lives she would have betrayed could be gone forever, because she was weak.

Her father was right the last time he had buried her. She was too weak to live. Too weak to survive in the world she had been born into.

Breathing out wearily, she kept her gaze on the faint impressions of Tanner's hiking boots through the tunnel, until they turned and stopped right at the stone wall.

Her eyes narrowed. He couldn't walk through a wall, dammit.

Reaching out, she ran her hands over the wall, frowning at the feel of it. It looked like stone, it almost felt like stone, but with a difference. Moving her hands from side to side, her fingers finally found the faint depression on one side. Hooking them into it, she tugged, surprised at the faint scraping sound as a rock-lined panel slid open.

This was the scraping sound she'd heard when he left. A false wall opening, and she hadn't been able to find it. It was narrow, short, barely five and a half feet tall and maybe three feet wide. Tanner would have had to tuck and turn to pass through, but he could have easily done so quickly.

She paused there, knowing she would find an exit on the other side, somewhere. And she had to force herself forward. Force one foot in front of the other as she tightened her lips and moved into the next tunnel.

She felt the regret tearing at her now, a sense of loss. Had she ever felt as safe, as secure as she had felt cocooned in those caverns with Tanner?

She knew she hadn't. She had found a haven in his arms, below the earth, and letting go of it was surprisingly difficult.

She felt as though she were letting go of Tanner. As though by finding that hidden panel, she had betrayed him. Hadn't trusted him.

Shaking her head, she had to force herself to keep going. She wasn't betraying him, she assured herself. She was saving him. If he wasn't the spy, she was saving his family and his pride nephew. She wasn't betraying anyone but Cyrus Tallant, and God above knew he deserved the betrayal.

Her hand flattened at her lower stomach. There was a slight burning sensation, a warmth that had begun to become noticeable the day before and didn't seem to be easing.

Of course, she and Tanner had been fucking like minks; that could explain it. Her body wasn't used to the pounding it had taken. The pounding it loved. Craved. Needed.

A bitter smile touched her lips. She had never known pleasure as she had known it with Tanner—fierce, hot as hell, and all-consuming. She hadn't had sex with him. She hadn't fucked him. She had made love to him, and she knew it.

Each touch, she memorized. Each taste, each of those growly little sounds he made, she loved. Like a cross between a snarl and a purr, sometimes when he was irritated with her, mostly when he found pleasure with her. And she knew he found pleasure with her.

Her suspicions that he could be in league with her father always faltered there. She knew he needed to be with her. She could feel it in him, see it in the hard, corded strength of his body each time he held back and let her touch as well.

God, what was she doing? She was convincing herself, even as freedom was so close, that maybe he loved her. Just a little bit?

She was willing to trade her life, and the lives of so many others, on a maybe.

Her taste in men sucked and she knew it. Her first lover, Chaz, had been an assassin. The second hadn't been much better. The only difference was he wasn't part of her father's organization. He just wanted to be. The third. Oh, there was a real winner. The lover she had become acquainted with at one of the clubs she frequented had actually been an undercover federal agent. Actually, a married undercover federal agent.

Cyrus had really enjoyed punishing her for that one. At least he hadn't killed the agent. Oh no, Cyrus Tallant didn't murder useful talent right off. Nope, the married agent was still being blackmailed by Cyrus Tallant.

She'd had two other lovers, short affairs, men whose names she forced herself not to even remember. Nice, plain men whose saving grace had been their warmth. For a few short weeks she had let them keep her warm.

Rounding the curve in the tunnel, she moved into another. How fucking far did this damned underground path lead, anyway? She felt as though she had been walking forever.

And each step hurt more. The closer she came to escaping Tanner, the more it hurt. A physical, burning ache in the center of her chest.

Her common sense was screaming at whatever weak-kneed little romantic was whispering that she turn back. Return to bed. Wait on Tanner. He was just checking on the soldiers surrounding his cabin, that unknown voice whispered in her head.

Stupid twit, shut the fuck up, her common sense screamed. He was probably reporting to her father even now.

But he had hasn't hurt you. He was worried for you.

He wants answers, not your old-assed body.

She sighed. She felt old. So old that at times her soul felt shriveled, dry.

Until Tanner touched her.

Rounding another curve, she saw the way out. There, set in the stone, was a metal ladder leading to the ceiling and a light indention around what seemed to be a stone covering.

Freedom.

A tear slipped free of her eye.

Scheme brushed the dampness away slowly before rubbing her fingers together, absorbing the sign of weakness as she stared up at the exit. It was time to face destiny now. Fate. Karma. Whichever it was, it was time to pay for the lives her father had taken.

Wasn't there a scripture in the Bible? Something about the son paying for the father's sins? Well, she wasn't a son, but she was the only child capable of paying.

She grabbed hold of the ladder and pulled herself up it, using the flat of her hand to push the stone above her aside.

Freedom.

So why did it feel more like a return to captivity?

◆   ◆   ◆

"Tanner, son, we got problems."

Tanner crouched just behind Jackal and Cabal, his narrowed eyes piercing the early morning mists rising from the cliff-shrouded valley to envelop the high ridge his cabin sat on.

"What are you two doing here?" he murmured, his eyes following the delicate dance between a half dozen Council soldiers and the four Breed Enforcers moving around the small building several miles from the caves.

"Checking a few things," Jackal's ruined voice murmured. "We expected the Council soldiers to watch the cabin. We didn't expect Jonas's men to be there too."

"He knows you're here?" Tanner was aware that Jonas had

ordered them to remain on active duty. Hours later, Cabal had flipped him the finger and walked out of the Bureau. Jackal had followed with a smirk, Cabal related.

"He shouldn't know shit," Cabal growled. "We went to Sanctuary first and slipped out from there. By the way, Callan said you're getting your ass kicked when you get back."

Tanner grunted as he slipped the noc's, the short-range, multiuse glasses used for ground warfare, from Cabal's face and set them over his eyes.

Son of a bitch. Council soldiers and enforcers were each pretending they didn't know the other group was there.

"Wild," he muttered. "What the fuck is up with this?"

"The Council crew is half a dozen of their best," Jackal whispered. "Men they only call out in extreme circumstances because they charge an arm and a leg for the service. The Breeds playing patty-cake with them are part of what Jonas calls his Alpha Team. They're the best of the best. Jonas recruited each one personally."

"The other half of Alpha Team is concentrated around the comm shed at Sanctuary, and some of the equipment they're using is definitely not standard issue."

"Like?"

"Like short-range transmission locators and translators." Cabal stared back at him. "They've been listening to every frickin' message coming in and going out, and Callan wasn't informed. That equipment wasn't even through R&D last we heard."

"If they're everything he says they are, then they can be programmed for specific words or phrases while monitoring every damned frequency known to man at one time," Jackal continued.

"What about encryption?" Tanner knew the few transmissions they had actually picked up from Sanctuary to Tallant had been intricately encrypted.

"All you need are the encryption keys," Jackal said. "And I bet you they picked up something here. Does your princess have a radio?"

"Not possible." Tanner shook his head. He knew beyond a shadow of a doubt that nothing had come out of those caverns.

"Agreed." Cabal's voice was less than a whisper. "So tell me what the party is here?"

"They know about the caverns," Jackal suggested. "It's the only reason for both teams to be pussyfooting around like that. They're looking for the same thing."

"Jonas went to Sanctuary night before last," Cabal mused. "You could hear him and Callan roaring at each other, but not much else."

Tanner winced. "They're looking for her." He pushed his fingers through his hair ruthlessly. "I can understand Tallant putting out the effort, but why Jonas?"

Cabal glanced back at him worriedly.

"You got the op from hell goin' on here, Breed," Jackal said and sighed. "How we gonna play it?"

Jackal turned to look at him. The wicked scar that ran from his temple across his eye and the bridge of his nose, then down the opposite cheek gave him a brutal appearance. The navy blue eyes, so dark they were nearly black, and shoulder-length black hair didn't help things.

At thirty-nine, he kept swearing retirement was at hand, but his gaze glittered with glee at the mere thought of taking on Council soldiers, supremists and their inbred purist cousins.

Tanner had opened his mouth to speak when he felt the silent alarm vibrate on his belt.

"Breach," he hissed.

Council soldiers and Breed Enforcers were forgotten as the three men turned and melted into the forest, racing back toward the cliffs and the caverns.

Scheme had been searching for the damned exit every day she had been there, he knew that, but he didn't believe she could have found it. He didn't believe she had the desire to find it. And even if she did, he had made certain to never take the same tunnel to it twice, and that she was asleep each time he left.

That meant, possibly, someone else had managed to find the hidden entrance.

And Scheme was undefended.

It could barely be called daylight. And was she in a forest? Trees, grass, dirt ground, with bugs and slimy forest things?

Ewww.

Grimacing, Scheme stood at the narrow entrance to the cave she had entered from the cover stone and stared out at the misty, wet-looking land beyond.

This wasn't smog; she could have handled that. She was used to that. This was a wet mist hanging in the air and dampening everything it touched.

And there were birds. No pigeons. She wondered if birds really did crap on your head just for the hell of it. She had heard that—somewhere. At the moment she couldn't remember exactly where.

The minute she stepped out of the caves' narrow opening she was going to get her socks irreparably messy. They would never come clean. The damp would ruin her beautiful velvet lounging pajamas, and they really were her favorite pair. Unfortunately, there was nothing more durable in her luggage.

She was in a bona fide freaking forest. It took a few minutes, but she knew the general area she was in, several miles from Tanner's cabin. Far enough away that the Coyotes there would never know she was in the vicinity. They weren't in the area of the caves, according to Tanner, just the cabin. And the wind direction was with her. It was flowing from the cabin and back down the valley. And she was headed up.

She knew the direction to take to get to the main road. There were several houses on that road. At the most, she was a half hour's walk from one of those houses.

There was just no help for it. She was going to have to make herself walk through the forest. Damn, it was a good thing she hadn't known where she was before she attempted escape. She might well have stayed in Tanner's comfortable, warm bed.

At that, her lips tilted mockingly. She knew better, escape was too important, but it was really nice to tell herself otherwise. It made taking that first step not so hard. Maybe.

Who was she lying to? She didn't get along with nature. She liked her cement jungle. D.C. and New York were the perfect habitats for her. Cyrus preferred the Pennsylvania estate, but even it was nicely landscaped, with all the modern conveniences, and set just outside the limits of a very nicely populated city.

She doubted there was a Starbucks within a hundred-mile radius of this place, let alone an actual city. But all she needed was a phone. A half hour at the most and she would have that taken care of.

Okay, she didn't have a choice. Tanner rarely stayed gone more than a few hours; he would be returning soon. She had to find a phone before he did that.

She peeked out again.

She put her best foot forward and stepped outside the cave, immediately grimacing in distaste as her foot came into contact with the loosely packed leaves, grass and soil layering the ground.

Her sock immediately dampened.

This was not going to be pleasant.

Breathing in deeply, she forced herself out of the protective stone shelter and began to make her way along a faint path leading up.

The caverns were down. No one would surely live in the bottom of this mess, and she couldn't see a single house. So they had to be up. Simple. She could do this. All she had to do was go up.

Way up, it appeared.

Too bad there wasn't an elevator.

◆   ◆   ◆

"Son of a bitch. She found her way out." Tanner scanned the entrance cave, drawing in Scheme's scent, her determination, her hesitance, her sorrow. The scents lingered, fresh, strong. "She won't be far."

"Yeah, and she's cutting a path like a sumo wrestler," Jackal growled. "Get out there and find her while I clear out her tracks. I'm betting every Breed, Council soldier and enforcer has caught her scent by now."

"Who needs her scent? You can hear the disturbance in the air," Cabal snapped, fast on Tanner's heels.

And Jackal was right; she had made a damned mess heading up the mountain. Leaves torn from the ground, grass smeared from where she had slipped, broken branches, leaves and bramble. Cleaning this up and keeping the damned entrance safe from detection was going to be a pain in the fucking ass.

He was going to paddle her ass.

"Get back with Jackal." He turned on Cabal, snarling as the other man drew up short. "I want you two to draw the Council and enforcers off her scent. I don't care how you do it."

He couldn't bring Cabal and Scheme face-to-face yet. Not yet, not until he could get a handle on the animal screaming inside him.

As Cabal turned back, Tanner lifted his head, scented the air and headed up. A hard smile slashed across his mouth. It would be harder for the Council Breeds or Jonas's enforcers to catch her scent this way. Once he got her back into the caverns, the entrance cave would be sanitized and her scent dispersed. Even Cabal would be unable to tell where she was if he didn't know. The cover stone fit the entrance into the caverns perfectly; no scent, no sound, nothing to indicate what lay below the rock would be detected.

He just had to get her back to the caverns.

◆   ◆   ◆

Traipsing along the faint path up the mountain, Scheme kept her head down and fought to keep her eyes clear. This was a mistake. Everything inside her was screaming that one glaring piece of information back at her.

Leaving Tanner wasn't the answer. Trusting him. That was the answer. As illogical as it seemed, as suspicious as she had been of him, every particle of her being was crying out for him.

She had to trust him.

Reaching a flat bench of land farther up the mountain, Scheme paused and wiped at the perspiration on her forehead before bracing her back against a tree and staring up at the glimmer of the sky beyond.

She didn't want to go any farther.

She stared back along the valley below and blew out a weary breath. She was tired of fighting it. Tired of fighting the need for him, the feelings for him. She was tired of being alone. So alone she couldn't trust; she couldn't laugh or love.

She had to fight to hold on to what Tanner seemed to be offering her. Safety. Security. His love. Maybe his love. A big enough maybe that she was ready to turn around and run back to him. Right now.

Straightening quickly from the tree, she turned and came face-to-face with death.

"Stupid bitch." Dog, her father's most merciless blood soldier, had stepped from behind a massive boulder to her side. His cruel face was enhanced by steely gray eyes, his lips pulled back in a snarl, his curved canines flashing in the weak sunlight that penetrated the dawn light.

"Lapdog," she snapped back. Show no fear. She had learned that a long time ago when it came to Cyrus's pets.

His lips twitched. They always did that, just seconds from a smug smile, from gloating satisfaction. He was literally the top dog within her father's organization. He controlled the Coyotes and the assignments going out, as well as the preparation of them.

He was as evil as her father, and twice as dangerous.

"You must like being buried alive."

His gray eyes were constantly scanning, watching, his nostrils flaring as he drew in the scents around them.

Where the hell was Tanner? She could use a little help.

"Gives me time to think," she sneered, moving back, nearly stumbling as her knees actually trembled. Of all her father's Breeds she would have to meet up with this one.

Rather than following her, he crouched, his gaze narrowed on her. Six feet, two inches tall and corded with muscle, he would have been imposing without the cloudy gray eyes and black-streaked gray hair. He was said to be the most merciless Coyote the Council had ever created.

"If I bring you in alive, I get to fuck you before your daddy buries you." He smiled in mocking pleasure. "I'd have to bathe you first. The smell of cat just offends my senses."

She'd rather be buried first.

"You can fuck?" She widened her eyes mockingly. "Since when did Cyrus stop castrating his little pets?"

His lips tightened.

It was one of Cyrus's favorite control measures. "I didn't come to Tallant from the main labs, little girl," he snarled. "You're forgetting that."

Okay, mistake on her part. Maybe Dog did still have his manly parts. Which only made him more dangerous. And he was right; he hadn't come to her father from Tallant-controlled labs. He had come from the Council itself. Who or what had trained him, no one knew, at least Cyrus didn't, but there was no denying he was one of the most proficient killers created.

She moved back a step. Running from him wasn't going to do her any good.

Oh, this had just been a bad idea. Bad. Bad. Bad.

"Your daddy's not going to like having the smell of that Breed all over you." Amazingly, Dog felt into his shirt pocket, pulled a slim cigar free and lit it before straightening.

"My father's not a Breed. He can't smell me." She backed up farther.

Surely Tanner had returned to the caverns by now. He would know she was missing. He would be following. He had to be here somewhere.

She looked around frantically.

"*Tsk, tsk,* little princess," Dog murmured. "So, you want to tell me where you've been hiding for the past week? I might be able to talk your daddy into just shooting you rather than letting you die in that casket again. This time forever."

His voice was cold, brutal. God, she hated him. She had seen him calmly walk into a room and snap the neck of one of Cyrus's soldiers for nothing more than the sloppy care of his weapons.

And he had enjoyed it. She had seen the pleasure in his eyes, in the tight grimace of his expression. She had made certain never to attend another operation meeting from that day on.

"You haven't answered me." His voice dropped dangerously low.

"Oh, here and there." She waved her hand about, encompassing the forest. "One tree looks like another, you know."

So why hadn't she slipped one of those kitchen knives out with her again?

Oh yeah, because she thought Tanner would stop her. That was right. For some reason, she just thought he was Superman.

Dog's lips quirked as he looked around. "Yeah, I guess it does." He drew on the cigar, blowing out a line of smoke rings before turning back to her.

He didn't make a move to jump for her. She tilted her head and watched him curiously as he once again glanced down the trail she had used.

"Hello, Tanner," he drawled.

Scheme twisted around, crashing face-first into a broad, so familiar chest. Her heart rate picked up, her fingers curled into the material of his shirt and a small cry broke free of her lips.

She tried to crawl into him.

His arm tightened around her, muscles contracting, allowing her to nearly climb his body in an effort to hide from the sense of danger smothering her.

"I'm going to spank your ass." He did the growly thing at her ear. "You know that, don't you?"

"Promises, promises." She was latched onto him like a leech and had no intentions of letting him go. "Just get me away from him. Now would be good."

One strong arm surrounded her, holding her to his chest, allowing her to soak up his warmth, the sense of security, of protection. She was shaking in reaction and so damned glad to see him she had to blink back tears.

"How many are with you?" she heard Tanner ask the Coyote.

"Half dozen. I took scout position," Dog answered with a trace of amusement.

"How many Breeds?"

"Just me," Dog answered. "Get her the hell out of here before your enforcers start investigating the crash and bang through the forest though. Didn't you tell her how sound carries in these hills?"

Scheme turned her head slowly, her eyes narrowing.

Dog hadn't drawn his weapon. He was leaning against the boulder enjoying that cigar, for all the world like a man taking a nice, leisurely hike into the woods.

"Is *she* Jonas's too?" Tanner asked

She, Scheme assumed, meant her.

"That one only Jonas can answer." Dog shrugged. "I don't belong to Jonas, cat. Don't make that mistake." There was an edge of danger in his voice. "I just don't see any reason to torture her further. If you can save her from herself, then more power to you. Saves me the trouble of putting a bullet in her brain." His smile was cruel.

Tanner growled, and it wasn't that low, purring rumble he used for her; this one was pure danger.

Dog inclined his head slowly before turning his back on Tanner and beginning to move back up the mountain.

"Hurry, cat," he suggested smoothly. "My good moods don't last for long."

When Dog turned back to look, they were gone.

◆   ◆   ◆

Dog shook his head grimly as he clamped the cigar between his lips and headed back to the top of the cliff. Not that he had a hope of catching sight of the bastard again. Tanner knew these hills like most men knew their own bodies. But he could try. Finding the Breeds' hidey-hole in these mountains would be a hell of a feather in his cap. His boss had been searching for it for years.

Damn, whatever the hell was going on in these mountains was about to get ugly. If he wasn't mistaken, Scheme Tallant and Tanner Reynolds were mated.

The scent of it had filled the air like a soft, intoxicating brew. It was subtle, barely there, but unmistakable. She was Tanner's mate. And mated Breeds were lethal. They were a hell of a lot more dangerous than unmated ones; he had reason to know.

Shit was getting deep. Dog prayed he could keep himself from getting stuck in the quagmire here. He fancied holding on to his balls if it was all the same to everyone else. And his boss wouldn't have a problem whatsoever cutting them free of his body if anything happened to that girl. No problem at all. His boss, Bollen, wasn't exactly a man you wanted to displease. And Bollen's boss, Jonas Wyatt, was even more dangerous. Damn. Shit was just getting too deep lately. Way too deep.

CHAPTER 17

Tanner didn't bother to lead her through the forest. The minute Dog turned his back on them, he flipped her over his shoulder and began to move. She didn't dare scream or cry out. She could feel the tension emanating from both men, the air of danger and lethal violence. So she held the required protests back until they entered the small cave that held the cover stone to the tunnels.

Why Dog had just let them escape even she couldn't guess at. She was in shock over that one. Dog never showed mercy, and he never failed a mission. Ever. Until now. He had just let them go without a gun at his head.

"Not a fucking word," Tanner hissed as he set her on her feet, his nose nearly touching hers, his golden eyes burning with subdued flames. She swore there were veins of red flickering in his eyes.

She nodded slowly, eyes wide, almost holding her breath at the unusual phenomenon. No one, period, had ever returned to the Council with a report of seeing Tanner enraged. Playfully murderous, if there was such a thing. And with Tanner she was certain there was. But never truly angry. Never enraged.

He was enraged now.

Snarling, he turned, snagging her wrist to drag her to the open entrance.

"Down." He pointed into the hole.

With pleasure. He didn't have to tell *her* twice.

Scheme plopped down on her butt, swung her legs into the hole to find the ladder with her feet, and she was gone.

"Oh my God!" She screeched like a frightened little mouse when she came face-to-face with the hard, savage expression of someone she didn't know.

She knew all the Breeds.

Jerking back, the back of her heel caught on the edge of the ladder, taking her off balance and throwing her against the wall.

A second later freaking Catman dropped into the tunnel, crouched, snarling. The sound of it sent chills up her spine.

"Whoa there, big boy." The man stepped back, his hands held carefully in front of him. "I was just here to make sure she didn't fall."

"I know how to climb down," she snapped. "Tanner, where the hell's the flashlight? I can't see."

She was seriously afraid that whoever the hell the other man was, his existence was definitely in question if the sounds coming from Tanner's throat were any indication.

He was still growling. A dangerous, not-so-comfortable sort of sound that had her stomach cramping in fear. Not for herself.

He whirled on her, his eyes practically glowing in the dim light as he stared down at her.

"You're seriously starting to piss me— *Oomph*."

Before she could say anything more, he lifted her. He didn't jerk her or drag her; he lifted her into his arms before snarling over his shoulder at the surprised stranger.

Or at least he was a stranger to her.

"I'll just, uh, put the stone back in place." The other man cleared his throat. "You go ahead and just do whatever. I'll wait here for Cabal."

Tanner's body tensed further.

"Stop it." She slapped his chest sharply. "That sound is really starting to get on my nerves. I don't like it."

Surprised, he stared back at her.

"The growly thing when you're getting hot and wild is one thing. This let's-kill-somebody rumble really makes me ill. I'm going to throw up on you if it doesn't stop."

There was a snort of laughter from behind Tanner. She threw a frown over his shoulder before bringing her gaze back to the dangerous Bengal Breed.

His lips were curved, maybe into a smile. Well, at least he wasn't snarling anymore. Not that the smile on his face was much more comforting. It was a bit hard, calculating, laced with a fair amount of anger.

"I'm in trouble, aren't I?" she asked, flattening her hands on his chest as she stared up at him. "How much?"

"Plenty."

She licked her lips nervously.

"I have a very good explanation."

"No, you don't." With his arm around her waist, he picked her up off her feet, just that easy, and began moving down the tunnel.

"I can walk."

"So I saw," he growled. It wasn't the growly, but it wasn't the death-is-coming sound either.

"I really do have a good explanation." She cleared her throat, wondering just how bad this was going to get.

"There were Coyote soldiers breaching the tunnels?" he asked.

"Umm, no."

"Of course, how stupid of me," he snapped. "You wouldn't have reached the cover stone if there had been. One way in, one way out."

"That's rather foolish of you," she pointed out. "Anything could happen. A secondary escape route is always advisable."

That might not have been the best thing to point out. A second later she found herself pressed firmly against a wall, her feet still dangling above the floor, staring into fierce, gleaming eyes.

"Dog kills: over three dozen reported. Mercy level: zero. Proficiency level: off the fucking charts. Your father's senior blood soldier." His voice deepened, roughened, became savage as he spoke of the Coyote. "Do you have any fucking idea the danger you were in?"

Well, duh! She had seen the bastard kill. Her heart had nearly stopped at the sight of the Coyote. Right now, he looked a shade more understanding than Tanner.

She licked her lips. "Pretty much."

She ran her hands from his chest to his shoulders, softened against him and bit her lip at the warning growl that rumbled in his chest.

"Pretty much?" he snarled, furious. "Pretty much?"

His hands tightened on her hips as she stared back at him, wondering if she wouldn't have been better off facing Dog than Tanner at the moment.

She licked her lips again and let her knees lift, bending to brace on his hips as his body jerked, nearly slamming against her.

He was hard. Thick and hard, his cock driving against her pussy, shifting, stroking over the velvet lounging bottoms and the silk of her panties. And it felt really good.

Even if she was just a bit concerned. Tanner really looked just a shade pissed.

"I missed you." And she had. Like chocolate, like coffee. The farther she had gotten away from the caverns, the more she had been certain she was making a terrible mistake.

And she had been.

His gaze flared, sexual heat burning with the anger now.

"You ran from me," he rasped. "You nearly got your ass killed, Scheme. He could have taken you, so easily."

"You wouldn't have let him." Her fingernails scraped over his shoulders to his neck, pushing beneath the collar of his shirt as the muscles in his jaw bunched.

His fingers flexed at her hips again as he lifted her, rubbing her against the erection behind his jeans. And he was really filling out those jeans.

"I might not have been able to stop him!" he bit out, his

voice rough, violent. "He reached you first, Scheme. He could have killed you as easily as he let you go. Do you understand that?"

"More so than you," she cried out. "I've seen him kill."

"And you dared to fucking leave the safety of the god-damned caves?" he roared.

Damn. Whoa.

Scheme blinked back at him. Maybe he was a little bit more than pissed.

"You wouldn't let me go," she whispered as she gripped the collar of his shirt and jerked at it.

"I can't let you go," he grated, one hand moving to her hair, tangling in it and holding, pulling her head back roughly. "Even for your sake, I can't fucking let you go."

His lips came down on hers in starving demand. As though he had to have the taste of her. And she had to have the taste of him. To live. To breathe. To go on for another second she had to taste him, hold him. She had to be a part of him.

She had nearly walked away from this. From the one thing she had believed she could never have. And yet the one thing she had always craved. Deep down inside, where she hid the hopes and dreams, the needs that festered within a wound that never healed. This was what she craved.

"I can't lose you," he muttered against her lips, and her heart tripped, speeding up, nearly smothering her with the excitement racing through her as he nipped at her lips. "I can't, Scheme. Not now. I can't lose you."

✦　✦　✦

He was dying inside. Her kiss was every fantasy he had ever dared let himself imagine, and a few he hadn't. Her hands in his hair, her tongue meeting his, licking, rubbing against it. Rubbing against a damned tongue whose mating glands were dormant, normal, and refused to swell with the mating hormone that would mark her as his forever.

What the hell was he going to do? How was he going to survive letting her go to another man?

He knew his kisses were desperate. As his lips slanted over

hers, hunger clawed at his guts, his balls. The need to mark her was so overwhelming that when he found his teeth opening over her shoulder, it sent a surge of shock tearing through him.

Not his mate.

Fighting for control, he dropped his forehead against the silken flesh instead and closed his eyes. Instantly, his sense of touch and smell sharpened. He could feel her need for him, smell her arousal, but something was different.

Scheme never relaxed against him until those minutes after her orgasm when she had no other choice. She was wary, always cautious, always on guard. Until now.

"I knew I shouldn't have left even before I saw Dog," she whispered at his ear. "I shouldn't have left you."

A part of his soul was dying at her admission. Trust. He could feel her beginning to trust him, and he was going to have to let her go. He couldn't ignore the truth any longer. There were no mating signs. *She wasn't his mate.*

He pressed his lips to her neck though he stepped back, forcing her legs to release him as he found the courage to lift his head and stare down at her.

"We'll talk later." He scowled at the effort it took to force his hands to release her hips and allow her to stand on her own.

"I don't want to talk later, Tanner. I have to tell you—"

His fingers covered her lips. He could sense what she wanted to say. The sweet spice of the emotional storm brewing within her would rip his soul out. If she whispered the words, he would never survive what he had to do.

"Later," he whispered, feeling the words tear from him. "Come on, Cabal will be here in a few minutes."

"Cabal?" Confusion filled her eyes.

"That mountain out there is a fucking war zone, Scheme." He grabbed her wrist and began to pull her through the tunnel. "You're damned lucky you didn't run into more trouble than just Dog."

He had to push the thought back. He had to force himself to do what had to be done here. He had never shirked his responsibilities; he had never tried to hide from the truth of his life, no matter how much it had sucked at times.

Right now, he wanted nothing more than to hide. To find a place outside of reality where he and Scheme could exist together forever.

And it wasn't going to happen. No matter how much he wished it could. Which left only one last resort to save her. To give her to her true mate.

Other than the color of his hair and eyes, Cabal St. Laurents was identical to Tanner. The difference in the hair was a matter of transposed colors. Tanner's was black with burnished gold streaks. Cabal's was a burnished gold with black streaks. Tanner's eyes were deep, rich amber with flecks of brilliant green. Cabal's were green with flecks of amber. Both men were exactly six feet and two inches tall. Both men were hard, muscular and had the looks of a fallen angel. Neither could, by any stretch of the imagination, be called angels though. They were equally dangerous.

Scheme's father had once had extensive files on the two Bengal Breeds, their training and strengths, as well as their weaknesses. Scheme had nearly memorized those files. During his stay in the labs, Tanner had played the game perfectly. He had excelled at every obstacle he was pitted against, killed with proficiency and proved to the psychologists that he was a loyal Breed Killer, even at a young age.

He was considered one of the labs' greatest failures now, and one of Callan Lyons's greatest weapons in rescuing the Breeds from the New Mexico labs.

Cabal had been another story. His training had been filled with pitfalls. He refused to practice the maneuvers taught to him, and used his own. He refused to kill when ordered, but had no problem killing soldiers and trainers. He refused to talk to the psychologists and was labeled psychotic by the doctors working with him.

At the age of twenty-five he was declared a failure, without hope of training, and listed for cancellation along with nearly two dozen other Breeds. He had survived weeks in a pit designed to kill with torturous precision.

"I don't think your friend trusts me, Tanner," he commented hours after his arrival, as Scheme moved slowly from the bathroom into the main cavern.

Tanner stood by the counter, a beer in one hand, the other tucked into the pocket of his jeans while Cabal sat at the table, relaxed in his chair, his beer sitting in front of him.

"Is my trust required?" Scheme finally asked as she moved to the refrigerator and pulled free a bottle of water.

She had bathed and changed clothes and, for the first time since walking out of the caverns, felt warm again. Safe. God, she hadn't realized the toll her life had taken on her over the years, until now.

And now she had to wait just a little while longer. Cabal would leave soon, and when he did, she could talk to Tanner. She could explain why she left, and why she needed so desperately to talk to Jonas.

"Perhaps not." Cabal shrugged, his gaze boring into her. "At least not right now."

She gave him a distrustful glare before moving past Tanner and heading to the seating arrangement located in front of the television.

"You know, your daddy was on the television last night," Cabal announced. "His cheeks even got wet with tears as he begged for your return."

She paused before turning to face him.

"Cabal, let it go," Tanner ordered him softly.

Cabal's green eyes flicked to Tanner before returning to Scheme with a gleam of predatory interest and satisfaction.

"Let what go?" she asked them both.

Her heart was heavy, sluggish, bordering on panicked. She hated that feeling, the premonition of danger, a sense of warning.

"Nothing," he finally murmured, a mocking grin tugging at his lips as he glanced back at Tanner. "It can wait."

Tanner shook his head as though in resignation, while Cabal's grin deepened.

"Call me the impatient sort then," she responded tightly.

"I already had that one pegged." Cabal lifted his brows mockingly. "You know, I *can* smell your arousal as well."

She didn't flush or blush. Instead she sighed.

"It takes a lot more than that to humiliate me, Mr. St. Laurents," she informed him. "Try again."

"I think I could come in my jeans just watching his cock stretch your pussy," he responded. "It would be enough to make a hungry man lick his lips in anticipation."

She glanced at Tanner, watching the way his brows lowered and his stare toward his brother became dark.

What the hell was going on here? It was as though Cabal were deliberately trying to piss her *and* Tanner off.

"Those lips are the only thing you're going to be licking where I'm concerned," she told him sweetly. "If you and Tanner have an itch to play more of your games, then you can play them somewhere else."

"It won't be the first time you've let your lover share you, Scheme," Cabal pointed out. "What made you trust that assassin more than you trust the Breed that saved your ass?"

She turned slowly, staring back at Cabal silently, furiously. Why bring this up? The fact that Chaz had shared her with another man shouldn't be anything to Cabal. Had Tanner shown him the videos? They had shared women, she knew. Had they shared viewing the video feed Tanner had watched?

"He didn't see the surveillance, Scheme." Tanner's voice held a note of resignation. "It was in my report."

"You reported on what you saw?" she asked past the tightness in her chest.

"When needed." He shrugged. "Allowing St. Marks to bring

an FBI agent believed to be loyal to the Breeds to your bed was of interest to Security."

"What was St. Marks paying him for?" Cabal asked. "And I should point out, that while you showered, the agent thanked St. Marks nicely for the two of you meeting his price so easily."

She stared back at them blankly. It was one of the last times Chaz had touched her. Not that the experience hadn't been pleasurable, but the hollow sense of shame that had filled her later had followed her for years. And now it was back.

"I had no idea Chaz was paying him for anything." She forced herself to retreat mentally, emotionally. She couldn't afford to feel shame or pain at this point. "All I knew was that he was a friend of Chaz's."

"Man, the men in your life managed to keep some hellacious secrets from you." He clucked in mock sympathy. "Were you just too stupid to see how you were being used? Or did you enjoy it?"

"I enjoyed it," she crooned, burying the flash of pain deep enough inside the dark little corner she reserved just for such occasions. For the times when the knowledge of her own stupidity cut into her like a hot blade. "Maybe Tanner should have let you watch. The two of you could have jacked off together while you played your little spy games."

Cabal grimaced sarcastically. "Now, that's just sick. You do have a twisted little mind, don't you, Schemer?"

A knife slammed into the table in front of Cabal, point first, vibrating with an innate violence as Scheme's gaze flew to Tanner.

"Keep it up, Cabal, and we'll have words," Tanner warned him. "Is that what you really want?"

"No, what I want is to figure out why the hell we have enforcers and Council soldiers jacking around in this mountain. How did they figure out who has her and where you're hidden?" Cabal jerked the dagger from the table and stared back at his brother angrily.

"You're a big boy," Tanner informed him. "You'll survive not getting exactly what you want. They'll leave when they realize they're not going to get what they want."

"And both of you are beginning to get on my nerves," she snapped as she turned to Tanner. "We need to talk. Get rid of Mr. Hyde here so we can do that. I believe your vacation is nearly up. We don't have all year."

"Does that make you Dr. Jekyll?" Cabal mused mockingly as he glanced at Tanner.

"Shut up, Cabal," Tanner rasped again.

Scheme stared back at him, miserably aware that he was holding himself distant from her now. He hadn't touched her since they entered the caverns, and now that Cabal was here, she could feel the chill in the air.

The sense of safety was rapidly evaporating.

"Tanner, please," she whispered. "We need to talk."

"Is that one of those hidden female messages for fuck me?" Cabal broke in. "Do I get to stay and play?"

Tanner stared back at him warningly.

Cabal grinned. "I think he's waiting on permission from you, gorgeous. Can't I play too?"

He was already playing, or attempting to play her by making her angry. Cabal wasn't the joking sort. The only question was, was Tanner playing the game with him?

Of course he was. These two didn't play alone, no matter the game. She should have expected Cabal to show up. Should have known he would be there. She was slipping bad, trusting a man, a Breed, when she knew better than to trust anyone.

"You two can play together all you like," she informed them both coldly. "I'm not up for more games myself though, so you'll have to count me out."

Cabal's grin widened, while Tanner stared back at her thoughtfully.

She turned and moved to the couch, lifted the remote for the television and pushed the power button. She flipped to the History Channel and settled back with her water, her mind running, plotting.

Tanner would make him leave soon, she told herself. Wouldn't he? Surely he didn't seriously mean to attempt to share her with him. Not now. Not when she needed to tell Tanner

the truth, when she needed to accept everything he had been trying to give her for the past week.

Uncapping the water, she sipped at it as she focused her
gaze on a documentary rerun on the marines, and her mind
tried to deal with this new, surprising development. Her life
was, quite literally, going to hell, and as of yet she had found
no way to stop it.

Tanner had finally brought his brother in. Surprisingly, she
hadn't thought of that. As though some part of her had actually believed that he would consider her exclusively his. That
he would maybe suggest using the mating clause in the Breed
bylaws to protect her. If he claimed her as his woman, he
could have taken her to Sanctuary and placed her under the
Breeds' protection rather than Breed Law.

She mentally kicked herself. What had ever made her even
halfway believe such a thing would happen? She was hated.
She was Cyrus Tallant's daughter, his assistant, part of the organization that had created and tortured the Breeds for decades.

It didn't matter that she had nearly given her life a dozen
times over to save them. That on at least one occasion she had
actually died from the torture her father had inflicted on her.

She blinked back the dampness in her eyes.

She should have known better. To claim her, he would have
to love her. And that wasn't going to happen. Ever. And no
matter how hard her heart ached, no matter the regret that
twisted through her and made her throat tighten, love wasn't
going to happen for her.

Her hand flattened on the warmth in her abdomen, an uncomfortable sting that didn't make sense any more than the
arousal building inside her did. Or the pain in her soul.

She was tired, she realized. Not weary, not exhausted, but
so mentally and emotionally tired that she wondered if she
could push herself to survive until Jonas found her.

He would find her. Alive or dead. He was the most determined, stubborn Breed she had ever known or heard of. He
would have known when she requested the meeting that
she was ready to come in, that she would need protection. Just

as she had known for years that it would take pretty important information to gain that protection.

She had what she needed now. The names of every purist and supremist group working with the Council as well as the names of the heads of the organizations. The proposed plots to systematically take out the Breed community and the spies working within the government to aid the Council's plans.

The only thing she didn't have was the identity of the spy working within Sanctuary, plotting to destroy the freedom the Breed community had found.

She could have made it to Jonas and had her freedom by now. If her father hadn't somehow learned that she had betrayed him.

"She knows how to be quiet, Tanner," Cabal observed mockingly long minutes after she had sat down. "She surprises me."

Tanner murmured something she didn't catch. Something she wasn't certain she wanted to hear. All she could feel was her own rioting pain. Suddenly, she felt lost, alone. More alone than she had ever been in her life.

✦   ✦   ✦

Cabal was pushing and he knew it. He wanted Tanner pissed. He wanted that superhuman control his brother possessed to break. He wanted the animal inside the man to claim his mate. Because it had obviously not happened yet.

It would have been laughable if it weren't so serious.

And if the cold steel blade of a butcher knife weren't lying at his throat. Not exactly a comfortable position for the sharp weapon in his estimation.

Tanner was enraged. His eyes were brilliant with it, his expression savage.

"Back off, bro," Cabal warned him. "We're not going to fight here."

"Leave her the hell alone," Tanner growled, his voice too low for the girl to hear where she sat across the room, on the couch that was turned away from them, but the dangerous demand was clear to Cabal.

He sighed. The poor bastard. The scent of the woman's pain was making *him* crazy. God only knew what it was doing to Tanner. It was their curse. They could smell emotion like other men could smell bacon frying or coffee brewing. Emotions other Breeds missed, the soul-destroying emotions that scarred and crippled the mind, they could pinpoint with amazing accuracy.

Some scents were subtle, he thought, as Tanner slowly removed the knife. Like Scheme's. A part of her was so dark with pain, with a hunger to be free, that it swamped his senses. He was certain it shredded Tanner's. Cabal was hoping that by pushing it, he could shred his brother's control as well and force the animal he could sense lurking beneath the surface free.

It was one of the reasons Cabal had used every means at his disposal to keep Tanner away from her over the years. The first time Cabal had gotten close enough to draw her scent in, he had known several things.

First and foremost, she was Tanner's mate. And that should have spurred him then and there to contact his brother and tell him. Tanner searched constantly for the woman who would bind his soul, while Cabal prayed to never meet such a creature. His soul was bound enough.

But Tanner. Tanner would have killed to take her. Or died. And at the time, she had been carrying another man's child. And later. Hell, later it had become more dangerous than ever. The time had to be right. And when it was, luckily, the opportunity had presented itself for Tanner to take her.

"We need to talk," Cabal nearly whispered as his gaze met Tanner's again. "Jonas is going nuts searching for her, Tanner. Every team available has been pulled in to help on this."

Tanner glanced back at Scheme, his jaw flexing spasmodically.

"Bring her in, man," Cabal growled. "Call Jonas. He'll send the helo in. Get her to Sanctuary."

"And have her jerked into Breed Law?" Tanner snarled. "Why the fuck do you think I have her here? The only way to save her is if she's my mate. She's not."

Bitterness filled the air, as did the scent of mating heat.

Cabal shook his head. "I smell the scent of it."

"And I thought I did." Tanner swallowed tightly. "Our DNA is so close . . ." He paused, his jaw working spasmodically. "I smell the scent of heat, but maybe not because she's my mate."

Tortured—it was the only way to describe Tanner's expression and the pain that blended in with the scent of hunger and desire.

"Meaning?" Cabal was almost wary now. Oh hell, Tanner couldn't mean what he thought he did. Could he?

"Maybe she's your mate." Tanner glanced back, keeping his voice so low that only Cabal could hear. "The heat could rise with my DNA. But perhaps that's the reason for only the scent of heat. The barb shows itself with full mating. If she's your mate, then that could explain it."

Cabal glanced at the back of Scheme's head, knowing Tanner's explanation did not explain why the barb hadn't shown itself for Tanner. Tanner would know his mate. He would never share his mate. It was something Cabal had known, but Tanner had always doubted.

It was almost amusing. Tanner, always so supremely confident, so sure of himself and his place in the world, now doubted his very nature. His own mate. But fixing this for his brother was going to be a bitch.

Cabal understood now why he had been born first. And it had been proven Cabal was the firstborn. He took that position seriously. It was his job to protect Tanner, no matter the cost to himself. No matter how much it sucked. No matter how much it hurt Scheme Tallant.

"And we should resolve this how?" He buried his amusement, knowing his brother would sense it if he weren't very careful.

Sometimes, it wasn't a good idea to let Tanner know that his big brother was better at deception games.

Tanner swallowed tightly. "I'll walk away, give you some time alone with her. When you mate her, I'll let her go."

Let her go?

Cabal watched as Tanner's eyes flared with an inner rage. Oh yes, this was funny as hell. Tanner share that pretty little thing? He looked back at Scheme. There wasn't a chance in hell he would be given the chance to slide his dick into that hot little pussy.

But some things were worth fighting Tanner for. Once Cabal touched her, he had no doubt the animal Tanner kept so deeply hidden inside him would break free. It could get messy. Tanner would lose all control and try to destroy the man touching his woman. But it would be better than laughing in Tanner's face at the very idea that Scheme wasn't his mate.

"She seems unwilling to be shared, Tanner," he pointed out. "How do you suggest we do it?"

"She's your mate," Tanner whispered bitterly. "She'll want you. We won't have to deceive her."

Poor Tanner.

Cabal lowered his head to hide his knowledge. If the barb was taking its own time to show itself, then Cabal could understand the mistaken conclusions his brother had drawn. It didn't change the facts though, facts that even Sanctuary would have to take into account. Tanner and Cabal might be brothers, but there were still distinctions to their scent and their DNA. Slight ones, he admitted, but there all the same.

Things such as the fact that for ten years Tanner had been consumed with fantasies and thoughts of Scheme Tallant. Cabal had been amused, but not in the least fascinated. She was pretty enough, but nothing exceptional.

Crossing his arms over his chest, he leaned back and met Tanner's gaze directly.

"Okay." He nodded easily. "I'll accept her as my mate."

He nearly flinched from the wave of savagery that swept from Tanner. His brother was perfectly calm. Neither his expression nor his gaze altered, but Cabal felt the animal inside. And to say it wasn't pleased was an understatement.

Poor Tanner.

Tanner meant to leave. He really did. He pulled himself through the opening at the top of the farthest tunnel and crouched in the back of another series of caverns that led to the small cliff-sheltered valley beyond, before forcing himself to move to the exit.

He couldn't stay here. His hearing and sense of smell were too strong. He would hear Cabal taking her, smell the mating heat, and he feared for his own sanity if he did. The animal within was clawing for freedom, enraged, desperate to force him to return, to jerk her from Cabal's touch.

How many women had he shared with his brother? Dozens. Neither of them had been monogamous in the least, and the sex games they played with their women had always been bold. Hot.

Yet he couldn't stay in that damned cavern with Cabal and Scheme. He had forced himself to leave, ignoring her confused tone when she called out his name, forcing himself to leave as fast as he could go.

His and Cabal's DNA was too closely linked. It was nearly identical. They were just short of clones of each other. It made sense that he would hunger so desperately for Cabal's mate. That he would burn for her. Lose his mind for her.

He was losing his mind now.

He paused at the exit of the caves, drew in a deep, hard breath and stared up at the cliffs that sheltered the narrow valley.

The mountains in Sandy Hook were littered with cliffs and caves and hidden pockets of tunnels. Callan's scientist mother had played in the cliffs and caverns as a child, and had used them several times to hide Callan. But it was Callan who'd found the small, narrow tunnel beneath the main caverns, and the caverns connected to it.

They were completely hidden, even from the satellites in orbit equipped to see beyond the surface.

Tanner stared up at the jagged overhangs, through the pine, oak and locust trees that filled the area. Inhaling deeply, he fought a battle within himself, one he wasn't certain he would win. The animal he fought to keep hidden roared in outrage, clawing at his mind, his flesh, demanding his return.

That he take what was his. *His.*

His jaw clenched as he shook his head with a quick jerk, fighting back an impulse so primal, so bestial, it shocked him.

A growl rumbled in his chest as his lips pulled back from his teeth and he fought an enraged roar. It was a battle he almost lost.

His woman.

The primitive declaration raced through his head.

His woman.

His to touch, to hold, to take.

He had watched over her for ten years. Had been forced to watch other men take her, control her sexuality. He had watched another man take her, hating himself, hating her, forcing himself to steer clear of her despite the hunger that beat at him.

And because of it she had been tortured. Nearly killed more than once. The man who should have protected her, her father, had fucked with her sanity and her life. It was a wonder she had survived intact.

And Tanner had never known the hell she was going through. He had ignored every demand that he kidnap her, that he take her out of the games being played between the Council and the Breeds. He had let himself believe she was a monster, the same as her father was. And he had known better. Just as he knew better now. And yet still he was walking away.

He had paid his dues, for what? To give her to Cabal? To let go of the only woman he had ever— He stopped, clenched his eyes closed and snarled with primal anger.

He loved her.

Cabal didn't know her. He hadn't watched her all those years. He hadn't seen the loneliness on her face as she lay down to sleep each night, or the dissatisfaction and desperation each time another man had touched her.

Cabal hadn't watched her cry into her pillow. Not often, only a handful of times, but Tanner had watched her cry, and he had ached with her, for her.

He rose to his feet, determined to stalk from the caverns, to find a bar and get just as damned drunk as he could get before returning.

But he couldn't move. He willed his feet to walk, but the animal screamed out inside him, outraged.

His woman.

He breathed in roughly. He could still smell the scent of her on his flesh, the taste of her kiss on his tongue. His skin itched with the need to feel her again, to hold her beneath him, to take her, to fucking mark her.

He hadn't mated her. She wasn't his mate. She had to be Cabal's. But he loved her. God, he loved her.

Before he could regain the control the animal inside him had stolen, he turned and moved through the caves once again, fighting the growl emanating from his chest, the rage building inside him.

He had never let the animal free, not since his escape from the labs. He had fought it, caged it, imprisoned it at all costs. Until now.

He could feel it breaking free of the bonds he had placed on it.

My mate, the animal screamed.

She couldn't be his woman, his mate. His steps increased. It didn't fucking matter. She belonged to him. Fuck the mating heat, she was his woman, and he would defy any attempt to take her from him. He would kill the man or the Breed that attempted to take her, to harm her.

Reaching the hidden access, Tanner jumped back into the tunnel. He had to reach her before Cabal took her. Because God as his witness, if he took her, Tanner just might have to kill him.

◆   ◆   ◆

Scheme stared at the entrance to the tunnel Tanner had taken as he stalked from the room, feeling the coils of panic gathering in her gut. Cabal St. Laurents watched her curiously.

Her lips trembled as she inhaled slowly, deeply, her skin suddenly crawling with an impending sense of doom. The same feeling she always had when her father smiled at her.

Cabal was smiling now. A small quirk to his lips, his green eyes probing as she glanced at him.

Tanner hadn't said a word; he'd just left. She wouldn't have known he was going if Cabal hadn't bidden him a rather sarcastic farewell.

"Tanner." She raced for the exit. "Tanner, don't you leave me here with him."

She skidded to a halt as Cabal moved in front of her, blocking the exit, his arms held easily at his side, his body prepared.

He was going to stop her. He wouldn't let her leave.

She backed up slowly, her breathing harsh in the stillness of the cabin as she stared back at Cabal.

"Where is he going?" She continued to back away, only to stop abruptly as her rear met the back of the couch.

His smile deepened as his green eyes gleamed back at her in amusement.

"He decided to give us some time alone."

Scheme swallowed tightly, her fists clenching at her side as anger began to churn inside her. She had been here before, she thought with a sense of building shame. Chaz had done this to her. He had informed her that an associate would be joining them in their bed, teased her, dared her, then shared her.

She couldn't even remember his name. She fought the memory of the act. It hadn't been horribly unpleasant, but the hollow shame that followed her afterward still haunted her.

"We don't need any time alone." She stared back at the exit, feeling betrayed on a level that made no sense to her.

Tanner had made no commitments to her. Quite the contrary. They wouldn't matter if he had. There was no doubt he was her father's spy. Why else would he believe she would agree to this?

And why did it hurt? As though some part of her had hoped he wasn't that spy. Some too-stupid-to-live part of her that even her father hadn't been able to kill. The part that dreamed of a white knight when she slept, that continued to believe that somewhere there was hope.

She blinked back her tears. She would not cry in front of this man. This Breed.

"Unfortunately, we do need time together," he said softly, moving toward her as she sidled to the edge of the couch.

"For what reason?" she snapped back, not bothering to tamp down the anger or the fear.

She had been strong for so long, far longer than she had imagined she would survive when she first began working with Jonas. She had survived far longer than she could have ever guessed.

Cabal sighed again, tilting his head to watch her inch around the couch. Yeah, so, he could jump and take her at any moment; that didn't mean she had to make it easy for him.

"We need to talk, Scheme." His voice hardened. "Jonas has been waging quite a battle to find you this week. Why?"

She fought to breathe, but the fear was pounding in her head, through her bloodstream. And she wanted Tanner back. If one of them had to kill her, why couldn't it be Tanner? Surely he would do it without hurting her.

"Tanner!" She screamed his name as a dry sob tore from her throat.

"Tanner left," he drawled. "Come on, let's do this the easy way." Now where had she heard that before?

"The easy way?" she snapped, her breathing rough, panic edging through her.

She was so stupid. Stupid. She was actually shocked that Tanner had walked away and left her to die by another's hand. She should have ceased to be shocked by anything years before.

"Why the hell should I make this easy for either of you?" she hissed, glaring back at him as he watched her with calculated interest.

"Why is Jonas sweating over your disappearance, Scheme?" he asked her again. "Could it be that you're the spy enabling him to track Tallant's movements so accurately? Is that why your father sent an assassin after you?"

"Why do you care?" she asked, edging back farther, knowing she would run out of room soon. "Afraid of something, Breed?"

His lips quirked.

"You know, I remember seeing you in person once, years ago." His eyes narrowed on her. "You were standing with your assassin boyfriend, the breeze carrying the scent of you to me. You were pregnant."

"Don't." She shook her head. She couldn't bear this.

"Does Tanner know you had a child aborted, Scheme?"

She shook her head desperately. "I didn't," she moaned. "I wouldn't."

"Then where is the child?"

"You son of a bitch." Her control was shredded. She wouldn't be tortured like this. "Do you think you're torturing me?" she sneered. "You don't know what torture is. Go ahead and kill me, Cabal. Stop fucking with me."

His eyes widened. "You think I'm going to kill you?" he asked in amusement. "Not unless you can expire from orgasm."

"You think you're going to fuck me first?" she sneered back at him. "Does rape fall into your list of talents? Because that's the only way you'll have me."

He stopped, no more than a few feet from her as the wall stopped her backward retreat.

"Tanner didn't mate you," he said then. "That leaves me, sweetheart. Might as well get used to it."

"Excuse me?" He was crazy. Psychotic didn't even come close to the insanity this Breed possessed. "I think you know damned good and well I did have sex with Tanner."

White, sharp incisors flashed at the side of his mouth as he smiled—a wide, amused smile as his green eyes became brilliant with it.

"You had sex," he agreed. "But you didn't mate. He's decided I get to take care of that one."

"Oh, has he?" She was shaking with fury, with fear. "Are you going to rape me to do it?"

"Do I have to?" The smile was gone. His expression hardened with purpose as he stepped closer. "Are you going to force me into doing it, Scheme, or are you going to make it easy for both of us?"

She shook her head slowly. "I won't let you rape me."

"I guess that means you're going to make it easy for me, then," he said, the curve of his lips feral now. "Be a good girl then and take your clothes off. We'll just go ahead and get it over with."

"No." She shook her head, feeling the pounding fear and fury filling her head. "I won't make anything easy for either of you."

"Mates can't deny one another," he said, confusing her further as he stepped closer to her. "I promise, honey, once it starts, you won't want to deny me."

His smile was sarcastic now, his body corded and tight as he stalked her.

"You're crazy," she accused, fighting to breathe as she stared around the room desperately. There had to be a way out of this. She couldn't bear it if he touched her, she knew she couldn't.

"Just close your eyes and pretend I'm Tanner." His voice gentled. "It won't be that hard."

Her heart was beating so fiercely against her breast that she was certain it would burst through. It tightened her throat, made breathing hard, made thought almost impossible.

"I won't hurt you, Scheme." He advanced further, moving closer.

She wasn't going to get out of this, Scheme realized. He was waiting on her to move, to run. He was prepared for it. She wouldn't make it a single step.

"Don't do this," she whispered when he was but a step away. "Please."

"Why?" His voice held a crooning purr, a dangerous, subtle savagery.

"I don't want you." Her voice was thick with the tears she refused to shed. "If you're going to kill me, just do it and get it over with. Don't do this."

"I'll ask you again. Why? Why shouldn't I take what Tanner gave me? He wants your protection, nothing else. The only way to protect you against Breed Law is if one of us mates you."

"What are you talking about?" she cried out angrily. "I've spent a damned week in that bed with him. What kind of demented rules do you bastards have for sex anyway?"

His head lifted, his nostrils flaring as his gaze became calculating. "I'm sorry," he whispered a second before he was on her.

His fingers curled around her arms as his lips moved over hers, his tongue sliding against the seam as she lost the last of her sanity.

Wild. Desperate. She screamed out in rage, kicking, trying to bite, feeling her flesh crawl at his touch as she fought to escape him. She couldn't bear it. Not after being with Tanner, feeling things she had never thought she would feel with a man, being warm, whole in his arms, even if he was destined to be her executioner.

She couldn't stand for this man to touch her now. It didn't matter who he was or what he was to Tanner, he wasn't Tanner. And it wasn't his touch she was dying for, bile rising in her throat as pain welled in her soul.

In all the years she had deceived her father, he had never had her raped. And Tanner had walked away and left her alone with a man determined to do just that.

"Tanner!" She was screaming his name as Cabal held her easily, his lips at her ear, touching her, whispering something. Something meant to be soothing, though the words made no sense.

She screamed Tanner's name again, struggling, fighting to be free from the impossibly hard grip of Cabal's hands on her arms, the breadth of his chest which kept her pinned to the wall, the force of his powerful legs pinning hers in place.

Panic raced through her system as she shrank from his touch, her sensitive flesh prickling with distaste as he held her to him.

"I don't want you," she cried out furiously, bucking against him, fighting his hold. "I don't want this."

"It's going to be okay, sweetheart," he crooned at her ear, yet he still held her to the wall, touched her, nipped at her ear and had her screaming in rage.

"Son of a bitch!" Desperation lent her strength, but it didn't help her escape. His hold was unbreakable.

"You're a wildcat." His chuckle was soft at her ear. It wasn't cruel or hard and it was all the more frightening for it.

Panting, exhausted, she held herself still, trembling in his hold as she felt a single tear fall. She wouldn't cry over this, she told herself. Not this. Tears wouldn't change his course, and it wouldn't help her find the strength to endure whatever he had planned.

"Do you love Tanner, Scheme?" Cabal whispered at her ear, his voice so soft it was barely heard.

She closed her eyes, knowing any lie she told he would smell.

"I love him." And it made no sense. How could she love the man who had left her to be raped by another?

"Why do you love him?" He nuzzled her neck, his hold never weakening, the careful readiness in his body never changing. "Tell me why you love him, Scheme, and I'll let you go."

He wouldn't let her go. She knew this trick, the insidious promise of freedom for something so little, so destructive.

She leaned her head away from him, the fear rising sharply within her as she felt his incisors rake her neck, felt the subtle threat in the action.

"Because I'm too stupid to live," she whispered. "Too stupid to know hell when I see it."

Oh God, his touch hurt her. It was agonizing. The lightest of touches, but suddenly it felt like daggers digging into the flesh of her arm. She screamed out in agony as his hands quickly released her, but his body still held her to the wall. The knowledge that she couldn't fight him sent a surge of insanity through her mind.

"It's okay," Cabal whispered, his voice gentle. "He'll be back for you, Scheme. One more second, he'll be back."

She wasn't in a coffin buried beneath dirt, but the same suffocating, terrifying fear racked her mind. She wouldn't survive this; even if she lived, she would never survive this man taking her.

As she bucked, fought, she was certain she didn't have the strength to scream again, but an enraged snarl, a roar of fury, echoed around her as she was suddenly free, the momentum of her fight throwing her to the floor, her hair cascading over her face as she caught herself against the stone.

The sound split the air again. An animal's roar of killing rage.

Swiping her hair back from her face, Scheme stared across the room in shock.

Tanner. He had placed himself between her and Cabal, snarling back at his brother as he crouched protectively in front of her.

"I didn't tell you to rape her." The sound of his voice was horrendous. Animal and man, a snarling, graveled sound rife with violence.

Cabal flicked her a glance, amusement glittering in his eyes for but a second before they jerked back to Tanner. Scheme could feel the throb of murderous rage in the room now, hear it in the rumbled growls coming from Tanner's throat.

"You gave her to me," Cabal reminded him gently. "How I take my mate is my decision. Isn't it, brother?"

Tanner's responding roar was filled with challenge and fury.

"Mine!" The single word that left his throat had Scheme flinching in shock as Cabal tilted his head and watched his brother carefully.

He raised his hands slowly, a gesture of surrender.

"I won't fight you for her," he said softly, gently. "She's all yours, Tanner. She always was."

He backed slowly to the doorway, throwing Scheme a cocky wink as Tanner watched him carefully.

It had been deliberate? Cabal had been deliberately goading Tanner? Pushing him? Why?

Scheme moved slowly to her feet, shaking, watching the two men carefully. Breath sawed in and out of her lungs as she tried to understand what the hell was going on. She could feel the undercurrents of a savage fury and, when she glimpsed Tanner's face, the savagery of a naked, primal lust.

His eyes glittered gold as he watched his brother back slowly from the room, the primal growls that vibrated in his throat more animal than man. As though some inner demon had slipped its leash and taken control of the man.

Rubbing at her arms, Scheme backed away, wondering now if there was a way to escape Tanner. This wasn't the Breed the world knew, the soft-spoken, smiling, public relations wizard. This was the animal the Council had created, the killer it had trained.

He swung around to her sharply, as though he had somehow heard the thought.

"Do you think I would hurt you?" he snarled, his lips pulling back from his teeth as he straightened from the dangerous crouch.

There was nothing relaxed about him though; danger pulsed around him, as did lust. It gleamed in his eyes, naked and intense as he ate her with his gaze.

"I didn't think you would leave me to be raped by another man either," she panted, but where she had retreated from Cabal, she held her ground with Tanner. "You left me here to be fucked by another man, Tanner."

Anger slammed through her. Unfortunately, there was

nothing on hand to throw at him. Her fists clenched at her sides as she faced him, shaking with emotion, betrayal.

"You are mine," he snarled, stalking close to her, his movements fluid, filled with animal grace and sexual intensity.

She sneered in response. "Am I yours? I don't think so. I belong to no man."

A hard, carnal smile crossed his lips. "Not a man, a Breed."

She jumped to avoid him, but he was fast, faster than she gave him credit for. As she turned to run, his arms surrounded her, his chest cushioning her as he jerked her against him, his cock pressing into her lower back.

"My mate." Growling, intense, the words were followed by his hand jerking the neckline of her shirt aside and his teeth sinking into her shoulder.

He bit her.

Scheme screeched, not so much from pain, but from the sudden overriding certainty that he had done more than mark her physically. His incisors were lodged in her flesh, his tongue flickering over her skin as his mouth sucked at it.

It hurt, but not as it should have. A sexual intensity she hadn't expected bloomed within her as her head fell to the side and her nails bit into his wrists. It shouldn't ride a hard edge of pleasure; it shouldn't send ribbons of electricity to strike at her nipples, her womb, her clit.

She shouldn't be burning for more.

"What are you doing?"

He was growling behind her. His hands, her nails still digging into his wrists, moved beneath her top, slid over skin so sensitive she moaned from the touch of calloused flesh running up it, until they cupped her breasts.

Her nipples were hard, hot, pressing into his palms pleadingly as his fingers tightened on her flesh.

"Mine," he growled again, his teeth sliding from her flesh with an erotic shift of pleasure so intense that her vagina flexed in hunger.

"Tanner," she whimpered, feeling a slow, pulsing burn in her shoulder as his tongue licked over the wound. Heat and

liquid-hot sensation began to move from the four small punc-
ture wounds to weave through her body.

As though some powerful narcotic had hit her bloodstream,
her knees weakened and her womb clenched with a sudden
hunger so intense, so driving, she gasped at the strength of it.

◆   ◆   ◆

Cabal had to swallow the bile rising to his throat as he escaped
through the tunnels, putting as much distance as possible between himself and what he had just done.

Had he pushed too far? He had terrified her. He had sav-
aged her emotions. And he had known before doing it how
horrifying she would find it.

It was the bond. The animal could sense the mate's pain.
He had sensed it between other mates. It wasn't a conscious
thing; it was something the mates never truly recognized, but
it was there. Just as it was there with Tanner and Scheme. He
had to force Tanner back to her. He had to force the animal to
claim her.

But had he gone too far?

He had gone too far for his own comfort. He just prayed he
hadn't gone too far for his brother to ever forgive him.

CHAPTER 20

His mate!

She belonged to him.

Tanner knew he was out of control. Knew he had lost the self-imposed restraint he had always forced on himself and that he was teetering on the edge of complete primal melt-down if he didn't manage to pull back. Just a little.

He threw his head back, his knees bending to press the tor-tured length of his cock against Scheme's buttocks as his hands curled around her breasts.

He had bitten her, tasted her blood and licked the wound with a tongue painfully swollen, the glands at the side of his mouth spilling the sweet, dark taste of lust into his mouth.

Each time he swallowed, he burned.

He bit off an oath as he thrust against her buttocks, feeling the heat of her flesh through the soft velvet of her pants and the denim of his jeans. If he didn't get inside her, if he didn't fuck her, he was going to die.

She was his woman. His mate.

He had known it. For years, despite his denials, he had known this woman belonged to him, and yet he had stayed back. Some impulse, some knowledge he couldn't make sense of, had kept him from taking her, from stealing her away from her home and hiding her for his pleasure alone.

The animal inside roared in triumph as he turned her, wrapping his arms around her and slamming his lips to hers. There was no time for finesse. No time to consider each touch for pleasure or pain, no control to temper the animalistic lust with tender words or with comforting kisses.

There was hunger. God, the fucking hunger was going to kill him. He speared his tongue past her lips, growling in satisfaction as she immediately enveloped it, her mouth tightening, suckling it.

Sweet God.

His hands tore at her pants, ripping fragile material, hearing in a distant corner of his mind the rending of the material. But he felt her flesh, naked, soft as satin, hot and arching toward him.

Pleasure burned through him as she sucked the sweet hormone from the glands in his tongue, and with each pulse of the liquid she moved with deeper sensuality, moaned against his kiss with strident need.

It was burning her. He could feel it. Smell it.

This wasn't just mating heat. This was more, so fucking much more.

He had been insane, crazy to think that he could ever allow Cabal to touch her without losing his mind. To believe that another could ever mark her, hold her, and he would survive it.

He could barely survive having Cabal in the same room with her. He had forced himself to walk away. Forced himself to do what he thought he had to do.

The animal, though, had known. He had pushed that beast so far back into the darkest corners of his mind that when it slipped his bonds, there had been no stopping him.

His nails raked over her back before he clenched his hands in her top, ripping it from her. He wanted her naked. Wanted her hot and wet and dripping over his cock as he slammed inside her.

And she was dripping. His fingers tucked beneath her buttocks, thrusting inside her pussy, feeling the slick hot cream covering his fingers, easing his way inside her.

Her hands were in his hair, her arms bracing against his shoulders as she reached for him, trying to climb against him as his lips slanted over hers and she sucked deeper at his tongue.

Mating heat was slamming through him now. Grasping control of the animal and the lust was impossible. Tanner had never known a time that he didn't control the animal and the sexual hungers. There hadn't been a woman he couldn't control, couldn't finesse. Until now. There was no controlling this.

He didn't bother to pull his shirt off. Pulling it off required breaking the kiss, the suckling heat of her mouth that was spilling more and more of the hormone into both their systems. He couldn't allow that.

He ripped the buttons apart before shrugging the material from his shoulders. His hands moved immediately to his belt, tearing it loose before loosening his jeans, pushing them just past his hips and freeing the engorged length of his dick.

He had to fuck her. If he didn't get inside her hot pussy and screw the painful need from his system then he was going to implode. He was melting beneath the heat burning through his body, causing sweat to drip from his pores and growls to vibrate unceasingly from his throat.

He gripped her thighs, spread them, lifted her.

A primal, muttered snarl vibrated from his chest as her pussy settled on the tip of his cock. Fuck yes. Her cunt was hotter than fire, lava-hot, melted-iron-hot, and he needed more.

She was tight. The wide crest pressed inside her, parting clenching tissue and muscle as he pumped his tongue in her mouth and staggered to the wall.

No time for the bed. It was too far away. He had to get inside her now. All the way inside her.

He tore his lips from hers to breathe, his lashes lifting to check her face. God, she had to need this. He couldn't bear to see the pain in her face that he had smelled as he raced through the tunnel to the cavern.

There was no pain. No expression of it, no scent of it. Pleasure, rich and vibrant, suffused her expression, tilted her eyes further and gave her an exotic, otherworldly appearance that had his hips jerking, forcing his cock deeper into her snug pussy.

"I won't let you go," he snarled, his hands clenching on her hips. "Ever."

Her eyes were so dark they were nearly black, staring back at him languorously, damp with tears, stark with hunger.

"What are you doing to me?" She panted for breath, her nipples raking his chest as her pussy flexed and spasmed around his burrowing cock.

He lowered his head until his lips were brushing hers, his eyes staring into hers. "My mate," he whispered, almost wincing at the guttural, primal sound of his voice. "Just mine."

Her lips parted as she moaned, a low keening sound of pleasure as her tongue swiped over her lips, his.

"Something's wrong." Her lashes fluttered over her eyes a second before a harsh cry left her lips and he felt her orgasm.

He had penetrated no further than halfway into the snug depths of her pussy and she was already coming for him, washing his dick with the heated cream flowing around it.

"No. Nothing's wrong." He couldn't breathe. He couldn't hurry. It was so good, so fucking hot and good, sliding into her, working his cock into the clenching muscles milking at him. "It's right, Scheme. It's all just right."

"Tanner. I'm scared." Soft, subtle, the scent of her fear infused her pleasure.

"Trust me, Scheme." His chest clenched at the scent. "Please. Just this once. Just right now, sweetheart. Trust me not to hurt you."

"I can't . . ." A sharp cry left her throat as he pushed inside her to the hilt, his cock pulsing, throbbing with the heated grip she had on it. "Oh God, Tanner, I can't stand it. What are you doing to me? You can't do this." Her fingernails were pricking at his scalp sensually, her hips writhing against his, her legs tightening around his back as her pleasure began to increase.

"You can't control this, Scheme." He wanted to smile. She

was as much a control freak as he. She needed to know every step she was taking, needed to acknowledge it and understand its consequences. There was no understanding this. No controlling it.

"I have to." She was gasping as he moved against her, stroking his dick inside her, caressing her, driving them both crazy as sensations built, one atop the other, pushing them headlong into a dark, unknown center of lust.

"Give to me, Scheme." He didn't want her frightened. She had feared too much in her life, known too much pain, too many betrayals. "Just here, just now, little love, trust me."

She stared back at him, tears welling in her eyes as he pulled back until only the head of his cock remained inside her, before he slowly, with agonizing pleasure, penetrated her once again.

"Just don't hurt me, Tanner. Please don't hurt me."

And he knew she didn't mean physically. She was begging him not to betray her.

He smiled sadly. The beast had known his mate, but he hadn't. The woman Scheme kept hidden deep inside her, the woman that wept, that feared, trusted him. It was the conscious woman, the one who had known unbelievable pain, who feared.

"My mate." He paused, buried full-length inside her, his cock throbbing, surrounded by hot, tight silk. "I would die for you."

He licked at her lips, slid his tongue inside her mouth, growled as she opened to him, her tongue tangling with his, tasting the dark brew that released from the mating glands and giving herself to him.

No fear. She accepted him, if only as this, for now.

His hands clenched her buttocks, his hips moved and he was lost in her. Pleasure burned and built. It raced through his body and left him climbing, reaching . . . dying in her arms.

She couldn't make sense of the pleasure. But she never had. From the first touch, days before, knowing he could kill her, destroy her, the pleasure that came from his touch hadn't made sense.

Her body trusted him; she couldn't stop it. She couldn't

hold on to the distrust and the fear when he touched her. And now. Something was different now. From the moment he had bitten her, his teeth sinking into her flesh, his tongue numbing the wound and then burning it—it had changed.

The need, the hunger, wasn't just indescribable pleasure any longer. It was a firefight inside her body. Whipping lashes of burning sensation that bordered on pain increased the pleasure, forced her to ride a boundary between the two so fine it was terrifying.

Swirling vortexes of lightning resounded beneath her flesh. Charged with erotic intensity and weakening carnality. It was like sinking into a whirlwind of such heated delight that the senses exploded. There was too much pleasure.

His lips on hers, his tongue tasted of a storm, lightning-charged, damp and earthy, sweet. There was nothing to compare it to, no other taste she had ever known that even came close.

And she needed more. She tangled her tongue with his, sucked at it and let herself fall into the wicked vortex overtaking her.

The pleasure would kill her. Her arms tightened around his neck, her legs around his back, and she moved against him, forcing his cock deeper with each stroke inside her swollen, overly sensitive vagina.

She had never been so sensitive, so swollen. His cock felt like a fist inside her, stretching her, stroking sensually as she felt her muscles spasming around him.

"Tanner." She could barely breathe, let alone speak. Yet she couldn't stay silent. She couldn't process the pleasure fast enough to find a steady shore amid this storm.

She was going to come again. She could feel it racing it toward her, like a tidal wave preparing to swamp her.

"Tanner. Help me." Her hands clenched in his hair as it began to beat at her womb, convulsing it, tightening it. "Please, Tanner," she tried to scream. "Help me."

He thrust harder inside her then, faster. Heat seared hidden nerve endings, pushing her closer as fingers of blistering sensation began to clench in her womb.

The orgasm ripped through her. Arching, tightening, she screamed his name, her hips writhing, pushing harder on the impaling flesh, fucking him back with mindless hunger. It tore through her senses and flung her through a velvet-dark landscape of such ecstasy she didn't know if she could ever survive without it.

"God yes, sweetheart," he was growling at her ear. "So tight. So hot. Fuck me back. Damn you, yes! Fuck me, Scheme."

They were moving. The cold wall became the cushions of the couch. Her lashes fluttered open as she felt her thighs being pushed back, her hips lifted and his cock spearing so deep inside her she screamed again from the pleasure.

It was too much. Too much for her body. Too much for her mind. His touch was like fire, the stroke of his cock inside her like pure energized sensation. Wicked, destructive, carnal, his expression was dark with it.

"It's not over," he grated, growled. "More. Come more for me."

She was dying from the pleasure. Her hands gripped his forearms as she shook her head, feeling perspiration running along her body, the burning heat inside her spiking to a point that she wondered if she would combust.

"Tanner . . ." It was building again; she could feel it, the need unlike anything her brain could process.

"All of you," he snarled. "I'll take all of you."

He came over her, pushing her legs around his back, pumping his cock hard and deep inside her as one hand moved around her rear, his fingers caressing, stroking, then finding an area so sensitive, so erotic, that when his fingers parted the little entrance and slid home, she lost her mind.

Her teeth locked on his shoulder, mindless guttural screams leaving her throat as his fingers pumped inside her ass, his cock pumped inside her vagina, and she was destroyed.

She thought there could be no greater pleasure. She thought she had reached the pinnacle. Until she felt his release.

His cock throbbed inside the tight muscles of her vagina, then seemed to swell, just beneath the thick crest, like a thumb reaching out, locking into an area inside her that had never been touched, just behind the convulsing muscle, stroking, pulsing and burning with destructive heat as she felt him begin to spurt inside her.

He was locked inside her. His teeth at her shoulder again bit into her even as her teeth locked on his flesh. Growls left his throat. One hand clenched on her hip as two fingers of the other stretched her rear, and Scheme knew she was lost.

Destroyed. The woman she had been buckled, and the wall between innocence and pain collapsed beneath the orgasm that swept not just her body, but her soul, as she realized in one blinding second that not only had the man's body taken her, but the animal he was had just marked her forever.

Tanner sat on the couch, his head lowered, his hands clasped between his knees as he turned his head and stared at the bed.

Scheme had cried. She hadn't sobbed. But as he laid her carefully in the bed, her slight body had shuddered as tears ran from beneath her closed lashes. And he couldn't comfort her. She wouldn't let him.

"Just leave," she had whispered. "Please. Just leave."

He couldn't leave. He had covered her with the quilt and retreated to the other side of the room instead, trying to make sense of what he sensed inside her.

There was no pain. Weariness. Resignation. But no true pain. And love. The scent of that emotion was unmistakable. He had smelled it between other mates, sometimes, even before the mating. It was a scent unlike anything else. Summer and heat, chocolate and liquor. It was pure emotion, addictive and soothing, yet Scheme wasn't soothed. And neither was he.

The mating hadn't been easy. Son of a bitch. He grimaced at the knowledge of what he had allowed to happen. The animal inside had gained its freedom in a way he had never expected. It had taken over, claimed him and his mate in a way

Tanner couldn't have anticipated. In a way he would have stopped if he had the control to do so.

He ran his fingers wearily through his hair, his head lifting before he pulled himself painfully to his feet.

The torn edges of his shirt draped over his chest as he turned to face Cabal, seeing the heavy knowledge in his brother's face as he entered the room.

Tanner moved slowly, wearily, to the cabinet, where he pulled out the whiskey and two glasses and gestured to the tunnel. He moved ahead of Cabal, leading the way to another smaller cavern farther into the system of caves.

Lights flickered on as they entered the cave, revealing a secure communications room equipped with computers, camera monitors and surveillance equipment that linked to the hidden remote cameras scattered around the properties Callan owned.

Scheme had found this room days before. Tanner's lips quirked at the knowledge of the time she had spent in there trying to get the equipment to work until she realized it was fingerprint, DNA, and pupil-scan protected.

But she had tried. He had to give her give her credit for her persistence; she wasn't a quitter. She was strong and courageous, passionate and sassy. And he loved her. God, he loved her until it broke his heart in half.

A couch, table and several comfortable chairs sat in a rounded corner of the room. Tanner threw himself in the couch, leaned forward and poured himself a healthy drink.

"Liquor affects the mating heat, Tanner," Cabal reminded him softly as he took a seat in one of the chairs opposite the couch. "You know it makes it worse."

"It can't get worse." Tanner wiped his hand over his face before tossing back the burning liquor, grimacing as it burnt its way to his gut.

Rubbing at his beard-stubbled chin, it suddenly struck him that for all the Breed males' lack of body hair, none of them had a problem growing a beard. Sometimes he wondered about the genetic mix they were learning they were. Was the world truly better off without them?

Lifting his gaze to Cabal, he breathed out roughly. "You knew."

His brother had known Scheme was Tanner's mate; there was no other explanation. Cabal would have never walked away from the woman his soul screamed out for.

Cabal leaned back in the chair and sipped at the whiskey, his gaze somber as he stared back.

"I've suspected it for years," he said. "I caught a scent of her just after I'd healed from the pits. My first assignment under the new Bureau was to shadow her for a few weeks. Each time I caught a scent of her, I could sense a connection. It just took a while to figure it out."

"How long since you've figured it out?" Tanner growled.

Cabal's gaze flickered. "Six, seven years maybe."

"And you didn't tell me?" His jaw clenched in anger. "Why?"

Cabal leaned forward, lowering his head to stare into his glass before sighing deeply and lifting his head.

"Jonas," he finally said as he lifted his gaze once again. "I went to Jonas. He convinced me that if you kidnapped her then, as I knew you would, it could be too dangerous. He had suspected himself, I think. He knew your fascination for her. He also knew how deep the hatred for Cyrus Tallant ran in our family."

"He thought I'd hurt her?" That surprised him. He had always controlled the animal inside him, had never killed rashly.

"I don't know, Tanner." Cabal shook his head roughly. "Jonas was determined that we wait. I accepted that decision, because it felt right."

"Betraying me felt right?" Tanner asked him curiously, his expression twisting with his inner rage. "Do you know what her father did to her, Cabal? Did you have any idea the hell she was going through?"

Cabal's eyes narrowed, the green gaze flickering. "She was his daughter," he said slowly. "His right hand. But what she said earlier . . ."

Tanner leaned forward. "He buried her alive, Cabal, more

than once, and unless my senses are wrong, after he killed her baby, he had her sterilized."

Cabal paled. "He buried her?"

"The power shut off to the lights the other day when I was checking the cabin. When I returned, she was nearly insane with hysteria and the fear of being buried alive. She hasn't mentioned the sterilization, but my sense of smell doesn't lie. She wouldn't have done that to herself."

He couldn't explain how he knew she wouldn't, but he knew for a certainty.

"God." Cabal tossed back his own liquor before refilling his glass and downing it as well. "Jonas couldn't have known." He shook his head jerkily. "He couldn't have suspected. He would have done something."

"Would he?" Tanner leaned forward slowly. "He advanced to director of the Bureau because of the spy he managed to acquire inside Tallant's organization. What if his spy was Scheme?"

It made sense. Instinct gathered inside him, laying the final pieces together in the puzzle that was Scheme.

"She was Tallant's assistant," he continued. "Closer to him than anyone else, able to access any file she needed. She knew the rumors in the Tallant ranks as well as the truths and the plans the bastard was creating to strike against the Breeds using the various racist groups."

"And Tallant suspected," Cabal whispered. "He would have tortured her, tried to make her admit it; it's his favorite game."

Exactly. Tallant always wanted proof if possible.

"He sent the assassin after her why?" Tanner asked then. "Why did he stop torturing her and decide to kill her instead?"

"Either he's figured out he can't break her, or she has something he can't risk going further. Something he didn't anticipate her finding out," Cabal mused. "But what?"

Tanner refilled his own glass, sipping this time rather than downing the liquor. It was harder to think; the mating heat was building inside him, the glands at his tongue becoming sensitive again. It wouldn't be long before he had to have her again, before the heat became so blinding that nothing mattered but fucking her.

"How did Jonas react to her disappearance?" The answer was there somewhere; he could feel it.

"Every available Breed Enforcer as well as recruits are searching for her," Cabal said softly. "He's pulled Breeds off imperative missions and sent them looking for this woman instead."

"How did he know she was here?" Tanner narrowed his eyes on his brother.

Cabal grunted mockingly. "With Jonas, who the hell knows? I followed the second half of Alpha Team out here as fast as I could. It just took me a while to shake a few shadows I had before coming here."

Tanner stared back at him questioningly.

"Callan refuses to tell Jonas where you're at. I think he suspects where you are, but he's possessive of the knowledge of these caves."

Callan would be. It was their last sanctuary if things went from sugar to shit for the Breeds and the children born of matings needed to be concealed. The information was so closely guarded that besides Cabal and a Wolf Breed—Dash Sinclair—no one outside Callan's original pride knew of it.

"Have you talked to Callan?" Tanner asked.

"Let's say Callan talked to me," Cabal snorted. "He's worried, Tanner. Her death is being placed at the door of the Breeds. You can't keep her here forever and you know it."

"I will protect her," Tanner snapped with a primal rasp. "Nothing can happen to her." The animal rose to the surface, beating at his brain with the imperative demand.

"Do you have a plan?" Cabal asked.

Tanner's sharp laugh was mocking. "Plan? Since I pulled her out of D.C. I haven't been able to figure out anything except how many different ways I need to fuck her."

He swiped his fingers through his hair again in frustration.

"If we take her to Sanctuary, then the spy Tallant has there will stop at nothing to kill her," Tanner said. "I can't keep her locked up forever."

"It could be the only way to flush Tallant's spy out," Cabal pointed out.

Tanner growled. For once, the animal didn't have to push to the surface; the man was there and he wasn't pleased with that suggestion.

"You said you can't keep her locked up forever, Tanner," Cabal bit out. "What other choice do we have here? The only way to ensure her safety is to get her to Sanctuary and flush that bastard out."

"We have no idea the direction he would take in attacking her," Tanner snapped. "Every Breed on the place is armed to the teeth. I won't take that chance. Even if she had something we could use to take Tallant out, it wouldn't be enough. His spy wouldn't stop until Scheme was dead."

"We need that spy, Tanner," Cabal growled.

Tanner's hand flashed out, wrapping around his brother's throat, tightening as Cabal stilled.

"You will not risk my mate," he snarled, leaning closer for emphasis. "Not now. Not ever."

Cabal never broke his gaze. "Do you think I would risk your mate unduly?" he retorted. "No more than you would mine. But keeping her here forever won't work. You know that as well as I do. Use your head here instead of your heart."

Tanner jerked his hand back before rising abruptly and pacing the room. He couldn't do it. If he took her to Sanctuary, he couldn't protect her. There was no way to protect her.

"Tanner, there's no other choice." Cabal rose, facing him. "If we don't show proof that she's alive, everyone will suspect the Breeds of having killed her. Bringing her to Sanctuary and holding a press conference we can control, assuring the world of her safety and her protection against the monster that tortured her, will only aid our cause. Striking against your *wife* will afford Tallant the same consequences as striking against you."

The world loved Tanner Reynolds. It was set in stone. He was the face of the Breeds, the laughing, easygoing playboy. Would it protect his mate, to the world, his wife?

They knew orders had gone through the Council as well as

Tallant's organization that due to public sentiment for him, no strikes were to be made against him. It was amusing sometimes, watching the Council agents that often trailed him, the hatred on their faces, their need for blood restrained.

"It wouldn't stop them," he said softly. "They would kill her. She knows too much."

"Do you have a choice?" Cabal asked.

"I'll find my own choices, dammit," he snarled, his fists clenching as pain raged through him. "I won't let them take her from me. Not now. Not knowing what that bastard has done to her over the years."

It tormented him, tortured him. The thought of being buried alive, her slender fingers clawing at a narrow casket, it sent rage pulsing through him, ripping at his control and sending a growl rumbling from his throat.

"Tanner. I would stand in front of her," Cabal told him imperatively. "As God is my witness, I will protect your mate as though she were my own. It's the only choice we have."

"And you think I would trade my brother's life for my mate's?" Tanner snapped, burningly aware of his limited choices. "Do you think I would ask that of you, Cabal?"

Cabal's lips quirked in bitter knowledge. "You wouldn't have to ask it of me. You saved my sanity after you rescued me. You made me live as a man instead of an animal, Tanner. Do you think I wouldn't die for you or your mate?"

Tanner stilled, staring back at Cabal as he inhaled roughly. It was there, the scent of Cabal's determination and something more. A hint of emotion, sadness, resignation, regret. They had always assumed they would mate the same woman. From the day Tanner had pulled him from that pit, the need to share the finer things in life with his brother has risen to the fore.

Food, wine, song and women. Playful teasing, a child's laughter. Tanner had shared it all with him, and now they had found something Tanner couldn't bear to share. And he couldn't regret it. Nature had given him something that belonged to him alone, something he had marked, something he would give his soul for.

"I don't want you to die for me or my mate," Tanner said simply. "I want you to live to help protect my children."

Cabal frowned. "She was sterilized."

"So was Sherra," Tanner pointed out, speaking of his pride sister.

Sherra had had herself sterilized after the loss of her first child, but once she had been reunited with her mate, somehow nature had repaired the separation of her fallopian tubes and her pregnancy had resulted.

"You believe the hormones are forcing her body to repair it as they did Sherra's?" Cabal asked.

"Something is going on," Tanner sighed. "There's a difference to her scent; there has been for days, as though something were changing inside her. I could smell this on Sherra when she was fighting the heat with her mate, Kane. The scent is the same, Cabal."

"The healing process took much longer than a few weeks." Cabal frowned heavily. "Dr. Jacobs guessed it had been in progress for more than a year, from the moment Kane reappeared in Sherra's life. It won't happen overnight."

The mating heat and hormonal effects on the body were still unknown for the most part. There were too many anomalies for the Breed doctors and scientists to keep up with. It was one of the reasons they were so desperate to find the first Leo. Reports were that he existed, in his prime, still a strong, amazingly healthy male at nearly a century in age. And his mate was said to appear as young.

"What the hell am I going to do?" He sat down heavily in the couch, covering his face with his hands wearily. "How am I going to protect her?"

"We will protect her." Cabal's voice was cold, hard.

Lifting his head, Tanner stared back at his brother in surprise.

"Listen to me, Tanner," he growled, his incisors flashing dangerously. "We know those who are most loyal to us. This damned spy is good, I'll give you that, but we can protect her and flush him out at the same time. You don't have a choice. And neither does she."

"How?" The heat was messing with his mind now. All he could think about, all he could feel, was Scheme.

"We take her back to Sanctuary. We'll place our enforcers around her, keep her under house protection and see who gets curious. Whatever she knows, once she knows she's truly safe, she'll reveal it. It will flush out Tallant's spy."

He would have to risk her to save her.

Tanner shook his head. "I don't know if I can do it, Cabal."

CHAPTER 22

"And I don't know if it's entirely your decision."

Tanner jerked around, a growl rumbling in his throat as Jonas and three of his enforcers stepped into the room. How the fuck had they managed to sneak up on him?

Jonas's lips tightened as he tested the air, his strange silver eyes flashing with anger.

"You should have smelled us coming the moment we dropped into the tunnels," he snapped. "Mating heat is making you weak, Tanner."

Tanner lifted his lip in a sneer. "Not so weak that I can't take your throat out, Director," he snarled. "Why the hell are you here?"

Jonas snorted at the question. "Callan did a good job of hiding you, but you forget, I hold my position for a reason. Tracking you wasn't as hard as you would have imagined. It's a goddamned wonder the Council hasn't already found this place."

"It's a goddamned wonder a Breed hasn't killed you yet," Tanner growled.

"Several have tried." Jonas shrugged, staring around the room. "Where is she? Don't make me go looking for her."

"Touch her, cause so much as a flicker of fear to ignite inside her, and I'll kill you." Murderous rage brewed in Tanner's gut as he stared back at the director of Breed affairs.

Jonas's lips flattened. "Don't sign her death warrant here, Tanner. Let's protect her together."

The animal awoke with a roar. Tanner could feel blood pumping through his body, tightening his muscles, sending a surge of adrenaline-laced rage to race through his head.

His head lifted as he stared back at the taller man, not in the least intimidated by Jonas's six-six frame or the glowering menace in his expression.

"You signed yours," Tanner rasped, "when you recruited her rather than rescuing her."

"It was her decision," Jonas refuted coolly. "I offered her safety; she chose revenge for the death of her child. You can't fault her for that."

"I don't care how you've excused ignoring a woman's torture," he snarled contemptuously. "And neither will the Breed Cabinet when I request asylum for my *mate*."

Jonas's eyes flickered, his jaw hardening. "I ignored nothing," he finally retorted. "She never reported it."

"She gave her soul for the Breeds," Tanner hissed. "How old was she when you recruited her, Jonas? Nineteen? Twenty?"

Jonas stared back at him coldly. "She was twenty-two."

Tanner's smile was savage. "A child. You recruited a child, Jonas. One likely already scarred by a father's torture. A woman you should have sensed needed your help rather than your exploitation."

Jonas's expression never changed. "We do what we have to, Tanner, to survive."

"You son of a bitch!" Tanner's fist flashed out, connecting solidly with Jonas's jaw and knocking him backward.

A hard lion's roar left Jonas's lips as he moved to counterattack, only to draw himself up short, his expression twisting with fury as the enforcers beside him tensed for action.

Cabal stood beside Tanner now, a warning growl echoing in the room as Jonas's eyes flashed toward him.

"My mate"—restraining the killing rage surging inside him was nearly impossible—"is not a tool to survive."

As the words left his throat, his senses exploded with the scent of Scheme, his gaze moving to the doorway as she stepped into it slowly.

She was pale, her dark eyes wide, tortured.

"Unfortunately, that's exactly what I am," she said as she faced the six Breed males that had turned to her. "First a tool against the Breeds and now one for them."

Her voice sounded calm; her expression was stoic, but Tanner could smell the pain and the fear twisting inside her.

"Not any longer." He pushed past Jonas and his enforcers, growling warningly as he tossed Jonas a furious glance.

Tanner pulled her into his arms, sheltering her against his chest as his hands tucked the sheet she had wrapped around herself more firmly about her body.

"You should be sleeping." He didn't want her here, didn't want her facing Jonas's cold, hard objectivity. It was the reason he made such an excellent director of a bureau created for the covert operations the Breeds were forced to use to survive.

"No, there will be time to sleep later." Her words had his heart jerking in his chest. "It's time to finish this now."

◆ ◆ ◆

"You're late." She felt the nervous smile trembling on her lips as she faced the director of Breed affairs, the man who had once saved her life, who offered her a chance to destroy the monster haunting her.

She watched as he breathed out heavily, regret flashing in his silver eyes.

"Finding the caves wasn't easy," he growled as Tanner's arms tightened around her. "I knew who you were with. I thought we had time."

"And what changed that?" Tanner snapped behind her.

He really was protective. It surprised her, the warning and fierce protectiveness in his voice.

Jonas's silver eyes flicked to Tanner before returning to her. "And here we thought he was the calm Breed," he commented. "Go figure."

"Jonas, I'm going to kick your ass," Tanner warned him.

"No." Scheme tightened her hand on the arm surrounding her. "You don't understand, Tanner."

"Probably because you never explained it to me, Scheme," he bit out mockingly.

"I tried. Right before you left me alone with Cabal."

Silence filled the room.

"He saved my life," she told Tanner then. "Right after I lost the baby. He found me." She swallowed tightly, trying to dislodge the grief in her throat, the memories of the loss and of her own weakness.

"We were trying to get a few bugs in her home at that time. We thought she and St. Marks both were still at the Tallant estate. Scheme had returned." Jonas began the explanation only to stop as Scheme shook her head harshly.

It was her weakness and it was time she faced it. "I was sitting in the dark, in the living room, staring at a handful of pain pills." Her lips twisted in disgust. "I couldn't run. I would have been found and punished. I knew that. And I needed to escape. I just wanted to escape."

She remembered that night clearly.

A shadow had moved at her side. Her gaze had lifted to meet the silver eyes of what she knew was one of her father's greatest enemies.

Go ahead and kill me, she had whispered. *Saves me the trouble.*

He had crouched to sit on his heels, staring at the pills in her hand.

I can take you out of here. The offer had been tempting.

Finally Scheme had shaken her head. *I don't have the information you want, Breed. Not enough to stop him. Not enough to convict him. Saving me is more trouble than it's worth.*

Then get me the information, Scheme. Find it. Get what we

need and we'll take him down together. Do you want to die?
Or do you want to see him suffer?

"I wanted to see him suffer," she whispered then, refusing to see the effects of her explanation on Tanner's face. "I wanted to see him destroyed. So I stayed. And I worked for Jonas. And he never knew of the punishments I received. He never knew the lengths I was going to. All he knew was the proof I sent him. And I could never get enough."

Her father had been smarter than she was, it seemed.

"Why did you call for pickup?" Jonas asked then.

Scheme breathed in roughly. "In roughly one week, the spy at Sanctuary will have everything in place to kidnap the pride leader's son, David Lyons. I found the reports on this just before I called you."

And then she waited. There was so much information she didn't have. Promises she had made to Jonas that she hadn't kept.

He watched her now, his silver eyes flashing with satisfaction.

"You have enough." He suddenly nodded. "We'll get you back to Sanctuary and you can start making the lists of contacts and resources that you can pinpoint. You did good, Scheme. You know that, don't you?"

Had she? Tanner hadn't said a word. He was silent behind her, his hold on her less fierce now, though the tension in his body was much higher.

"I did what I could," she answered faintly, suddenly feeling self-conscious, and terribly aware of Tanner's silence. "I wish it had been more."

"We have the heli-jet waiting outside," he announced. "We have to get you back to Sanctuary. Then we can make our plans from there."

"Not yet." Tanner's voice was frightening. "Scheme and I have a few things to settle before we leave. Wait outside."

"Tanner." Jonas's voice was warning. "We need to leave."

The primal snarl that came from Tanner's chest caused Scheme to flinch and Jonas to stare behind her with a suddenly wary expression.

"Leave," Tanner ordered him then. "I'll deal with you later. Right now, I'll deal with my *mate*."

Jonas stared back at Tanner for long moments before nodding shortly. With a brief flick of his hand, the room began to clear and Tanner was releasing her, jerking his arms from around her and stalking to the other side of the room.

She had known this was coming. He was furious; she could feel the waves of anger ricocheting around her and sparking a defensive reaction inside her soul.

"You couldn't tell me." He swiped his fingers through his long hair as he turned back to her, his eyes glowing with anger, his expression suddenly hard, savage. "You would have let David be kidnapped and the first Leo murdered before you told me."

Scheme shook her head as she swallowed tightly.

"I tried to tell you this morning, before you left me with Cabal. I was going to tell you everything."

His jaw clenched.

"And before then? Why didn't you tell me when I first kidnapped you? When I couldn't decide if I was going to fuck you or kill you?" His voice rose perceptively; the fury building inside him was frightening to watch.

"Father's spy," she said faintly, knowing what she was about to say would only add fuel to the anger. "I don't know who he is. All I know is that he holds a position of trust within the main pride. Your profile fit the spy's."

His expression went blank. No emotion. It wasn't cold; it wasn't furious. It was just without emotion, period.

"You thought I could betray my family?"

"I didn't know you, Tanner," she cried. "All I knew were your files and the public persona you project to the world. The information I've managed to find on the Breed working within Sanctuary coincides perfectly with your training and your escape from the labs. I was too scared to trust you simply because you wanted to fuck me."

He shook his head slowly. "You knew better."

"And I thought I knew better than to believe Chaz would help abort my baby." Her fists clenched as pain tore ragged wounds into her soul. "I couldn't risk it. Not then. You have to understand that."

She could see the struggle in his face now, the fight to accept her distrust, to understand how she had held back.

Would she have understood? She knew the betrayals he would have felt in his position, the personal sense of failure. But it would have been personal. Emotional.

"I tried to be logical," she said faintly. "I did my best to protect them."

"As you've done your best to protect the Breeds for eight years?" He growled. "How would your death have served us, Scheme? It would have served us no more than remaining silent now. You could have spoken up. You could have told me about the plan to kidnap my nephew."

"And risked having it changed? Risked something going wrong or the timetable moving up?" She yelled back, frowning as arousal began to pound inside her with the same force as her anger. "I couldn't risk his life or anyone else's because of my stupid need to be touched by you."

She snapped her teeth shut with those last words, whirling around as she held the sheet close to her body and strained to hear something in the silence behind her.

"I made that mistake once," she finally whispered. "I needed. Needed to be held. Needed to be loved. I needed— and because I needed, my child died. I wasn't about to risk someone else's child because of that need."

She turned back to him slowly, meeting the predatory gaze that seemed sharper, more savage than before as she continued. "I was going to tell you before you left earlier, but you didn't want to listen. You didn't want to hear any more than you wanted to admit that I belonged to you. You gave me to another man."

And that sliced deep. It hurt in ways she was still reeling from.

"I came back," he bit out harshly.

"You were willing to give me to another man."

"To save your damned life I would give my own soul away." The fury was free once again.

Tanner stalked across the room, jerking her to him before she could avoid him, pulling her against his chest, the erection beneath his jeans pressing hard into her abdomen as he glowered down at her.

"I risked everything to bring you here. To hold you. To find a way to save your life, and you were working with Jonas all along," he snarled.

"I tried to tell you I would be safe," she protested against the anger she could see glittering in his eyes. "I tried to do what was right, Tanner. Just what was right. That was all I was trying to do."

"What was right, Scheme, was trusting me," he retorted. "But trust wasn't something you could give me, was it? Just this. This is all you were willing to give."

On the heels of those words, one hand tangled in her hair to pull her head back, and a second later, the taste of spicy passion and dark lust filled her senses.

His kiss.

Her senses ignited instantly.

Tanner's lips were on hers as he backed her against the wall, soft, stroking, his tongue caressing over the parted seam of her lips as she fought the whimper of need building in her throat.

This had defeated her. This need, whatever it was, shook her to the core and left her desperate for more. She should protest, but she couldn't risk losing it, not yet, not until the hunger had been fulfilled, until the need eased.

Her arms stole around his neck, crossing, holding him close as his tongue parted her lips and slid against her own. She had to hold him to her.

Spicy heat exploded in her mouth; sweet temptation swept through her senses.

She needed him.

"You are mine," he snarled against her lips as she whimpered into the kiss, desperate to get closer. "Damn you for not trusting me. Damn you!"

She could feel his anger, but she could also feel his need.

The same need that tormented her, burned her, that kept her in his arms despite her need to explain.

He lifted her against him as he moved to the couch, holding her steady as he shrugged his shirt from his shoulders, then struggled with his jeans. All the while he made love to her with his lips and tongue, his groan vibrating into her mouth as she felt him, suddenly naked, his cock hard and hot against her stomach as his hands removed the sheet.

She had waited on this, she realized. All her life, growing more cynical by the day, harder, more disillusioned, certain it didn't exist. Only to find it where she had expected to only find death.

"Don't let me go," she moaned against his kiss, feeling him sit on the couch, pulling her over him, her legs straddling his lap, the feel of his cock pressing against the tender folds of her sex.

"I'll never let you go," he promised, his teeth catching her lower lip as he stared into her eyes. "Now take me. Suck my tongue like your tight pussy sucks at my cock. Now."

His tongue slid into her mouth as his cock slid deep inside her vagina. Her cry was lost in the wild, wicked taste of him. His tongue fucked into her mouth with the same hunger that he worked his cock inside her. Slow, deep, filling her, feeding the hunger ravaging her as she began to move above him.

Her arms tightened around his neck as his hand gripped her rear, parting the smooth cheeks, his fingers massaging the sensitive inner flesh. The calloused tips slid in the juices easing from where his erection filled her. He used it to ease the path of his fingers, working them slowly around the tight entrance to her rear.

With any other man, she would have been shrieking. She hadn't allowed a man's touch there since Chaz had brought another man to their bed. It was an act she had sworn she would never allow again. Now she craved it.

This was Tanner, just Tanner. His touch spread fire; his kiss was wicked sex; the movement of his hips between her thighs disintegrated control and thought.

He brought her nothing but pleasure. No man had ever brought her nothing but pleasure. None had ever stood between her and danger or had so much as thought to protect her.

Her breath hitched in her throat on a ragged cry as she sucked at his shuttling tongue, drawing more of the wild taste into her mouth.

Cabal had forced her to admit her love for Tanner, but Tanner had forced her to feel it. Despite all logic. Despite fear and suspicion.

Had she loved him even before she met him?

His lips slanted deeper over hers as his movements became harder, his thrusts driving his cock to the hilt, sending rapid, burning flares of pleasure to attack nerve endings never touched before.

"Don't stop." Her weak cry came as his lips lifted from hers, reminding her to breathe, to survive. She had to survive for this.

Her head tipped back on her shoulders as she felt his finger enter her ass. She shuddered, trembled. Sensations attacked her with near violent intensity as a long, low wail left her lips.

He was fucking her harder now, deeper, as though that small surrender had spurred his own lusts. She could hear his growls—he growled a lot—and feel the sweat gathering on the hard shoulders beneath her hands, and she gave herself to the orgasm suddenly exploding through her.

Tanner's hoarse shout was barely recognizable, but the feel of that thickening beneath the head of his cock, the thick extension reaching out, locking inside her, spilling a heated warmth as his seed spurted inside her—that she understood.

She understood the sudden, secondary orgasm tearing through her, riding hard on the back of the first. She knew the blinding heat, the shaking, writhing motions of her own body, the need to milk every drop of semen from his cock, to cool the need raging inside her womb.

She even understood the tears this time as Tanner pulled her against his chest. She understood the emotions he had ripped free of her, the frightening realization that for the first time in years, she felt. Love. Hate. Hunger and need. They weren't buried any longer. They were free, and they had the potential to destroy her.

"I love you," Tanner whispered at her ear. "I loved you before I touched you, before I knew you. Know that, Scheme. Before I ever suspected your true worth, I still knew you were worthy."

She shook her head wearily against his chest. He couldn't have known. He couldn't know now.

Scheme swallowed tightly, aware that he hadn't shifted, hadn't moved. His cock, still half-hard, was buried inside her.

"Father sedated me," she whispered, forcing the words past her lips. "They drugged my drink. When I woke up, I was in a private clinic and he had taken my baby."

The dark place inside her opened, the pain tearing through her, splitting through her soul. "They took my baby."

His arms tightened around her as he held her head to his shoulder, his head bent over her, sheltering her.

"I was six weeks pregnant." The tears fell then. "It was Chaz's baby. But Father didn't care, and neither did Chaz. At the time, he couldn't afford having Chaz singled out in public. A known assassin marrying his daughter?" She nearly strangled on the bitter laughter. "And there wasn't a chance his child was going to be a single mother." Her fists clenched at his shoulders. "I didn't know what they were doing."

"Stop. God, Scheme. Please." His voice was rough, ragged. "Do you think I don't know that, sweetheart?"

She shook her head, the movements jerky. "I was going to leave when I found out about the baby. I begged Chaz to take us away. I didn't know what he was. Who he was . . ."

"Scheme . . ."

"It was my fault." She pulled back, staring up at him, years of regret and loss burning her soul to ashes. "Don't you understand, it was my fault. If I had run when I saw how angry Cyrus was over the baby. If I hadn't told Chaz . . ."

"Then he would have killed you both," he sighed against her hair. "You're alive. And when this is all over, you'll have a chance at living. Hang on to that, Scheme. You'll make him pay."

Her head lifted as she stared into his eyes then. She would be free, but would she still have Tanner? That hard core of ice still glittered in his eyes; anger still sparked in the muted green flecks within the brilliant amber. She hadn't trusted him and she should have. Would she now lose him? And if she did, would freedom really matter?

❖ C H A P T E R   2 3 ❖

CYRUS TALLANT'S ESTATE
PENNSYLVANIA

Cyrus stared out the windows of his office, his gaze roving over the well-manicured lawn, perfectly symmetrical trees and lush flower gardens. A soft dew had settled on the land overnight. Soon, it would be frost. Fall was moving in; the leaves were already turning, spreading their blazing color across the forests surrounding the estate and flashing their warning of the winter to come.

"Have you found her yet?" He clasped his hands behind his back, standing military erect as he watched the Coyote Breed who entered the office.

Dog. That was what he called him. Cyrus didn't allow his Breeds to have identifying names; he had warned the Council of that decades before. Giving them even a small measure of humanity had resulted in the mess they were in now.

Breeds were breeding with pure-blooded humans, diluting God's creations. Not that he was a particularly religious man, but he believed in pure blood. Blood would tell, he always said. Look at the world. The result of mixing pure blood and that tainted by poverty, criminal minds and diseased psyches.

"You haven't answered me," he reminded the Coyote softly, feeling a surge of disgust well inside him.

"We haven't found her yet," Dog answered. "She has to come to ground soon though. We'll get her then."

"What of the soldiers in Sandy Hook—have they learned anything there?"

"Nothing." Dog shook his head. "The heli-jet flew into the area several hours ago though. There's no report of why they were there."

"I want her dead, Dog," he reminded his pet calmly. "She can't be allowed to talk. God only knows what the bitch would tell if she had the chance. Are you certain there are no files missing? No information accessed by her?"

"Nothing, sir," Dog answered. "The files haven't been accessed and nothing left with her. Mr. Bollen believes her escape was unplanned."

John Bollen, Cyrus's heir and second in command, was out in the field when he should be on the estate overseeing the various functions they funded with Council money. This had to get cleared up soon. John was needed here. There were too many plans to destroy the Breeds being left unattended.

Cyrus turned slowly, watching as Dog's bearing became stiffer, more military than ever as Cyrus stared back at him.

"Breeds?" he sneered.

"Breeds were on the mountain, but they seemed to be searching for something as well," he answered.

Cyrus restrained his grimace. He should have had Chaz dispose of her while he had her at the estate, but she was his child. He had raised her here, listened to her laughter and played with her when she was a toddler. Killing her in the home she had been birthed in had seemed distasteful at the time. A lesson learned, he thought with a sigh.

She was flawed. Weak. Only the strong could survive in this battle, and he refused to allow the weakness of his love for his daughter to stay his hand. She had betrayed him. There was no love in her for him, to have betrayed him this way. He had taught her better. Trained her better. But she was weak. Too weak to be allowed to destroy him.

"Do you believe the Breeds have her?" It was his fear, his greatest fear, that the animals would offer her asylum in exchange for what information she might have. If this happened, he would have no choice but to risk his spy within Sanctuary before they could complete the kidnapping of the boy. Scheme knew too much of his organization; she would be a liability to his plans and the Council's needs.

"We believe so, sir," Dog answered. "We believe she's been with Tanner Reynolds. Our Sanctuary contact reports that an emergency call came in before the Breeds' heli-jet flew out to Sandy Hook. She should be there within hours if she is."

Cyrus tightened his lips in fury and turned back to the window. "You can leave now," he barked. "I'll take care of this from here on out."

"Yes, sir." Dog turned and beat a hasty retreat from the office as Cyrus turned and sneered at the animal's back and the door closed behind him.

Chaz had been one of his greatest assets, and now he was gone. Had he lived, Scheme would have already been dead. Instead, the bitch had disappeared and Chaz was dead, with no sign of who had killed him.

She had to have been conspiring with those Breeds long before now. He knew it. He could feel it. How else could they have secreted her away so quickly?

She was a woman, weak, too easily led astray. Just like her mother. A whore, just as her mother had been, Scheme had proved that when she not only allowed herself to become pregnant, but allowed Chaz to bring another man to her bed.

He shook his head. Just like her mother. The bitch that had whelped Scheme had been intelligent, well placed in society, but her bloodline had been tainted by her dockworker grandfather. She had dared, actually dared, to aid in the escape of several Breeds from the lab where she worked.

He had killed her himself, just as he should have killed Scheme. Teaching her to fear him, to obey him hadn't worked. Somehow, she had overcome her fear.

He stared at the picture of her on his desk. The long sable hair, the serious brown eyes, the restrained line of her lips.

He'd thought he had succeeded in raising her properly, but he'd been wrong. So wrong.

Moving to his desk, he picked up the secured cell phone he used to contact his spy at Sanctuary. A Breed. His lips tipped into a smile. For once he had succeeded in the training he believed in so implicitly. If Scheme showed up at Sanctuary, then her stay would be very, very short-lived.

He punched in the text message.

Delay mission. Betrayer of prime importance. Report soon.

The moment the message left the device, the encryption would send it in coded form. A short little note saying hello from a friend. Nothing more. The Breeds would never know it for what it was intended.

He sighed regretfully. He had looked forward to beginning the training on Lyons's son himself. The Council had approved the plan to kidnap the child. He was a first-generation Breed child conceived naturally. They were all curious to see how his genetics differed from his father's. Should the boy prove to be the specimen they were hoping for, then he would be given into Cyrus's care and his training program.

The boy was nine, a little old to be inducted into training, but Cyrus was confident of his chances of success if they could manage to steal him from the secured compound the Breeds used as home base. Sanctuary had the best security, the most merciless guards, but Cyrus had his spy and his spy knew their weaknesses. Knew, because she was one of them.

The Council couldn't stop the breeding of the animals with their human counterparts, but they could use them in their attempts to find a way to destroy the Breeds.

They must be destroyed. At the very least, confined to prevent their attempts to mix with society. They were animals. Animals had no rights, no souls. And he would prove it.

◆　　◆　　◆

Tanner didn't take any chances with Scheme's safety. He might be furious with her, betrayed by her, but her life meant more to him than his own. Enough so that when the heli-jet landed, Callan's personal guards were waiting at the landing pad to escort her to the main estate in the secured Hummer normally used for Callan and the main Breed Cabinet when outside Sanctuary.

He could tell by the look on Jonas's face when he spotted the Hummer that Jonas considered the move a waste of time. Tanner didn't. His gut was on fire with the warning flares of danger slamming into it. His survival instincts were amplified, stronger than they had ever been before, and they were assuring him that no protection was too great right now. No precaution too extreme.

"I've called the Breed Cabinet together." Jonas looked back from the copilot's seat, his silver eyes flashing with steely determination. "They need to be apprised of the situation immediately so we can get additional security in place."

"How do you know the spy isn't on the cabinet?" Scheme asked then. "I've seen the profile associated with this Breed, but no personal information. They were trained just for this. To infiltrate the inner circle of their target and wait. They weren't trained for direct or covert warfare as many of you were. Their tactics are more subtle."

"The cabinet isn't a threat." Jonas shook his head. "I trust every one of them with my life and there are very few that I trust that far. I've been tracking this spy myself, Scheme, I have it narrowed to several parameters, but not the main estate. You'll be safe there."

"Have you pulled Alpha Team back to Sanctuary?" Tanner asked then, referring to the group that had surrounded his cabin in Kentucky and the Breeds Cabal had reported were skulking around Sanctuary.

"Alpha Team is in full force on Sanctuary," Jonas said and sighed. "But I would prefer if that information doesn't leave here. They are our last defense in this endeavor, Tanner. If all else fails, they'll succeed."

"They're watching David?" Tanner asked.

"They're tracking. Callan refuses to change David's bodyguards at present. We'll see how he feels once Scheme makes her report."

Tanner doubted that would change Callan's mind. David's bodyguards were men the pride leader trusted above anyone else. He wouldn't trade them for Jonas's Alpha Team, period.

Beside him, Scheme remained silent. She hadn't said a dozen words since they left the caverns, and her eyes were haunted. He could smell her pain, her fear, her need. Despite the time he had spent trying to slake the mating heat before leaving the caverns, it was only growing again. With each mile the scent of her arousal infused the cockpit of the heli-jet, putting every Breed in it on edge and making Tanner's mood worse.

As the heli-jet settled on the landing pad and the Breed guards rushed to the lowered door as the steps folded out, Tanner placed himself in the doorway, ignoring Cabal's attempt to stand in his place. His eyes scanned the perimeter of the landing pad, noticing the absence of Breeds milling about as they normally were.

His orders to clear the way to the estate had been carried through.

"Let's rock and roll," the commander of the team growled, his dark eyes scanning the area as well, while holding the powerful semiautomatic rifle he carried with relaxed readiness. "The Breed Cabinet is in residence and awaiting your arrival."

"Scheme." Tanner turned to her, holding his hand out, watching as her gaze touched on it with a second's hesitation. Then she placed her slender fingers within his hand, breathing in deeply, doing nothing to still the scent of her fear as he led her from the heli-jet.

Behind him, Cabal, Jonas, Jackal and three of Jonas's main enforcers followed close on their heels, ranging around them as they left the heli-jet and rushed to the Hummer.

"We'll be right behind you," Cabal stated as Tanner pushed Scheme into the backseat of the Hummer.

Tanner nodded quickly before jumping in beside Scheme, his arm going around her to pull her close into the shelter of his larger body as Jonas jumped in beside her.

"Don't touch her," he growled.

Jonas snorted. "I'm well acquainted with mating heat, Tanner."

"Meaning?" Scheme finally spoke.

"Meaning that until the heat lessens, normally within a two- to four-week period, then the touch of any other male is agonizing. The hormones that create the heat sensitize the flesh to the point that only the mate can touch you. No other. Even another woman's touch is painful," Jonas explained.

"Great," she stated mockingly. "And you were of course going to explain all this to me before you decided to mate me, right?"

Tanner shifted in his seat, knowing she wouldn't like the answer. "I had no intention of explaining it to you, unless the mating heat arose."

Anger was overriding the scent of fear now. He could feel her gaze on his profile, searing him with the accusation he knew would be in her eyes.

"In Tanner's defense, there's a ban on revealing that information to anyone as yet unmated," Jonas revealed as Tanner clenched his teeth at the explanation. "Many of the Breeds are aware of it, but no one talks about it."

"And you intend to hide this for how long?" Her voice was strained, a product of her anger and the arousal.

"As long as possible," Tanner informed her. "We've managed to keep a lid on it for ten years. We just need a little longer."

"A little longer for what?" Incredulity filled her voice. "Do you have any idea the outcry knowledge of this is going to produce? What I'm feeling right now is hell, Tanner. And it would effectively shut down a woman's life for the time it lasts. Not to mention the fact that it takes away free will."

His gaze sliced to her. "Have I taken your free will?"

She was breathing hard, her eyes gleaming back at him fiercely. "I'm aware of how furious you are right now and all I want to do is find the nearest bed. So yes, it has. Because otherwise, I'd stay as far away from you as possible until you calmed down."

"You know, Scheme, this idea you have that I'm going to hurt you is starting to piss me off."

"This has nothing to do with thinking you'll hurt me. It has to do with the fact that you have no right to be angry, and I have every right to be offended that you are."

Female logic? It had to be. Tanner stared down at her in disbelief as the Hummer came to a stop in the rear of the estate house.

"I'll figure that comment out later," he growled as the other vehicles pulled in ahead of them and behind them and the Breed guards surrounded the Hummer.

Pushing the door open, he lifted Scheme from the vehicle, careful to keep her in the center of the Breeds surrounding her.

"Son of a bitch, Tanner," Jonas growled at the precautions. "Why don't you just send out a notice that we know for a damned fact we suspect Tallant's mole of trying to gun for her. It would be a hell of a lot simpler."

"Simple never was my way," Tanner snapped as he moved Scheme quickly to the back door that led into the home of the pride leader. "I don't know what made you think it was."

Scheme was fuming as she was led into a large, well-appointed meeting room. Soft lighting lit the shadowed interior, courtesy of the windows that were heavily curtained and shaded. If she wasn't mistaken the small black boxes above them were infrared and thermo heat jammers. Beside them was another device with several digital displays, insurance against any listening devices that were slipped into the room, or any outside attempts to listen in.

A long, wide table filled the center of what Scheme knew had once been an opulent ballroom. The estate had once been held by a group of Genetic Council scientists. Deep beneath it was a labyrinth of cells and medical labs once used to splice the Breed genetics and create the soldiers that the world was never meant to know about.

There were twelve people sitting at that table. The members of the Breed Cabinet, one of which was a lone Wolf Breed that had apparently disappeared off the radar after news of his existence was released. She recognized the faces and knew the profiles of each of them. She trusted none of them.

As they stood to their feet, Tanner led her farther into the room, his hold suddenly gentling as she felt a shaft of humiliation rise inside her. Her father had tortured several of those Breeds. He had been instrumental in the attempted murder of the lone human on the cabinet, Kane Tyler, the brother to the pride leader's wife and the husband to his sister. And he had attempted to use the miscarriage of his wife's child at that time against her. As an experiment. To see if she could conceive again.

Scheme met each of their gazes, lifting her chin as her breathing became heavy and the pain in her chest increased. These men and women had fought to live, to love. They had wanted nothing more than their freedom, and it was something her father was determined to see destroyed.

"Callan." Tanner held her close to his side as he addressed the Breed at the head of the table. "I would like to present my mate, Scheme Tallant."

The silence was deafening. She watched as two of the women, Sherra Tyler and Dawn Daniels, exchanged glances, before Dawn pushed her fingers through her short, golden brown hair.

"Scheme, welcome to Sanctuary." Callan's voice was calm, distant. "Jonas, it seems, has been lax in informing the cabinet of your work on our behalf. Let me be the first to thank you."

She was shaking her head even as he was speaking. "Don't," she whispered, ignoring Tanner's warning grip on her side. "Don't thank me, Mr. Lyons. What I've done isn't that much. And my presence here could only complicate your lives. I'm sorry for that."

Callan breathed out heavily before waving his hand to the empty chairs. "Please, sit down. Would you like something to drink? A snack?"

"Coffee?" She was dying for coffee.

"Yeah, fix her a cup of coffee, Sherra." Dawn picked that moment to speak, her smile mocking as she stared back at Scheme. "One of the large cups."

"Dawn," Tanner snapped as he dropped into the chair beside Scheme.

Dawn rolled her eyes.

"You don't drink coffee?" Scheme swallowed tightly as she glanced at the amused expressions of those around the table.

"Mates in mating heat don't drink coffee, Miss Tallant," Merinus Tyler announced from her husband's side. "It makes the symptoms worse. We have decaf if you like, water, or a specially blended tea that we drink during the heat phases."

"Phases?" This was starting to sound worse by the second.

"We'll get back to the mating heat later," Callan announced. "Have the tea, Miss Tallant. Merinus seems to thrive on it."

Sherra rose from her chair then, walked to the sideboard and poured an amber-colored liquid into a glass of ice before moving around the table and setting it by Scheme's side. Scheme had no intention of touching it. She stared at it for a moment, feeling the dryness of her throat, her mouth, wishing she didn't feel like a lamb in the middle of a carnivore's feast.

"Here." Tanner picked up the glass, brought it to his lips and took a healthy drink. "I promise, it's safe."

She was going to collapse. Scheme could feel something buckling inside her. A need to reach out to him despite the anger she could still feel in his gaze.

"We wouldn't poison you, Scheme," Sherra announced, her ice blue eyes warmer than Scheme had expected. "Jonas had his assistant relay your file once he realized where you were and how to breach the caves. We're aware of what you've lost, and the sacrifice you've made for the Breeds. We wouldn't re-pay that by poisoning you."

Scheme's gaze moved to Callan. "Did he tell you what I re-ported?"

Callan's gaze flashed with merciless fury.

"Tallant is going to attempt to take David?" he asked, though she could see he well believed it. "It won't be the first attempt that has been made, Scheme. I doubt it will be the last."

As he spoke, his wife reached over, laying her slender hand on his arm as his voice echoed with a primal growl.

Merinus Tyler had just passed her thirty-fourth birthday, not that one could tell. She didn't look a day older than she did the day she stood beside her lover, Callan Lyons, and announced to the world that Breeds existed. There were no lines at her eyes or lips. Her skin was still fresh, youthful. Only her eyes appeared older.

"In the past ten years, Cyrus Tallant's spy hasn't been in a place of trust within the Breed community," Scheme stated firmly, adopting the brittle shell she had used all her life when confronted with a situation guaranteed to throw her off balance. "His spy is now in place. Within a week, perhaps a few days more, that spy will make his move to take David. There were no details; the only clue I have of when or how it's going to happen is a conversation I overheard between Cyrus and his second in command, John Bollen. The pickup point isn't heavily defended because of the difficulty of accessing the compound on foot or by vehicle. Cyrus will fly in, pick up your son and his kidnapper, and fly out before you have him on radar because of a particular blind spot. And the spy knows the location of the transponder you've placed just below David's skin in the event of a kidnapping."

Surprise, shock, fury. It all erupted in the room as Merinus turned to her husband with a cry of distress.

"Only a few people know about the transponder," he snapped. "It's undetectable."

Scheme nodded. "A prototype that you acquired from Vanderale Industries in Africa." She nodded. "He knows that much, though he's not been able to learn who created it, or if there are more."

Callan's lips flattened as he turned to Kane Tyler.

The ex-military head of Sanctuary's security was staring back at Scheme with brutal gray eyes as Callan spoke softly to him. Kane nodded sharply before his gaze moved behind her.

"Jackal." He said the name coldly.

"I got it, Commander. I'll get on him now." Jackal, the scarred, bass-throated stranger Scheme had fallen into when Tanner had returned her to the caverns had entered the room with Jonas, Cabal and several Breed Enforcers.

Scheme glanced back in time to see him leaving the room quickly.

She turned back to the cabinet. "I have names, locations and profiles of the contacts Cyrus has that I've met. Jonas has most of them, but lately, there's been a stream of purist and supreme race leaders and commanders passing through the Tallant estate. I don't know if he's gaining support or planning to make a larger attack than he's attempted before. I know the Inner Council is losing faith in him."

"Bastards!" Callan cursed. "Why do you think they're amassing?"

Scheme licked her dry lips. "I think they're awaiting the kidnapping of your son and the chaos it will cause. Every Breed alive will be out looking for him. Breeds will begin striking Council strongholds and hitting their members. It's what they want. They want the Breeds to shed blood, they want to prove to the world how vicious, how merciless you can be. And they believe David Lyons's disappearance will do that. Once you're destroyed, they'll then use your son as a base for the new generation of Breeds. Ones they can control. They feel they've learned from their mistakes and that the killers they envision are finally within reach."

It was insane, but Scheme had never believed there was any sanity within the Council to begin with. The scientists that created and oversaw the labs were cold, without emotion. The Breeds were an experiment to them, nothing more. They were disposable because they were created rather than born. They saw them as animals, without soul.

The Breeds were their chance to do the experiments they dreamed of. Learning how far the human body could possibly be pushed, how to immunize against particular diseases, how the brain and the body functioned together. The Breeds were stronger, more enduring than normal humans, which made them perfect for such experimentation.

"Do you have any information that can shed any light on who we're looking for?" Callan asked then, leaning forward intently. "We need more than this, Scheme. We need something to catch one of our own. That won't be easy."

"They're trained in subversive infiltration." She rubbed at her head, trying to think past the arousal that filled it. Tanner was too close, his body too much of a temptation. And she needed. She needed so desperately. "The spy he recruited posed as a Breed that followed his trainers to gain information, when in fact he was no more than a double agent of sorts."

"The same training Tanner received, then?" Callan asked. "The same training many of the Breeds received. We weren't all trained as assassins."

Scheme sighed. "The profiles are similar from the quick glance I caught of it."

Callan chuckled at Tanner's growl. "Let me guess. You were afraid Tanner was our spy?"

Scheme glanced at Tanner. The question didn't set well with him.

"I was."

Callan shook his head, his expression somber, concerned.

"Miss Tallant, I would be pleased to offer you Sanctuary," he said then. "I understand that this moment isn't the best time for what we're doing as far as the mating heat is concerned, but I hope you can stay here and talk to us a bit longer?"

She stared back at him in surprise.

"Yeah." Dawn spoke up then, her voice amused, her gaze cynical. "We can all smell how bad you want to bed the little Bengal."

Scheme felt her face flaming.

"Dammit, Dawn," Tanner retorted. "Drop it."

Dawn rolled her expressive whiskey brown eyes and restrained the smile tugging at her lips.

Scheme hated having something so personal, so uncontrollable being so easily detected by these fierce men and women. Strangely, she didn't hate the arousal that was continually building. The sensitivity of her flesh, the sharp awareness of Tanner sitting so close beside her.

"We need to reschedule this meeting," Tanner said. "Scheme needs to eat and change clothes and rest for a while. She's not going to be able to give you what you need as clearly as she could if she had a break."

Callan glanced at the others before sighing deeply. "Agreed. We'll meet back here in a few hours." He turned to Jonas.

"Get me the rest of those files together, then you can sit down here and explain to me why the agents you and Tanner had in place didn't pull her out of that damned coffin when her father buried her. I'll expect something a bit more than I read in the reports you supplied before heading out to find Tanner."

Tanner froze in the act of helping Scheme from her chair. She went still, the smell of her fear slamming in his face as he stared into her eyes. She knew. She had known there were Breed agents within her father's inner circle that could have helped her, and she had refused to ask for that help.

He knew her now. Knew she would have died rather than ask those men or women to betray themselves. His gaze lifted to Callan, and he saw the condemnation in his brother's eyes. In Merinus's. Kane's. They thought he had known. They thought he had left an innocent woman to suffer, to possibly die in a way that they all knew was filled with horrendous fear and suffering.

And Jonas. Jonas had kept those reports from him.

Tanner loosened his hold on Scheme, turning slowly to face the director of Breed affairs, a low growl building in his chest as Scheme's soft voice whispered his name, only adding fuel to the rage building inside him.

"Tanner had no knowledge of the abuse being perpetrated within the Tallant estate against Miss Tallant, Callan," Jonas said then. "That information was confined to myself."

"Why?" Tanner snarled. "Why didn't you tell me?"

"Because I suspected she might be your mate," he said softly. "Cabal had already made the connection and we needed the information—"

Deliberately, purposely, Tanner loosed the animal clawing inside him on the Lion Breed who had dared to allow Scheme to suffer in such a way. To allow her to be tied *hand and foot with a cold electronic voice counting down her oxygen allowance* within a coffin and buried beneath dirt.

He plowed into Jonas. They hit the wall, plaster cracking then falling away as the force of the two heavy male bodies crashed into it. Before Jonas could recover, Tanner found his feet and righted himself as he jerked Jonas back and slammed his fist into the other man's face. He was pulling back for another strike a second before restraining hands were jerking him back, grappling with him, strident orders barking into his ear.

Tanner roared in outraged fury, struggling to break free as Jonas pushed himself slowly to his feet, a smug smile almost tugging at his lips.

"I said enough, goddammit." Callan was suddenly in his face, amber eyes blazing, his expression furious as Tanner snarled back in his face.

"My fucking mate." Rage was burning hard and hot inside him. Bucking against the hands holding him, he nearly broke free, nearly threw another punch at Jonas before Callan was in his face again, pushing him back as whoever dared to retain their hold on him jerked his arms back and wrapped his powerful arms around his neck. "You knew what that bastard was doing. You fucking knew and you didn't save her."

"No." Scheme's cry diluted the haze of red in front of his eyes; her soft hands slapping into his chest drew his gaze to her furious one.

"It was my choice," she screamed back at him, her cheeks pale with fear and anger and damp with tears that still welled in her eyes. "Do you understand me! It was my choice to make. I knew Jonas's men were part of Father's soldiers. I knew and I didn't ask them to save me."

"Dammit, Tanner, do you think I didn't try to get her to come in?" Jonas yelled back at him, the growl in his voice filled with anger. "Do you think I didn't give her a choice?"

He snarled back at Jonas before leveling his fury back on Scheme.

"Why?" he bit out with primal fury. "Why would you let him do that to you?"

Agony was racing through him. She hadn't just allowed her father to bury her, but she had done it when she had a choice to escape.

"To convince him I knew nothing." Her chin lifted, her brown eyes glittering with furious intensity. "To prove to him that I wasn't betraying him. That my mistakes were mistakes rather than the deliberate attempt to destroy him that they were. Because seeing him destroyed meant more to me than my own life."

Tanner shook off the hands holding him, restraining him. Violence pounded through his bloodstream, created a buzzing in his head that threatened to drown out the voice of reason in his mind.

"Never again," he grated out. "You will never again place yourself in that kind of danger."

Her expression shifted then, became cold, calculating, filled with determination.

"I will do whatever it takes to see that monster destroyed," she declared hoarsely. "This isn't your choice now any more than it was your choice then. Don't make the mistake of thinking for one moment, Tanner, that you can, or will, be allowed to dictate these choices to me. Because it will not happen."

"And don't you think for one moment that I won't tan your hide should you ever, *fucking ever*, make such a choice again."

CHAPTER 24

He'd had enough. Tanner admitted to himself that he had reached the point where he could deal with this situation in a sane and logical manner. His mate had lived in fear, in pain, under the threat of an agonizing death for ten years and he hadn't known. Jonas had known. The Coyotes they had managed to recruit within Tallant's organization had known and reported it to Jonas. But Tanner hadn't known.

"Cabal." He heard the guttural sound of his own voice but couldn't find the need to care that the animal part of his nature had risen so close to the surface.

Cabal had made the suggestion in the caves as they were preparing to meet Jonas at the heli-jet. To keep the pride confused about the mating, to allow them to believe that both of them had mated her. Even Jonas wouldn't know any better. Their scents were too similar, their natures too extreme for the Breed community to ever doubt that it could have happened.

Not that Tanner would allow Cabal to touch his mate in any way. He couldn't handle it. But her protection meant more than his comfort. If the spy thought he and Cabal both had mated her, then they would believe Cabal's senses were too frayed by the mating heat, as well, for him to be watching closely.

He needed Cabal to be able to watch very closely indeed.

"I'm right behind you," Cabal answered as Tanner gripped Scheme's arm and pulled her to the door.

"Tanner." She jerked at her arm, sending a firestorm of possessive determination racing through him. "Stop dragging me around like this."

He could smell her heat, her arousal. He could smell the need and the anger and it spurred his own. But he could also smell her fear, her pain, her discomfort and a sense that the world was falling apart around her.

She had survived her father's abuse because she understood it. She had survived it and dealt with it even as she worked toward his destruction. But she didn't know how to handle acceptance. She had no idea how to handle love.

And he couldn't afford to argue the point with her here. Not while everyone was watching. Not that the cabinet would ever speak of anything that happened inside this room, but he needed their confusion where the mating was concerned. He needed their reactions to the uncertainty of whether or not he and Cabal had continued their games with Scheme.

Before she or anyone else could object, he had her over his shoulder, her squeak of surprise following her hands bracing at his back as she struggled against the dominant hold he had on her.

"Stay still." He tapped her rounded little fanny, smiling tightly as he stalked through the room and headed at a quick lope for the stairs.

"Are you crazy?" she screeched from her upside-down position.

"It's a popular opinion," he assured her tightly as Cabal moved ahead of them, entering the suite before Tanner followed him.

As the door closed behind them, Tanner set her upright on the floor, and before she could voice what appeared to be a very loud protest, he pressed his fingers against her lips indicating silence.

She was fast. Smart. A frown instantly formed between her brows as suspicion filled her eyes.

Turning, she watched as Cabal began checking the room for electronic devices. Several minutes later he stored the small device he was using away and shook his head.

"It's clear," he finally said.

"They're smarter than I thought they were," Tanner muttered as he moved across the room to the electronic jammer at the side of the windows. He found two loosened wires when he disabled the device and lifted the protective covering from it. That wouldn't have disabled it, but it would have severely weakened it.

Shaking his head, he replaced the wires, reset the device and secured it back to the wall. Propping his hands on his hips, he growled low in his throat as he lowered his head and shook it wearily.

"Whoever it is can get into the house easily," Cabal said then. "I didn't expect that."

Tanner lifted his head and stared back at Scheme. He hadn't truly expected it either.

Scheme wrapped her arms over her breasts and stared back at Tanner uncertainly. She could see the concern in his gaze now as he watched her, just as she had seen the hope that she had been wrong. That whoever the spy was, he wasn't in a position that would afford easy entrance into any part of the estate house.

"This is going to be a problem," Cabal said softly.

Scheme looked from Cabal to Tanner. "What's going to be a problem?"

"Convincing the Breeds here in Sanctuary that both of us have mated you." Cabal's grin was all teeth.

Scheme narrowed her eyes back at him. She hadn't forgotten the terror that had filled her the night before when he had held her against the stone wall, acting for all the world as though rape were nothing new to him.

"Good luck," she said sweetly. "It's going to be hard to do when I won't let you within a hundred feet of me."

Cabal grimaced at that, his gaze shifting to Tanner.

"Don't even look at him like that," Scheme ordered roughly as she turned to Tanner. "Tell him to leave, Tanner."

Tanner crossed his arms over his chest. "Cabal, you can spend some time in the bathroom." He nodded to the door that led into the other room.

Scheme stared back at him in shock. "Are you insane?"

"Probably," Tanner grunted. "But everyone in Sanctuary knows us. They know the games we play with our women, and there's been speculation for years that we would end up mating the same woman. I need them to believe that's exactly what happened so Cabal won't be suspected to be watching for danger. Mating heat burns through the senses, Scheme; it makes us weak for a time. Cabal can watch our backs if we play this correctly."

She shot Cabal a glare. "And I'm just supposed to accept that?"

Cabal's expression shifted, became suddenly more relaxed, less cool and hard to read. And regret lay in his eyes. "I had to frighten you, Scheme; otherwise dumbass over there might have convinced himself he really wasn't your mate. He wanted your safety, your protection bad enough that he would have kept hold on that primal part of himself to achieve it. I would never have hurt you."

Her eyes narrowed on him. "I had that part figured out. That doesn't mean I want you in the bed with us."

"Can I watch?" Amusement glittered in his eyes. And a dare. A challenge.

Scheme rolled her eyes. He was serious and she knew it. She glanced at Tanner in time to catch the incredible heat that flared in his eyes at the thought.

These two men had been sharing their women for ten years. They had established a reputation for it, an easy, playful air of sexual amusement. Strangely, that didn't bother her. And it appeared Tanner was more than willing to allow his brother to watch.

Playfully.

Tanner seemed more relaxed, less intense, amusement glittering in his gaze as he stalked to her, his eyes darkening with desire and hunger as his hands suddenly gripped her waist and he picked her up.

She bounced on the bed, gasping as Tanner's fingers went to the snap of her jeans.

Her eyes widened.

"Tanner." Her fingers curled around his wrists. "What are you doing?"

"Too many clothes," he growled.

She tried to bat at his hands as the zipper released and his twin leaned against the door and grinned rakishly. "Are you sure about this? Cabal's still here." He stopped, his head swinging to the side. A warning snarl curled his lips.

"I have no intention of touching," Cabal murmured wickedly. "I'll content myself right here."

Tanner growled again. God, she loved that growl. The way his incisors flashed, that wild light that lit his amber eyes. It was almost an orgasm by itself.

"As long as he just watches," he panted, literally tearing his shirt from his shoulders before his hands went to the belt of his jeans, ripping it free.

"Oh God, this is insane," she wheezed, and she should have been outraged. But she wasn't. She was getting wetter.

A tight smile curved his lips.

"You like that," he purred. Oh my God, he actually *purred.*

He kicked his jeans free of his body, revealing the thick, heavily veined, luscious length of his cock.

Her thighs parted as she licked her lips.

"Kiss me too," she moaned. "I need you to kiss me."

His lashes swept over his eyes as his tongue licked over his lower lip.

He leaned closer. "Can you feel him watching you?"

It was turning him on. It was really turning her on.

"It turns you on," she accused, her eyes trained on his lips. She needed that kiss now.

"I'm a helluva pervert," he admitted, pushing her legs back as he jerked her to the edge of the bed.

Her breath caught as he bent forward, licking at her lips as the head of his cock pressed against the saturated, swollen folds of her sex.

"I can be a pervert too." Her thighs strained against the hold his hands had on them.

He paused, a slow, rakish grin curving his lips.

"Good girl," he purred, the rumbling sound raking up her spine with invisible claws of erotic pleasure. "Show me, pretty thing. Show me the wicked in you."

His lips slanted across hers then, his tongue sliding past her lips, the taste of him exploding in her mouth. And he tasted so good. Wicked, erotic, a banquet of lust, irresistible and combustible.

She sucked his tongue into her mouth, her own twining with it, milking as she discovered the tiny, swollen glands at the side of his tongue and the rich, tempting taste that gathered there.

Moaning, certain she had found ambrosia, Scheme licked, sucked and drew more of it into her mouth. She needed that taste. She needed it to breathe, to live.

Her hands threaded into his hair as she held him to her, writhing beneath him as she tried to impale herself on the thick width of the cock still poised at the entrance to her desperate, needy vagina.

She ached. She ached until the need was a pain. She was certain she would go insane from the need to be fucked. But he didn't fill her, except with his tongue. His tongue pumped into her mouth; his lips moved over hers; his kiss sent a fireball of sensation racing through her.

"Damn you," she cried out weakly as he pulled back, staring down at her with narrowed, glittering eyes. "I need more."

"You need to be spanked." Whiskey-rough, purring with pleasure, his voice and his declaration had her hips jerking, her womb spasming.

"I'm a bad girl," she agreed roughly. "Fuck me first. Then you can spank me."

A wicked smile curled his lips. "Oh no, baby. First, I'm going to spank that pretty ass of yours. I'm going to watch it blush, smell your heat, and then maybe, just maybe, I'll bank all those hot little fires burning inside you."

Her eyes widened as he jerked back from her.

"Tanner, I can't take this." She was burning now, flames erupting beneath her flesh, searing through her as the wracking spasms of need shook her frame.

"Oh, you'll take this, baby," he growled. "And you'll love it."

Before she could fight him, before she could protest, he was sitting on the bed, pulling her over his knees. She was about to come from the heady dominance she could feel rising from Tanner—and the surprising pleasure her submissive position sent whipping through her.

Spankings were a tease. She had been spanked erotically before; it was pleasurable, but with no real clash and bang.

Then Tanner's hand landed on her ass in a short series of sharp, burning caresses. She couldn't call them painful. They were agonizingly pleasurable.

"Oh my God, Tanner. Please. Don't do this to me." Vibrations of sharp, near-orgasmic sensation tore through her womb.

Two more sharp little taps, each on the rounded curve, just above her thigh. They stole her breath. She was so aroused, so ready for him that the primitive submissiveness washing over her was like a heady drug.

His hand fell again. Again. One strike to each cheek, heating her flesh further.

Scheme tossed her head, flipping her hair from her face as her eyes opened and locked with the man standing in the bathroom doorway.

Oh God. She shuddered, feeling her juices easing from her vagina, heating her thighs. Cabal was Tanner's twin in almost every way. Tall, hard, his expression savagely aroused, his jeans cupping and conforming to the impressive erection beneath. And he was watching. His arms crossed over his hard chest, his fists clenched.

A spasm shook her core, rippled to her clit, her womb, then shuddered through her.

Cabal's gaze flickered to Tanner, then to Scheme's ass.

"I won't touch." His voice was savage. "But I'll watch."

There was no denial from Tanner. His hand smoothed over the cheeks of her rear as Cabal's green eyes glittered with hunger as he watched.

Tanner's hand fell again.

"Mine!" he snarled. And once again she felt the declaration clear to her soul. Then she felt his possession in the next caressing tap delivered against her ass.

And it wasn't enough. She needed it harder, hotter. She writhed on his lap, fighting his hold, her hands bracing against his leg as she fought him.

His hand landed harder.

"He can smell your need." Cabal's voice was guttural. "I can smell your need."

Tanner's hand landed again, burning against the cheek of her ass as she stiffened, her eyes drifting closed as savage pleasure swamped her.

Yes, this was what she needed.

A keening cry left her lips as his hand fell again. Again. She was riding an edge so sharp, so high, she was almost terrified. Almost. She needed it, she realized. The overwhelming need for a harder touch, a more savage possession had tormented her for years, leaving her dissatisfied, searching, reaching.

She wasn't searching any longer. Each slap on the cheeks of her ass sent her higher, built the fires hotter.

"Damn, your ass blushes pretty." Tanner's voice was a primal snarl. "Soft and silky and such a pretty burning pink. Like sunrise."

She was hotter than sunrise. She was blazing like a comet.

"Like a peach," Cabal whispered then, his voice almost reverent. "Ripe and ready to bite into."

Scheme whimpered as the lust suddenly spiked hotter, brighter. She had never done that, that she knew of. Never had sex while she knew another man watched.

The hollow shame wasn't there, as she would have expected. The discomfort that she had to fight was absent.

This wasn't about the sexuality alone. She could see the need in Cabal's eyes. He had been such an integral part of

Tanner's sexual life for years, immersing himself in the pleasures his brother allowed him to share in, that he needed this.

She could feel it as sharply as she felt Tanner's hands on her rear. Cabal needed at least this much. Just for a while.

And she needed it. Something to wipe away the memory of years of shame, the knowledge that what she had with Chaz hadn't been love, but a degrading enforcement of control.

This wasn't about control. Tanner had somehow sensed her needs from the start, and he was giving her what she craved.

She writhed on his lap, crying out in pleasure, each slap sending her higher until she was nothing but a mass of lust, need, hunger.

She was dying in his arms in the midst of a pleasure she couldn't control, and for the first time in her life, she didn't want to control.

Scheme gave herself to the whipping ecstasy rushing through her system. Tanner's sharp caresses were firm, then soft, gentle then burning. Each slap vibrated to her clit, causing it to swell further, throb, ache. Her hips writhed over his thighs, clenching together, forcing friction against the little bundle of nerves as she felt the spirals of release building in her womb.

She was going to come. She could feel it. She was going to explode.

"There you go, pretty girl." Tanner's voice was so rough, so graveled, it was primal. "Feel it burn. All the way into that tight pussy. Feel it, Scheme."

The sharp caresses were more rhythmic now, a steady, hard vibration of flames that began to pulse in her clit.

"You're so wet I can feel it on my thigh," he snarled. "So fucking hot you're going to burn me."

Slap. Slap.

"Come for me, baby. Spill all that sweet cream. When you do, I'm going to lap every drop of it up."

She exploded. Cords of lightning wrapped around her clit, electrifying her, tearing her senses from her mind and sending her into an explosion of fiery, desperate release.

She heard her own strangled scream as she arched in his

arms, feeling his fingers force their way between her thighs, plunging into the impossibly tight confines of her cunt.

She was losing her senses. Dying. Her vagina convulsed, raining the silky spill of her release to those thrusting fingers and jacking her higher into her orgasm.

She was limp, shuddering violently, and she needed more. Oh God, she needed more.

CHAPTER 25

The animal was free inside Tanner. As he felt the wash of her release soaking his fingers, smelled the complete submission to her pleasure and the burning, desperate need inside her, the animal tore free.

It was a part of himself he had always feared. He kept it locked away, hidden, fearing that releasing it would return him to the creature he had been before Callan had saved him.

There was no locking it away now.

Lifting Scheme from across his legs, he laid her back on the bed, knelt on the floor and buried his lips between her legs.

God, her pussy was sweet. Like cream. Like syrup. It clung to his lips, drew his tongue and made him drunk on the taste of her.

He loved eating her. Licking her, sucking at the pearly clit, feeling the soft, silky curls covering her pussy. Rounded thighs clenched on his cheeks, and he loved that too. The way she writhed beneath him and he had to clench his fingers on her hips to hold her still.

She didn't want gentleness; she needed all of him. He

could feel it, smell it. She wanted the animal taking her, and it
was a damned good thing, because he couldn't restrain it.

Lapping at her, he drew the sweet taste of her cream into
his mouth, growling at the addictive sweetness as she shuddered and bucked beneath him again, spilling more. She was
all soft, liquid heat.

The glands in his tongue were throbbing, so engorged and
swollen it was painful. He needed her kiss. He needed her
sucking the hormone from him as he fucked her.

He had to fuck her. His cock was so engorged, so tight he
was in pain. Delicious pain.

Dragging himself from the delicacy he was consuming, he
pushed her further up the bed before settling himself between
her thighs.

He was growling and there wasn't a damned thing he could
do to stop it. His lips had pulled back from his teeth, and the
rumbling animalistic sounds were pouring from his chest.

Rather than terrifying Scheme, as it should have, her
brown eyes glittered with another surge of lust. Her hips lifted
to him, her lips opened, and the world exploded in a haze of
incredible, incurable lust.

Tanner slanted his lips over hers, spearing his tongue into
the heated, hungry depths of her mouth as he thrust his cock
into the milking depths of her pussy.

Sweet heaven. It was good. It was nirvana. It was ecstasy.
He worked his hips, circling, rotating, pushing his dick inside
her as the muscles clamped on it, sucked at it. Just as her
mouth, hot and sweet, sucked at his tongue.

Her hands clamped on his ass, her body bowing toward
him, gasps of primal hunger leaving her throat as she forced
him deeper.

God, he didn't want to hurt her. He didn't want it like
this . . .

A rumble of a snarl left his chest as his hips slammed forward, burying every hard, desperate inch of his erection inside
her. To the hilt, his balls, tight and hard, pressing against her
ass as he tore his lips from hers to breathe.

He needed to breathe. To think.

"No." She followed, her head lifting, one hand snagging the long strands of his hair, tangling in it and jerking his mouth back to her. Eating at his lips, her tongue licking at him, searching for more of him as her hips writhed beneath him.

He was lost. Lost.

His tongue plunged into her mouth as his body became controlled by one thing only: the animal marking his mate, taking her, slamming his cock inside her with primal, primitive force.

He wasn't going to last. Not long enough. He wanted to fuck her forever. Linger in the brilliant heat of her pussy and memorize every sensation whipping through his body.

Next time, he promised, growling as his lips left hers and moved to her neck. The hormone had eased from his tongue, but the need hadn't eased from his body. Moving his arms beneath her, he cupped her ass in his hands, came over her and gave her everything he had never given another.

All of him. Desperate, growling, surging hunger. His hips churned into her; sweat dripped from his body and his senses focused on one thing. Only one thing. Scheme.

Her release was building, whipping through her. He could sense its peak nearing. Just a little further. A little harder. He could only give her what he needed and rush into the flames along with her.

His lips opened, his teeth sinking into her shoulder as she ruptured around him. Her pussy clenched, spasmed, grabbed hold of his dick and milked it until he had no choice, no will.

He felt the barb extending, a thickened, stiff extension pressing out from beneath the hood of his dick, locking into the back of those tight, gripping muscles, and spurting inside her as his release swept over him.

Deep spurts of his semen filled her snug pussy as the barb spilled the soothing, heat-easing hormone that would give her a small respite from the hungers gnawing at both of them.

Tanner kept his head buried in her neck, his tongue lapping at the bite he had left on her, smelling his scent inside her, moving through her veins, filling her body.

His scent.

Tanner growled in satisfaction at the presence of the mark, both on her shoulder and now a part of her very essence. She was his. She belonged to him and him alone.

As the last pulsing, desperate shudders eased from his body, his head turned, eyes opening to see Cabal where he stood by the bathroom door.

His brother was aroused, desperately aroused, but a glimmer of satisfaction raged in his eyes. Cabal could sense it, Tanner knew, the primitive marking, the satisfaction that glowed through himself and Scheme.

As Tanner sighed wearily, the heat temporarily stilled, his senses replete, he realized he was leaving his brother behind. Again.

Drawing from Scheme, he wrapped his arms around her as she cuddled against his chest and drifted into sleep. She would rest for a while. Then, he would have to make certain she ate before taking her to Ely. The tests had to be done; he knew that, though he hated it.

Cabal caught his gaze again as he moved in the doorway, indicating the connecting room on the other side of Tanner's. Cabal's room.

Tanner tucked the blankets around Scheme, keeping her warm as she slept, before rising from the bed and pulling his jeans on.

Barefoot, he followed Cabal into the other room, moving instantly to the small refrigerator his brother kept in his suite and the sandwich meat there. A loaf of bread sat on the tray on the small side table beside the bar, as well as small packages of condiments.

Pulling a paper plate from beneath the table, he piled the bread with sliced meat, squeezed several packs of mustard onto it and then bit in with relish before pulling a beer free.

"I don't think so." The beer was snatched out of his hand and replaced with water.

Tanner frowned.

"The alcohol only increases the mating heat," Cabal explained. "Listen to me for once or you'll exhaust her more than necessary."

Tanner shook his head, but he didn't argue. He took the sandwich and the water and moved back to the doorway to check on Scheme.

"You'll know if she wakes up," Cabal commented behind him. "We have to talk."

Tanner finished the sandwich in silence before polishing off the water and turning back to Cabal.

Ten years. He had spent the past ten years making certain his brother knew he was part of something. Not just a family, but an integral part of something. For years Tanner had assumed they would mate the same woman, continue on as they had started when Tanner had brought Cabal his first woman. Cabal had been twenty-five, and he had never known a woman's caress or her soft kiss. Had never spilled his pleasure or given himself up to the erotic, exotic scents of a woman's desire.

"Stop regretting, Tanner." Cabal sighed. "I don't. This is right, and I'm not feeling left out."

Tanner's lips quirked.

"I would have felt very left out," he admitted. "I would have been pissed, Cabal."

Cabal grunted on a soft laugh. "You're too spoiled, Tanner. First Callan and the girls spoiled you; now the world spoils you. You haven't heard the word 'no' since you left the labs."

"Sure I have." Tanner grimaced. "Scheme tells me no every chance she gets."

"Oh yeah, she counts." Cabal chuckled as he moved to his dresser and pulled free a clean shirt.

"What happened to your shirt?" Tanner knew he had been wearing one when they entered the bedroom.

"It's in shreds." Cabal shrugged. "Restraint isn't my strong suit."

Tanner shook his head. "Why did you stay and watch then?"

"You need someone to watch your back." Cabal flicked a look over his shoulder. "Because both our scents needed to be in that room to make this work."

"Ely's tests will prove the mating," Tanner pointed out. "There's no way to keep it a secret from her."

"Ely doesn't have to do our damned tests," Cabal retorted. "Not on us. Just on Scheme, and just enough to create the hormonal supplement she'll need to function through this. If we're going to keep her alive, Tanner, then we're going to be careful." Savage fury flashed in Cabal's eyes. "I won't lose you, Tanner, and I won't allow you to lose her. We're going to catch the bastard this time. I can feel it."

"I don't want to lose you any more than I want to lose my mate, Cabal," Tanner warned him.

"No danger." The confidence in his brother's voice never failed to amaze him. "I didn't survive that damned pit that long, Tanner, just to eat an assassin's bullet. My senses are sharper than yours, especially now that you're in mating heat. With the spy believing both our senses are dulled, my job will be made that much easier. While the two of you are in the cabinet meeting later, I'll begin checking a few things out, and watching to see who comes upstairs. They won't expect that."

Tanner pushed his fingers through his hair as he stared back at Cabal. It made sense. There were rumors about the brothers, suspicions that their animalistic abilities went much deeper than anyone suspected. And they were right. Tanner's were sharper, a hell of a lot sharper than most Breeds, but Cabal's were even stronger. So strong that sometimes he worried about what his brother actually sensed from those around him.

Tanner breathed out tiredly. "That doesn't fix the problem that you aren't in mating heat."

Cabal's lips quirked. "Doesn't matter, the scent is all over me. Only a Bengal would know the difference, and since there are no other Bengals here, we won't have a problem."

Tanner inhaled sharply, separating the scents in the room and narrowing his eyes. The scent wasn't just on Cabal; it was a part of him.

"What's going on?" he asked the other man. "And don't lie to me, Cabal. You'll just piss me off."

"Hell if I know." Cabal shook his head in irritation. "The hunger isn't there, Tanner. I'm not in mating heat for your woman. But the scent is there, like it's weeping from my pores. Let's just see what the hell happens."

"We need Ely on this," Tanner argued. "It could be important."

"Do you trust her with Scheme's life?" Cabal asked. "That's a question you better answer before you bring anyone into this."

"We have to get Callan up here," Tanner decided. Damn, this was beginning to get complicated. "We can't do any of this without his cooperation. And we have to make it work."

"We'll make this work." Cabal's voice was hard. Savage. "No matter what, Tanner, we *will* make this work."

· CHAPTER 26 ·

There were few times in her life that Scheme could say she had been warned about the hell she was getting ready to step into. Until she arrived at Sanctuary.

Tanner, Cabal and Callan had warned her about the examination she needed to allow. It was an examination. How freaking painful could a simple examination be? Some blood samples, some swabs, a poke and a prod here and there. No big deal.

Yet, something had warned her. She had declined eating until afterward. The sight of blood being drawn from her arm always had the power to make her slightly ill. It was much more comfortable without food lying heavy in her stomach.

But had she eaten, there would have been no way to keep it in her stomach. The pain didn't make sense, even after the explanation. That the Breed mating hormone made her flesh so hypersensitive that no one other than her mate could touch her. Nature's insurance, the Breed doctor theorized, to make certain that the mates were given time to bond emotionally while the hormone worked to make certain the small amount of human-compatible Breed sperm had a chance to fertilize the female eggs the hormone forced from the ovaries. Eggs whose DNA was altered by the hormone, which acted as a virus at the genetic level. The process was similar to the one used to change the human sperm during the genetic alterations to create the Breeds.

She had become one of nature's experiments; unfortunately, her body was a defective testing ground.

Dry heaves still wracked her, long minutes after the doctor, formerly a Council-trained scientist, Elyiana Morrey, finished her exam.

Tanner stood to one side of the cot Scheme still sat on; Cabal lounged against the wall on the other side of the room. Both men were tense, dangerously so. It would have been hard to tell which was the supposed *mate* from the way the two men were acting.

"You need to go outside," Scheme told Tanner, growing more nervous by the minute with the subtle rumbles of a growl in his chest. "Both of you." Cabal wasn't much better.

"Get used to it." Ely's smile was warm, if slightly uncomfortable, as she glanced at the two Breeds. "Breeds become slightly intense when they mate."

Scheme was so getting tired of that word. Mate. She might love that insane Breed, but she was on the cusp of killing him. The word *mate* just irked her that much worse. Because he hadn't warned her. Because he had taken her, driven her insane with need and then decided to change all the rules on her and play her game without being willing to allow her to participate. She had gone through hell more than once in her efforts to find the identity of Cyrus's spy. Now, Tanner and Cabal both wanted to wrap her in cotton and keep her from the final inning of the dangerous confrontation they all knew was coming.

"I don't want to get used to it," she grated as she forced back the dry heaves and gripped tighter the sheet that covered her breasts. "Is this finished yet? Can I get dressed?"

"You need a hormonal injection first," Ely argued. "Tanner and Cabal are trained medics though, so I can allow one of them to give the injection. It won't cause any pain that way."

She glanced up at Tanner, watching as his jaw flexed. When Ely turned back to him with the syringe, Cabal had paced to the door of the examination room, appearing to listen to something in the corridor.

"The door's locked, Cabal," Ely informed him, not for the first time.

Cabal continued to stand with his back to them, his head tilted as Tanner took the syringe.

"The upper arm works fine, Tanner," Ely instructed him.

With two fingers, Tanner stretched the flesh tight; then he laid the auto-syringe against her skin. There was barely a sensation of heat before he was lifting it away and handing it back to Ely.

"And these hormones do what?" Scheme asked tiredly.

"They ease the mating heat. I'll have the capsules prepared by morning. One each day, with food if you don't mind," Ely ordered. "The mating heat can leave you defenseless without it, unable to function under even the most peaceful circumstances, let alone the surprises we sometimes get at Sanctuary."

"The examination is finished now," Ely announced. "You can dress and leave."

Scheme slid from the cot.

"Scheme." Ely stopped her as she moved to step away. Turning back to the other woman, Scheme watched as the doctor's gaze flickered with indecision. "It was very brave of you, what you've done for the past ten years."

"Brave?" Scheme shook her head at the word. "It wasn't bravery, Dr. Morrey, it was fear. He won't stop until the world bows to its knees before the Genetics Council. That's what I fear. Bravery had nothing to do with it."

She had been sired by a monster. A creature so evil, so immoral, that even she couldn't make sense of it.

Breeds were animals, he always said. Creations. They had no souls and therefore they felt nothing but topical pain. They were weapons, tools, and as such had no rights, not even that of a peaceful death.

"However you define it." Ely shrugged. "It took an incredible amount of courage. And we thank you for it."

And that made Scheme highly uncomfortable. They were thanking her for what? For the Breeds that had died because she wasn't fast enough, smart enough or deceptive enough to save them? She didn't need thanks for what she had done, because there was much much more that she had been unable to do.

But rather than arguing the point, she only nodded tightly before moving behind the privacy screens to remove the hospital gown and dress. She pulled on the light gray sweats emblazoned with *Breeds Rule* across the front of the shirt and pushed the sleeves up on her arm impatiently.

Rather than focusing on Cyrus Tallant and what she couldn't change, Scheme chose to focus instead on the irritation rising inside her. She began with the clothes Tanner had brought in for her. If she didn't focus on something mundane, then she would lose the last shreds of her control over the worry and fear that somehow she was going to fail in saving David Lyons, just as she had failed in saving her own child.

So she thought about the sweats. Something she never, ever wore. She hated scratchy materials. Sweats were just scratchy. She pulled the ultra-soft velvety socks over her feet and hoped she could find some decent clothes today.

Soft materials soothed her. They caressed her with comfort. They endured and gave her joy.

"I want to go shopping." She stepped from the curtained area and faced Tanner and Cabal. "I need clothes."

Ely's gaze raked over her as she stepped from behind the screen. "The sweats look fine."

"The sweats don't feel fine." She pulled at the snug, *scratchy* material. "I need something soft. Where are my clothes?" She looked at Tanner.

He grimaced. "Cabal didn't bring them."

Cabal wiped his hand down his face, obviously hiding a smile as he glanced away from her.

She leveled a dark look on Cabal.

"My little striped kitty," she crooned. "You are dead meat."

His brow arched.

She wasn't comfortable with Cabal playing her mate as

well, but as long as he was, she could at least have some fun with it. Her chances at light entertainment were rapidly dwindling.

She caught Ely's surprised look. "You haven't seen the stripes?" She opened her eyes wide. Obviously, Ely hadn't seen Cabal without his shirt on. "They're amazingly erotic."

And if she wasn't mistaken, the lightest of blushes was tinting Cabal's cheeks. Interesting. After all it was reported he and Tanner had done with their women, he could still blush.

"I've seen the stripes," Ely sighed. "I just hoped Jonas was wrong and these two hellions hadn't mated the same woman. Sharing is all well and good, but this just takes it to the extreme."

"You seem disapproving, Ely." Scheme frowned. "This mating heat stuff is biological, right? It's not like they could help it. Or can they?" She gave both men a suspicious gaze, though her gaze lingered longest on Tanner and promised the most retribution.

"The Breeds have no control over the mating heat, Scheme," Ely agreed as she crossed her arms over the front of her white lab coat and watched the three of them with a frown. "This was just something I had hoped wouldn't happen. Especially in light of the fact that I knew neither of them would allow me to examine them, or to take their blood."

Cabal's expression became closed, Tanner's resigned.

Now, this was interesting. "Why?" she asked both of them.

"I don't like needles." They both answered at the same time. A very well-rehearsed answer.

"Hmm," she murmured disbelievingly. "You can explain that one in the room. While I'm ordering my clothes."

If she was going to take the chance of dying by an assassin's hand, she was going to do it in silk, not in scratchy sweats. A person needed a little style, even in death.

"Ely, I hope you don't need to do this again," Tanner remarked as Scheme headed for the door. His voice didn't sound comforting.

"One week," Ely announced. "But by then, it will be easier for her.

Tanner grimaced. "It better be."

"Every Breed mate has a weekly examination, no matter what. I'll send you the schedule for the next few months in a couple of days."

Taking Scheme's arm, Tanner moved to the door as Cabal unlocked it and ushered her into the hall.

"Where now?" She had been dragged from one end of the stately mansion to another today. The century-old plantation home had had several wings added to it and, even now, was being added to by the Breeds. Its sprawling, graceful design accepted the additions easily, but made for a hell of a walk when you were being shown around.

"You said you needed some clothes," Tanner reminded her a little too smoothly.

"Yeah. I did. But you didn't seem inclined to go shopping at the time."

His hand pressed warningly against her back. As though she didn't know how to watch what she said. She wasn't a complete moron. She had survived betraying her father for ten years, that should qualify her as rocket scientist intelligent.

"So where do I get to go shopping?" she asked him, her voice sweet, her gaze promising vengeance if he didn't stop with the big bad Breed routine.

"What's your favorite clothier?" he asked as they moved into the first floor of the estate.

"Vilado," she answered, naming the exclusive Italian designer she had a fondness for.

"Barring Vilado."

Now, didn't that just figure?

"Why don't you just tell me my choices?" She sighed as he led her to the curved staircase leading to the second floor and their suite of rooms. Behind them, she heard Cabal snicker.

Tanner named off three less than satisfactory choices. The major chains were overpriced and underquality. She pursed her lips in dissatisfaction but reminded herself that she could at least find a few outfits that would make her feel less like an orphan castoff.

"You can give me your sizes and we'll call the outlet in

Richmond. I'll have one of the pilots fly in and pick the clothes up. They'll be back by the end of the evening," he announced as they stepped into their room.

And came up very short in surprise.

"Oh, there you are, Tanner." Frazzled, appearing slightly off balance and guilty as hell, Tanner's female assistant, Jolian Brandeau, straightened from the papers laid out on a table that sat in the middle of the small sitting area just inside the room. Jolian, or Joley, was a regular at news conferences with Tanner, though she rarely had much to say.

Tanner pushed Scheme behind him quickly, his body tensing, a growl rumbling in his throat as the dark-haired assistant paled, her blue eyes blinking owlishly behind a pair of slender-framed glasses.

"Jolian, what the hell are you doing in here?" Cabal came around them, his body vibrating with anger as he faced the short, rounded young woman who stared back at him with a flicker of her own anger.

That anger rapidly receded as she blinked once more, her gaze then staring back at them with a hint of confusion.

"I was looking for the notes Tanner had done a few weeks ago on the interview he wanted to do with National News." She gripped her hands in front of her, her fingers twining together nervously. "He said they were in here." She waved her hand nervously around the room.

"And you couldn't ask me for them, why?" Tanner questioned brutally.

She licked her lips as Scheme forced her way around Tanner and watched the young Breed.

Jolian Brandeau. She was a panther Breed that the French labs had created and had declared a failure in nearly every area she had been tested in. Scheme recognized her easily. She was always silent when she accompanied Tanner on an interview or during a news release. Barely five-four, rounded when other Breeds were lithe and well toned. Scheme believed she remembered the girl's age as twenty-four, as well as her training: infiltration.

Tanner and Cabal obviously remembered it as well.

"You don't have clearance to be upstairs, Jolian," Tanner reminded her harshly.

Jolian tucked her ribbon-straight hair behind one ear, shifted and let her gaze fall to the floor. "No, sir," she whispered before flicking a miserable glance toward Cabal.

She didn't even act like a Breed. She acted like a soft, cuddly little coed. If this girl was a spy, then she was the least likely spy Scheme had ever laid her eyes on.

"I didn't want to mess the interview up, Cabal." She turned to Cabal rather than facing Tanner. "I thought I could get the notes. I forgot them before Tanner left, and I knew he would be upset."

"He's even more upset now." Tanner's voice lowered to a primal rasp as the bedroom door suddenly opened and Dawn stalked in dressed in her enforcer uniform, several other female Breeds flanking her, weapons drawn.

"You set off your alarm, Tanner?" Dawn stared at Tanner in confusion, as did Scheme. Where the hell was an alarm?

"Oh God," Jolian whispered, staring at Cabal beseechingly now. "I swear to God, Cabal, I was just looking for those notes."

Jolian looked like she was going to start crying any second.

"She was up here without clearance." There wasn't a shade of remorse in Tanner's voice. "Take her downstairs until I can question her."

"Jolian?" Dawn stared at Tanner in shock before staring back at the young Breed. "Searching your room?"

"Cabal?" Jolian whispered his name faintly. "I was just looking for those notes."

Scheme glanced at Cabal. His expression was closed, cold as he stared back at her.

He repeated Tanner's order. "Take her downstairs, Dawn. And put a guard on her."

Jolian's face went white, her blue eyes darkening with something akin to agony. Scheme knew that look well. Betrayal. If she was a spy, then there was no damned wonder she had stayed hidden in Sanctuary for so many years.

"Come on, Jo." Dawn shook her head as she gripped the girl's arm, confusion and a shadow of disbelief in her eyes as she glanced at the shorter girl. "Let's go downstairs. I'm sure we'll figure it all out."

Dawn stared at Cabal for one long, silent moment, until he turned his back on her and moved to stand on the other side of Scheme.

Interesting. Very interesting.

Jolian's shoulders fell before she lifted her gaze to Tanner. "You left the notes on the table," she said faintly. "I forgot them. I didn't want to disappoint you again."

"Then you should have asked me for them."

"Come on, Jo, we'll figure this out downstairs." Dawn led her to the door before glancing back at Tanner. "Don't take all day, okay? I have work to do, and if I don't get it done, I'm not going to be in a good mood."

Tanner chided her then. "Are you ever in a good mood? I'll be down later. Make certain Jonas is around as well. I need to talk to him about his guard's lack of diligence in letting unauthorized personnel on the family level."

The door closed behind Dawn with a snap as Scheme felt the tension emanating from both men now.

"Not her," Scheme muttered as Tanner stalked to his dresser, jerked the electronic bug detector from inside and began running it over the room.

Cabal moved to the small table and began sorting through the small stacks of paper there.

"You don't know it's not her," Cabal responded, his voice grating. "You didn't see a name on those files, remember? And she was trained in infiltration."

"And failed." Scheme rolled her eyes in exasperation. "Do you have any idea how many kill orders I shredded on that girl? She failed every program they put her in. What is she? Twenty-four now? She was lucky she didn't have a stroke during the rescues. The girl is terrified of her own shadow."

"No, she's not." Cabal flipped a notebook to the love seat beside him. "There're the interview notes." His gaze was cold as they latched on to Scheme. "Don't let her fool you. I've seen her when no one is watching. She's rather organized when she thinks she's alone."

Scheme shook her head. "It's not her."

"Drop it," Tanner ordered firmly. "You don't know who it is and neither do we."

"Cabal just found the notes she was looking for. That poor girl, you nearly scared the life out of her, you know."

"And she could have nearly fucking killed you." Tanner gripped her arm, turning her to face him as the fury in his eyes lashed at her. "Stop protecting someone you know nothing about."

"And stop treating me like a twit that doesn't know any more than that scatterbrained little Panther you just terrorized." She jerked away from him, striding across the room before facing both of them with cold resolve. "I'm a profiler, Tanner. I know my job. And I know that girl is the last one who would ever attempt to spy on anyone. The damned notes were on the table, just like she said."

"Convenient." His lip lifted in a snarl.

"Convenient or not, you're wrong. I know my stuff, and I know it's not her."

"Good, you know your stuff, Miss Profiler," he growled. "Use it. Tomorrow evening Callan and Merinus are hosting a little party for our mating and upcoming marriage. Find our spy, then I'll stop suspecting every Breed trained in espionage and infiltration that I catch going through my personal room. How does that one suit you?"

"About as much as sleeping alone tonight," she informed him sweetly. "Just damned fine."

"Sleeping alone?" His arms crossed over his chest as he glanced at the bed. "You go ahead and try it, sweetheart. You're already burning as hot for me as I am for you. Neither one of us will make it another ten minutes before I have you flat on your back and my dick buried as deep inside your body as you can take me."

Her face flamed almost as hot as her body.

"Cretin," she snapped.

Tanner growled, his lips pulling back from his teeth as he

pushed his fingers through the fall of sun-streaked black hair that fell around his face. Cabal grunted before moving to the connecting door between the two suites.

He didn't speak. No good-bye, go to hell, catch you later or anything similar. When he entered his own room, the door closed so quietly she didn't even hear the snick of the latch.

"Look." Scheme finally inhaled deeply. "Just give her the benefit of a doubt before you do anything harsh. You asked me to trust you; now I'm asking you to trust me. I'm telling you, you lock that kid up in a cell and terrorize her, and you'll regret it."

"Beats regretting the possible consequences if I don't. Your death," he pointed out.

"Trust me, Tanner. She's not your spy."

"Are you willing to bet your life on it?" he asked her then.

Was she? Was she ready to put herself that firmly on the line for a Breed she knew only through her lab files? Lab files filled with failures, punishments, and years of living with the knowledge that she would die because of those failures. Even the psychologists assigned to try to mend whatever was broken within the girl to make her productive hadn't been able to fix her.

Jolian Brandeau was one of the few Breeds that clearly stood out in Scheme's mind. Because everything in her initial psych files had pointed to a strong, adaptable Breed female. But nothing in her performance had proved it.

"At this point," she finally answered him, "I'm not willing to bet my life on anyone but you and Jonas. But something tells me you and Cabal had better walk a very fine line with that kid, because breaking her would be easier than you believe."

"And you say that because of her files," Tanner pointed out. "Files that could have been wrong, Scheme. I could smell her guilt while she stood there facing us. I could smell her attempts to hide something. Files are not always right."

"No, I say that because of her eyes," she said softly. "She has very sad, very old eyes, Tanner. And whatever was going on here, whatever she was hiding, it wasn't an attempt to kill.

Your harsh attitude with her hurt her. That's not something that can be faked as easily as you think it can be. Don't focus on her and risk overlooking the real threat."

"I'll overlook nothing. No one." Before she could evade him, he had her in his arms; his hands were tugging at her sweatshirt as he pressed her against the back of the love seat, jerking the sweatshirt up and over her head before he moved to her pants. "Because I'd die without this."

His hand cupped between her thighs, causing her to lift to her tiptoes as sensation slammed inside her. Pleasure. Oh God, the pleasure was so intense that sometimes she felt she would die from it.

"Feel that," he rasped, his fingers massaging her wet flesh, stroking her, sending tendrils of sensation to race through every nerve ending. "Feel it, Scheme. Do you want to lose this forever?"

Before she could answer, before she could form a coherent reply, his lips were on hers and he was bracing her on the back of the love seat, spreading her thighs, releasing his cock and pressing between the saturated folds of her sex.

Her arms wrapped around his neck, her knees tightened on his hips, as he began to work inside her. Stroke her, stretch her. And bind her soul tighter to him.

She could feel that each time he touched her. Each time she felt his kiss on her lips, ravishing her, sipping at the passion that rose between them, hotter, wilder, more intense than anything she had ever known in her life.

Yes, the mating heat stole control. But Tanner had stolen her control before this heat had ever begun. He had stolen her heart. No matter what came later. No matter what happened in the future, she knew she had found something more than blinding desire and heated lust.

She had found Tanner.

She had found trust.

As his hips moved between hers, his tongue tasted her, let her taste him. The mix of rich, dark desire and stormy passion filled her senses. The taste of him was exquisite. She needed more. She craved more.

His pelvis caressed her clit with each stroke, rasped against it, sensitized it as his cock began slamming inside her, thrusting so hard and deep she was screaming her pleasure into his kiss. Screaming, begging with each cry, then tearing her lips from his as her orgasm exploded through her.

The pleasure was rich and hot, washing through her with the force of a tidal wave and leaving her shaking, shuddering in the wake of a release she still couldn't get used to. It was like this every time. Each time he touched her, took her, possessed her. Riotous and soul-deep. Profound satisfaction and an intimacy that shook her to her core.

"Be careful, damn you," he panted at her ear then, his hands caressing over her as he lifted her and carried her to his bed. "Please God, Scheme, let me protect you. Let me keep you safe."

She smiled as he lay down and pulled her close to him, tucking her against his sweat-dampened body as his arms held her tight, possessively.

"How about I let you help protect me?" she asked then. "Don't discount me, Tanner. I've survived ten years on the Tallant estate. I can't just sit back and wait for you to fix everything now."

"And I can't handle the thought of you being in danger," he argued. "Your father will stop at nothing to kill you, Scheme. He deals in positives. He didn't kill a Breed without proof that he was a failure. He doesn't kill his people without proof of betrayal. He knows you've betrayed him now. He won't miss an opportunity to take you out."

"But it will have to be dealt with personally. I'm his daughter. He won't tolerate another killing me now. Not after I escaped Chaz. Chaz was the only one he trusted to kill me with mercy, other than himself. He'll have to do it himself, Tanner. Nothing else will satisfy him."

She had given it a lot of thought, had considered each possibility and the placement of the spy in Sanctuary. It was dangerous, and there was always a chance she could be wrong, but she had never been wrong before, despite her deliberate mistakes. She was a better profiler than even her father understood. And she knew, beyond a shadow of a doubt, that Cyrus would have to kill her himself. He might not realize it yet. And Tanner might not believe it. But when it came right down to it, it would eat her father alive. He would have to punish her himself. He was her father. No one else had the right.

"He'll never get you out of Sanctuary," Tanner swore.

She hoped he couldn't. But she knew her father, and she knew he had managed to do many things that others had believed impossible.

· C H A P T E R   2 7 ·

Sanctuary was a cross between a loose-knit community and an armed camp. All around the twelve-acre main compound was a thick iron fence posted with guards. Outside that area, small cabins sprawled in an orderly abandon into the mountains surrounding the main estate.

The cabins were built to blend into the forest, rather than forcing the forest to accommodate the small cabins. Everything was orderly and neat on the outside, but Scheme knew that on the inside, the souls of those who lived here screamed out at the horrors they had escaped.

Enough time hadn't elapsed since the Breed rescues. Many still moved around as though uncertain of their freedom, always looking over their shoulders, crouching at the least sign of danger. And many were so young.

Most of the surviving Breeds had barely been in their early twenties when they were rescued. As Breeds aged, the Council had learned, they were much harder to control. It was extremely rare for a Breed of any species to survive past thirty. As though that age clicked some mental switch within them, they became deadly.

"The fenced area holds the house, communications, supplies, weapons and the garage." Tanner pointed out the buildings. "Seth Lawrence, the majority shareholder in Lawrence Industries, has supplied most of the building supplies."

"And Vanderale Industries supplies weapons, vehicles and satellite access," Scheme finished for him. "That's aside from the various corporations that donate money yearly for food, clothing, travel and other expenses. Sanctuary also lines its coffers with the exorbitant rate it charges for Breed support in a variety of operations both military and private. Sanctuary has learned that it holds several exceptional artists who, through their paintings and drawings, have depicted the horrors the Breeds endured in captivity for the world, gaining it multinational support."

Oh, how Cyrus Tallant hated those paintings and the high prices they brought.

"You're very good." He sighed.

"Unfortunately." She stared around the main grounds. Behind the house, a pool, patio and small play area for the children had been covered with a camouflaging screen to allow a measure of safety for the inhabitants of the house. But nothing was foolproof.

"Why do you stay here?" she asked. "Vanderale offered the Breeds a sizable portion of land in Africa. The conflicts there have eased, and Vanderale land has always been safe. Why not relocate?"

"We have the right to live," Tanner answered. "We shouldn't have to hide, Scheme. Hiding will not further our acceptance in the world."

"Racial wars are never easily won," she pointed out. "This war could become more brutal than any other in history. A lot of Breeds will die, Tanner. And there aren't many of you left now."

"Could die." His expression turned predatory. "If done correctly, propaganda will do for us what it could never do in other racial conflicts. We'll succeed. In the past several years we've begun talks with the Wolf Breeds in Colorado that we learned had escaped as well. With the free Coyote Breeds, they number several hundred."

"Three hundred forty-five as of last month. They've lost many of their numbers as well in the past few years. Together, your numbers fall far short of a thousand. The numbers of purists and supremist society members are only growing by the day."

"We'll survive this battle, Scheme. Public support means everything, and we hold it."

"And you've decided this simply because it's the way you want it to go?"

"Because we're strong enough." He led her around the side of the house as Cabal moved in carefully behind them. "We're strong enough to keep the support we have and to build upon it. We're making ourselves important to several different governments and proving our humanity. We're winning the battle."

"What about the children?" she asked carefully. "They're isolated here. Callan's son David is taught at home, and he doesn't have the chance to interact with other children. That's dangerous."

"What are you getting at, Scheme?" He was cranky and becoming more so by the moment.

Scheme restrained her smile. She knew exactly why he was cranky. She could feel it herself, the heat building inside her. If it could get this bad with the supplement, she wondered what would happen without it.

"My study of society, interactions and racial conflicts showed me one thing. Without real interaction, the Breeds will never become a part of society. Look at the past. When nations conquered each other, what's the first thing they did? Soldiers married or raped those they conquered and bred their women. Breeds seem to be succeeding there. But to truly interact, to become accepted, it begins at childhood. The children of those nations mingled, interacted, worked together and fought together. You don't have that."

"We have less than a half dozen children born of the matings. There's no sense in building schools."

"They should be in public school." She stopped then and stared up at him. "Each Breed child should be in school and taught to interact. They shouldn't be trained to kill; they need to be trained to avoid the conflict of racial, or in this case, species distrust."

His gaze was hooded. "That's a long way off."

"Then peace will be even further away," she informed him bleakly. "The reason I was valuable to the Tallant organization is the fact that I can see the threads that bind events. Where to cut them, where to strengthen them. Because I knew how to profile people and events. If you don't begin building that critical thread now, then you're screwed."

"You tell us in one breath that David is in danger of being abducted by the Council at any time, and you say send him to public school in the next," he accused.

She shrugged philosophically. "The President's children have attended school with their Secret Service agents in tow. Create a force just for the protection of these children. It would be easy to do. Buffalo Gap, the small town outside Sanctuary, is very small. Build them a new school, fund it, bring in the supplies they need to better educate their children, and they will cooperate with you."

"Which will cause the town to grow," he argued, his golden eyes swirling with frustration. "Which provides a fertile ground for the Council to lay in their soldiers and their killers."

"That's the risk you took when you based yourself in the States rather than hiding in Africa." She turned on him, staring back at him in determination. "You have Breeds that could be trained to teach school. Several files I read marked them as perfect teachers. They're not just trained to kill; they're trained to teach. Make them available to a new school with new supplies and better opportunities. Until you do this, the Breeds will never fit in, Tanner, and timing is crucial at this point to keep the pure blood societies from gaining ground."

She didn't mention the mating heat, but she knew from what Jonas had said at the caverns that it was the Breeds' most destructive secret. If Cyrus ever gained this information, he would destroy the Breeds with it.

"The Breed Cabinet convenes monthly for ideas," he told her then. "You can attend the meeting and propose it."

Her lips twitched. "I can just see Jonas embracing it, let alone the parents of those children. Breeds are very stubborn, I've noticed."

"So are you." He gripped her arm, turning her toward the sheltered, camouflaged area farther behind the house. "All you have to do is fight for it."

She might have a chance if she had a hope of having children herself.

"Live for it," he whispered a second later.

Scheme jerked her gaze away, staring instead into the dappled sunlight that pierced the netting into the yard.

"Tanner," she began to protest.

"Scheme." He crowded her. His larger body seemed to surround her as he backed her into a small grotto of flowering bushes.

"I'm not trying to die, you know," she bit out, frustrated by the needs of her own body and the need to learn as much as she could to figure out the identity of the assassin within Sanctuary. "This isn't helping me do my job."

"I don't want you to do your fucking job," he growled. "I want you back in the house. I want you safe until this is over."

"And how is it supposed to be over?" she hissed back. "I can help here."

"Not until that spy is caught."

"I'm the only one who can draw that bastard out." Her whisper was frustrated. "He won't try to kill me; he'll try to take me. Try working with me for a change."

They had raged over this argument since early that morning, and still Tanner refused to see sense. The only reason she had made it out of the house to begin with was because Cabal had finally out-argued his brother. And Tanner hadn't been pleased over it.

"I've had enough." His lips drew back from his teeth, red

flickering in that golden gaze. "We've been out here for more than a half hour, plenty of time to draw him out if he was going to be drawn."

Her eyes narrowed. "You know better than that, Tanner," she argued. "I need more time."

"Time for him to load his rifle and get in place for the shot?" he asked, his voice dangerously calm.

She scoffed. "Not hardly. Time for Cabal to see who's watching and how close. That's all the spy will do until he makes his move."

She lifted her hand to touch his face, marveling at the perfection of it, at least to her. The strong planes and savage angles. The fallen-angel sensuality and long, shielded golden eyes.

"I don't want to die," she said. "I want to live and laugh, and fight with you for years to come, but we won't have that chance if the spy doesn't show himself." Her voice dropped. "You know that as well as I do."

"You terrify me," he growled. "Waiting around on a bullet is no way to fight back."

"Trust me Tanner, there will be no bullet." She let her lips twitch with amusement. "But he will make plans. He'll watch. He'll test security. All we need is one mistake and then you can take him down. I promise not to interfere in that."

"That's big of you." He wasn't in the least placated.

Scheme shrugged as she stared around the grounds. "It will never be easy for either of us, Tanner, you know that. Father will always be waiting for me."

"He doesn't have to live forever." His head lowered, the red in his eyes deepening.

Scheme backed up sharply, her eyes widening. "What are you talking about? For God's sake, Tanner, what are you planning? You can't kill him any more than he can kill you without it backfiring."

His expression instantly closed. "All I'm concerned with is keeping you alive," he snapped, his fingers curling around her arm as he headed to the back door. "Nothing more."

"I'm getting sick of you dragging me around like this." She

jerked at her arm. "And I'm getting really sick of you treating me like a dimwit."

"You are a dimwit," he snapped as he pulled her into the house. "You just put yourself in danger like tomorrow doesn't matter." The back door slammed behind him. "Just fuck it, as far as you're concerned it's going to be done your way, period."

"It's not like that."

"The hell it's not," he yelled back at her. "You needed a damned keeper. I'll be damned if I have any idea how you survived this long. You are so fucking stubborn you make me rabid."

"I'm getting really tired of your insults." Her teeth clenched against the need to fight back. She was not going to get into a screaming match with a damned Bengal in the middle of a Breed kitchen. "And you were born rabid."

"Then prove me different." He threw his hands up at his sides as he turned sharply away from her and headed for the coffeepot. "Go on, Scheme, tell me how fucking wrong I am."

She turned to Cabal. "Could you help me out here?"

His brow lifted mockingly. "I've learned not to argue with him. As you said, he was born rabid. It's best to let him blow off the steam, then start wearing him down again."

"Just tell me if you saw anything or if that little trip outside was a fool's errand?" Tanner growled.

Cabal's lips thinned. "A faint glint of the sun off metal farther up the mountain. Just for the slightest second and consistent with the gleam of the sun on the new telescopic scopes Vanderale sent last year. They have a single vulnerability. If the sun hits them just right, then it will reflect back for a millisecond before the computerized lens detects it and shifts the shading within the lens. We've only just discovered the vulnerability. Not all the Breeds are aware of it yet."

"And you caught that?" Scheme blinked back at him. She knew of only one Breed in her father's organization that had been able to pinpoint that one millisecond of light reflecting back from those lenses.

"I'm rather good at some things." Cabal shrugged. "That's one of them."

"Someone had a scope on her!" Tanner's voice was a low growl of rage as he glared back at her. "No bullets, huh?"

She shrugged placidly. "None were fired."

"She has a point, Tanner. I had a team move into the place where I detected the reflection, but it was clear. We didn't even get a scent."

And that had Scheme's blood running cold. No scent. That meant a Breed had learned how to camouflage himself.

"Who's accessed the scent neutralizer Ely created?" Tanner shocked her as he questioned Cabal.

"You have a scent neutralizer?" She turned back to him in surprise. "Since when? Even the Council scientists couldn't come up with anything to keep Breeds from detecting Breeds."

"Vanderale Laboratories has been helping us with it." Tanner poured a cup of coffee, his voice still tight, his body tense. "We developed it with their help just this past month and just started testing it. Evidently it works."

"Only Ely's supposed to have access to that," Cabal said. "But according to her, Jolian had been in the labs lately chatting with her."

"Chatting with her?" Tanner asked dangerously.

"Chatting," Cabal said coldly. "Passing the time of day. Ely says they're friends."

Tanner turned an accusing eye on Scheme. "Harmless, is she?"

"We don't have enough to confine her yet, Tanner," Cabal informed him, his voice still hard. "Until we do, all we can do is watch her."

"Then you watch her," Tanner ordered harshly as Scheme leaned back against the kitchen island, crossed her arms over her breasts and waited.

She wasn't going to debate this one.

"By the way, Scheme's clothes came in this morning." Cabal surprised her with the announcement. "She has several dresses in there to choose from for the party tomorrow night."

"Finally, some decent clothes." She straightened and headed for the door as she glanced back at the two men following her.

"Has it ever occurred to you two that sometimes you get a little intense over things?"

She caught their confused looks.

"What the hell do you think we're too intense over now?" Tanner bit out.

Scheme paused, turned to them, and smiled sweetly. "The wrong person."

And she wasn't wrong about Jolian. There had been a few Breeds that Scheme had taken a personal interest in over the years. Jolian had been one of them.

"Has it ever occurred to you that you can be too damned trusting?" Tanner retorted harshly.

"Yeah. It has." She nodded somberly. "Every day of my life for the past eight years. But this isn't one of those cases."

With that, she turned on her heel and entered the foyer, before striding quickly to the stairs.

She had been too trusting many times, but not since Chaz. Chaz had taught her the value of questioning any trust she had. She no longer trusted in people; she trusted in herself. In her ability to profile.

She hadn't failed in suspecting Tanner of being the spy; his profile had fit the *possibility*. Jolian didn't even come close to a possibility.

"God forbid we ever give her the chance to say 'I told you so,' " Cabal muttered.

"Don't tempt fate," Tanner growled. "Because I have a feeling she would exact payment out of our hides."

Scheme smiled. Of course she would.

As they topped the stairs, Callan was heading from the end of the hall, where it turned to his family suite, his expression tight, his eyes glowing with fury.

"We have a problem," he grated, stopping at Tanner's door as Cabal moved ahead of them and entered the rooms.

Scheme watched as Cabal grabbed the electronic detector and began moving over the room, finally nodding the all-clear.

"Your father has just held a press conference." Callan directed the disgusted comment to her. "He's claiming you've been kidnapped and brainwashed. Reports are already coming through of the pure blood societies arming and preparing to go hunting. They're going after Breed hides."

"We expected this," Tanner pointed out to him. "The party tomorrow will alleviate a lot of the suspicion."

"Callan!" Jonas stalked into the room. "We just blocked a transmission out of Sanctuary. Someone's attempting to up-load information on the mating heat. We broke the encryption on it; it was sloppy for a change. They have everything."

"And if it gets out, we're fucked!" Callan's growl was a pri-mal, furious rasp. "I want a complete blackout on transmis-sions out. Cell phones, sats and landlines as well as Internet. Whoever our spy is, they're getting ready to make their move."

"I'll get a statement together and prepare for a news con-ference after the party tomorrow announcing the engage-ment," Tanner informed them quickly. "Jonas, have you tracked where the transmission came from?"

"We're working on it. It was bounced around Sanctuary like a damned ball. It's just a matter of time."

"And the spy knows that," Scheme informed them. "He's getting ready to make his move. He's trying to get the infor-mation on mating heat to Father to create chaos within Sanc-tuary when it's released. That will allow him the break he needs to take David and get him out of the estate."

"Move." Callan nodded to Jonas. "Do whatever it takes. I want that bastard found. Now!"

Jonas's gaze was fiercely intent as he turned and left the room, the accompanying Breeds following quickly behind him.

"Tanner, get that statement ASAP," Callan rasped. "Let's defang this bastard before I have to kill him myself."

And he could do it. Tanner watched as the pride leader stalked from the room, his expression savage, his eyes cold amber. Callan had protected them for nearly ten years before the world ever knew they existed. He had killed, silently, re-morselessly, and he had assured the safety of the other mem-bers of his main pride as they healed and grew to enjoy the freedoms he ensured for them.

Tanner knew Callan wouldn't hesitate to go hunting Coun-cil members or collaborators again if the need arose. It was a risk they couldn't take. Not now, while the world was watching them so closely.

Grimacing, he turned to Cabal as his brother made his way to the connecting suite.

"Cabal, find that bastard," he growled.

His brother shot him a cold smile. A smile of promised agreement. "I'll slip out of my rooms and go hunting."

Tanner blew a restless breath out before turning to Scheme. She had the television on, working the remote to show several major news channels at once on the screen, searching for threads, for hints of how her father would attack next.

"It's only a matter of time," she murmured then. "News of the mating heat is going to break. Ten years is too long for anything that explosive to stay hidden."

"We'll counter it." His eyes narrowed as she shifted, subtly pressing her thighs together as the scent of her heat filled his sense once again.

She had been burning for hours and refused to sate the need. He could smell it building in her now. Hell, he had scented it building within her the first hour after they had left their bed that morning.

She shifted again, finally sitting down in the chair at her side and leaning forward as she watched the news. Her gaze was restless as she scanned each view on the television screen, listening to the alternate statements, one of which was a review of General Tallant's accusation that the Breeds had kidnapped his daughter and were now brainwashing her.

"He always has a fallback position," she murmured. "What's his fallback this time?"

"Hell," Tanner suggested, moving to her as he stripped his shirt off.

He was tired of waiting. The scent of her need called out to him, stroked over his senses like vibrant fingers of an electrical charge. Like static. Sensitizing him and reminding of the pleasure he had only ever found with her.

He pulled his boots off behind her chair, released the belt of his jeans as he straightened, and released the snap and zipper as he rounded her seat. By the time he was beside her, she was turning to him, her brown eyes like rich milk chocolate, melting and heating as he stripped the jeans from his legs.

"I should be watching this," she breathed out as he knelt in front of her and lifted the remote from her hand. "I have to figure out what he's planning."

"In a minute you can watch it," he promised. "The playback works really well on that model. You won't miss a thing."

His fingers gripped the bottom of her sweatshirt and lifted, revealing her creamy tummy as she leaned back in the chair, her hands going to his bare shoulders.

Her nails scraped at his flesh, reminding him of a cat's kneading. Smiling tightly at the thought, he leaned forward and nipped at the skin he revealed, drawing her shirt up and over her breasts before she lifted her arms and removed it herself.

Her braless breasts were swollen, the hard tips of her nipples lifting out to him. They made his mouth water. Made need claw at his balls. But the glimmer of emotion and need clenched at his heart. God, she made him relish every moment that he breathed. He had never felt so alive, so filled with power as he did when she looked at him like that. Like he was the center of her existence at that moment, the forefront of her focus. Like he belonged to her as much as she belonged to him.

It hit him then. As her slender fingers eased the material of her sweatpants down her thighs, it slammed into him. He belonged. To someone. For someone. He was a part of a whole, rather than a cog in a community fighting to survive. If he died today, the world would go on without him. If he died today, this woman would always remember him. His touch, his kiss, his warmth as he held her at night. She would be alone. Forsaken by the heat that bound them. Unable to ever love again as she loved at this moment.

And he couldn't allow that. He would survive for her. And he would make certain she survived for him.

He took the material of the pants from her hands as they

cleared her knees and finished removing them before he spread her thighs and stared at the dew-laden curls between them.

She was so wet that her cream glistened on the soft pink folds and silken curls.

"Don't leave me," he whispered.

"Never," she whispered. "You make me whole."

He had to clench his teeth against the emotions that swept through him. She made *him* whole.

His hands slid up her thighs, then to her hips, pulling her forward as he moved closer. He wanted to worship her. He wanted to show her all the pleasure she gave him. He had every intention of lowering his lips to the sweet essence that eased from her pussy, but he found himself pressing into her instead.

Her breath caught. He heard it.

Her womb spasmed with pleasure as the head of his cock snugged inside her. He could smell it. That pleasure. Racing through her, making her wetter as she stared back at him from beneath hooded eyes, her hands wrapped around his wrists as she watched him begin to work his erection inside the sensitive flesh of her heated sex.

Tanner paused there, his eyes closing at the feel of her surrounding that sensitized crest. Beneath the head he could feel the barb throbbing just beneath this skin, preparing to swell, to erect at the point of his release and lock him inside her.

"I love your soft curls," he whispered as he pressed deeper into her, grimacing at the flexing of her inner muscles, at the tremulous sigh that left her lips. Those soft curls were clinging to his shaft as he retreated, drawing his gaze, holding him mesmerized with the wondrous sight of her response to him. Silky soft cream glistened on the head of his cock before it disappeared inside her once again.

"'Cause you don't have any," she gasped.

"Maybe." He had to fight to breathe. To keep from taking her hard, fast. To work his cock inside her with slow, steady thrusts, a little deeper each time, feeling her shift, lift, her legs wrapping around his hips as her hands smoothed over his shoulders.

Why had he never taken her like this before? he wondered. In this big overstuffed chair, on his knees before her, watching as each inch of his erection possessed her. It was the most erotic sight of his life.

"Tanner, I'm dying." She was panting.

"In a minute."

He knew her need for release was escalating rapidly. Each slow thrust inside her and she was tightening further on him, her inner muscles caressing him, drawing him deeper into the vortex of need that threatened to consume him.

"Now." She tightened again, flexed, rippled, and he had to grind his teeth to keep from coming for her then and there.

"Naughty Scheme," he grated out, clenching his teeth to hold back.

But he couldn't resist moving inside her harder, faster. The pleasure was like a whirlpool sucking him in. His eyes lifted from where he was pressing inside her to meet her gaze. Melting chocolate. That's what her eyes reminded him of. Hot, rich, glittering with the hunger and need as her hand lifted to his face.

"All my life," she gasped. "All my life, I've prayed for you."

"All my life, I've loved you." He bent to her, taking her lips with his, giving her the spicy, erotic taste of his kiss and sharing the burning need threatening to sear his nerve endings.

Nothing mattered now but stilling those flames. Taking the kiss deeper, letting it get wilder as he began to thrust powerfully between her thighs, taking her cries as his own and throwing them both into the tempest racing through them.

He felt her orgasm first. The steady tightening, the tension building until she bucked beneath him, screaming into his lips as her nails dug into his back. Then he gave in to his own, tearing his lips from hers to throw his head back, a primal snarl leaving his chest as his semen pulsed from his cock and the barb became painfully erect, locking him inside her, stealing his mind.

He felt reborn within her. Renewed. Locked inside her, spilling his seed into the heated depths as he spilled his soul into hers. His head lowered, a growl rumbling in his throat as he locked his incisors into the mating mark he had given her at the caves.

She cried out again, spasmed around his cock, and spilled more of the sweet release that he knew was his alone. Just his. His mate. His woman.

Moments later, he collapsed against her, sweating, panting, drawing her against him as his tongue lapped at the wound on her shoulder and his senses filled with the taste and scent of her.

This was what he lived for now. Not revenge or hatred, but this. For love. For Scheme.

CHAPTER 28

Scheme hadn't expected that the Breeds would ever throw a party such as the one she prepared for the next night. Of course, the fact that there were several reporters there to report on the "engagement" of Tanner Reynolds and Scheme Tallant had nothing to do with it. The only thing missing inside the opulent mansion was the news crews parked outside the iron gates of Sanctuary's main entrance.

She hadn't expected this. When Tanner had said "party," she had assumed he meant some sort of small event. Just the main families within the estate house, not the guests that had arrived in heli-jets for the past few hours.

Of course, she should have known better. This was what she would have done herself to counter General Tallant's accusations. And they had grown in the past twenty-four hours.

Her father was frightened. She had seen it in his eyes in the last news interview. He was terrified of what she was going to say, what she was going to do. What proof she might have of his actions. And she had plenty. Proof that she knew Jonas was now downloading from the secured site she had been storing it on over the years. Her insurance, she had always called it, just in case she needed it.

As she swept her hair into a fashionable twist, she met her own gaze in the mirror and nearly flinched at the grief in her eyes. Why should she feel grief that the monster that had haunted her living nightmare would soon be falling? It wasn't as though he had been a loving father.

In his eyes though, he had been, and she knew that. Her father was a psychopath of the worst sort. He believed in what he was doing with total conviction. He believed he had done the best by his daughter—the daughter betraying him in what he considered the most heinous matter.

He had killed her mother, and Scheme knew he would have killed her given the chance. He would have done it with love in his heart and belief in his soul that he was saving the world.

She shook her head at the thought before securing the last pin in her hair and surveying her image carefully. She was known for her scarlet dresses, and she wore one now. Scarlet silk with a daring slit cut to the thigh and black stockings peeking through. The silk swept over her curves and molded her breasts before the straps tightened at her shoulders and crisscrossed behind her back.

Having checked her makeup one last time, she slid her stocking feet into scarlet pumps, picked up the little evening bag that matched her stockings and left the bathroom.

"Ready?" Dressed in a tux and looking sexier than any man or Breed had a right to, Tanner rose from his seat at the bottom of the bed, his gaze moving over her with slow appreciation.

"You look good enough to eat."

"I'm nervous as hell." Her skin was sensitized, warning her that the mating heat was playing hell with the nerves, as Ely had warned her it would.

"Just remember to keep enough distance between you and others to keep them from accidentally touching you. You know the reporters. You've dealt with them before. You know how to work them. Everything's going to be fine."

Everything was going to be fine.

"Cabal will be keeping watch from outside," he continued. "David is secure in Callan and Merinus's suite. There are about two hundred guests; none are known associates of your fathers or the Council's, but they're influential in politics and financial affairs. The reporters are well respected and known for their impartiality where the Breeds are concerned."

"I'll be fine." She was assuring them both.

She lifted her chin, reminding herself that she had done this countless times in other settings without so much as a twinge of nerves.

Tanner's hand rode low on her back as they left the suite and moved to the wide, curving staircase that led to the crowded foyer and ballroom. Breed Enforcers were en masse, stationed with silent watchfulness every few feet up the stairs. Below, they had positioned themselves at the doors leading into the house and the ballroom, as well as the other rooms that led off the foyer. Only the ballroom was open. All other doors had been closed and carefully locked.

The ballroom doors were thrown open, and she knew the French doors leading into the gardens beyond would be open, allowing the guests to wander out for fresh air in the heavily secured and well-lit gardens.

No sooner had they stepped from the stairway into the foyer than the three reporters invited were striding toward them. Cassa Hawkins was a reporter and newcaster for INS, the International News Service; Joel Briggins from CNN was there, as well as Philippe Augustan of ENI, Euro-News International. Each reporter had his or her own cameraman following behind. The small recording devices normally uploaded their video feed live to the stations, but with the communications blackout at Sanctuary at the moment, they were on record only, to be uploaded after Jonas had previewed each disc.

"Scheme, you don't look drugged to me." Cassa Hawkins made a little moue of disappointment as she stepped past the Breed Enforcer that had stepped closer as they entered the foyer.

Cassa was in her thirties, cool and polished. A natural

blonde with steady gray eyes and porcelain skin. She could be amusing but frighteningly sharp.

"Of course I am, Cassa." Scheme smiled as Tanner tucked her hand into the curve of his arm and glared at the reporters. "Tanner can be quite addictive in certain areas."

They had no clue how addictive.

Cassa's agreeable laughter was soft, but her eyes missed nothing. Not Tanner's good looks or the way he seemed to hover over Scheme protectively.

"He could be indeed," she agreed. "Do you think he would allow us a few moments alone? He's glaring at me, you know."

And he was. Glaring at her and the camerman behind her.

"Tanner, I'll be fine." She slid her hand from his arm and glanced around. "There are enough enforcers here to fight a small war. And I could use a drink if you don't mind."

His amber eyes gleamed down at her, rich with amusement and a shade of disapproval.

"I won't be far," he promised her, warned the others.

"He's very protective," Cassa said softly as Tanner moved to Sherra, resplendent in a smoky gown as she stood beside her husband, Kane Tyler.

"He's had reason to be." Scheme let her gaze harden as she stared back at the reporter, then her cameraman, before moving back to Cassa. "Turn him off."

Cassa sighed. "Go get a drink, Monty, and some nice shots of the party."

Monty mumbled and moved away before Scheme turned to the other two reporters. "Sorry, guys." She smiled. "Girl talk. Can we chat later?"

The promise to chat later had them smiling agreeably, if suspiciously, before moving away.

"General Tallant is frothing at the mouth," Cassa said as Scheme led her to the far end of the foyer with a small indication to the enforcers to keep others at bay. "And word is that the pure blood societies are arming to attack any Breed they come across."

"They do anyway." Scheme sighed. "Now let me ask you something, Cassa. Whose side are you on?"

"The truth." The answer was given without hesitation. And Scheme believed her. Cassa was a fanatic about the truth. It had nearly cost her her job and her life on more than one occasion.

"Excellent." Scheme stared back at her in focused determination. "You and I have talked often in the past. Do you believe General Tallant, or what you see now?"

Cassa's lips twitched. "Honey, I doubt the devil himself could brainwash you. So why don't you tell me what's going on and if the rumors are true that General Tallant is fighting to keep the skeletons in the closet, or just his little girl close to his side. And if it's okay with you, let my cameraman back in here."

The last was said with subtle mockery. Cassa wanted an exclusive, but she was willing to play nice with it.

Scheme nodded to the enforcer a few feet away, who waved the cameraman over.

With polished expertise, Cassa turned to the camera. "I'm talking to Scheme Tallant, General Cyrus Tallant's daughter and rumored personal assistant. We're at Sanctuary, the home of countless Feline Breeds and the main base of operations, where Miss Tallant and Mr. Tanner Reynolds are preparing to announce their engagement on the heels of her father's accusations of brainwashing and coercion." She turned back to Scheme. "Miss Tallant, I must say after knowing you for several years, you don't look in the least brainwashed. Why is your father claiming you are?"

Scheme put on her "public" face and gave Cassa a practiced, charming smile.

"To hide the truth."

"And the truth is, Miss Tallant?"

"That he would do anything to silence the truth that will be revealed in the coming weeks. The truth that he's murdered countless Breeds, and had Tanner not moved quickly, he would have murdered me as well."

Her heart ached, and she didn't know why. He had never been a father. He had never cared for anything other than his fanatical dreams of controlling the Breeds.

"Why would your father want you dead?"

"Because I know the atrocities he's committed. Because, Ms. Hawkins, for the past eight years I've been a double agent for the Bureau of Breed Affairs, working directly with Jonas Wyatt. I know my father's secrets. And he would do anything to silence me."

The interview with Cassa went smoothly, despite the constant interruptions the other reporters tried to make. The enforcers held them off dutifully though, and once she finished with Cassa, Scheme gave the others a few minutes with their questions. It wasn't much, but they would have airtime. Tanner had also talked with them, and before they entered the ballroom, Tanner and Scheme were interviewed together.

But she couldn't shake the feeling that her father was up to something more. That he had an ace he hadn't played yet and was just waiting on her. The communications blackout had kept the spy's transmissions from going through, and Jonas had whispered to Tanner that they were narrowing the location of the attempted transmissions further in the mountain.

Which left the estate house safe, at least for now.

"One of these days," Scheme commented as they left the reporters, "one of those reporters is going to catch onto your lies."

He chuckled at that, pausing as he moved to a small group of women gathered around one tall, blond-haired cowboy.

"Scheme, I'd like you to meet some friends," he announced. "Tamber Mason." A tall, well-toned brunette with twinkling brown eyes reached out to shake her hand with a murmured, almost too soft hello. She appeared shy. Restrained. Though the low-cut, almost too short silver dress she wore was anything but restrained. "Tamber is our resident communications expert. She runs the comm shed like a little drill sergeant."

Tamber ducked her head as though embarrassed with the praise.

"It's good to meet you, Tamber." Tamber nodded, mumbled again and offered a small smile.

"This is Shiloh Gage." He introduced an auburn-haired Jaguar Breed beside Tamber.

This Breed, Scheme remembered.

"The brat?" Scheme's lips twitched as the other girl stared back at her with brazen curiosity.

Shiloh Gage had been known for several things in the labs she had been created in. Among them was her ability to work the scientists and trainers in a manner that screamed princess brat. Tonight she was dressed in snug tan breeches and a sleeveless, deeply cut vest that revealed a generous cleavage.

She should have been killed within the first five years of her life. Instead, the scientists had written in their reports that they kept her alive for study purposes. They were trying to figure out where she had managed to get the idea that she deserved life, and why she assumed they would care. Personally, Scheme knew that the scientists in that particular lab had a sense of humor.

"That's me," Shiloh agreed archly.

"And she doesn't mind admitting to it." The tall, blond-haired Southern charmer, human, ex-mercenary and general bad ass, Simon Quatres, spoke from beside Shiloh. "I assume you know who I am?"

"Not everyone knows you, Simon," Shiloh informed him querulously.

"Actually, I have read several reports on him," Scheme agreed. Thankfully, he didn't insist on shaking her hand. The pain would have been hard to hide. "It's good to meet you."

"And it's fine to finally meet you, ma'am," he drawled. "Ole Tanner seemed to do well for himself after all. He's surprised us."

Tanner grunted in reply.

"Callan's motioning for us now," Tanner told her, gripping her elbow as she offered her good-byes to the small group.

"Meet and run. An interesting concept," she told him as they headed toward the front of the ballroom.

"Cabal's watching," he murmured in her ear. "You'll meet a lot of the others the same way."

"Tamber's much different from her files," she said. "I wouldn't have thought she would be so shy."

"Pissed is more like it," Tanner sighed. "We had to order

her out of the comm shed tonight. She's been installing new equipment this month and didn't want to leave her babies."

Shaking her head, Scheme drew in a deep breath as they neared Callan and stepped onto the podium erected for the band at the far end of the ballroom. Time to smile and play nice, she thought as her gaze swept the room, seeing the distrust, and in many cases the animosity, that filled the eyes of those watching. It was going to be a very interesting night indeed.

◆　◆　◆

Moving through the ballroom after the announcement of their engagement, Scheme spotted Jolian slipping quietly through the French door into the gardens beyond. She knew Jolian had taken a hell of a mental beating from Jonas earlier yesterday, and if the girl's pale face was any indication, she still hadn't recovered.

Why she should care, Scheme wasn't certain. But she did. As Tanner stood talking to Jonas, Dane Vanderale and several politicians, she slipped away, certain he would never allow her to go after the little Panther Breed otherwise.

And slipping away from Tanner wasn't an easy thing to do. She stopped by several clusters of guests, chatted, smiled, made certain she wasn't touched, because the first brush she'd had against someone other than Tanner had felt like knives tearing through her flesh.

Long minutes later she edged around the French doors though and stepped onto the patio where Jolian stood silently. And alone.

"Jolian." Scheme tilted her head, watching as the Breed female tensed at the sound of her voice.

"You should go back inside," Jolian told her firmly, if a bit huskily. "Cabal would be upset to find us near each other."

Cabal would be. Strangely enough, Jolian wasn't worried about Tanner.

"I don't believe you mean me any harm. I warned them they were making a mistake."

Jolian's head lowered, her hands gripping the stone rail that edged the marble patio.

"They think I'm a spy." Her mocking laughter was a thread of pain. "I could see it in Cabal's eyes. They were filled with disgust."

And Jolian was filled with pain because of it.

"You're in love with him," Scheme guessed.

"And you're mated to him and his brother. Damn, some people just have all the luck, don't they?"

Jolian didn't turn around. Her hands lifted from the balustrade though and wrapped around her breasts. The loose cream-colored gown she wore wasn't particularly flattering on her frame, and it was evident no one had taken the time to try to advise her on her dress. Most likely, the other Breeds were steering a path far clear of her at the moment.

"I'm sorry," Scheme said softly. "About Cabal and about what happened yesterday. If you would let me, I could make it up to you."

Give her some hair and clothes advice to start with.

"How could you help me?" Jolian turned to her, anger marking her face, her gaze. Then her eyes widened, rolled back in her head, and she slumped to the ground.

Scheme rushed toward her, without thinking, without considering the consequences. In the next second, blinding pain shot through her head, sending a blaze of white-hot light to explode in front of her eyes as she felt herself crumpling over the other woman. And wishing to hell she hadn't come out here without Tanner.

◆　◆　◆

Tamber Mason.

She was trained in communications, and she had been a part of the inner circle of the pride since Sanctuary was first inhabited by the Breeds. She was Merinus's friend and sometimes bodyguard and Callan's most trusted communications expert. She often went shopping with Sherra, sparred with Dawn and was rumored to have slept with Tanner and Cabal on several occasions.

She was also Cyrus Tallant's spy.

This was why the spy was so confident. Why Cyrus had

such a hard time controlling her. Her place within Sanctuary had been firmly established years ago. She was, in essence, a part of the family.

Scheme had seen all their files. The Breeds at Sanctuary as well as those now working in the law enforcement and military areas. She had gone over them, studied them, learned all she could about them before they were destroyed. And she had somehow managed to let this one blip past her radar.

Because Tamber was plain. Unassuming. There had been nothing in her files to indicate a connection to Cyrus Tallant or to anyone within her father's organization. She was simply a well-loved member of the Lyons' extended family.

But all Scheme had had was her picture to go by. Once she fully heard Tamber Mason's voice rather than the mumble she had been given at the party, Scheme knew exactly who she was. Her father's second in command's former lover.

Scheme had only heard her voice; her father's wannabe son had never mentioned her name or her expertise.

"You know they're going to track you," she warned Tamber as the jeep moved over the uneven road leading through the woods. "They'll know you were the one who attacked Jolian and took me."

"It really won't matter." Tamber flashed her a hard, cold smile. "I won't be returning for a while. I've just taken care of my mission, two in one; John will take me in for a while."

Scheme wanted to turn, to check on the unconscious child in the back of the jeep, but she didn't dare. If she looked at him, she might not survive it, she would break down, and she couldn't afford that.

"You really think John is going to allow you freedom?" she asked Tamber instead, working at the rope binding her wrists. "Do you think you're the only spy he's fucking, Tamber?"

"Actually, I know I'm not." A smug smile curled Tamber's lips. "But working in Breed communications isn't the only thing I'm trained for, Scheme. The Breeds don't have my DNA; all they have are my fingerprints. DNA is voluntary, you know. In six months, I'll be right back, working somewhere else within Sanctuary, with a new name and a new face as well as new fingerprints and a different scent. The Council scientist can work with the scent neutralizer and make it whatever they want it to be. I am a chameleon. The Breeds will never know."

Like hell. Scheme knew that unknown to the Council or to other Breeds, Tanner and Cabal's sense of smell would easily detect her. And they would be looking for her. She would never survive returning to Sanctuary.

"You're too confident, Tamber." Scheme braced herself against the door as she shook her head sadly. "Ego goes hand in hand with failure."

"I'm confident, period," she snapped. "I've been working on this for years, you stupid bitch."

There had to be a way to escape. They were following the exact path she had laid out on the map for Callan; all she had to do was find a way to delay Tamber, to make her stop.

Scheme struggled harder with the ropes, feeling the burn of her wrists, the slickness of her own blood, but the ropes were loosening, closer to coming free.

God, she prayed the child slept through this. He was so small still, innocent-looking as he slept in the backseat. Of course, if he were awake . . .

She stilled as she felt something at her wrist. A faint touch, a tug at the knot. He was awake. Oh God, he was awake. She felt her breathing hitch in her chest at the fear he must be feeling.

But he was working the knot free, slowly, his fingers quick and sure. They weren't trembling like hers. And hers were trembling. She was shaking like a leaf. And behind her, a nine-year-old baby was working the knot loose on her bonds.

"You're such a dumb little twit, Tamber," Scheme announced, feigning amusement. "John is going to chew you up and spit you out, you know that, right?"

Tamber's fist flew out, connecting with Scheme's jaw, knocking her sideways into the jeep as a mini growl erupted from the backseat and David Lyons pounced.

Tamber wasn't expecting the attack. She cursed as her hands jerked on the wheel, throwing the jeep against the sharp incline that ran alongside the road. The jeep tilted, wheels spinning as Tamber's hand flew back and connected with the face of the child locked onto her neck.

A hiss of pain sounded from the little boy, but he didn't let go. The jeep tilted again as Scheme fought to get to the wheel to right the vehicle. Tamber had her hands full with a miniature Lion Breed hybrid that seemed to be everywhere at once.

And cursing. Scheme hoped she lived to laugh about the less than childish language he was using. But it wasn't looking good. Oh God, it wasn't looking good at all. The jeep was tilting, pitching.

The child. She had to protect the boy. As the jeep finally lost its battle to stay upright, she pitched herself toward the little boy, hoping to cushion him, to break the roll as it came.

Her elbow connected with Tamber's head, her fingers grasping frantically to grab hold of David as she bounced, her back hitting the seat, before she was tossed again, slamming her into the dash as she heard Tamber scream and the mini-Lion's almost grown-up roar.

Another flip of the jeep and her head slammed against the windshield, darkness flickering over her consciousness as she fought to keep from being sick or passing out. Or both. She could have easily done both.

Dammit, where was Tanner anyway? He was supposed to keep this from happening, wasn't he? Protect her and all that macho stuff?

Moaning, she felt her fingers curl into something soft, cool. Dirt. She struggled to shake off the paralyzing pain that seemed to blaze through her body. It wasn't the stupid mating heat either; she had just been bounced around a jeep like a frickin' soccer ball.

David.

She forced her eyes open, seeing first dirt, crushed leaves, a hint of grass and trees. Moaning again at the effort, she turned her head to stare directly into David Lyons's golden gaze.

The kid was crouched beside her, his eyes, very much like his father's, peering into hers as he tilted his head, his shaggy light brown hair falling over his eyes before he pushed it back.

"Lady, we need to move," he seemed to sigh. "That stupid cat is just knocked out, I think."

"I have to move." Why didn't she figure that one out? "Where is a damned Breed when you need one?"

Damn. She hurt. She hurt bad. And if she wasn't mistaken, the gown she was wearing was ripping further up her thigh with each move she made and she had lost both shoes.

Forcing her arms beneath her, she struggled to sit up.

"You could help," she muttered.

David frowned a little. "You smell like Uncle Tanner when he's really mad," he pointed out. "I aint touchin' you for nothin'."

"Not touching me for anything," she automatically corrected him.

"That's what I said." He chewed at his lip worriedly, sharp little incisors poking out. "But we got to go. We're too close to the boundary."

"Okay, we have to go." She nodded.

"Uncle Tanner will turn the lions loose when he knows we're gone. Uncle Kane will have his soldiers out on the motorcycles. If we can get close enough, then we'll be okay. Uncle Tanner says the lions only eat people that are too close to the boundary."

"Oh great. Let me guess, they only eat my kind, not your kind."

He paused as she wobbled to her feet, his frown deepening as he stared back at her with a hint of hurt confusion. "Aren't we the same kind?"

Scheme winced as she tried to smile in agreement. "Yes, David, we're the same kind. But Breeds have a different scent from non-Breeds, just like a male smells differently from a female."

"Oh." He moved around her, nodding thoughtfully before he picked up a thick stick lying on the ground and handed it to her. "Here. We better hurry. I can feel a chopper in the air, and I know our heli-jet isn't in Sanctuary right now."

"Great," she muttered. "How far away is it?"

And it was dark. Cold. The moon was full, the canopy of trees above them was pretty thick.

"We need to hurry." He hitched his jeans up on his lean body and moved ahead of her. "Uncle Jonas says the sound of a heli-jet carries for a ways for a Breed. But we can't stay here."

"Uncle Jonas, huh?" she asked.

"Yeah, he smells kinda like Daddy, but Daddy doesn't like it when I say that, so I don't tell him." He shrugged his thin shoulders. "I can hear the lions. Let's go this way."

Lions. They eat people. Scheme whimpered. She was not having her best week here at all. Just not at all.

CHAPTER 29

"Tanner, we have a heli-jet on radar coming over Buffalo Gap and moving in fast," Kane reported over the earwig Tanner wore. "We're putting the chopper in the air, but it's not going to be much defense against it and our heli-jet is currently unavailable."

"We caught their trail," Tanner shouted above the din of the dirt cycle's motor as he raced behind Dawn and her Lionesses. "The lions are moving in fast now, so we believe they're stationary."

He gunned the dirt bike harder, skidding around fallen logs as he raced up the incline of the old logging road that cut through the mountain.

In the distance he could hear Sanctuary's armed chopper lifting into the air and he prayed. He had been praying since the moment he realized Scheme was gone. Praying like he had never prayed, even during those horrifying years in the labs.

"Tamber's tracker was deactivated, as was David's," Kane barked in his ear.

Callan's snarling voice cut across the line. "The lions will find David."

Callan, his pride brother, Taber and Jonas were just behind him, gunning their bikes just as hard as Tanner was his. They hadn't spent the hours riding these mountains that Tanner and Dawn had. Tanner would get there first, and when he did, he would kill Tamber.

It was almost impossible to believe that the quiet, soft-spoken Lion Breed female had been part of Tallant's organization. The lab she had been rescued from had been one of the worst. The conditions had been horrid there for the Breeds. The Coyotes that oversaw them were some of the most vicious, the scientist depraved.

Tamber had been rescued as a teenager; she couldn't be much more than twenty-five now, and she had been betraying them all along. Her position in the communications shed, given complete trust simply because she was a Breed, would have given her all the access she needed to keep Tallant apprised of every move the Breeds made.

Tanner's hands clenched around the handles of the cycle, one wrist bending back, giving the cycle more speed as he raced up the logging road.

If they didn't get to Tamber's jeep before the heli-jet reached the boundary of the property, then Scheme and David could be gone forever.

"The lions are catching scent," Dawn called out on the channel. "We're moving in. The alpha is roaring his challenge now. We better hurry."

Releasing the lions with Scheme out there was a risky venture. They were trained to only respond to certain non-Breeds, only those who lived full-time within Sanctuary. Scheme was in just as much danger from the big cats as she was from Tamber. Unless she went to the ground and became completely submissive, making no sudden moves and not looking the animals in the eye. That would be the only way she could save herself.

"The jet is clearing Buffalo Gap, Tanner," Kane barked. "You have approximately five minutes before it reaches the only possible launching site."

Time was running out.

"We'll make it," he snarled, pushing the bike harder. They had to make it; he couldn't live otherwise.

◆   ◆   ◆

Scheme stumbled on the incline as she tried to hurry away from the jeep and the psychotic Breed hopefully bleeding to death inside it. Though she doubted it. For the most part, Breeds, even the foul ones, were amazingly resilient.

Holding on to the stick David had provided, she followed him as fast as she could, feeling her legs trembling, the pain racing through her body and the overwhelming knowledge that she might have failed.

"We have to hurry." David turned to stare back at her worriedly, his head lifting, scenting the air around him. As small as he was, as young as he was, he was already showing traits of an alpha Breed male. Sure of himself, confident of his surroundings and his family's ability to find him.

What would it be like, Scheme wondered sadly, to have that confidence? To know beyond a shadow of a doubt that if your family was near, then you were safe.

Her father was most likely near, coordinating the capture with his smug smile and self-satisfaction. But it wasn't for her protection. It was for the destruction of others. The Breeds who had escaped the torment he could have inflicted on them.

"Go." She waved her hand back to David weakly. "Get out of here, David. Find Tanner. He'll come and get me."

The boy didn't have many self-preservation instincts. If he did, he would be running like hell away from her.

He chewed at his lips in indecision, clearly eager to be on his way down the mountain. "The lions will eat you, lady," he explained as though speaking to a dimwit, his shoulders straightening and an invisible mantle of responsibility seeming to settle on them.

"Then let the damned lions eat me," she snapped desperately. "Do you think I went to all the trouble to get into Sanctuary just so they could take both of us?"

He rolled his eyes. "You're being melodramatic."

Melodramatic? A freaking nine-year-old had just called her melodramatic?

"Excuse me here," she snapped. "I'm stuck in the woods, I think I broke bones, and I've lost my shoes. This is not melodrama, *kid*. This is me getting ready to have a meltdown."

He stared back at her with a patronizing, totally male gaze. Good God, this kid was a hazard to himself.

"Meltdown when we get home. Mom keeps chocolate for meltdowns. Daddy always has them when Uncle Jonas visits." He frowned, glancing at the sky while he grabbed a handful of her sweats to steady her as she stumbled over something barky. A rotten piece of a tree maybe. She shuddered. Anything rotten should be kept well away from her.

"I don't blame your daddy," she muttered. "Jonas is a pain in the rear. Now run and tell him I said it. Go on." She waved her hand imperatively. "Go."

The kid shook his head.

"Uncle Jonas is cool. He knows neat stuff, like guns and knives and how to fight."

"So does your daddy," she reminded him impatiently. "Would you leave already?"

"But teaching hurts Daddy," he sighed, ignoring her once again. "I can feel it. So I asked Uncle Jonas to help me, and Uncle Taber and Uncle Tanner. It hurts them too though, but not like it does Daddy."

"It's for your protection," she pointed out.

"I know. I think that's why it hurts them," he shrugged. "It's why I can't go to the regular school or play baseball."

There was a note of sadness in the boy's voice, of loneliness. Hell, the Breeds were no freer now than they were in the labs; they just weren't tortured. Unless they were caught.

"We have to move faster," she muttered, trying to force her legs to obey her. It was obvious the kid wasn't going anywhere without her. "We don't have much time."

She could hear something coming herself now, could feel the vibration of it.

"The lions are close." David's voice rose in excitement as

they passed a thick growth of foliage. "All we have to do is get to the—"

Scheme stopped in shock as Tamber erupted from behind the brush and jerked David to the side, her pistol lying at his temple as his eyes widened in alarm and fear.

Blood smeared the other woman's face and hands as she blinked several times to clear the sweat that dripped into her eyes.

"Oh man, Daddy's going to be really mad now," David mumbled.

"Brat." The gun slapped the boy at the side of the head as Scheme flinched, reaching instinctively for him.

"You stupid bitch." The weapon turned on her. "Your father said dead or alive. I'm just going to kill you and get it over with."

"You kill her and I won't be nice." David struggled, though his eyes were a little dazed now, his face pale. "And my daddy is going to kill you."

"Shut up, you little bastard." She whacked him again, causing him to stumble as she dragged him closer to her.

"Stop hitting him." It was hard to breathe for the pain in her ribs, the agony streaking up her arm and the fear she could feel crawling inside her. "You knock him out and he's going to be dead weight."

"So?" Tamber sneered, her plain face twisting into a grimace of anger. "Who really gives a fuck? He's going to be wishing he were dead by the time General Tallant finishes the first stage of training. Let him get used to the pain now."

There was a smug glint in her eye as her gaze flickered to David.

"Let him go," Scheme whispered. "I have something more important than the kid. Something my father will want much more than he wants that child." She waved her fingers toward him.

"There's nothing you could have," Tamber snapped.

And Scheme prayed for forgiveness. She sent the prayer winging to heaven and begged for protection. Not for herself.

"I know where the first Leo is," she whispered painfully.

It was a secret she had sworn to herself she would never reveal. If the Leo wanted to reveal himself, then that was his
business. It wasn't her place to do so. No one else knew the
secret; it was information she had destroyed long ago. It was
information she had thought she would die before revealing.

"Shut up, Scheme!" David suddenly cried out. "Daddy's
going to be pissed."

Tamber tangled her fingers in his hair and pulled. Hard.

"You're lying," she snarled.

"Breeds can smell a lie, Tamber," she reminded her harshly.
"You know I'm not lying."

"Then you'll just have to live. I'll take you both." She leveled the gun at Scheme. "Move."

Scheme shook her head. "It's not going to happen. Let
David go and I'll come with you. But I'm not moving as long
as you have him. He'd be better off dead than with the general. And if you kill him, you'll have to kill me."

Her gaze flickered with indecision.

"The first Leo and his mate, Tamber. They're both still alive."

Her eyes gleamed.

"Let David go."

She loosened her hold as she waved the gun to indicate that
Scheme should move back.

David jerked away from her.

"Man, Daddy is going to be so mad at you. He's going to
roar," he said and sighed, stumbling.

"David, get down the mountain," Scheme ordered harshly.
"Now. Go."

He stumbled again, righted himself and started running
down the track, glancing at her over his shoulder as the low,
vibrating hum of a heli-jet on stealth mode began to fill the air.

"Let's go." Tamber jumped to her, grabbed her arm and began pulling her back up the track. "Bitch. You are so dead anyway. And I'll just come back for him."

A lion roared. Scheme's gaze jerked to the side, watching
as a huge, four-legged, sharp-toothed, fully grown male lion
opened his mouth and roared a challenge before disappearing
into the brush a second before Tamber fired.

There wasn't a chance in hell Scheme was going any farther. She knew these lions, remembered the reports her father had received on them. They were trained to attack and kill intruders. The only time they wouldn't attack was if the victim was on the ground, unarmed. Tamber's bullet would hurt a hell of a lot less than those teeth. Scheme wasn't going anywhere near that border and she wasn't running any farther.

She shuddered before stumbling and letting herself fall to the ground. Her arms went instinctively over her head as she prayed not to feel the mercilessly large, sharp teeth of the predator.

"No, you don't," Tamber screamed, her foot driving into her ribs, sending shafts of agony to tear through Scheme's body. "Get up."

Oh God. That hurt bad enough.

Snarling, Scheme reach out, gripping Tamber's foot before the second blow fell, struggling to stay on the ground and at the same time to keep the bitch from breaking her bones. Dammit, this was not the way that party was supposed to end tonight.

"Whore, I'll kill you," Tamber shrieked as she managed to kick free.

A hard punch to Scheme's stomach came as a gunshot splintered her hearing and black agony raced through her mind. Better to die here.

CHAPTER 30

Tanner rounded the curve in the old logging road, cursing as he threw the cycle to the side and jumped off in a crouch to grab David and haul him to the side of the road, out of the way of the cycles moving in behind him.

"Get her, Uncle Tanner," he was screaming, crying, his bruised face twisted in fear and anger as he struggled in Tanner's arms. "Tamber's going to kill that lady. She's going to kill her."

Turning, Tanner saw Callan pull his own cycle to a stop, jump from the seat and run to David.

"Tamber has Scheme ahead," Tanner yelled, as the other bikes skidded to a stop. From the corner of his eye he watched Dawn's Lionesses take off on foot around the mountain as Dawn jerked her rifle from the scabbard at the side of her bike.

Pushing David into his father's arms, Tanner took off at a run. He could smell them now. Scheme's pain and rage sliced into his senses, as did Tamber's killing rage.

A second later his roars followed the lions' as he watched Tamber aim the deadly pistol at Scheme's head.

"No!" He was too far away. He couldn't save her. He wasn't going to make it in time.

The shot came out of nowhere. He was within twenty feet of them when the bullet tore into the center of Tamber's forehead, throwing her backward as her eyes widened in disbelief.

"Scheme!" He raced for her as the lions converged on the area, roaring, enraged as they paced the perimeter, the sound of the approaching heli-jet warning them of the danger coming.

"Spread out," Dawn was yelling to the female Lion Breeds she commanded. "I want that heli-jet down. Go!"

They all packed small, cylindrical rocket launchers on their backs, which they tore free as they ran to take up defensive positions.

"Scheme." Tanner fell to her side, his hands touching her, moving over her, shaking her as pure terror raced through him.

She was bloody, bruised, but she was alive. He rolled her over carefully, a roar ripping from his soul at the sight of her heavily bruised face and the blood that seeped from a wound in her forehead.

She was breathing. Thank God she was breathing. He buried his face in her neck. She was breathing.

At the sound of gunfire, he waved several Breed Enforcers over to her as he jerked the automatic rifle from his back and began to return fire.

The border was within sight, and somehow Tallant had managed to get his men in place with no advance warning. Which meant he had to have had help in Buffalo Gap.

"Cover her!" he yelled to the enforcers braced around Scheme and returning fire across the ravine. "Nothing touches her."

Several more raced in to circle her as David was pushed into the circle as well. Tanner covered the circle of men, motioning other enforcers racing in to cover them as well as more gunfire began to echo through the mountain.

"The heli is gunning," someone yelled as the rapid fire of the heli-jet's onboard guns began to cut through the forest.

"Get them the hell out of here. Now. Dawn, get a bead on that bastard and take out those guns."

Someone, a Breed, grabbed David as Tanner lifted Scheme carefully in his arms and ran for the chopper landing in the small clearing below.

Behind them, Tanner heard the retort of a mini rocket launcher. The shoulder-held device Dawn and her women carried would pack a punch if one of them managed to hit the heli-jet. The problem was aiming at a moving target and managing to hit it before the rocket's safety primer self-detonated in the air.

"Jonas, I want Tamber's body back at Sanctuary," Tanner snapped into the earwig. "Take no chances that she's carrying any info."

There could be hidden chips or any manner of other ways of hiding sensitive information on her body. "I want a complete examination and autopsy of her body."

"Got it," Jonas snapped. "Just get Scheme and David out of here. Go."

Tanner was going. An enforcer tossed David to the pilot while another braced Tanner as he jumped into the cockpit. The doors slammed closed as the chopper was lifting into the air, angling sharply and rising above the trees.

Checking for the heli-jet, Tanner watched in satisfaction as one of Dawn's rockets hit the tail, swinging it off-kilter before it righted itself and banked away from the area, shuddering before the pilot managed to engage one of the jets.

The heli-jet was still in the air but unable to fight now. It surged around the mountain, disappearing from sight as the Breed chopper maneuvered around the opposite hill and headed back to Sanctuary.

Shaking, Tanner stared down at Scheme, smoothing her hair back from her pale, bruised face as he realized his tears were staining her face.

"She was very brave," David said beside him. "But you need to train her. She doesn't know how to fight, Uncle Tanner."

He didn't want to train her, but he knew he had to. If she woke up. God, if only she would wake up. He wanted to protect her; he wanted life to be secure and happy; he wanted the threats she faced gone forever.

"I love you," he whispered against her ear. "Don't leave me, pretty girl. Please God, don't leave me."

◆　　◆　　◆

It was like being buried alive. Scheme fought for consciousness, moaning as she felt her body being jostled, firepoints of pain erupting along her arms, ribs, legs.

"Easy, Scheme." Ely's voice was soothing, comforting as her gloved hands pressed against her stomach. "I just want to make sure there's no internal bleeding. There are no broken bones, though there's a hairline crack in your left arm. You took a beating." Her voice was soft, though husky, as though she had been crying. "I've given you more of the hormone to allow for the exam and to give you time to heal."

Scheme struggled against the blackness surrounding her, a whimper leaving her lips.

"You're not buried, Scheme," Tanner whispered at her ear again. "Ely had to place coverings over your eyes while she swabbed around them. They'll be off in a minute."

She tried to shake her head. Now. She wanted them off now.

"Easy, pretty girl," Tanner crooned at her ear. "Would I lie to you, baby?"

In a heartbeat, if he thought it was for her own good.

He chuckled huskily. "I would never lie about this, Scheme." A light touch to her cheeks, beneath her eyes, her forehead, proved his words. "See, you're fine. Just in Ely's lab. You took a beating, baby."

"David." She managed to push the word past her lips.

"Safe and sound." His lips brushed over her ear as his hands smoothed to her bare shoulders. "Tamber is dead. We got to you in time."

Did he? She couldn't see; she couldn't be certain. She whimpered in dread, terrified it was another trap. Did Cyrus have her again? Was he tricking her somehow?

"Take the coverings off her eyes, Ely," Tanner ordered. "Now."

Soft latex brushed her cheeks, and an instant later the pressure was gone. Her eyes flickered open as the lights dimmed in the exam room.

"You look like shit," she whispered as Tanner's face came into focus.

He looked haggard. Pale, his face streaked with grime, his hair tangled.

"Keeping up with you is hell on my appearance," he said, his amber eyes gleaming with . . . love. They were filled with love. Soft, warm, rich with emotion.

"I love you," she whispered then, her lips trembling as his hand clasped hers and he bent closer to her. "I was so afraid I couldn't come back to you."

She had been terrified. In the midst of everything rushing around her, in the back of her mind, the awareness that Tanner could be lost to her forever had been more horrifying than the thought of being buried.

"I've managed to dull the mating heat for the time being," Ely spoke. "But it's only going to work if you two try to keep a handle on yourselves here."

It was then that Scheme noticed the machines she was tied to. She recognized most of them, but the one her right index finger was attached to had her brows drawing into a frown.

"Hormonal indicator," Ely explained. "I had to readjust the hormones and trick your body into thinking Tanner had been doing the nasty with you." She waggled her brows suggestively.

Scheme stared back at her suspiciously before turning back to Tanner.

"This isn't the doctor who checked me earlier. Someone should look for the real one."

Ely's smile was self-deprecating. "I was wrong about you," she said simply.

Scheme snorted. "I'm really not willing to go through this every time someone here gets in a snit. And put a leash on that kid; he's dangerous." Her eyes drifted closed. "You guys need to learn how to avoid conflict," she muttered. "Go to school."

"Do what?" Tanner chuckled.

"Go to school. Teaches you all kinds of neat stuff. Public school, hell of an invention."

She drifted, aided no doubt by the drugs dripping into that IV in her arm. She liked drugs, she decided. She really liked them.

"I'm gonna sleep," she mumbled, frowning. She had done something really bad; she knew it. "Tell David mum."

"Mum?" Tanner's voice sounded far away.

"Mums thaword," she slurred. "Tell David mum."

And the curtain swept over her. It wasn't dark, frightening or smothering. Just a gentle silken veil that covered her and eased her from the pain and the worry.

She would deal with David later.

"Ely?" Tanner whispered as he smoothed Scheme's long hair back from her forehead and watched her worriedly.

"A week, she'll be good as new." Ely shrugged. "The hormones will rush to heal her body first. It will delay the symptoms of the mating heat to allow the body enough time to strengthen for it. Ain't Mother Nature great?"

Tanner sighed in relief. He couldn't bear to have to take her in the shape she was in. It would have destroyed him.

"She's strong," Ely said. "I was listening to Jonas debrief David as the nurse checked him out. He said she fought to get him out of there, to get him away from Tamber. Then she traded herself for him, claiming she had information no one else had."

Tanner narrowed his eyes on her. "And Tamber believed her?"

Ely shrugged, but Tanner could detect the scent of her concern. She was bothered by this, more than she should have been.

"And David didn't know what it was about?" Tanner asked her.

She shook her head. "He said he didn't." The scent of nervous fear was a subtle fragrance now. She didn't believe him, and neither did Tanner.

If Scheme was still holding secrets, then she would never be safe from Cyrus Tallant. Not that she was anyway.

"How long will she be out like this?" he asked, staring at her face, his chest aching with the bruises that marred her creamy flesh.

"She'll be in and out for a few days," Ely told him. "She's hurt, Tanner, not dying."

"I want her in her own bed." He smoothed her hair back, feeling the silkiness of it even as he pulled free several more twigs. "I want her comfortable."

"I'll take care of it," Ely said softly. "She's going to be okay, Tanner. I promise."

"This time," he whispered. "This time."

He wiped his hands over his face, breathing out wearily. Tallant wouldn't stop. He would never let Scheme go. Not until she was dead.

"Once the mating heat stills, Tanner, we need to do a CAT on her ovaries and fallopian tubes. She has the same concentrations of an unknown hormone in her system that Sherra showed when her body was repairing the tubal. We need to check on that." Ely's voice was still soft, compassionate.

A child. Her body could be preparing to conceive. It most likely was preparing to conceive. Many of the hormones associated with Breed mating heat hadn't been completely identified. The research into it was slower due to the extreme need to keep the facts of the heat hidden from the world.

God help him, another attack like this, during pregnancy, would be disastrous. He couldn't let it happen again. But God help him if he knew how to stop it.

Shaking his head, he looked around the small medical room. On the other side of a curtain was Jolian Brandeau. She hadn't survived the surge of electricity Tamber had slammed into her brain with the tazer. She had died instantly, no doubt as Tamber had intended.

Cabal was behind the curtain with her, and the scent of his regret and pain washed over Tanner. They hadn't trusted Scheme where the girl was concerned, and now they would all pay for that. Cabal more so than others, Tanner suspected. They had all known Jolian fancied herself in love with Cabal. She was pathetically shy around him, yet the scent of her pleasure when he was near was like summer itself. But the smell of deception that centered around her had always thrown them off. The deception was the love she believed she had kept secret.

Ely's gaze followed Tanner's to that curtain, grief twisting her expression as she turned back to him.

"She was a good kid," she whispered.

"Yes." Tanner breathed out roughly. "She was a good kid. Take care of Cabal for me, Doc."

Ely looked at him in surprise. "He'll be fine, Tanner. The two of you have your mate—"

"Scheme isn't Cabal's mate," he revealed, staring down at the woman he loved beyond life. "She's mine. Just completely, all mine."

Ely blinked at him in shock. "We can smell the scent on him, Tanner," she suddenly whispered. "Is it possible—" She looked back to the curtain. "Dear God. Was *she* his mate?"

Tanner shook his head. "It wasn't her, Ely. And it's not Scheme."

"Then what?"

"Twins." Tanner's smile was sad. "He was almost Scheme's mate. Trust me, that's a hell of a place to be. It's hell, period. Now, help me get her to our room. I need to hold my mate."

✦   ✦   ✦

Cabal heard the door close, felt the absence of others and slowly sat down beside the cot that held Jolian's pale, lifeless form. The vibrancy, hope and shy quest for happiness that had always bloomed in her face was gone now. It now held frozen regret, as though she had known the moment she felt that shock hit her head that she would never awaken again.

I wouldn't hurt your mate, Cabal, she had told him tearfully as he interrogated her the day before. *Don't you know, I would die for your mate. I would give my life to make certain you never suffered again.*

Or would you destroy her out of jealousy? he had questioned her coldly, then watched as a tear trailed down her cheek.

But I'm not jealous. Her voice had been rough, aching with longing. *Envious maybe, but not jealous. Your happiness is too important for me to ever feel jealousy—*

His throat tightened now as he reached out, his fingertips smoothing back a lock of silky black hair from her forehead.

"I'm sorry, Joley," he whispered, using the name he had given her rather than the name she had chosen. "I'm so sorry."

And there he sat, his soul aching with the sudden knowledge that now he was truly alone. Tanner had Scheme, and for a while he had entertained the idea of giving little Jolian a few weeks, maybe a few months in his bed. She was soft. Sweet. And she loved him.

The selfishness of that thought slammed into his head now. She had loved him. He knew she had loved him, and he had waited, waited to see if Tanner's mate was his as well. Waited because he knew Jolian wasn't a woman that would ever take to the sexual antics he and Tanner played. Waited to see if his own future was connected to Tanner's, and if not, then he had Jolian.

And now he no longer had Jolian. He no longer had anyone.

CHAPTER 31

ONE WEEK LATER

Scheme stared in silence at the image on the television screen, her heart aching with regret and a sense of things that had never been. Jonas had offered to let her be a part of the team paired with government authorities sent to arrest her father for crimes against Breed Law, multiple charges of murder against non-Breeds and charges of conspiracy to incite civil unrest.

Cassa Hawkins had been chosen to cover the arrest and been given an exclusive interview with Jonas, Tanner and Scheme on the charges.

One of Cassa's questions to her had been about closure. Would she receive any closure with her father's certain conviction and death sentence for the charges against him? Closure, Scheme had realized, had come with her mating with Tanner and her acceptance in Sanctuary. There was no need for closure with a man who had never truly been a father. There was only a sense of sadness, of relief. The monster had been conquered.

"I love you, Princess." Cyrus Tallant looked tearfully into the camera after he was charged. "Always remember I loved you."

Tanner growled in fury at the declaration. "Do you have to watch this?"

He paced the floor behind her, his hands shoved into his slacks, his expression creased into a scowl.

"It doesn't hurt, Tanner," she told him, not for the first time.

"I hate it when you lie to me, Scheme," he rasped angrily. "So stop."

Was she lying? Maybe she was, not just to him but to herself.

"General Tallant, do you have a comment on the allegations by your daughter that you forced an abortion of the child she carried eight years ago?" Cassa asked the general as they stood in his opulent foyer and the officers snapped restraints on his wrists. "Doctors, both Breed as well as conventional, have verified the evidence of abortion as well as a procedure to ensure no future conception. Did you destroy your own grandchild?"

He gazed into the camera, grief-stricken, his eyes filled with tears. "I love you, Princess," he repeated.

"Guilt," Scheme said softly. "He thinks he can inspire guilt. He's already working his defense. Does he know yet that his lawyers have refused to handle the case?"

"I didn't ask him," Tanner snarled.

"He's breaking," she mused. "He won't live to see a trial."

Tanner paused behind her chair. "What makes you think that?"

"He knows too much about the inner council." She watched Cyrus's shoulders slump as he was led from his mansion. Behind him, his second in command and heir apparent stood stoically in the background.

"I never guessed he was working with Jonas," Scheme commented in regards to John Bollen. "He's a cold bastard."

"Yes, he is," Tanner agreed. "He and Jonas must get along famously."

He still hadn't forgiven Jonas for allowing her to do the job she had set for herself eight years before.

"I make my own choices," she reminded him, not for the first time.

"Wrong. You and I make the choices now. Remember that."

"And if I don't?" She glanced over her shoulder. Tanner's tension was so thick now it wrapped around her, tingling across her flesh as she picked up the remote and flipped off the interview. Some things, her mate couldn't handle. The regrets that filled her at times were perfect examples.

"Then I'll spank you!"

She leaned into the corner of the chair, aware that the position loosened the front of her robe that had only been quickly tied after her shower, and bared her lotioned legs. Tanner didn't miss the sight. His gaze sparked with lust as he moved around the chair.

Scheme didn't give him time to pin her in her seat. She rose to her feet, gripped his shoulders as she turned and pushed him back into the chair.

"What are you up to?" His eyelids drooped in sensual response, and the look seemed to stroke over her body.

"Loving you?" She loosened the black slacks. He was shirtless, his dark bronze chest rising and falling sharply as his hips lifted, allowing her to draw the material from his powerful thighs and down his legs.

"Hmm, very nice." She gripped the hard rise of his shaft with both hands before leaning forward and licking over the broad crest. "Have I mentioned lately how much I do love you?"

"I could stand to hear it again." He groaned, his hands threading into her long hair as she filled her mouth with the engorged head, working her tongue over and around it, moaning at the taste of his flesh, the dark lustiness that filled her each time she experienced it.

"I love you very much." She lifted her head and placed a kiss on the throbbing crown before rising to her feet and shedding the robe slowly.

His golden gaze flared as his hands gripped the arms of the chair, fingers digging into the padded softness as she smiled back at him.

She cupped her breasts, her fingertips thrumming over her nipples as he bared his teeth in arousal.

"I need you," she whispered.

328

L O R A L E Ĩ G H

"I'm yours, pretty girl," he growled. "Come take me before I have to spank you."

"It might be worth the spanking," she drawled as she straddled his lap and began to lower herself to him.

"I'll spank you anyway," he promised thickly as he gripped her hips, drew her down, then bit back a curse as the hard crest began to push inside her.

Flames were licking over her flesh even as he leaned forward, his tongue licking over her nipples as her hands gripped his shoulders.

Slowly, so slowly, he took her. Working inside her, stretching her, filling her, reaffirming the fact that she was alive and she loved. She loved and she was loved.

"Oh God, Tanner, it's so good." She moved on him, pressing lower, forcing him deeper until he was seated fully inside her and throbbing pulses of heat began to whip through her body.

It was always like this. So intense. So filled with warmth. With the knowledge that she belonged. Finally Scheme Tallant belonged.

"Beautiful," Tanner breathed out roughly. "So damned beautiful you steal my breath."

She couldn't speak; she could only feel. Feel his hands moving up her back, calloused fingertips stroking up her spine as his erection began to stroke inside her. She leaned to him, needing his kiss. The mating heat wasn't as harsh as it had been before Tamber's attack and the subsequent kidnapping attempt. But the need for his taste still filled her head.

He was there for her. His tongue licking over her lips, then flickering over her tongue and spilling the stormy taste of the mating hormone into her mouth. Within seconds she was desperate for more, arousal rising sharper, sweeter than ever before, and it had been damned sweet to begin with.

The mating hormone sensitized her further. It seemed to open each nerve ending in her body, allowing deeper sensation, more heat, more pleasure and, finally, an orgasm that tore through her brain with sharp, blinding pleasure and sent her flying.

She was flying. Free. Her cries echoed around her as she

felt the barb emerge, felt it lock straight into an area so sensitive, so filled with nerve endings that she exploded again. Over and over, flying higher, her soul opening and taking Tanner in ways she would have never believed possible before the night he kidnapped her.

"I love you." She tried to scream the words, but they were only gasps. "Tanner. Oh God, Tanner, I love you."

She collapsed against him, holding tight to him, only barely aware of his incisors locked once again in her shoulder, piercing the mark he had left there countless times before.

It should hurt, she had once thought. Now she knew it would never hurt. It was the proof that she belonged, that she was now a part of a whole rather than drifting along half-alive.

Tanner completed her.

"My Schemer," he finally whispered roughly at her ear. "Forever, my Schemer."

She was Tanner's Scheme. But she was her own person as well. And beneath his love she had come to learn that being her own person meant giving her soul where it belonged. Within Tanner's care.

✦　　✦　　✦

As Scheme slept, Tanner moved across the room to the phone, picked it up and dialed a secure number.

"I don't have much time," John Bollen announced as he answered the call.

"Were you contacted?"

"Right after the arrest," John revealed. "I'm under scrutiny."

The inner Council needed the Tallant organization to carry out its objectives, and now John controlled it.

"Did the order go out?" Tanner asked.

"An hour ago. He'll be dead before the week is out. The Council can't afford to have him talk. They're taking care of it."

A cold smile pulled at Tanner's lips before his gaze sliced back to the bed to see his mate watching him knowingly.

"Let me know if you receive warning."

"Jonas will let you know. Now go away, I can't afford these calls this close to success. Practice patience."

Tanner disconnected the call and stared back at Scheme.

"Patience was never one of my virtues," he informed her unapologetically.

Her arms opened wide for him. "Mine either. And mine has run out. I need you again."

They wouldn't speak of it, he realized. She was smart. She knew what would happen. She knew that if he could, Tanner would kill the bastard himself. And she understood, because she knew that monsters couldn't be allowed to roam unchecked.

Speaking of it wasn't something he wanted to do anyway. Sometimes, it was best that his Scheme be allowed to ignore the merciless animal that lurked just beneath the flesh of the man. The animal willing to kill to protect all he held dear.

The animal that understood that sometimes, only blood could ease the rage beneath, and assure the safety of the woman that held his soul.

His woman. His mate. His Scheme.

LORA LEIGH is known for her deliciously intense and satisfying erotic romance. Her characters come to her in her dreams, inspiring her with the possibilities of *What If* . . . Most days, Lora can be found in front of her computer weaving daydreams while sipping the ambrosia of the gods, also known as coffee. When not writing, thinking about writing, or plotting what to write, Lora, a Kentucky native, enjoys gardening, fishing, and hiking with her husband and children. You can find Lora at www.loraleigh.com.